Birthright

MARI FREEMAN

Happy Reading

Mari (signature)

ELLORA'S CAVE
ROMANTICA PUBLISHING

What the critics are saying...

&

"*Birthright* is a riveting, exciting book that hooked me from the first word and held me in its grip until the last." ~ *The Romance Studio*

"**Birthright** flows and comes together without anything to hinder it from being a superfluous story. Recommending this novel hands down is the best compliment as a reviewer/reader I can give to this author." ~ *Joyfully Reviewed*

"An exciting journey that shouldn't be missed."
~ *ParaNormal Romance*

An Ellora's Cave Romantica Publication

www.ellorascave.com

Birthright

ISBN 9781419958854
ALL RIGHTS RESERVED.
Birthright Copyright © 2008 Mari Freeman
Edited by Kelli Kwiatkowski.
Photography and cover art by Les Byerley.

This book printed in the U.S.A. by Jasmine–Jade Enterprises, LLC.

Electronic book Publication October 2008
Trade paperback Publication February 2009

BIRTHRIGHT

∽

Chapter One

ℛ

I felt like death but the warmth of a bed was proof that I was, in fact, still among the living. I pulled a pillow closer, hugged it to my chest, and buried my aching head in the softness. The unfamiliar velvet-covered down and soft cotton sheets felt good sliding against my skin as I tested the movement of my feet.

Hospital…must be in a hospital. Fuzzy voices floated around the room but I couldn't make out exactly what was being said. Comforted by the ease at which my toes wiggled, I tried to drift back into sleep.

Then memories came flooding back, slamming into me. Strange men in flowing black capes and the stale smell of old, wet carpet played in my mind, along with flashes of a big, ragged knife held to my throat. I blinked hard. *Where am I? No hospital bed feels this good.* I held my breath, trying to concentrate on the voices. My head hurt and my eyes burned, dulling my focus. *Slow, steady breaths. Get your bearings, woman.* As my heart rate slowed, so did my breathing. My concentration steadied and the muffled conversation started to make sense.

"She'll be fine, just a knock on her head. A Slaugh wound is always more painful than it should be." An older woman's voice, with a calming, almost musical tone.

"How long has she been out, Manus? I don't want her to get too weak. This is all going to be traumatic enough." Another woman's voice, stern and tough sounding. I shivered at the dominance in that voice.

"It's been almost forty-eight hours. She should come around soon," a man's voice replied.

Trying to remain still, I peeked under my lashes to find myself on my side, facing a stone wall. Prison? Dungeon? The gray stones looked very old, hand cut, not hospital walls or even cinder blocks. *Where the hell am I?*

"I'll wake her this evening if she's not up on her own," said the male. I listened for other sounds, anything that would help me identify my location, but there was nothing but the voices from the other side of the room.

The tough-sounding woman spoke again. "Don't leave her side. The Weres are meeting in Austria and I've agreed to be there. She should be safe here, but I want no chances taken until she has come fully into her powers."

"I have not left her side in eighteen years, my lady, I do not intend to now." The man sounded offended. *What the hell? Eighteen years!* My head pounded. I slowly ran my hand through my hair and found a small bandage taped to my temple.

I must be on some good drugs. That's it. I'm in some kind of coma or something. I moved a little bit at a time and managed to get into a sitting position. My head throbbed harder. Looking around the room, I praised the narcotics after getting a look at the scenery. "*Really* good drugs," I said aloud, looking around at more stone walls.

Sitting up hadn't brought reality back to me like I'd hoped it would. I closed my eyes tightly and held the heels of my palms over them. Maybe moving even slower would have been better.

I took my time opening my eyes for a second look around. The room was huge, with only two small windows that were covered in the same velvet as the comfy bed. The bed was so big it wouldn't have fit in my bedroom at home. Luxurious, emerald-green velvet set off the deep amber hues of the intricately carved posts and headboard. The smell of fresh rain wafted through the room on a breeze that rustled the heavy velvet drapes.

Thick white candles sat on hip-high, twisted, black-iron stands in two corners, bathing the room in a glowing light. There was a small table at the far end of the room made from the same carved wood as the bed. Two more candles burned there, the flames dancing and reflecting off several crystal wineglasses.

"I assure you, Ke— Mary, you are not under the influence of narcotics," the taller of the two women said. She was the one with the authoritative voice, I realized. Her face was long and beautiful, with delicate lines and a hint of wrinkles around her eyes. I couldn't have pinpointed her age if I had to. She was dressed in a fabulous silver-gray dress that accentuated her shape. Man, I hoped to age that well. Her eyes were light amber and her hair was a glistening golden brown that made me conscious of my own mousy locks. "You are completely safe," she said with an air of assurance. Her face contorted into a smile that I suspected was rarely seen.

"Mary," the man said. I caught his gaze. *He was there, with the guys who had jumped me.* Flashes of the attack came to me again. Two figures on my back porch, both with big knives. One grabbed me from behind. The other fought someone else, someone with deep green eyes—like the man moving closer to the bed.

"How's your head?" As he moved closer I scooted back farther against the huge oak headboard. "It's okay, Mary. We're here to help you."

"Help me what? Where am I? Who are you?" I spilled the words out so quickly it made my head throb again. The man stepped closer. He moved with a certain grace that seemed somehow familiar. I'd seen his eyes before, and not just from the attack. I couldn't look away. Their familiarity was making my skin tingle.

"Take it easy." He sat on the bed beside me. I felt a sense of ease from his presence that I knew I should trust, even though I didn't know why. He gently ran his hand over my forehead, lifting my bangs to look at the bandage. "Bevin," he shouted.

Or maybe it wasn't a shout, but the sound certainly rang through my pounding skull like one, making the throb stronger than ever. The woman moved closer to the bed. Bevin, I guessed. She was short and round. Her back was slightly hunched over but her face was bright, her cheeks cheery. Her hair was pinned up in a tangled bun that bounced as she moved. She reminded me of an aunt that used to live with my family.

"I've got it Manus, calm down. I like you better as a cat. You're not so bossy." She was the one with the nice voice. She handed him a gold necklace with an intricate charm of a soaring bird of some sort, with an amber stone in its body. The glowing stone hummed ever so slightly. My gaze darted between the charm and the man's green eyes.

"Hush! She's not ready for all that yet." He took the necklace from her and held it out toward me.

The old woman tsked. "She *needs* to be ready. We're short on time, my feline friend." She scuttled to the far side of the room, bun bouncing as she went.

The man leaned toward me and lifted the necklace. Startled, I put up my hand, but even that movement seemed to hurt.

"I'm asking again. Who are you people and where am I?" Ignoring my protest, he placed the necklace over my head. Who was I to argue? I was a captive. There were three of them between the door and me.

As soon as the metal of the necklace hit my chest, the pain in my head subsided dramatically. I put my hand to the charm, shocked.

"Bevin, I would like to do this as gently as possible. Can you make sure that we have no surprises in the next few minutes?" The taller woman nodded toward the door. Bevin mumbled something and the door slammed shut, the large iron latch creaking as is slid into place and locked the door—all on its own. "Bevin," she huffed. "I didn't...oh never mind." She turned to me.

"Kee— *Mary*, there is no delicate way to do this, my dear, so I'll just jump right in."

I looked into her eyes—she was trying for a look of empathy but the way she carried herself screamed power.

"I am Doran, High Priestess of the Winds. I'm the leader of all Witches—"

I barked out a laugh but she wasn't even smiling. I bit my lip to combat the fit of giggles about to overtake me. *I'm in a coma and this is a drug-induced hallucination. Not a problem*, I told myself, *just go along. Don't fight the madness.*

"And the spiritual guide of the Kith in general," she continued, hesitating for a heartbeat to let her statement sink in completely and presumably prepare me for the rest. "You are my niece." She waited for some sort of response. She was regal in the way she held herself. She was fit and strong. I could see it in her posture.

"Sure," I said. *Don't fight it and you'll wake up in no time*, I told myself again as another giggle slipped.

She started again, not the slightest hint of sarcasm in her voice or any acknowledgement of my state of amusement. "You've been late coming into maturity but it has now begun, and we have brought you back to us for the rest of the indoctrination."

Indoctrination? That sobered me up. *So I'm not a coma. I've been kidnapped by some wacko cult. Maybe I'm in more trouble than I thought.* I could feel my heart rate speeding up. I tried to brace myself up on the bed with my arms.

"This," she said, motioning to the green-eyed man on the side of my bed, "is Manus, your guardian. He's been with you since you were twelve. He is the one who brought you home after the Slaugh attacked you." I was starting to get a little scared. "We had hoped that some day your magic would mature. As such, Manus has stayed with you."

"Uh-huh." I looked back and forth rapidly from her to the man she called Manus. He was an attractive man with a strange sort of light-gray hair. It wasn't the gray men get from aging, but more the gray of a stormy night. He was well built, but not in an overly muscled way.

The guys in the black capes were scary enough. At least they *looked* like bad guys. These people looked mostly normal.

He smiled tenderly at me. "I'm glad to finally meet you in my human form."

"Human form?" *I'm dead. These people are loonies and they've kidnapped me. I have got to get out of here!* "Look, my family doesn't have much money. If you want ransom money, you took the wrong girl." I started to move away from him, which on the huge bed was pretty easy.

Bevin came closer. Her bun flopped to the side. "You are a Witch, young one—"

"Bevin!" Doran snapped.

Bevin tilted her head and her bun flopped to the other side. "Doran, we don't have time to be delicate. She is not a child as her sister was. She will understand."

Doran bowed her head and made a face that I thought looked like concern...or was it disgust? I couldn't decide.

Bevin continued, "You are one of two who were born to a powerful Witch and then hidden. We sent Manus to you at the age of twelve, when we found your location. Manus is a Shapeshifter, and he has spent the last eighteen years as your guardian in the form of a gray cat." I looked into his eyes again. The green was the same shade as Clyde's. His face held the slightest feline shape. It took nothing away from his masculinity, but it was there. "You didn't come into your powers at puberty as most Witches do," Bevin explained. "I suspect it's your Demon blood, or maybe the human, we're not sure."

"Excuse me? Demons...Witches?" I rubbed my eyes again, grateful that the pain had subsided some.

"You aren't yet convinced? Manus, please demonstrate." Bevin stood up straighter, maybe reaching five feet at her full height. The action sent her bun to the far side of her head.

Manus stood and raised his eyebrows in question. "Don't you think we can demonstrate another way? We don't have to frighten her to death."

"If she is the Priestess of the Wild, she must learn not to be frightened every time she encounters something that is unfamiliar." She and Manus both looked to Doran, who bowed her head slightly in agreement. He shook his head and closed his eyes...

And began to distort!

Memories from the attack at the house rushed over me. Clyde, my beloved cat, under the patio table hissing as his face contorted...

I shook off the memory as, before me, the man's form shifted, bones buckling and body shrinking.

Impossible as it was, there on the floor, surrounded by piles of clothes, sat my precious cat. He was the same cat who had been with me through all the good and bad times of my life, the only creature on Earth that loved me unconditionally. I had talked to that cat when I was happy, sad or frightened. Clyde had been the only thing that had remained constant in my life. He jumped onto the bed and circled close to my legs on the down comforter before reclining and starting to purr.

It was him. There was no way it wasn't. I'd have known him anywhere.

A sickening feeling came over me. "You've seen me pee!" I squeaked. "Slept in my bed." This was just getting worse and worse. "Oh. My. God! You've been in the room when I had..." I glanced briefly at the sophisticated woman, Doran. "When I had *company*!"

"Manus!" Bevin scolded.

"I was to protect her! How could I do that if I wasn't near?" His protest came out slightly slurred and hissing in his cat form.

He made his way into my lap and stretched his neck, nuzzling my own with his head, the way he had comforted me for years. "I didn't mean to impede on your privacy, my lady, I only wanted to protect you and act as any cat would. It was natural for me to be so close to you. It still is." Softly, he spoke into my ear, "What we are telling you is true. I wish we could have done it a better way, but there it is. You *are* a Witch."

I pushed him back to the bed, trying not to think of anything else horrifying that he may have witnessed. *Everything!* He'd been there for everything.

"Your true given name is Keena," Doran said softly as she sat on the end of the bed. She was trying to be non-threatening but it wasn't working. Supremacy rolled off the woman like an expensive perfume. My stomached burned in response to her closeness. "Haven't you always felt like you were different, someone not quite like the others? Stronger than the other children, longing for something in relationships with humans that wasn't there?"

She paused, watching my face. I looked away from the three of them, gazed across the room to watch the flame on one of the fat, dripping candles. I thought back over all the times in my life when I'd felt as she'd described. She was right. I didn't fit in anywhere, even in my own home. I loved my parents, but it was true—I was never really at ease with them. But it was still hard to believe they weren't my real parents. This couldn't be real.

I had been a good athlete in school but too embarrassed to surpass everyone so easily. Everything else about academic life had bored me. Everyone else seemed to be in on something I wasn't. *Or had it been the other way around all along?* I blinked a couple times, my brain feeling overloaded.

Doran's strong voice brought me out of my thoughts. "You have longed for your own people, Keena. Without magic, you've not been complete. You couldn't be. It is similar to sensing something wrong but not being quite able to pin it down." Her pleasant face looked sympathetic. "We feared it would never come to you, until last month when Manus started to feel your magic."

"Magic? I don't have any magic." I was confused and getting angry, but at least I no longer felt threatened. I looked at Clyde-Manus, curled against my hip. "Could you change back? I'm a little freaked by you right now." He shrugged his kitty shoulders, something I'd never seen him do as a cat, and moved to the edge of the bed and changed back.

I preferred him in his cat form, actually. It was comforting—but I really wanted to see the change again as a reinforcement of my sanity. And he did it, changed with a smooth stretching of bones and flesh before nonchalantly picking up his clothes and redressing. "Either this is the result of really good drugs or…"

I couldn't think of another or.

Bevin cackled a little and finished for me. "Or the things that go bump in the night are real. Believe me, dear. They *are*. We're real. *You're* real. You will find out you have true magic. Witches use far more of their brains than humans do, you know. Everything about you will grow stronger." She smiled, which made her dark eyes twinkle in the candlelight. "Have you had a burning in your lower abdomen?"

I know my eyes were bulging in disbelief. "Yes. How did you know that?" My stomach had been burning off and on for weeks. I'd chalked it up to work, but… "I thought it was stress."

Bevin came closer and put her hand over my lower abdomen. The burning turned to a surge of warmth. "That is your power, child. It comes from your womb. You will learn to channel it…use it. It will grow stronger, as will your sense of being and your confidence. Once you are brought into your full powers you will be a great Witch."

Her lovely voice seemed to echo through my head. *Witch.* I couldn't get the image of the Wicked Witch of the West out of my head. Yet these women were graceful and beautiful and I could feel something in the air around them. I let my hand cover the charm around my neck. It seemed charged with the same force I felt in my abdomen.

"Did you say something about a twin? What about my mother? Is she a Witch?" The questions were coming faster than I could get them out. "I look just like her. How would she not have known this? *Did* she know? Why did those things attack me?"

Bevin turned a sideways smile to Doran before turning back to me. "You were given to…your human mother when her biological child died at birth, we think. She knew no different. Your real mother—your Witch mother—spelled you to take on the human characteristics of your adoptive mother." She looked out into space with an expression resembling awe. "Quite an impressive spell, actually. No one has been able to replicate it since. It was more like Fairy glamour than a spell."

Manus leaned back against the headboard next to me, his hand falling on my thigh. Even in his human form it felt natural having him close, touching me. "You noticed that your pants were getting shorter and looser?" I answered with a small nod. "We think the spell started to break as your powers started to emerge. Your hair is getting darker, even more so since you have been here with us."

"You are starting to look more like my sister, Trevina, your birth mother. Your *real* mother," Doran said.

"Where is she, my real mother?" When no one answered, I looked to Manus.

"She died after finding a safe place for you and Feldema, your sister," he said, his eyes cast down to the floor. There was more to that story, to be sure.

Doran spoke loudly and with authority. "You need your rest Keena, and some food." She raised her hand and the iron latch clicked undone, the door falling inward.

I shrieked and raised the covers to my chin as a little creature stumbled abruptly into the room. The eavesdropping little creature was perhaps waist high and bluish-gray. His eyes were black but I could see a tiny ring of bright blue around the irises. His head held a tuft of blue-green hair that stood in a little mohawk. Iridescent, feathery scales covered his blue skin.

Once he recovered from his stumble, he presented the room with a formal bow. He looked at me with a big, toothy smile. "I am Hogan, of the valley Kell. I am at your service, my lady." I blinked hard at the little thing and looked at Manus.

He gave a small laugh. "Gnome. He is your sworn servant. He will care for your chambers."

"Gnomes, Witches…what else do I need to know about?"

Hogan scrambled to the edge of the bed, being careful not to bump Doran. "Weres, Vamps, Gremlins, Slaugh—" I must have looked as horrified as I felt because Doran put her hand on his shoulder. The Gnome fell to his knees and shut his mouth.

"Hogan, please get Keena something to eat and run a bath." As she spoke, calm emanated from the powerful woman. The feeling wrapped around me like a warm towel.

"Yes, my lady." He bowed again to me and then scurried out of the room, his little legs moving him faster than I would have thought possible.

Doran stood. "I hate to leave you at this time, my niece, but I have an urgent meeting to attend. Manus and Bevin will attend to you. They'll begin your training and answer all your questions, after you've had some time to rest. Bevin will also begin to help you learn your spells. You are starting very late, so I hope you are up to the accelerated teachings. I will be back in a few days. If you need me in the meantime, Manus can get in contact with me."

I nodded acceptance because I had no other real response. I wished it all *was* a drug-induced hallucination, but I was awake and this was as real and as solid as the stone walls of the room.

Hogan returned with the food—barbecued pork and a diet soda, my favorite. I stuttered a weak "thank you" to the Gnome. Hogan winked, and his unimaginably long blue eyelashes sparkled in the candlelight.

Manus took the plate to the small table. "Hogan is pledged to you Keena, but you must watch the Gnomes. They have a strange sense of humor and it tends show up at inappropriate times."

The food smelled divine from across the room and my stomach grumbled. I got out from under the covers and realized for the first time that I was dressed in a silk gown that was very low cut on the top and very high cut at the bottom, showing most of my thighs. It was a deep golden color that worked well with my skin tone and it fit like a glove. Though the garment was beautiful, I felt uncomfortable in front of the audience. Manus obviously read my discomfort.

"We have different sensibilities about nudity here, Keena. You will have to adjust to that as well. We value our bodies as a great gift. They are part of our magic and hold no shame among our kind. Some of the species you are going to meet would be insulted by your shyness." Hogan, I noticed, looked truly disappointed. His little face was actually cute with his tuft of blue hair falling in his eyes as he pouted. "Hogan is also responsible for your wardrobe. I assure you everything he chooses will be flattering and in the proper fashion for the occasion."

Hogan was still looking at the ground and standing very rigid. It occurred to me that I had hurt his feelings and, even given the unusual circumstances, I didn't want to offend anyone.

"It's beautiful, Hogan, thank you. But...do you think I could have a robe?" His head popped up, the mohawk quivering from the quick movement, and a smile full of tiny, sharp teeth covered half his adorable face.

I had just given a compliment to a Gnome for a sexy nightgown. Shaking my head, I decided that I needed the food before I fainted.

He mumbled a few words I couldn't really hear and a robe that perfectly matched my nightgown appeared at my feet. He handed it to me. "I'll prepare your bath," he said with a wink, bowing and backing into an adjoining room.

Chapter Two

80

Manus fell on me hard, knocking my last dagger from my hand as he pinned me to the stone floor with his body, the steel of his own blade cold against my neck. He was only slightly taller than I was, but his weight was much greater than I would have suspected from his appearance. He was tight and compact in his human form, much like he was as a cat.

"Shit!" I pushed on his chest, trying to dislodge the Shifter. "You get me with that move every time!" I was covered in sweat and breathing hard from the long workout. I'd been able to get one dagger from him today but he had completely disarmed me. Again.

Even so, battle training was coming along well, which was more than could be said for my spells. Bevin was getting more and more irritated with me. Yesterday, when I tried to use an easy spell to block a book she threw at me, I misspoke the incantation, letting the book conk me on the head. A late surge of misdirected power then sent the book flying at her face. She got up and circled the room, muttering as she paced. Her bun floundered from side to side, punctuating her ire. After two rounds, she left me with a glare. That was the end of the lesson.

"You're doing fine, Keena." Manus had been working with my fighting skills. I had always been better at sports than the delicate stuff. I had little grace. But who'd have thought I was a natural fighter? As I lay on the floor, the strangeness of this new life washed over me again. I'd seen and done too many weird things in the castle to *not* believe it all for truth, yet there were still moments that made me question my own sanity.

Manus took in a breath. "You're not insane, Keena. It's all real. You're doing great," he said as he helped me to my feet, reading my mind once again. He was used to reciting this speech, and always patient in reassuring me.

"I wish my magic skills were as good as my right hook. Bevin's about to give up on me, you know," I complained as Manus ushered me back to my chambers. Hogan hurried along in front of us, grumbling about yet another tear in the black leather vest he'd fashioned for my workouts. The Gnome opened the door to my rooms and stopped short, making me bump into his back as he ducked, more than bowed, to the people in the room.

In front of Hogan was an amazingly tall, willowy woman with hair so blonde it was almost white. She was draped in a dress that was the liquid blue of a tropical lagoon. The dramatic satin affair was made in a Victorian style with white braids and tiny golden ribbons at the bodice. Her skin was creamy, her eyes sparked a blazing blue I had never seen before and her facial features were delicate and full of confidence. She didn't smile as she looked up from the stumbling Gnome to me.

Manus put his hand on my lower back to ease me forward. Following his urging after I caught my balance, I moved into the room, laying my blades and the shields on the table, one at a time, using the familiar actions to give me time to recover from being surprised.

"So," she said in a tone that could only have been interpreted as disgust. "*You're* Keena." She didn't look impressed as she circled around me, looking me over as if I was some ugly stain on her new white carpet. She stopped to face me and two men moved up close behind her. Until they moved, I hadn't even realized they were there. That wasn't very smart on my part. Manus would be so disappointed if he knew. We'd spent a good amount of time working on opening my senses to my surroundings and I missed two men in my own room. Bad.

The taller of the two looked like a stereotypical Vampire from the movies. I'd learned they were real, but somehow I hadn't pictured the beings Bevin and Manus spoke of with such reverence and respect looking like this guy. Hollywood didn't get many things right about the Kith, but they had nailed it with *this* Vamp. Slicked-back hair and a black, velvet cape draped over a crisp white shirt gave him a comical look. But his height and the fact that he was looking down his long, narrow nose at me with a cold sneer took away from the ridiculous effect of his attire. Standing there, he seemed to take up more room than he should have, given his slender build. His dislike of me was very evident.

I shifted my attention to the other man. A young blond whose face was that of a boy — but the rest of him proved he was a man. His naked, perfect chest was clean-shaven and his stomach held a fabulous six-pack, which was displayed nicely above a tight pair of tan leather pants. From the stretch of leather in the front of those pants, it was easy to guess what *his* particular talent was.

The group looked me over as if I was somehow substandard. I felt suddenly self-conscious in my sweaty and torn black leathers. I unconsciously tried to straighten my hair. Manus pushed past me into the room and made a halfhearted bow.

"Feldema, you've come to meet your sister. How…nice of you." I noticed he didn't use a title. Everyone else I had met in the last few weeks had held some sort of title and first introductions were always formal. His intentional dismissal of her title showed a great amount of disrespect. "May I present Keena, Priestess of the Wild." He then turned to me and bowed deeply, swinging his arm under his chest. I didn't like what was going on or the feeling that I was being left out of something important.

"Manus, you insult me again and I'll make your face green for a month." Her voice was light but her cold blue eyes said she meant it. I hadn't seen anything like that in my spell books yet, so I wasn't sure if she could really do it. Looking at her cold features and callous eyes, I had little doubt that she had the temperament to do it, if not the spell.

I felt a small tingle of her power calling to mine. Not much, just enough to test me. I had to fight the urge to answer her call and struggled to hold back my burgeoning powers. If she wasn't showing me all of hers, I wasn't showing her mine at all.

She turned to me, silent for a moment, taking another scathing look up and down. "You still have no *real* power or I'd feel it. You realize you have mere months." It was a statement, so very matter-of-fact. I had no idea what she was talking about but there was no way I was going to let *her* know that. She went on, "I've looked forward to this, sister. I had heard of your coming and I have to say, I was a little worried." She smirked and looked back to the Vamp, flinging her white-blonde hair. "Misplaced concern."

I didn't know what to say, so I watched her and tried to keep my face from showing my growing confusion.

"Feldema, you should go. The priestess is in need of a bath. You'll be properly introduced soon enough. Doran will be back from another pack gathering this evening and I'm sure she won't be happy to find you and your...friends here." Manus opened the door wide for them, making it clear it was time for the trio to exit.

As she stepped through, Feldema looked back to me with a blatantly fake smile. "See you soon, sister."

Manus slammed the door behind them and warded it with a few flicks of his wrist and an annoyed grumble. At least I knew a ward when I saw one these days. No one could use that door unless he wanted them to. I'd successfully drawn a few wards in my work with Bevin, but not one strong enough to block an entryway. I stood looking at the closed door and realized that I hadn't said a word while she was in the room. I had only stared at her, dumfounded.

What a great first impression I must have made.

Hogan led me to the bath and removed the leathers with a mumbled incantation. I stood naked before him and Manus. I was finally getting used to them dressing me and helping me bathe. It had taken many uncomfortable moments and several screaming fights, but they had finally convinced me it was the norm. Now it almost *felt* normal. Turns out I like being pampered.

"That's my sister? Nice girl." Hogan held out his hand for me as I stepped into the tub. The water was perfect, as usual, and scented oils and freesia petals floated on top of the water, soothing my sore muscles as I sank deep into the tub.

"She is your twin half sister. The archaic Vampire was Kendrick, one of her consorts." Manus was still grumbling.

I turned the former piece of information over in my head but I couldn't get it to make any sense. "Clarify the half sister bit, please."

Hogan cleared his throat. "Your mother acquired seed from two men into her womb and held it with a powerful spell to conceive the two of you at once." I looked at Hogan as if he was crazy. Which was in itself crazy. After all, a Gnome and a Shifter were helping me bathe. Why would anything be crazy to me anymore?

"Your mother was a very wise Witch, Keena. She knew that her child was to be High Priestess and leader of the council. Because she had two girls, she also knew they would have to fight for the right to be High Priestess and the strongest would hold the title."

"Fight?" I looked at Manus. He nodded and let the Gnome go on.

"You will battle Feldema in the ancient ways. By might and by witchcraft to prove you're the true heir to the throne of High Priestess."

I put my head down on my knees. I knew I should have had some compassion for the woman. After all, she was my sister. But Blondie threw the first stone and I wasn't in any position to try to make amends for whatever the last thirty years had created between us. If I had needed to be her friend, Doran would have said so. Right? "Great. I think I could take the skinny bitch in a fight but when it comes to even basic spell work, I suck."

They both laughed as Manus washed my hair. Bevin came around the corner scowling. She'd obviously heard my last comment. "If you don't soon choose a man, well…"

That got my attention away from my twin. I jerked my head up so fast that water and petals sloshed out of the tub. "Choose a man? Choose a man for what?"

Manus chuckled again, shaking his head. "You didn't realize all the Magicians and half-Demons that Bevin and Doran have been introducing you to were for your selection? She's had some of the most powerful Kith in the castle and you haven't shown the slightest interest in any of them."

"I've kinda been busy trying to accept all this." I gestured around the cavernous black marble bathroom, sloshing even more water. "And all the training. The last thing I want is a man." I suddenly felt self-conscious, vulnerable, and pulled my knees up, hugging them to me to cover my breasts.

"Pardon me for saying so, Keena, but your previous life was…*is* gone. You don't have to love this one anyway. You just have to join with him so your magic will mature. Then spells will be no problem." Hogan was getting towels ready as he spoke.

"Tell her all of it, Hogan," Manus said. He was working a sweet-smelling shampoo into my hair as he eased me back against the tub. His hands felt so good as they massaged my scalp. The caresses relaxed me a little and I let my head fall back.

"By 'join', you mean sex?"

Hogan gave me his wicked, toothy smile and nodded.

"I have to have sex with someone to bring my full powers out?" I was shocked—and after three weeks of Gnomes, Weres and all sorts of Imps and such, that was really saying a lot.

"Yes, dear," Bevin said, as if I should have known. "But there *is* a catch to it."

"There always is," I said, sinking farther into the tub as she dug a pain amulet from her pouch. I needed it for the aches and bruises from the battle training. Manus let go of my hair long enough for me to hang it around my neck.

"The one you choose will be spelled to love you all his days, whether you return that love or not. He will never take another. The spell that binds him to you will prevent him from abusing his ability to take in some of your magic. Joining for creatures of magic is quite different from human sex. We exchange power, share magic in our couplings. Your first lover as a Witch is an awakening, a call to your power."

"That doesn't seem fair. I get full powers and he gets zilch. Do I have to marry him then?"

"Absolutely not! We don't marry in the sense that you understand. And he *will* benefit from your coupling. The spell merely prevents him from using your own magic against you. You can keep him as a consort as long as you like, but you can send him away whenever you please," Bevin explained.

"Consort?"

Manus answered, "You should have two consorts at any given time. They are sworn to you. But your first experience with a member of the Kith will awaken your powers completely. Your powers as a Witch are part of your essence as a woman. The first lover, or *la graine* as we call him, will simply bring on the bloom of your full abilities."

"La graine?"

"The seed," Bevin said. "It is the bringing of life to your power as a Witch."

I thought on that for a moment, not sure how sex could manage to awaken my power. Yet I had no choice but to believe.

"Can I have Manus as a consort?" I looked at him, then Bevin. His face brightened and those green eyes shone as he smiled.

"No, Keena," Manus said with a soft lilt. "I am honored deeply that you would consider me for a consort, especially as *la graine*, but I have sworn my life to you as your guardian. I pledged an oath to you and your mother. I will not go back on that oath no matter what may come."

I had a hard time imagining having that kind of relationship with him anyway. He was my friend, my strength...my *cat*. And he'd seen me wax! "Never mind." As it all settled into my brain, I put my hand on Bevin's arm, suddenly panicked about my lack of magical skills and the subtle threat from Feldema.

"How long do I have to find a consort? When is this battle with the wicked half sister? She mentioned something about 'mere months'!"

They all smiled at me—the Shifter, the Gnome and the Witch.

I had daydreamed of a life where I was fuller, more complete. And now I had it. I was given attendants, clothing fit for royalty, magic and a huge suite in a *castle*. I was getting used to it—but they had neglected to tell me I had to fight for it all. What if I didn't have the power to beat Feldema?

"You may not believe this, Keena, but you are stronger then I ever imagined you would be, my child." Bevin's wrinkled face was soft but a shadow of concern shifted across her eyes. "But the sooner the better. We have no idea how strong your powers are going to be. Feldema's magic...her powers are great. You need all the practice you can get before you have to face her." She handed me another amulet. I groaned as I eased it over my head. Manus had stopped pulling punches in our sparring and I hurt all over.

Bevin continued, "Doran is back this evening and we will be heading home tomorrow. There will be more men to choose from there. Don't worry, my child, your body will tell you when the time is right—*if* you open yourself to your senses. You still don't trust yourself, your new magic. It will come when you open up to it and accept it."

She turned to Hogan and the bun in her gray hair wobbled. "Something formal this evening, our host will be here as well." Hogan gave her a little bow.

"Our host? This isn't home? You people don't tell me anything," I said with a pout. This lack of information was getting very irritating and I had every intention of speaking with Doran when she returned.

Bevin gave me a confused look. I guess she assumed I knew. "This is the home of Lord Tynan, of course. He's been very generous to house us for this long while we helped you to adjust. But we leave for the homeland tomorrow night. All the Kith will welcome you and you'll feel more confident. It will feel like home."

I thought about that last statement. I'd never really felt a sense of home anywhere in my life. I hadn't realized how much I wanted just that until I was flung into this strange world. I'd grown comfortable with these people, these beings, so easily. I couldn't explain it, even to myself, except that I felt like this was home already. *They* were home. I belonged—and had even grown to love them in this small amount of time.

It was Manus, Hogan and Bevin who made this feel like home, I told myself. Some other place wouldn't change that.

* * * * *

Manus, Bevin, Hogan and I sat in a large dinning room and made small talk as we ate. The mysterious Lord Tynan and Doran had not made it in time for dinner. We enjoyed a fabulous meal of exotic fish with strong spices that made the candlelit room smell like an incense shop. Imps flitted gracefully about, refilling wineglasses and serving the courses. When I complained that I would gain a hundred pounds eating like this all the time, Hogan told me I wouldn't easily gain weight anymore. Evidently my metabolism was different as a Witch.

I stretched back and rubbed my tummy. "Well, with our workouts, Manus, I probably wouldn't gain weight anyway, Witch or no."

Manus gave me the once-over. "You've not really looked at yourself lately, have you?"

I rolled my eyes. There were only a few mirrors in the castle and even those were small and dingy. What with all the training, and with Hogan doing all my dressing and attending, I hadn't really concerned myself with my appearance. I knew my hair had grown and darkened, though.

"Hogan, a proper mirror please," Manus said. Hogan motioned to a corner of the dining room and a full-length, gold-framed mirror shimmered into existence. My magic was so pathetic that I had to stare at the mirror for a moment and wonder if my craft would ever be up to par. I opened myself up to get a feel for Hogan's energy as it lingered around the looking glass. I felt the glow in my belly as my magic responded to his.

Manus got up and offered his hand. "This way, priestess," he said and stopped me beside the mirror to brush a loose bang from my forehead. "Feel your magic. Pull it from within yourself. Experience it." I closed my eyes and let the feel of it rise, opening to my own sense of being. "May I present to you, the Priestess of the Wild," he said, turning me to face my reflection.

I took a breath so quickly it was actually a gasp. I heard Bevin give a little chuckle.

I'd seen myself—but not like this. My hair had grown at least six inches and it was a shiny auburn, falling in cascades around my face. A healthy golden glow radiated from my skin, making me look as if I'd just come off the beach. Since I had been in this castle for most of the last three weeks, it was startling. I was also several inches taller. My face was thinner, and although I could still see the hint of resemblance to my human mother, the spell my real mother had cast to make me look like my adopted parents had mostly faded.

But my *eyes*! Still hazel, yet with tones of brown that were glowing as if there was a fire behind them, bringing them to life. It was still me in the looking glass but from head to toe, I was brighter.

The gown Hogan had created for me this evening was midnight blue and stunning. By now I had gotten used to his method of dressing me. As he mumbled his spells, a pile of fabric would appear at my feet, and after mumbling again, the garment for the occasion would wrap itself around my body and be right the first time, buttons or zippers done and all perfectly fit. But this particular gown was the most beautiful thing I had ever seen. It lifted my breasts so they appeared larger than they were and it clung tightly around my waist, making me look every inch a woman.

I'd never felt beautiful in my life—until this moment.

"Your powers are glowing within you, priestess. You just need to open yourself up to them." Manus was smiling like a proud father with his hands resting on my shoulders. He leaned in and kissed me tenderly on the head.

A strange feeling filled me as I stood there and looked into my own eyes. I felt wholly myself, looking at the woman I had been born to be. The Imps, Gnomes and Witches, all of them were my family. I was a Witch and I had a fire in my soul that belonged there and it was burning to be freed. I felt tears welling as my abdomen burned with those powers that I suddenly knew were truly my own.

I opened fully to my power for the first time. I could sense it as it reached out and flowed through the room. Hogan and Manus closed their eyes and inhaled to take it in, to let it mingle with their own. Bevin's voice echoed in my head, *Yeeesss, Keena.*

"I-I need to go for a walk," I said as I turned from the mirror and headed for the archway leading away from the dining room.

Manus bowed. "Please stay inside the castle." I looked away before the tears came fully. I heard Hogan asking why I was crying as I left the room. Manus sniggered and told him that his question was why he was still an unmarried Gnome.

* * * * *

I found myself on the roof of the castle in the early spring night. I had gone there often to think and get fresh air. It was one of my favorite places in the castle. The forest below spread out for miles and I could just barely see the twinkling lights from a village in the distance. The moon was high and bright but not quite full. The air was very cool, but my tolerance for the cold had gotten stronger along with everything else. The night was alive and I felt it.

I ran my hands over the fine bodice of the gown, leaving them on my stomach. I opened my mind as Bevin had been trying to get me to do and inhaled deeply. That glowing feeling started in my womb. I felt on fire but nothing hurt...it was a wild warmth that came *from* me, through me. I gave in to the force I felt growing and concentrated on it, pushed at it. I let it search outward to the night, feeling the life force of the creatures that rummaged through the forest far below the castle tower. Each one responded to the call, sending a small acknowledgment to the life force within me.

Bevin was right. Letting the power be part of me opened a new level of understanding of this world. Of myself, of what it meant to be Priestess of the Wild.

"Priestess."

The deep growl came as a plea from behind me. I turned to find a new life force and — wow! *What* a force. It was

33

attached to a tower of a man who was looking up at me from a bowed position.

"Forgive me for intruding on your private time, priestess. I'm sure you've had precious little of it since coming here." He stood and the moonlight hit his eyes. Black Vampire eyes. Thick, golden hair was neatly tied back, showing off the strong lines of a powerful jaw. He wore a perfectly tailored black suit with a crisp white shirt and gray tie. The cut of the jacket enhanced broad shoulders and an expansive chest that tapered down to a trim waist. Even with my new height, he stood a good six inches above me. I swallowed hard when I realized he was looking me over as closely as I was him. I blushed like a schoolgirl.

"Tynan," he said in a sultry voice that flowed over my skin like silk. "I hope my home has been to your liking." He moved farther out of the shadows and I got an even better look at him.

Bevin was right again. No sooner had I opened my mind than my body started talking to me in ways it never had.

I was lusting for this man—this *Vampire*! I felt his gaze right down to my slipper-encased toes.

I tried to steady myself enough to speak. "Lord Tynan," I squeaked. He smiled at me, making my pulse race. "Thank you for your protection. I've been very comfortable here. Someday, maybe I'll be able to return the favor." Thankfully, the last part came out sounding somewhat normal. His gaze stayed on my face, making me a little nervous. I adjusted the long skirt of the gown to have something to do with my hands.

"I see little Hogan has not lost his touch in dressing beautiful women. That gown is a piece of art. The way it brings out your eyes is breathtaking." I swallowed hard. My body was aching for him and I couldn't manage to find any real control over the sensation or any ability to hide it. Damn this new discovery! He turned away from me to look over the stone walls into the night. "This is my favorite spot to come in the evenings when I'm here."

"Where exactly is *here*?" I relaxed a little. Having something casual to talk about made the feelings inside me less frightening.

"You were not told?" He let out the tiniest of snorts, humor playing at the corners of his lips. "You have been living in the Castle Dracula." He watched to catch my expression.

"No freaking way!" I blurted it out before I could restrain myself. He chuckled slightly and I blushed again. "I'm sorry. That wasn't very ladylike. I just meant...I would have thought that Dracula's castle would be some kind of tourist trap these days."

"Hmm. One would think, but it's too remote, very few venture past the village below. Those who do attempt the trek are easily frightened away by the staff."

I studied him again. Vampire. He didn't seem scary at all. Delicious, yes—scary, no. "I bet," I said. "Hiding in plain sight."

"I'm glad you appreciate the irony. It's lost on many of my kind." He looked over the countryside. "It's actually a sanctuary. I spend far too much time among the humans and their hurried world. I come back here for the quiet."

I had a million questions for the sexy Vamp—most of which had to do with the instant attraction I felt for him. Was he looking at me that way for the same reason I was drooling over him? Or was it just bloodlust? Would he hurt me?

He obviously saw the uncertainty on my face and lifted one finely sculpted brow. "You *do* know that most Vampire lore in modern fiction is untrue?"

I looked down, embarrassed. Most everything I thought I'd known about Witches had turned out to be wrong. The only Vampire I'd seen was Feldema's consort. I should have known not to use that campy Vamp as a guide.

"I've had so much to learn in the last few weeks, Lord Tynan. I'm sorry I don't know the true nature of the Vampire. I hope I haven't offended you." I kept my eyes down in respect.

Bevin had taught me much of the politics within the Kith. He held a title, was a member of the council—and I had insulted him. Not a good thing. Time to play submissive and apologize.

He took my face in his warm hands, lifted it to his and took a step closer, so close I could smell his skin. It was the same scent that filled my bed, a rich, fresh forest...

I've been sleeping in his bed. I knew at once the thought was true. My knees felt suddenly wobbly as he looked into my eyes.

"You haven't offended me, priestess. Your concern for my feelings is a great compliment. I thank you for it." He didn't move away and I didn't have the will to pull back. I wondered if he could feel my attraction. It was all *I* could feel at the moment. I wanted to be in his presence, in his arms, his life.

"Would it be rude to ask the true nature of your kind, my lord?" Still staring into those dark eyes, I could see now that they weren't truly black but a deep, luxurious blue. A shade darker than the gown I was wearing. The gown that suddenly felt far too confining.

He let go of my face and smiled. "Of course not. We—"

"Keena, are you all right?" It was Manus. He darted around the stone wall behind us. "Oh!" He stopped short and bowed deeply. "Lord Tynan. I didn't realize you had returned."

"It's a good thing I'm not a threat, Manus...I have been with the lady for some time." The tone in his voice held a great deal of authority, marking his displeasure over being able to be in my presence undetected.

"Yes, my lord, but the emotions I was sensing from Keena were not of a dangerous nature." Manus kept his eyes cast down.

"True." Tynan smiled at me. He *did* feel my infatuation with him! I blushed again and could see the smile on Manus' bowed face.

Lord Tynan turned fully to me once more. "Until later, priestess." He lifted my hand to his lips and pressed a very gentle kiss on my knuckles, his thumb gently rubbing across them. He winked and walked away.

And I stood there, smitten, holding my hand out in front of me. Never before had feelings so overwhelmed me. It felt as if I understood the man completely, knew him without knowing him, his character, his strengths, his weaknesses.

"Keena seems to have found someone she's interested in, Hogan," Manus said to the Gnome as he scuttled up behind him. Manus held his arm out for me to take.

Hogan giggled. "That would complicate things, wouldn't it?"

I took Manus' extended arm. "Shut up."

"Yes, my lady." Hogan grinned like a mischievous boy.

* * * * *

Manus had changed into his cat form for the night and was kneading the comforter at the end of the bed as I brushed my hair in front of the beautiful mirror Hogan conjured in my chambers. *Lord Tynan's* bedchambers. The thought of him gave me a small shiver of excitement. I'd never responded to a man so strongly. I felt feminine from the intense desire and I was still spellbound by my appearance.

"You are simply more *you* now, Keena," Manus said as he circled around a time or two then plopped himself into a gray, furry lump. "You'll grow accustomed to it."

The truth was I had already grown accustomed to it. He was right. It was just more me. "Manus?"

"Yes." He lifted his head from his little paws and twitched his whiskers.

"Tell me about Vampires."

"What is it you wish to know?"

I did my best to keep my voice indifferent as I ran the brush through my hair. I loved looking at the vibrant auburn. No more mousy hair—and I didn't have to spend a fortune at a salon to get it. "You know what I want to know. Almost nothing I knew in my human life about any of the Kith races has been right. I assume it's the same with the Vamps. What's Dracula really like?"

His tail, wrapped around his body, did a little flutter beneath his nose. "Dracula was a monarch in the middle ages," he scolded. "He wasn't a Vamp at all. The locals just took advantage of the mythology to bring their lost monarch's memory back to life."

"Okay, not Drac, but what about *real* Vamps. Are they soulless fiends who feed on the innocent?"

He laughed, which from a cat, sounded more like he was hacking up a fur ball. "No. They were originally created by the Slaugh. Kind of an accident, really."

"The Slaugh? I thought they only gathered the souls of sinners and fed on the evil. What do they have to do with Vampires?" The Slaugh had been a good part of my instruction since they had attacked me before. They were a creepy species that survived by feeding on lost souls and were well known among the Kith for having a nasty habit of stealing. Collectors of secrets, souls and treasures, Bevin had told me. Politically, they wanted to regain the power they had enjoyed before the Kith went into hiding. They were foul creatures. Even if I didn't have a reason for personal bias, they'd still give me the creeps.

Manus kept talking as he cleaned his furry paws. "Their king, King Bran, got greedy centuries ago and tried to take the souls of some Greek soldiers because he craved their bravery and strength. Even though the men had killed in battle, Bran was unable to keep their souls. A soldier may be a killer, but that alone never makes for an evil or tainted soul. Anyway, those souls escaped Bran and tried to return to their bodies or move on to the afterlife. But King Bran cursed the escaped souls, preventing them from entering the afterlife or resurrecting their bodies completely. He cursed them to roam for ages as the undead. Lord Tynan was among the first."

"So they have their souls."

"Yes, but they *do* need to feed on human blood to exist. It was a side effect of the curse. Life force is needed to maintain their corporeal bodies. They don't have to feed every night like in the movies. They're gentle with humans to the point of being over-protective. The amount of blood needed to revive their flesh is minimal. They stand true with the council and the High Priestess. They are strong allies."

"Oh." I looked back to my reflection, remembering the depth of those dark blue eyes and the heat of his body so close to mine. I could feel the masculinity of him still lingering on my skin. My body felt tight with need.

"Keena." Manus sounded very serious for a cat. "Keep in mind, *la graine* will love you and no other for their entire life span."

I knew what he was saying. "A Vamp's life is an eternity," I whispered. If I were to let Lord Tynan become *la graine*, he would love me for a lifetime—a lifetime that would long outlast my own. Long after I was dead and buried, he would love no one but me. Too long.

I crawled into the bed, my body still aching for him, dreaming of those deep, dark eyes and those lips that had run over my hands. Imagining what they would feel like as he kissed my stomach, my breasts, my thighs...

* * * * *

I spun away from Manus as he lunged at me. My elbow landed solidly in his ribs, pushing him to one side. Stumbling only slightly from the impact, he turned just as fast and was balanced on his feet, his sword sweeping fast toward me. I countered the move with a sweeping kick from my right leg and hit his wrist hard, knocking his sword across the room.

Ha! He was now without weapons. I had already stripped his other two blades from him.

On fire, my mind saw nothing but the patterns of his movements, subtle hints of his next attack. Nothing beyond that mattered. It was as if the rest of the world had fallen away and there was only the dance of the fight, his will against mine. I was drenched with sweat and adrenaline pumped furiously through my body.

I lunged and he kicked me in the stomach. It hurt, but I was able to temper the reaction to the pain and spin to the right and connect my elbow with the side his face. He didn't flinch, just grabbed my arm as it withdrew from the blow. I cartwheeled away, twisting the hand that gripped mine. The pressure caused him to lose his grip and his balance for just a second, and I brought my knee to his chest, sending him backward to the ground. I pounced on his chest, my blade at his throat.

"Uncle!" he cried. "For Goddess' sake, Keena, *uncle.*"

I blinked and realized it was him almost too late. The haze I had entered cleared. He smiled up at me, bleeding from his nose, his hair dripping with sweat. "I think you got me this time."

I slumped down on his chest, exhausted. Every muscle in my body burned. At last, I had completely zoned out everything and saw nothing but the movements and the strategy.

Someone started clapping from behind us. I turned, still sitting on Manus' chest.

"Bravo...bravo! You have come so far, my niece." Doran's face was genuinely pleased. Lord Tynan also nodded his approval.

I struggled to stand and bowed to them both. "My lady, Lord Tynan."

She and Tynan stepped onto the matted floor of the sparring area. "You will do well against Feldema, Keena. She will not suspect you are warrior enough to take down a guardian. Most impressive." Doran bobbed her head, "Most impressive, indeed. You two have been fighting for over two hours. I was about to break it up."

Two hours? It felt like it. I was having trouble holding the short blade in my hand now that the adrenaline had started to fade. My muscles trembled as I looked at Lord Tynan. He was looking at my chest. I glanced down and realized that most of my top was torn away and sweat and a small amount of blood were trickling down my exposed left breast. I fought the urge to cover myself. That would be an insult. The expression of need on his face triggered the aching I had for him. His face twitched in response to the shift in my body and I knew he felt as overwhelmed by this yearning as I did.

It didn't matter. I couldn't have him. I couldn't ask him to pledge himself to me for ages. I would die and he would be left alone. That was that.

If only I could convince my yearning body...

Doran looked from me to Tynan. "We leave at sunset," she said to break the tension that suddenly filled the room. "I told Hogan to have your things sent ahead. He is preparing a meal and a bath for the two of you."

I needed both. I bowed again and Manus took my blade and led me out of the room.

Doran and Tynan had followed and were discussing a meeting with Werewolves. Something I should have tried to listen to, but I was far too worn out to pay much attention to Kith politics and fight the sexual urges of my body at the same time. Manus had a tight grip on my arm to keep me moving forward. I could feel Lord Tynan's gaze on my back. I bit my lip in an effort not to respond to the sensation.

We rounded the last corner—and were confronted by four shadowy figures in the hall.

My brain barely had enough time to register them as Slaugh before one ripped Manus aside and gripped me from behind around the shoulders. I was enveloped in the mist of the creature. Memories of the last attack came flooding back and fear filled me. I tried to struggle but I was pinned under a veil of mist and cloaks. Its bony body and scraggly ribs pressed painfully into my back. The thing wasn't much more than a skeleton wrapped in black gauze, its wasted fingers digging harshly into my shoulder. After the spar with Manus, I just didn't have enough strength to fight.

The Slaugh struck my face with its other skeletal hand and started to pull me away. My head reeled back from the blow and I saw darkness coming. I struggled harder, both to stay conscious and make the Slaugh's retreat difficult.

Manus impaled one of them with my small dagger and the thing disintegrated. The biggest of them had Doran in a headlock. The rage in the old Witch's eyes was frightening, even to me. She threw herself forward and the Slaugh was momentarily caught on her back. The profile of the lump of black gauze hanging over Doran's tiny back reminded me of a Halloween drawing of an old, hump-backed Witch leaning over a cauldron. I mentally shook myself at my own hysterical thought as my captor tightened his hold around my neck.

The last remaining Slaugh was attacking Manus from behind and blood ran from the Shifter's shoulder. Lord Tynan ripped it away from Manus and flung it against the wall with one strong arm while he grabbed the one holding me with his other hand. Tynan's eyes were black with rage. I studied his face, trying to concentrate on it to stay awake. The Slaugh that had me tightened his grip again and I lost the last bit of air I was getting.

Everything went black. Again.

* * * * *

I awoke in the huge bed, aching from head to toe and with a screaming pain in my throat. Timidly, I looked around the room through my lashes, afraid of what I'd find.

The Slaugh were gone and Lord Tynan was sitting at the table in the corner, Hogan pouring him wine. Hogan bowed respectfully and gave me a toothy grin and a wink as he turned to leave the room. I cringed, knowing what that wink meant. I looked down to find I was clean and wearing an outrageously revealing black-lace teddy. Damn. I blushed. I started to say something to the Gnome on his way out, but it caught in my tight throat.

Lord Tynan poured a glass of water and brought it to the bed — *his* bed. I took it with a trembling hand and sipped. It helped the dryness of my throat but not the tightness in my chest from being so close to him.

"Hogan's forward," was all I managed to squeak out as the door closed.

"I adore his taste." Tynan gave me a devilish, sexy smile and brushed a stray hair from my eyes. I tried to swallow but it hurt too much. He'd removed his jacket and his shirt was unbuttoned enough to reveal just a hint of his chest. I struggled to keep my gaze on his face. "Slaugh injuries are always more painful than they should be." He drew in his brows in worry. "They've never been able to breach the castle wards before. Doran is strengthening them now. We won't be leaving until the morning now and I want to assure you're safe tonight. I'll stay with you personally."

Oh goody. I didn't need this. I didn't think I could resist him all night. Hogan had left me in a skimpy bit of lace and the man smelled *so* good. "Manus?" I asked, getting a little more of my voice back.

"Bevin is healing his wounds, he'll be fine."

He sat on the edge of the bed and lifted an extra pillow, tucking it behind my head. His touch was gentle, his hand warm on my shoulder. I couldn't help but imagine them touching, exploring other parts of my body. His scent filled my mind. I couldn't control my response to his presence. I felt my power start to bloom in my abdomen, drawn to Tynan. I took in a deep breath, trying to settle the effect he was having on me. He saw my desire, probably felt it. I had no control over that part of my powers yet. I felt horrible, lying in his bed dressed to seduce yet I couldn't do it. I couldn't have him no matter how much I wanted him. I couldn't have him longing for me all his eternal life.

He leaned in close. "I feel your desire for me, priestess. I can't help it. It wraps around me and calls to my senses." His voice was low and husky, his breath hot on my cheek.

"K-Keena," I stammered. "My name is Keena."

"Mary didn't do your beauty or your strength justice. Keena fits you well." He gave me a tender look that made my heart race.

"I…uh…"

He put his lips lightly to mine. They felt like the soft petals of a flower. All the aches and pains in my body slipped away with his tenderness. He leaned in and the kiss went from light and gentle to hungry and needful. His arms wrapped around my back and I let myself melt into his embrace. His tongue plunged into my mouth, seeking, plundering. I felt it all the way to my pussy. His hand slid up the bare skin of my back. I groaned at the heat, the passion of the kiss. My tongue returned the passion — then it found his fangs.

I pulled back and away from the kiss, unable to speak from the desire burning up my mind.

He released me with a jerk and retreated back to the edge of the bed. I tried to talk but my sore throat just squawked. He handed me the water again without looking away from his knees.

"Lord Tynan. I'm sorry."

"My existence disgusts you. Keena, it is I who should apologize for assuming…" I felt his pain and self-hatred as clearly as I had felt his lust. But his tone was all business.

Disgust was the last thing I felt for this man. I wanted him more than I had ever wanted anyone in my life. Maybe even loved him. I didn't know why or how after only seeing him twice, but the feeling was there and I couldn't change it.

"Your...er...teeth only reminded me that I can't accept what you're offering." I was as matter-of-fact as I could be with a squeaky voice. He looked back to me with a wounded, questioning look. "I can't. I will *not* ask you to be *la graine*, my lord."

"Call me Tynan, please." His face had softened. "I don't understand."

"Tynan," I responded. "I'm told that now, as a Witch, the first person to share my bed will bring me to my powers. God, I don't know exactly what that means...they only tell me things on a need-to-know basis. But that man will be bound to me by a spell. He'll love me and no one else for his entire life." His face was still questioning and so wonderfully perfect. I hated the spell that would hold him to me at that moment. "I won't live nearly as long as you. I know I'll live longer than a human, but nowhere near the time..."

Understanding dawned on his face but his lips twitched up a slight bit. That little smile tightened my stomach and made me wet at the same time. I didn't know if I had the conviction to stand by my own words when he looked at me like that.

"I'm going to long for you for the rest of my life as it is." He ran his knuckles down the side of my face, sending chills through my whole body. "I felt the pull to you as soon as you smiled at me. You feel it as well. I know you do."

I had to look away from him, away from the desire in those eyes. "But you still have a choice, Tynan. You don't have to watch me grow old and die and then long for me. You can love whomever you choose. If I give in to my greatest desire, it would bind you to me so you could never choose another." I felt tears burning the backs of my eyes. "I can't ask that of you." I tried to sound stern and tilted my chin up. "I won't."

He wiped a single tear that had escaped onto my cheek and kissed me on the forehead. "You have given me the greatest gift, Keena. Compassion. No one has *ever* sought to protect my heart." He eased me back in the bed—and I saw something in his eyes that was breaking my heart. "Sleep, *mon guerrier.* I will watch over you tonight and I'll return you to your homeland tomorrow."

How could these feelings be so strong so fast? As soon as I thought I had a handle on all the changes in my life, something else came at me and I was lost again. Could he have the same feelings? Surely this was just a strong case of lust.

I felt his weight leave the bed. My argument had made sense to him. He didn't want to give his heart to me for all eternity and I certainly couldn't blame him. It was a good thing that one of us was thinking clearly.

I would *not* have been able to turn him away a second time.

Chapter Three

ॐ

Manus lifted me off the boat deck and onto the dock. My stomach was still queasy from the motion of the ocean.

Okay, maybe *queasy* was a grand understatement. I was definitely glad to be off the boat that had brought us from the Irish mainland to the island. The March cold of Ireland had been left far behind. The air here had the warm, thick feeling of the deep southern states. I felt the familiar burn start a low churn inside me. My power was reaching out to the magic that surrounded us — the same magic that allowed the island to remain hidden in the middle of the North Atlantic Ocean. Instinctively, I put my hand to my stomach.

"Welcome to WildLand," Doran said proudly as she moved to stand beside me. She looked a little younger in the afternoon light, whereas I felt tired and worn after a couple hours of seasickness. As I watched her breathe in, I felt the tingle of her essence stirring. As she raised her hands to the sun, the tingle quickly turned into a wash of power so strong I had to steady myself not to be knocked over by it.

Her magic filled the air, mingling with the native magic of the island. It was prickling as it danced over my skin. Wave after wave pushed through me, melting away into the trees, singing to the island, strong and true.

I was awed to silence, experiencing the true power of a High Priestess for the first time. How on earth would I ever become the Witch that Doran was when I was inept at the simplest spell, unable to direct or contain the budding power that rose from my soul?

Small sparks of other magics all around us responded and merged with her silent announcement. *I have returned*, it said. It felt as if the very trees themselves acknowledged it.

We all stood still, absorbing the glow of Doran's power.

Wondering what would come next, I glanced around the shore—and caught the sound of a low, rumbling thunder coming from deep within the forest. Curious, I took a few tentative steps forward and spotted a trail off to the left. None of the others seemed concerned by the approaching sound.

A faint recognition dawned on me. Horses. *Loud* horses.

Suddenly there came a white storm bursting from the trees. Two open carriages, each with a pair of magnificently matched white draft horses that took my breath away as they raced toward us. The driverless carriages drawn behind were also gleaming white and trimmed in bright maroon velvet, but they couldn't match the brilliance of the horses. The rigging that held the steeds was covered in shining silver and gold trim that gleamed in the early sun.

I stood transfixed at the sight as the teams skidded to a stop at the end of the dock. A deep, earthy magic rolled off the horses. I felt it rising above them like steam as they shifted and stomped in excitement. Surreal.

"Your chariot, my lady." Tynan reached out and used one of his long fingers to lift my jaw, closing my gaping mouth. He grinned and took my arm to escort me to the second carriage as Manus led Doran and Bevin to the first, where Hogan was waiting with the door open.

I sank back into the heavily cushioned velvet seats as the horses spun the carriages around. The rigging creaked and rattled. We took to the path at an alarmingly fast pace that made me cling to the seat, my hair whipping behind me. Tynan sat facing backward, unconcerned with the speed and the lack of a driver, relaxed and enjoying the ride. Bright sunlight spilled through the forest, sparkling on the dew-damp leaves and highlighting his golden hair. Having him so close was torture. I wanted to take the two steps across the carriage and crawl into his lap. I twisted in my seat to avoid his gaze, to hide the feelings that were lurking so close to the surface.

We passed a small clearing and several deer stopped their nibbling to watch us pass, unaffected by the thundering hooves of the horses or the jingling harnesses. After we passed, they stepped into the path behind, still watching us. Birds followed behind the carriages as well. All kinds of birds—brightly colored and drab alike. The largest, a hawk, swooped low over our heads. The path was starting to accumulate all sorts of animals. We were moving too fast for me to make them all out, but large or small, I felt the life force in them all.

"Remember who you are." Tynan murmured the words from across the carriage and I heard them like a distant echo. "Priestess of the Wild. They are all drawn to you."

I looked back to him from the path. "I feel them. All of them." It wasn't a feeling I could truly explain, but the prick of each of their lives reverberated in my mind. I closed my eyes and tried to see each one for what it was—and I could! I felt each individual presence, each life force. They were all part of me, attuned to my energy. I truly understood my title, Priestess of the Wild, for the first time.

All things here called to my soul—the loudest of which was the soul of the man sitting across from me.

When I opened my eyes I met Tynan's intense, appraising gaze. He bowed his head without breaking eye contact to acknowledge my revelation. Goose bumps arose on my arms from the desire in the depths of his eyes. Throughout the long plane ride from Romania to Ireland I had intentionally avoided looking into those eyes. Feelings more intense than any I had ever experienced overrode common sense when he was close.

The flight over on his private plane had only convinced me further that I indeed was wholly in love with Tynan.

"You have your father's eyes...or I presume you will when you've come into your full powers." The corner of his lips turned up just a little. "I knew him. A good man."

"Tell me about him. They've told me about my mother, but not him."

"Coyle was half-Demon," Tynan answered. He didn't offer more. Of course, truths had to be dragged out of this group. They shied away from anything that might bring me the slightest dismay, and I was tired of being treated with kid gloves.

"Okay, Mr. Silent Type, let's try a different question. If Mother had the seed of two men, how do they know which is *my* father and which is Feldema's?" Maybe I would have him on this one. It was a harder question to be vague about.

"*Her* father was a Magician. She came into her powers at the normal time for a Witch, so it's obvious she was the daughter of the Magician. Your father was half-human, half-Demon. We believe that's why you retained your human attributes until now." He leaned across and caressed my cheek. "Plus, those beautiful eyes are Demon. No question."

I blinked and felt myself starting to lean forward into his touch, pressing my cheek into his cool palm. His gaze drifted from my eyes to my lips and back. I was sure he could hear my heart pounding over the churning of the carriage wheels. He leaned in closer...

The carriage jerked and he lost his balance, breaking the moment. I pulled back as he straightened, turning away in a weak attempt to fight the heat of excitement that had rushed through my veins from his touch. I forced my attention back to the path as it opened into a vast valley of lush, open pasture. The speeding wheels left a swaying wake of purple and white Irish heather.

Tynan opened his hand to me and offered a gold coin. It looked like a Spanish doubloon, a real one.

"We'll come to the river shortly. Throw it in," he said.

I stared at the coin for a moment. My studies had covered all kinds of creatures and beings. There was only one I could think of that would be significant to the river. "The Trolls?" I questioned. He nodded. When the clatter of hooves hit the bridge, I leaned over the side of the carriage as far as I could. The river below ran strong and was about fifty feet wide under the bridge. I let loose the coin and it flipped and tumbled. As soon as it broke the surface, there was a disturbance and I saw a green, mossy mass. I watched the spot as we passed but couldn't see any other sign of the Trolls.

"You will be properly introduced," he said. I added questions about Trolls to the growing mental list of things I needed to ask Bevin.

That thought brought on another question. "How are you managing the sun?"

His deep chuckle raced along my nerves as much as his closeness had. "It's part of the collective magic of the island. The same magic that keeps the island hidden from the non-magical protects me. I can tolerate it for short periods before I must...retire."

The carriage raced around a bend and the forest gave way to civilization. The horses slowed as we got to the first of the buildings and we rolled along what I guessed to be the main street, where giant oaks lined the walks and hung over the road. Flowering shrubs dotted the front yards of the shops and houses. Made of creamy stucco or ancient, silvered wood, the structures looked like illustrations from a children's book. There were cottages and huts of all sizes, ranging from massive to the size of doghouses, the smaller dwellings haphazardly stacked on top of each other. The entire scene reminded me of a Seuss book.

Leaning over the side of the carriage, I looked down the side streets that wound off in both directions. Some were populated with more modern housing. Farther behind the storybook village stood warehouses and stores. As we came to the end of the street, the carriage meandered between more grand, old oaks dripping with Spanish moss and stopped next to the other carriage in front of a set of large, metal gates.

"Cold iron." Bevin gestured to the gates. "The metal of protection. Third-generation Fairies forged these. The old magic used in their production provides additional wards for the manor." The gates opened slowly, commanded by a wave of Doran's hand. I craned to look ahead, to catch a peek, but the lumbering oaks lining the path blocked any view.

"Your home," Tynan said as the carriages drew forward once more. The path finally opened to reveal a mansion that managed to keep the charm of the cottages on the main street while taking up several city blocks. The exterior was creamy, off-white stucco, accented with brick-red clay roof tiles. Natural gardens with walking paths and cozy seating areas sprawled on both sides of the driveway, further softening the palatial façade. The place looked welcoming. I'd expected something more ominous, like the Castle Dracula, but Doran's manor was gorgeous.

One could even say cute, if one looked past its size.

* * * * *

I had little time to settle in or explore after our arrival. After I was shown my rooms, Tynan went to retire and Doran disappeared to check arrangements for my formal introduction, which was scheduled for the next afternoon. Bevin set to the task of making sure I knew the history of, and what manner of courtesy was due for, each individual who would be in attendance. She grilled me on the details over and over to ensure I wouldn't insult anyone. After hours of study and quizzing, she finally left me.

Even after a full day of air travel, horrid seasickness and study time, I was restless instead of tired. I couldn't get the feeling of Tynan's hand on my face out of my mind. His presence was with me as I paced the room. The large bedchamber started to feel confining. I needed some time to sort out my growing feelings for the Vampire, and for that I needed some serious caffeine. Hogan and Manus were both elsewhere, so I was on my own to venture out of my suite.

The corridor was empty. The mumbling of a faraway conversation was the only sound to be heard in my wing at one end of the mansion. I suspected the kitchen to be closer to the middle of the manor, so I headed inward, feeling content to be alone for the first time in a long time. I followed the meandering halls with no Manus, no Hogan to tell me where to go. Heaven.

I rounded a corner and caught the unmistakable scent of baking bread. Even I could follow that smell. The aroma led me down another long hallway, close to what I thought was the back of the manor, to a swinging wooden door. I pushed it open slowly and peered inside.

The kitchen was large but not extreme, and it looked like a magazine layout. There were pots and pans hanging above a well-used chopping-block table. Cupboards lined the walls and a small stove sat in a corner, next to an oversized, lit fireplace with some large hunk of meat turning slowly, roasting on a spit. The garlic smell of the meat mingling with the aroma of baking bread made my stomach rumble. The back wall had large, double swinging half-doors that I could see led to a larger, industrial-looking cooking area.

Movement on the chopping block caught my attention. A tiny woman was pacing across the wooden table. The hinge squeaked when I pushed the door open a little farther and the woman spun around. She examined me, eyes wide, for just a second before falling into a very formal curtsey.

"I am honored to have you in my kitchen, my lady," she said, primly holding her arms at her side and keeping her eyes downcast.

"Thank you," I replied, entering and returning her curtsey. She rose up to her full height, which was about two feet tall. Her hair was a shimmering light green and looked as delicate as spun silk. It was plaited down her back and reached all the way to her thighs. The dainty woman's face radiated mischief. Her beauty shimmered in the air around her. I had no doubt that she was a very powerful Imp.

I smiled. "I was hoping to find some coffee. If it isn't too much trouble."

"Coffee this late, my lady," she tsked, looking truly concerned. "You need some sleep for your big day tomorrow." Her nose crinkled as she chastised me.

"It doesn't bother me." I slid onto a stool next to the chopping block as she waved her little hand, making a cup appear before me. The kettle from the small stove in the corner floated toward us.

Her face was beautiful. She had bright blue eyes that took up too much of her face and a warm smile with perfect, gleaming-white teeth. "Two sugars, I believe."

"Yes. Thank you." I put my hands on either side of the cup. "You are?"

"I am Abbey, the keeper of the kitchen here. Kitchen Imp." She sat down on a wooden box of onions and daintily crossed her legs. She leaned closer, over her knees, and gave me a serious look. "My lady, you must be wary, wandering these halls alone."

"Please, call me Keena," I said, and she nodded. "What do I have to fear?" I had assumed myself safe from the Slaugh while in the manor.

Her expression changed from a pretty smile to a worried frown. "Much, Keena."

I grumbled about being the last know everything and she rolled those big eyes. Lifting her hands above her head, she mumbled a spell I couldn't follow or fully understand. Her magic tingled, warm and inviting, and a shimmering bubble enveloped us. It was as if a large glass dome covered us and the table, down to the floor. I couldn't help but reach out a tentative hand to touch it.

"Don't," she said. "You'll break it. It's a sound barrier. We can talk without being heard...by most, anyway." I was impressed. I watched swirls of varying shades of blue shift and move within the bubble, like blood moving though a living thing.

She walked over and put her little hand over mine where I held my cup. "Until All Hallow's, you are not safe anywhere, Keena. The Slaugh are very determined."

"I wish someone would tell me what the hell is going on. I'm really getting tired of Bevin's half answers."

"Ask and I shall tell, my lady. If I am able." I was shocked. The others, even Manus, seemed so elusive when I asked direct questions. "I'm your servant. I will hide nothing from you."

"Really? How refreshing. Fine—what do the Slaugh have against me that they keep trying to kill me?"

She sat back on her onion box again and paused as she gathered her thoughts. "The condensed version is this. They, and some of the other Kith, do not mix with the outside world so easily." I must have looked confused. She tapped her finger to her head. "Think about a Gnome or Gremlin trying to live openly among humans. And most particularly the Slaugh. Yuck!"

When I nodded my understanding, she went on. "So some of them, especially the Slaugh, would like nothing more than to become the majority species, as it was in the early times, before the human population grew to dominance. In the meantime, some of our races have become very small. Given that we have more power than humans do, many feel that the magical should dominate the Earth. Some would see the humans destroyed or, at the very least, reduced to what amounts to slavery."

"Okay, so they want to wage war on humans. I still don't see the connection to me." Maybe I was just thick. I didn't understand the implications.

"You're as pure as I've been told. I'm pleased." She looked over her shoulders as if to make sure no one was around. "The High Priestess is the leader of the council. Doran has discouraged the Slaugh and others, like the Goblins, from their plans and though she is not their leader, they must follow the majority. The decisions of the council are binding to all the Kith."

"A supernatural United Nations?" I had to chuckle as I said it.

Abbey did too. A light tinkling sound filled the bubble. "Similar. The High Priestess's influence is weakening, because she will soon step down. The Slaugh are making sure their cause is taken up by her replacement. The council will be looking to you or Feldema to carry on the traditions and beliefs of the current leadership, and let fate take its due course. The Slaugh want their influence on the High Priestess's position. Then they can wreak havoc as they will." She looked to the tabletop, suddenly finding something interesting on her shoe, then back to me.

"And? I don't want to sound stupid, Abbey, but I still don't see—" Understanding hit me suddenly. "You mean that Feldema…she would allow the Slaugh to do what they want?"

She slightly bobbed her head.

I took a sip of the wonderful coffee and let the implications of what I'd just heard tumble through my mind. I had dealt with the Slaugh more than once now, and had Manus and the others not been there to protect me… The human population would break into chaos if the Goblins and Slaugh and God-knows-what-else were free to start attacking.

The implications were enormous. Doran and Bevin were looking to me to prevent a clash between the Kith and humanity. No wonder they didn't just come out and say it. I would have cracked under that kind of pressure, what with all the other changes I'd been through in the last few weeks.

I cursed. This still left me with more questions than answers. Why had my mother had two children? Why not just me if Feldema was weak or untrustworthy? Had she known this would come?

Abbey managed to change the subject and the tone of the conversation as she refilled my cup. We talked and gossiped for another hour or so and she told me more about WildLand and the races within it. Her demeanor was light and she made me feel very comfortable. I liked her immediately and knew she would be a true friend and confidant. Before we parted, she told me about those on the island who supported Feldema and her consorts—and among them, which would be in attendance tomorrow.

I left her to the preparations for the next day and ventured back to my room. Manus was asleep at the foot of the bed, just as he had been for years.

* * * * *

"Hogan, don't argue with me. I want to take a walk in the woods this morning. Please dress me appropriately." He wrinkled his blue face in frustration as he made himself busy in my adjoining bathroom.

"It is not the time for you to be running wild in the forest, Keena." He still only used my given name when he was trying to be serious.

I bent down to be at eye level with him. "I feel drawn to the forest, Hogan. I'll only be a while. Come with me if that makes you feel better. *Please*," I pleaded.

"Drawn" didn't even begin to describe the calling I felt. I *needed* to be out there. The forest offered peace and acceptance, and I needed that before I had to face the introduction ceremony. Hogan's face, covered in those crystalline, shimmering scales that changed his bluish hue to green in certain light, looked uncertain. He blinked and a pile of fabric appeared at my feet. It swirled around me and I lifted arms and legs to accommodate the moving fabric until I was wearing a pair of breeches that fit like a second skin, a navy top and boots.

"Only for a few minutes, my lady. The ceremony is but a few hours away."

I kissed his cute little head so hard he stumbled backward, and turned to head outside before he could change his mind or call Manus. He had to trot to keep up. I felt electricity snapping over my nerves as I stepped into the grass. It was nothing like what we experienced with Doran on the docks yesterday, but I felt it down low in my belly and my hand went to the source of that power. I smothered the urge to rip off my boots and walk barefoot in the grass. I'd have time for that later. For now I was drawn to the forest and moved quickly to be in it. I hesitated just at the edge of the manicured yard.

"Go on, it is where you belong." Hogan caught up to me and shooed me with his hands. "Just not long, my lady."

"I know. I feel it." And I did. I stepped slowly into the trees. They were a mix of pine, oak, ash and every other tree I had ever seen, and some I hadn't. The morning light spilled through the canopy and danced around me. I felt alive, alert and strong. I started running in joy. My blood was pulsing in my ears, the sound pounding in my head. Hogan couldn't keep up but I didn't care. I just ran. I had no trouble with the tangle of roots and broken, dead limbs. I moved carelessly through the forest, in it, part of the wildness of it, part of the energy that made it a living place. An energy I would have never felt while living in the human world.

It was exhilarating, humbling and freeing.

I came to small clearing and stopped to take a longer look, as if called by an unheard summons. On the far side, tucked behind a small, blooming dogwood, was a fawn. The tiny white spots on her back twitched as I slowly moved toward her but she stood her ground. Stopping a few feet from her, I held out my hand.

A noise came from behind me. *Damn it, Hogan.* The tiny doe turned and ran off into the forest. I spun around to scold Hogan for interrupting—and there in front of me, standing bold and brilliant in the little clearing, was one of the great white horses. He stepped gracefully on huge hooves toward me, lowered his head to my hand and tried to grab my fingers in his lips. The leathery feel of them tickled my skin and silky strands of luxurious mane teased my wrist. He pulled away smoothly, moved over to a large stone at the side of the clearing and stretched out his rear and front legs, parking out to lower his back. Sure of his intentions, I stepped on the stone and lifted myself quite ungracefully onto his back. He stood proud and tall as I centered myself on his muscled withers and ran my hands over his lustrous coat.

"Keena, that's not a good idea," Hogan warned, stumbling over a root and into the clearing. The horse took off in a gentle canter through the trees. I could hear Hogan's voice drifting after us but not his words. The mighty horse moved so smoothly that branches were always just out of reach. The feel of his muscles under my legs and the wind in my face was invigorating. There was no fear of falling, only exuberance. I held tight to his mane and clutched his sides with my knees. We ran on and on until I could see crashing waves in the distance.

The animal slowed to a trot and snorted from the exercise. I rubbed his shoulder and murmured thanks to him as we stood watching the waves on the empty shore.

I felt a tingle of nerves from the horse—right before he spun around and reared. I tried to gain purchase but slid backward off his rump, landing in a painful pile on the ground. I covered my head to protect it from his hooves as he reared again and then galloped back to the forest.

When I managed to catch my breath and look up, Kendrick, Feldema's Vamp consort, stood looming over me. *Shit.*

"Well, I see you've met the *ceffyl-dwr*, Keena." He spat my name. "You shouldn't be wandering the forest alone. You never know what you might meet."

As his sneer turned to an unnerving smile, I did a backward crabwalk away from him and tried to get my feet under me. He followed my movements and lunged. With fangs exposed, he fought to grab my throat.

I managed to drive a fist into his chin and roll away from him. My pulse was racing, my training kicking in, but he was too fast and got a hand on my arm before I could right myself. His other hand gripped my chin, pushing my face to the side. He was going in for the kill. So frightened that I forgot all my techniques, I could only think to knee him as hard as I could in the jewels.

It worked.

He let go briefly and I tried to run back into the forest. I was swiftly halted by his fist in my hair, the pain making me squeal. I reached for his hand as the searing pain of ripping hair pulled me backward to the ground. Kendrick fell to his knees, straddling me, his hands holding mine down in the sand.

I struggled against his grip but the hold was too strong. Dark eyes filled with rage held mine as he pulled his lips back, hissing to expose his fangs. I screamed and tried to break free again. Useless really, against his strength, but I tried anyway.

Before I could finish the scream, Kendrick was gone. Pulled off me and flung all the way the to water's edge. I was pulled to my feet just as fast and found myself face-to-face with Tynan. The intensity in his eyes took my breath.

"You're okay, *mon guerrier*?" It was both a question and a statement. The grip he had on my shoulders eased so he could turn my head from side to side to see if Kendrick had managed to bite. When he was sure there was no real damage, he tenderly rubbed the side of my face and pulled me into his arms.

I let myself feel protected by the strong body wrapped around mine. I still hadn't said anything. Pressing forward, I melted into the hardness of his chest. "The man is a monster."

With the adrenaline and the rush from my experience in the forest running through my blood, I couldn't fight the lure of his body pressed against mine. From the knees up, I could feel every hard line. I closed my eyes and imagined what his naked flesh would be like pressed against me like this. Not able to stop myself, I slid my hands around his waist and clung to him. The muscles of his back trembled slightly in response to my touch. His hands cupped my face as he pressed his cheek to mine. "Keena, we need to talk about this, about us."

The deep rumbling of his voice only made it harder to be this close. My body was crying for his. My pussy was wet and wanting and I had just escaped death. This was *not* right.

Shaking my head, I pulled away. "I can't—"

"Over here!" Manus shouted from the tree line. I could hear his movements as he joined us. It was a good thing he'd shown up. I didn't trust myself alone with Tynan. I attempted to shake away the barren feeling left in my heart, knowing I had to walk away from him. I would *not* give in and have him bound to me for eternity.

Oh, but I wanted to.

Manus ran to my side, sword drawn, still looking around for the threat.

"Kendrick. He's gone," Tynan growled over my head.

Manus sheathed his sword. "Here? That's rather bold, isn't it?"

"Not if he had succeeded."

Manus gave Tynan a terse look and turned to me, trying to change the subject. "How did you get all the way out here?" I saw his face change from real concern to mild amusement as he looked me over and calmed down.

Anger filled me at his question. They *still* weren't going to tell me about the plot against me after another attack! "I know about the Slaugh and my half sister's alliances. Kendrick was sent to kill me."

He took a step backward—and a deep breath. "It seems the Manor grapevine is wound deeper that I thought," he said, as he ran a hand through his hair. "You needed to know. I should have told you."

I glared at him. "But you didn't, did you? No. I heard it from someone else and I really didn't take it all that seriously. I figured if I needed to be so careful that I couldn't even take a walk on the grounds, my *guardian* would tell me."

"Keena." Manus had the decency to look regretful as he started toward me.

"Don't you think I could protect myself better if you guys told me exactly what's going on around me? If I'd heard the truth from you, even Bevin, I'd have taken more precautions! I'm not stupid and I'm not a child." Storming off toward the forest, I left with one last look at Tynan. I was trembling from anger, fear—and from the feel of Tynan's body pressed to mine, from the feelings I had no control over. Anger was easier to deal with, easier to control. Even predictable. This intense desire was something I had no control over. I concentrated on the anger.

Hogan stumbled from the woods, his clothing torn and tattered, his chest heaving from running. *Oh man.* He'd be furious at me for mussing his wardrobe, more so than for leaving him behind. I stopped to help him straighten himself, pulling his tunic straight and brushing leaves from his hair, straightening his mohawk. I kissed him on the cheek and gave him a wink that made him blush, which was really cute with his blue cheeks.

"She was riding a *ceffyl-dwr*," Hogan huffed toward the other men, trying to catch his breath. The two men looked from him to me, mouths gaping.

"Tattletale!" I re-mussed his hair and started down the path to the manor. Manus stopped me with a stern hand on my arm. "*What?*" I asked, brushing his hand off.

"The *ceffyl-dwr* are particular about being ridden, Keena. It's usually not safe. They take riders off and dump them. That beast brought you to Kendrick?"

No. Definitely not. The horse and I had been communing in the forest, sharing our love of the run and the wild. Coming across Kendrick was not the horse's fault. He wasn't part of some horsey plot against me. I knew it. They were *not* going to blame the horse. "He's not a beast, and we rode to the *ocean*, not the Vamp. Kendrick surprised *the beast* just as much as he did me. The ceffyl...cef...*whatever*...didn't do anything wrong.

"The bigger question is—how did Kendrick know I would be here?"

Chapter Four

ဢ

"Hogan," I said softly, looking at the shimmering gold fabric at my feet. It was beautiful but not what I wanted for the occasion.

Gnomes' magic was passed to them by their fathers and was geared toward a trade. Gnomes knew what they wanted to be as they grew up and trained their craft for that particular purpose. Hogan's mastery of fabric had won his position with the High Priestess at a very young age. He was a meticulous perfectionist, took clothing so seriously at times it was almost comical. A small imperfection in my appearance irritated him profoundly, so my question needed to be asked delicately.

"Yes, my lady?" The brilliant blue surrounding his dark eyes sparkled in the candlelit bathroom.

"Would it be an insult to your talent to request a specific dress for this occasion?" I watched his face for a hint of displeasure. Instead his smile was full, showing all his tiny, sharp teeth. His little green mohawk tilted to the left.

He bowed. "It is an honor that you liked one of my creations so. What would you like to wear?"

"If it's appropriate, I'd like the midnight blue and gold gown you made me the night Lord Tynan returned to his castle." I had felt beautiful in that gown, and needed all the confidence I could manage this afternoon.

"Very lovely." He looked pleased, almost giddy. He waved his little hand and mumbled. Piles of silky midnight blue replaced the gold at my feet. Another mumbled incantation and the fabric swirled through the air and wrapped around me. With an inspired grin, he mumbled yet again and gold and blue braided cording twisted into my hair.

In my excitement, I rushed to the mirror in the bedroom. He had done my hair up and twisted and curled it into the fabric. Long tendrils fell around my face and neck, giving me a very feminine look.

Manus came through the door and his face lit up. "You look divine, my lady."

"Divine?" Hogan tsked and crossed his arms over his own finely made gold suit. "She is a vision."

Manus offered me his arm. "It's almost noon. You ready for this?"

"Do I have a choice?"

* * * * *

We headed down the hall and I prayed I wouldn't forget the courtesies Bevin had taught me. The three of us stood waiting behind giant wooden doors carved with graceful Celtic designs. I studied the designs for a time before I realized that they were actually wards, carved into the wood to protect all who entered. I followed the designs with my eyes. I needed both the protection and luck.

Hogan was behind me, drawing a ward on my back with little fingers. The subtle sizzle of his magic calmed me. I took a deep, steadying breath. *This is my home, my place.*

The doors opened as if I had willed them to and Manus escorted me into the room, my hand tucked into the crook of his elbow. I thought it would have been an imposing space, since it was used for the political meetings and ceremonies of WildLand, but like the rest of the manor, the cavernous space was homey. Softly glowing lights and soothing sea-foam-green walls gave no hint of the power accumulated in the beings currently occupying the room.

A low murmur echoed off the cobblestone floor as I entered. All eyes were on me as I made my first appearance to the Kith and faced my first test. They knew my history, my parents, my world—but none knew me. I held my head high and looked around the room to meet the eyes of some of the guests standing around tables and along the far wall. Their assessment of me as a future leader would start now, and I wanted to make a good impression for Doran.

I turned my gaze from the tables and down the line of leaders. Feldema was glaring at me from the end of the line. Her blonde hair glowed around her sour face.

"Remember most of the men here are available," Manus whispered as we moved into the room.

"I'm aware of Doran's ulterior motives," I said under my breath. I smiled and nodded to Hogan as he took his place by the door. When Doran stepped forward to meet me, I released Manus and placed my hand on hers, hoping no one but her noticed the slight tremble. Her face carried a tinge of nervousness. It was gone as we approached the first in the receiving line.

"Simon James," Doran announced and gracefully turned me to face him. I did the smallest of curtsies. Simon was a Werewolf. The Were wielded some magic and the curtsey was a small show of respect to his rank. This particular Were was the Alpha male of the largest pack in America, located in the Mountains of North Carolina. He also ran one of the largest pharmaceutical companies in the United States.

"Mr. James," I repeated. His face was long and deliciously ferocious. Dressed in a well-tailored, chocolate-brown suit that complemented his dark-caramel hair, he looked like a sleek animal. Lean and extremely fit, Simon was a pleasure to look at.

I let my gaze roam from his head to his perfectly polished shoes as a show of appreciation of his prowess, making sure that my face expressed the fact that I found him attractive. And truthfully, I did. The Weres were very aware of sexuality and animal instinct. Showing him I found him physically worthy of his position as Alpha was a great compliment. I reacted to him strongly, a snap of energy sizzling between us.

When I met his gaze again I could easily see he was pleased by the exchange.

"I'm honored." His voice was thick and gruff. His amber eyes danced with heat and his desire had begun to show through the bulge in his slacks. The magic of the Were came from the animal side of his being, and that animal was attracted to my magic as well as my appearance. I felt the now familiar burn in my belly, the swell of my magic trying to reach to his, and concentrated on reining it in. I diverted my gaze to acknowledge the two other pack members that stood just behind him. It gave us both a moment to collect ourselves. I needed to get better control of my senses. If I continued to let my power flare so easily, things could get tricky.

Doran turned me to the next in line. "Deloris Matherson," she said as I turned to face the next guest. Definitely a Witch, bookended by two Magicians who were far more beautiful than me. Most of the purebred Magicians were beyond pretty. They wielded magic within them that was not as strong as the Witches', so Magicians were relegated to consort status within the council. Deloris sneered as I looked over her consorts. She was on the foe list, according to Abbey. Her son had been one of Feldema's early consorts and the two still held a strong loyalty to her.

"I am pleased to meet you, Deloris." Even though the woman was the leader of a large coven, only first names were used for Witches. She nodded slightly, and Doran quickly moved to the next in line.

"Lord Harkkas of the Trolls," Doran announced and turned me to face the Troll. Surprised, I sucked in a deep breath. The Troll was every bit of seven and half feet tall, with skin that looked like a cross between algae and brown leather. His face and head were rounder than that of a human, his eyes as dark as still mountain pools, and he smelled of the river. Lord Harkkas bowed deeply to me and I returned the gesture. The Trolls were on the friend list. They couldn't move openly in the human world but they weren't the violent Trolls of fairy tales. They enjoyed a good life and wanted it to stay that way. Trolls would fight to protect but otherwise, I was told, they were very gentle beings.

We stopped to greet several other Witches, Imps, Goblins and Gremlins. I had managed everything with grace and with the proper courtesy. Then we came to the Slaugh.

"King Bran of the Slaugh," Doran announced, keeping her tone as neutral as she had with the others. I hoped I could do the same. I made a small dip—to do otherwise was to show weakness to him. To look him square in the eye, I had to straighten to my full height and look up slightly. His crinkled, black face was tucked far back in a hooded cape. It looked more like a skull that actual flesh-and-blood and was beyond creepy, but I held his gaze and tried not think of the attacks and lose my temper. The stench of death hung around his form. His body took up a great deal of space but I guessed that without the voluminous robes it would be hollow and unsubstantial.

"King Bran," I said sternly.

"I am happy to see you in the flesh, little girl," he whispered, as the Slaugh do. The comment was a blatant insult, since there was nothing he would like better than to actually eat my flesh. I was now free to return the favor.

"You are as lovely as I imagined," I said so low that even those closest to us wouldn't hear, and I kept the eye contact. He winced and the haze started to thicken around his hooded features. I smiled. Doran turned me away before he could say more.

I caught sight of Tynan in the background with some others whom I had met previously. My heart leapt and my body tingled at the very thought of him.

I knew who was last in line, and was not looking forward to seeing her again at all. Doran turned me to my half sister. "The Priestess of the Seas, Feldema," she said in the same bored, formal tone she had used to introduce the others. Feldema bowed to Doran but not to me.

"Feldema," I said, intentionally leaving off her title.

She righted herself. "Keena." There were murmurs all around at the snarl in her voice. Kendrick stood behind her, his face bruised from this morning's incident with Tynan. I couldn't help but let a small smile cross my lips. Feldema's youthful, pretty face tightened. She leaned in as if to kiss my cheek. "You will not live to All Hallow's, old sister," she said for my ears only.

I clenched my teeth under my politically correct smile before replying, "You'd better hope not." I knew her powers were strong but I had no intention of letting her think I was afraid.

She drew in a gasp and pulled back. Pure hatred was painted in the lines of her face. Having no reason to feel the same for her, I didn't understand the intensity. Having been here on WildLand for so many years, and thinking I would never come to power, must have given her a sense that she would go unchallenged to the head of the council. That still didn't begin to account for such raw hatred. I had entertained the idea of trying to reach out to her. After all, she *was* my half sister. But there was no hope of making friends here.

Manus had explained that her foster parents had spoiled her as a child. Then the inhabitants of the island, who all assumed I was lost, doted on her as she grew into her powers. Feldema became even more spoiled, and those seeking power only boosted her swelling ego. My return challenged her—and Feldema had never been challenged. She didn't like the idea of having to prove her worth. *Well too bad.* I may have been new to the Kith but even I could see she was dangerous. Dangerous to us all.

Doran turned at the head of the room and we both made a small bow to signify that the introductions were complete and the feast could begin. All the assembled Kith started milling about and greeting each other. But my sister had other plans for the day.

"Doran, High Priestess of the Winds." Feldema's voice rose above the chatting of the crowd. "I call for the first Battle of Birthright now!" Gasps came from all over the room. I watched my sister's expression carefully.

"Feldema!" Doran exclaimed. Her brow was drawn and harshness that I'd never heard before colored her voice. "This is a banquet, not a council meet."

"I have the right and I demand the fight this day!" Feldema was absolutely seething. "I call for it *now* and you have no choice but to grant my challenge."

Doran looked to Bevin for assistance, to find a way out for me. When I had feared things would go badly today this was the last thing I had imagined. Doran's obvious lack of confidence in me hurt. I didn't want to fight today but there was no way I was going to let Doran think I wasn't ready. I stepped up next to my wicked half sister.

"I accept."

More gasps from the crowd. I looked to Manus and he came to my side and stood, legs spread slightly and arms crossing his chest. If little sis wanted to play today, we were ready. I may not be able to take her with magic yet, but I could take her in a fair fight.

I glanced at the tacky Vampire at her side and *hoped* the fight would be fair.

"Keena, you do not need to battle. This is your introduction and—" Doran began.

"I will not dishonor you or the council by not accepting this challenge." I lowered myself to one knee and bowed my head, my gown billowing out around me. With that statement, and the respect I was showing the council, I had drawn first blood. I'd taken the high road, making Feldema look like the spiteful child she was. I could feel hatred and anger emanating off her, along with power. It felt very different from the inviting glow of Doran's.

Her magic was cold and empty but her temper was hot—and that, thankfully, could be used to my advantage.

I raised my head to Doran. Several expressions crossed her face as she slumped into her chair on the dais. I could see she was impressed by my calm. "So be it," she said to me and then raised her voice to the others in the room. "In one hour's time. You have made the challenge, Feldema. Choose the location and the weapons."

"I choose here, in the meet room, to demonstrate for the Kith my superiority. Simple, short blades—so I can see her eyes as she cries in pain." Feldema was trembling in anger, her voice cracking. The murmurs around us echoed my surprise.

Doran leaned back in her chair and looked to me with a defeated expression. I bowed again and remained on my knee. "I accept the challenge and the boundaries."

* * * * *

Hogan and Manus diligently gathered my weapons and clothing. Neither seemed worried. When Manus finally spoke, his voice was calm. "You won't have your protective gear on. You're accustomed to the feel of the blows but the cut of a blade is going to be a new sensation. Be prepared for it."

I nodded my understanding. We'd had this conversation before. I wasn't sure if he was repeating his usual instructions for his comfort or my preparation. Hogan produced my black leather pants and tight leather tank top. We had planned on a special suit for the battle, but I was glad it was my usual workout garb. I had two short daggers with five-inch blades, one strapped to either thigh. A larger dagger was in a sheath at my waist and a little knife was tucked into my right boot. Feldema would be armed with an equal number of weapons.

As Hogan braided my hair back out of my face, I started to feel the adrenaline. I couldn't contemplate Feldema's motives for the abrupt call to battle, but I knew I was going to be fighting for real this time—real punches, real blood, real injuries and real consequences.

The stability of the supernatural world rested on the shoulders of the High Priestess. Feldema's erratic episodes made it easy to understand why most of the Kith wanted *me* in the position and not her. The woman was unstable and emotionally irrational. I shivered, trying to imagine her as head of the council.

No. She wouldn't win. This was *my* birthright, not hers.

"Ready?" Manus asked as he jerked the sheath at my waist one last time. I nodded.

The doors to the meet room opened as we approached. Tables that had been set up for the feast had all been removed. At the end of the room, Doran sat between her consorts on the dais, elevated above the cobblestone floor. With the tables gone I could see faded bloodstains on the old floor. This obviously wasn't the first battle to take place in the unassuming hall.

On either side of Doran were two identical sets of seating, each with three chairs. Feldema was already in her seat to Doran's right and dressed much like me, but her leathers were white. I guessed she intended not to spill any blood on them. Her shirtless blond and Kendrick were sprawled in their chairs on either side of her. The chairs to Doran's left were vacant.

So, there was more to this show than just the battle. It was a display to prove that I'd not chosen a consort. That I'd not come into my full powers yet. Doran followed the direction of my gaze and nodded in agreement of that assessment.

All the guests were now standing along the walls, still in their finery. The crowd looked bigger than it had earlier. I strode as confidently as I could to my seat and Manus moved to stand behind me. The chairs to my sides stood glaringly empty. Lord Tynan stood close but not on the platform. I could feel him there but didn't risk looking at him for fear of losing my composure.

Doran stood. All whispers came to a stop. "This is the first contest to determine the next High Priestess, to prove birthright. I had hoped we would not start the rituals until closer to the correct moon phase, but so be it." She paused, emphasizing her displeasure at the situation. "The prophecy continues. The daughters of Trevina will prove their worthiness, their strength and their cunning in battle. Agnus the Betrayed foretold the coming of the twins, and the ritual of birthright has been called for the first time in many generations. It is an important time for all Kith. May the Goddess bless these two Witches with her strength and wisdom."

She turned her attention to us. "The rules of the battle are very simple," she said, facing Feldema. "You are to fight until one of you is completely disarmed. This is *not* a duel to the death. *No* magic is to be used. Understood?" As she sat back down, her gown gathered gracefully at her feet. She'd never had to complete a ritual like this. No. She'd inherited her position when our mother died.

Feldema leapt to the floor, her movements abrupt and choppy in her haste. I assessed the crowd, got up slowly and tried to look as unimpressed with her as I could. My unhurried, calm appearance was making her mad. Her eyes narrowed, jaw tightened—and that was just what I wanted. She bowed deeply as I came face to face with her. The room was absolutely silent as I returned the gesture.

As soon as my face was up, she caught my jaw with a fast right hook. Reeling from shock, I spun backward from the blow but managed to draw one of the short daggers as I righted myself. She was fast but I recovered before she lunged at me with a swipe of her short blade. I jerked to the right and she missed. I gave her a mean blow to the face from my elbow as she passed.

She spun around and spat blood from her busted lower lip. Her eyes were burning with anger. With more bravado than I felt, I winked at her to rub it in. Those cold, steel-blue eyes connected with mine for a silent moment of blame before she lunged at me with a high-pitched scream.

I was easily able to get out of the way and followed her around as she passed, gouging her shoulder with the dagger. She shrieked again, not from pain but anger. She kicked backward, hitting me square in the stomach and knocking me off my feet. When I hit the ground, she threw herself on top of me, driving her blade into my side while forcing her knee into my pelvis. The cold sting of steel slicing through skin was more shocking than Manus could have ever prepared me for.

I bit my lip and closed my eyes against the nauseating pain taking over my mind. She twisted the shaft. Instinctively, I reacted to the additional pain by circling my leg over her head and striking her across the face with my knee. The force sent her tumbling. She lost one of the blades from her sheath in the roll.

"Oohs" and "ahhs" drifted from the onlookers. I stood holding my side as she tried to right herself. Her second blade was still in my side, stuck in the skin and protruding from my back. I grabbed the handle and pulled it out. I felt the warmth of my blood running down my hip as I tossed the blade to the ground. It skidded across the cobblestone floor and stopped just in front of Kendrick. Four to two — my favor.

She attacked again, bending and grabbing me around the waist, squeezing the wound in my side as we fell to the floor. I cringed but wouldn't give her the pleasure of screaming in pain, as I knew she wanted. In the struggle, she plucked the remaining short blade from its sheath on my thigh and threw it before I could knock her off. It was a coward's way to disarm but she'd taken it. "Easy way out, sis?" I asked as I got back to my feet. There were more rumblings for the crowd.

She growled and charged. I spun and hit her in the face with a roundhouse-style kick before she could reach me, cutting her forehead with my boot heel. Blood from both her mouth and the new cut streaked down her face and dripped onto her white leathers. She stood staring at me, obviously shocked. I took the opportunity to go on the offensive. She jerked away from my blade but I elbowed her hard in the stomach with my left arm. As she doubled over, I brought my knee up. It connected squarely with her face. The satisfying blow was hard enough to launch her to her back.

Her head smacked the cobblestones with a low thwack, knocking her out cold.

I walked over and stood above her, kicked her lightly on the thigh to make sure she was completely out before leaning down and removing her other blades, tossing them to the side. I stood tall, making eye contact with as many members of the Kith as possible as I turned to Doran. Our gazes held as I dropped to one knee. Blood dripped from my side, soaking through the leathers, down my leg and into my boot. The wound was bleeding freely, leaving a small puddle on the tile.

Kendrick's face was so tight I thought his skin would tear. "So you fight like a man—is that why you can't get one for your bed?" he hissed.

I reached down and grabbed hold of Feldema's white leather shirt, soaked with blood that had dripped from her face. I dragged my half sister's unconscious body to her consort. "You have no need to concern yourself with my bed." I dropped her at his feet.

"I would not dirty myself with a human the likes of you," he said quietly as I walked away.

The comment made me mad. I'm not truly sure why, but it did. I was part human, after all. I still had the adrenaline rush going and the jerk had attacked me with intent to kill the day before. I turned back and marched right up to his face. "Then dirty yourself with this!" I flipped my fingers, splattering his face and shirt with Feldema's blood, and turned away again.

The whole room gasped and then went silent.

That can't be good.

"I'll take that challenge, Keena, Priestess of the Wild." When I looked back at him, Kendrick bowed deeply to me.

"You will not!" Manus rushed toward Kendrick only to be held in check by Tynan. "She knows not what she challenged!"

Kendrick tilted his head and gave an evil smile to Manus then turned and bowed to Doran. "Her ignorance is of no matter to me. She made the challenge and I accept."

I watched them argue as the blood was draining from my side. I was tired, faint. Bevin came to my side and slid her arm around me to keep me standing.

"No!" Manus shouted.

"I am sorry, Manus...but I am bound by the rules of the council." With a solemn face, Doran turned to leave.

Manus picked me up and carried me to a small room not far from the meeting hall. He set me in a chair. "I've told you to hold your tongue time and time again, Keena!" He was angry and if my wound hadn't stung so much my feelings might have been hurt by his tone. Besides, I really didn't know what I had done.

Bevin was tending my side and saying her incantations as fast as she could. She had tears welling up in her eyes. That, more than anything, sent a chill of fear through me. I didn't think that the ever-bubbly Bevin could cry. She got mad, sure. But I was concerned with the tears.

I was about to ask what exactly I had managed to do when Doran flung the door open. "What have you done, Keena? What have you done?"

I looked up from my side and Bevin. "That was *my* question."

"You offered to allow Kendrick to avenge Feldema's defeat," she said, pacing behind me.

Bevin broke out into sobs but kept murmuring her healing spells.

"Oh. *Shit*." I was hardly in any shape to fight a Vamp. In top form I couldn't best a Vamp without magic. I was in another mess. "Did anyone tell me about this particular rule? I think I would have remembered this one."

Tynan stormed through the door, stopping when he spotted me. He shook his head and knelt in front of me.

"I will fight Kendrick for you." He took my bloody hands in his. Those dark eyes burned in anger.

"You are not her consort, so you can't." Manus couldn't seem to look at me. He spoke instead to the wall. I could hear from the rasp in his voice he was fuming.

"Keena, allow me this. Take me as your consort." Tynan tried to soften his face but his tone was stern, sincere. "Allow me this."

The consequences of my actions were sinking in slowly and I was so tempted to agree. But again I thought of him alone after my death, and shook my head. No. I couldn't.

Tynan looked up, still rubbing my hands in his. "Doran, talk to her. She will die."

"I can't let you do this, Tyn—" I froze when I heard his voice in my head.

Let me defend you.

A Vamp trick that was true from the movies. To have him in my mind was comforting and frightening at the same time.

The others were arguing around me. I couldn't bear the thought of him miserable and alone for an eternity. I spoke aloud. "I would rather die than have you bound to me forever. I can't do that to you."

He took my face in his strong hands. *I will love you forever anyway, mon guerrier. Allow me the honor of being yours, of fighting Kendrick for you. Allow me to love you while I can. Do not worry about eternity. I have left the love of women out of my life for more than a century and can do it again if I must. If you die tonight,"* his eyes closed, *"I will not love again. Somehow you have already taken my heart.*

I felt tears coming. I fought them. Doran was talking about Tynan to Manus behind me. I heard something else I didn't like.

"She will have other consorts."

"If I let him do this, I will not," I said firmly.

"You will *have* to," Bevin said, avoiding my eyes.

I heard her words but they didn't help me in this situation. I looked again at Tynan. "I can't…"

Tynan reached up and kissed me tenderly on the forehead. "You don't have a real choice *mon guerrier*, Kendrick will kill you easily."

"We're out of time," Manus said. "He's right. The decision is right."

"The prophecy…" Bevin sobbed.

I was too tired to ask. I felt weak from the loss of blood and fear for things that were yet to come. I looked at the man at my feet. He reached out and placed his hand over my stomach.

"Keena, open yourself to me. Let your magic guide your heart. It will know what to do. It will know who I am to you." A feeling of bliss overwhelmed me as my power answered the press of his. I gripped his shoulders as the strength of the surge caused me to gasp and close my eyes.

That was it. I knew. I was no longer able to fight it.

He didn't need words either. Tynan lifted me gently and carried me back to the meet room, which was now a battlefield, and set me in my seat. Kendrick stood in the center of the room, waiting with a satisfied smirk on his narrow face.

Doran took her place and announced, "Lord Tynan of the Sparta."

More gasps and some light applause came from the gathered crowd as Tynan took his seat in the chair to my right, making an official statement of his new position as my consort. I studied his chiseled features. His face was blank, his eyes cold, angry and not wavering from Kendrick. I looked to the Vamp in the middle of the room.

He paled as he realized his fate.

Doran moved to the center of the room and Tynan followed, standing next to his challenger. They spoke back and forth about the match to come but my mind was focused on the newly added stains, still fresh, on the cobblestones. I was struck by the seeming innocence of the room — with its flower boxes and light-colored walls — contrasted against the violence that had occurred here. How often were grievances settled in this matter, I wondered?

Kendrick's vehement objections brought my attention back to the situation at hand. Doran quickly negated his objections and reiterated that he had requested the right of vengeance and that my consort could stand for my honor if so desired. Feldema was absent from the room, so I assumed she remained unconscious.

The Vampires circled each other a moment. "This will be quick," Manus whispered in my ear.

The two Vamps looked so different. Kendrick still wore cheesy Goth clothing, minus his cape. The only thing that gave Tynan's connection to the past away was his shirt, a cotton tunic instead of a more modern button-down. It somehow blended well with the modern dress slacks that so wonderfully showed off his trim waist and strong thighs.

As I scanned the room, I saw King Bran watching with great interest from the sidelines, beady eyes glowing from under the dark hood.

Kendrick attacked first in an attempt to get the upper hand, and although even I could see how feeble the move was, my hands tightened into fists. Tynan seemed to stand still, waiting for the other Vamp to reach him—and then he was gone. His movements were so fast, so graceful, that watching him made me suck in my breath, feeling the now familiar warmth blossom in my belly.

Reappearing behind Feldema's consort, Tynan clutched the other Vamp's shoulder, violently halting his forward impetus. Then the two became a blur of swirling motion. I couldn't tell one from the other. I had to grip the chair to force myself to remain still. All I wanted to do was lean forward and scream Tynan's name.

There was a hiss followed by a wet gurgle—and all movement stopped. The room seemed to release a sigh as I blinked, trying to absorb what I was seeing. Tynan's eyes met mine and I could see the rage drain from them, just as the life was seeping from Kendrick. For a moment Feldema's consort hung like a rag doll, his throat a shattered mess, then he fell to the floor, released from Tynan's hand.

Dropping to one knee, Tynan plunged my blade into the heart of my sister's consort.

And still he held my gaze. The power inside me grew from a warm glow to a blazing inferno. He was magnificent. And now he was mine. A shiver of awareness passed over my skin. As if in acknowledgement, Tynan dipped his head toward me, his eyes seeming to echo the fire moving through my body.

The cozy room fell into an eerie silence for a heartbeat. Darkness threatened to overtake me again but I held fast to Tynan's face. He was still looking at me, his gaze intent, personal, not part of the fight that had just transpired. Neither of us heard the noise that started to fill the meet hall again. We stayed locked in a trance that was just between the two of us.

Briefly I broke the hold of his gaze to look again at the dead Vampire at his feet. One less foe to worry about—but Feldema would not be pleased when she woke up.

* * * * *

Tynan carried me in his strong arms back to my chambers, following Hogan. The Gnome's short legs were cranking fast in an effort to keep Tynan from running him over. The blur of gold and shimmering green amused me, in spite of the pain in my side and the weight of recent events.

Tynan stepped into the room—and stopped, hesitating for just an instant. But in that jerky halt, I felt a wave of joy wash over him.

When we had arrived at the manor, I had Hogan decorate my chambers to almost mirror Tynan's room at Castle Dracula. The only differences here were two large windows that connected me to the outside world. It was essentially the same room. I had loved the feel of the space, mostly because it reminded me of Tynan. The only thing that had been missing was the smell of him—and now it was here. He regained his composure and took me to the bathroom where Bevin and Manus already waited.

Bevin tended my wounds while Hogan ran a bath for me. Peeling the leather off without magic to prevent tearing at the cuts, she put a thick salve made of strong-smelling herbs on the stab wound. It stung and I cringed. Tynan was watching from the corner of the room, his own clothes covered in blood. I couldn't read the expression on his face.

"It's only through the skin. Lots of blood but she'll be fine," Bevin deduced as she worked.

Tynan closed his eyes. "Leave us." The sternness of his voice stopped all movement around me.

"She is in no condition to—" Bevin started, but Tynan held up a hand.

"I'll tend to her. Leave me your amulets." He didn't move or open his eyes.

She hesitated and looked to Manus. He placed some towels on the counter and motioned for Hogan. "She's in very capable hands this night." Manus looked at me and nodded before turning to leave. "Call if you need anything."

Once it was just the two of us, Tynan gently cut away the remaining leathers and let them fall to the ground with the bloody towels. His movements were careful and deliberate. Neither of us spoke but I could feel his pain for me, mingled with the smell of blood and fear. The concern clenched my heart. I reached out with a trembling hand and wiped some blood from his cheek. "Yours?"

"No. My wounds are minor, don't concern yourself." He had all my clothes off and hooked one of the golden chains that Bevin had left around my waist. The amulet in the shape of the fox—for a speedy recovery—dangled at my bellybutton. It glowed from her powerful healing spell when it touched my skin. Tynan's strong arms lifted me and gently placed me in the tub.

With a tenderness and gentleness that seemed alien to his ultra-male exterior, Tynan washed my wounds and the dried blood from my face and hair. I watched wordless as he caressed me and tended each scratch and bruise. I was tired but I knew as I watched his hands move over me, if he took me in his arms then and there, I could love him all night.

I didn't move to make that happen. I only watched his hands, his face. Bevin had said that Witches used more brain capacity than humans, were more sensitive to all things. I supposed I shouldn't have been surprised to find that I would love stronger and maybe even sooner than I ever had before. The feelings were there. I could no more deny them than I could the rest of this strange world to which I now belonged.

* * * * *

I woke up again in the softness of cotton sheets and velvet, moonlight shining through one of the large windows in my room. Images of the battle and Tynan rushed through my mind. I remembered the bath and his tenderness, and smiled into the pillow. I opened my eyes when I heard his voice, sitting up slowly to see Hogan pouring wine at the table. They both looked at me.

"This should be fine," Tynan said to Hogan, a polite way of telling him to leave.

"I fell asleep?" I asked, embarrassed. The man had agreed to be my consort, to give his heart to me for eternity, and then fought for my life—and I fell asleep on him.

I got out of the bed and started toward the table. Tynan's mouth curled in a sultry grin, causing me to stop and look down. Hogan had outdone himself this time. The short silk nightie was tight across my chest, pushing my breasts up so much they were bursting out. The shimmering, emerald-green fabric gathered at my waist and then barely fell over my hips. The panties were not much more than a ribbon. I blushed. "Hogan!"

"Keena." Tynan's voice was husky and he didn't try to hide his desire. I could feel it across the room, a calling from his magic that teased my senses like a small flame scorching my mind and body.

Hogan bowed as he backed toward the door. "I will take my leave. If you require anything else…" His grin was taking up his whole face and his little green mohawk wiggled as he winked.

"Go," I said, giving him a dirty look to back up my order. When the door closed I turned back to Tynan, who offered me some wine. I needed it. I took a tentative step toward him. He'd cleaned up and changed as I'd slept. The crisp white tunic was loosely laced from neck to mid-chest and the tight leather pants hugged his thighs nicely. His gaze moved over the nightie.

"I…I, um…fell asleep on you." I looked into the wineglass.

He let out a little laugh as he gathered the reason for my embarrassment. "The amulet, Keena. It's powerful magic. I knew you would sleep the day away. You needed it. You've done no damage to my ego."

"Oh. Good." Then I realized that my cut didn't even hurt. Fondling my side through the silk, I felt the wound tingle at my touch but for the most part, it seemed fine. He was still staring at me from his chair.

I put my glass back on the table and straddled his legs, sitting on his lap. "Then I need to take the time now to thank you for defending me." His hands stayed at his sides as I took his chiseled face in my palms and leaned in to lightly kiss him. I felt the surge of his magic spill over me and the slow burn of mine replying to his erotic call. I pulled back enough to see his eyes. The deep midnight blue was shimmering in the candlelight.

I slid my body closer to his, feeling the heat of his thick cock through the fabric separating us, enjoying the feel of his skin in my hands. I took his mouth with mine. No holding back. No fretting or concern over a faraway future. I made the kiss deep and demanding, searching his mouth with my tongue until I found his fangs. I ran the tip of it over them, no longer fearing the consequences of my decision. He tilted his head, letting me explore his mouth. Our tongues danced together as I tried to tell him with that kiss all that I felt.

Pulling back, ready to demand his touch, I realized something was wrong. His breath was coming in erratic bursts, his cock was rock hard in his pants—but he still hadn't moved his hands away from his sides. I ached with want for him but he seemed to be hesitating.

His gaze shot back to my eyes, the expression so intense, so full of hunger that I felt like the most beautiful creature on earth. I leaned in to kiss him again. This time his hands moved up my legs and slid around my back. His touch was heated even though his skin was cool. He returned the passion of the kiss, hungrily sucking on my bottom lip, pulling me against his chest. His skin warmed as his passion grew. His earthy scent filled my senses, made my pussy weep with desire. He stood effortlessly, lifting me, wrapping me in his strength, making me feel cherished. I held on with a grip stronger than I needed, as much to ground my reeling emotions as to dig my fingers into his sleek shoulders.

We stopped next to the bed and he pulled his lips from mine, not in hesitation but to let his gaze roam. It allowed me a moment to do the same. My God, he was beautiful. Tendrils of his silky hair had come loose from the band and a few stray golden curls fell over his eyes. I placed my feet on the floor and ran my hand up his stomach, feeling the tight, now-warm flesh under his shirt. Wanting to see him, all of him, I unlaced the top of his shirt and pushed it wide open, exposing those luscious muscles. His skin was the color of pearls and moonlight, and smooth to the touch.

I walked around him, taking my time, trying to slow my racing heart, trying to savor the moment. I stopped at his back. He looked over his shoulder and started to turn toward me. I stopped him by tugging his tunic down his shoulders, letting it pool at his waist briefly before pushing it to the floor. I ran my fingers softly down his back and around to his stomach. Goose bumps rose on his skin under my touch. He went stiff. "You're still holding back, Tynan." I sprinkled breathy kisses up his beautiful back.

"I don't want to hurt you, *mon guerrier*."

"Hurt me? You're the one who made the big sacrifice here. I'm afraid in the long run, you'll be the one who gets hurt."

I was still wrapped around him, my chest against his back, my fingers exploring his chest. He covered both my hands with one of his and pushed them down his torso. I had to take a gasping breath when I felt just what he was worried about. I smiled and kissed his back then let my fingers dance along the length of his cock. His back and shoulders stiffened. "We'll worry about that when the time comes, Tynan. I want you, all of you."

He turned and buried his face in my neck, placing a caressing kiss on the sensitive pulse point, sending delightful tremors racing down my spine. He hooked a finger in each of the straps of the teddy and dragged them forward until he had a strong grip on the green lace that barely covered my breasts. He clenched his fingers around the delicate fabric and jerked, ripping it all the way down. His lips curled in a satisfied grin before he released the ruined lace to join his shirt on the floor.

Tynan was no longer holding back.

I was on fire. My body felt as if it would go up in flames at the slightest spark. I made my own fist in an effort to keep myself from touching him again. I wanted to see where that sultry grin would lead.

He lifted me gently and placed me back against the velvet pillows, crawling up on the bed after me. Tynan ran his tongue along the gold chain still around my middle holding the pain amulet. I felt his magic, very different from mine, rushing over me like water pouring over polished stones.

I moaned softly, arching to feel more of his touch. One hand slid between my thighs, nudging them apart and lightly caressing the skin of my upper thigh. His tongue found its way to my breast and teased my nipple, making it stand at attention. I held my breath, concentrating on the warmth of his lips. Cradling his head against my chest, I pulled his hair completely loose from its band, reveling in the satiny feel of it as it spilled over my skin. His mouth became more demanding, his lips nipping and teasing my nipples. My pussy was swelling and throbbing. His smell, his magic, his touch were all causing their own spell over my senses.

I was writhing, ready to explode from just the play of his mouth on my nipples. He kissed his way up to my neck. I whimpered with need when his fangs teasingly scraped over my shoulder. "Do they frighten you?" he asked, his breath hot in my ear.

Sucking in air to be able to make a make sound, I barely got the words out. "No. I feel your powers through them." The essence of his magic flowed though me again, calling, stoking my nerves everywhere at once and overwhelming all my senses. Fighting the urge to both laugh and cry at the overload of intensity, I closed my eyes and let my head fall to the side, exposing my neck.

"If I frighten you, tell me."

I wasn't afraid. I didn't care at this point. "Bite me, fuck me. Whatever you want, Tynan—but *do it* for cauldron's sake!"

He laughed and started kissing his way back down my stomach. He tore the flimsy thong off and pushed my legs open farther to lower himself between them. My stomach tightened as he licked the inside of my thigh, teasing with his fangs. He kissed farther up my thigh until, with a flick of his tongue, he parted my pussy lips. I was already so wet. I gasped and bucked as I heard his voice in my head.

I do not need to bite you, mon guerrier. Your magic can touch mine without the blood exchange. After hanging so close to the edge of orgasm, I exploded from the first brief touch of his tongue as it brushed lightly over my eager clit.

His voice in my mind stroked me as surely as his tongue. As I screamed and tore at the sheets, he mercilessly teased with that sinful tongue, lapping and licking every crevice and paying particular attention to my clit, his fingers exploring my pussy, teasing the sensitive skin of my ass.

The pleasure was so intense, building so fast again that I couldn't take it. He held my hips tightly and kept me in his reach. Another powerful orgasm took me. I screamed his name into the night. He lifted his head, let loose my hips and I lay there as the ecstasy pulsed through me. Tynan rested his head on my thigh and watched me squirm from between my legs, grinning, pleased with himself.

When I calmed some, he leaned over and kissed me lightly on the stomach. "I've never been with a Witch. I didn't realize the effect of my powers. I'm glad to be able to please you in such a way."

I'd never been with anyone as a Witch before, but I was *very* glad he could please me that way as well. "Take off your pants, Lord Tynan."

"As my lady wishes." He was graceful as he stood, unlaced his leathers and pushed them off. He did it slowly, watching my reactions as he exposed his ivory flesh.

The sight of him nude brought a rush of excitement and apprehension over me. His shoulders were broad and strong, his stomach tight and muscled and his legs thick. His cock stood proud and erect. He climbed back on the bed and resumed a kneeling position beside me. I leaned over, kissing his chest and running little circles around his nipple with my fingers, enjoying the little tremors my touch spurred, the way his cock bobbed when he tensed. Tynan groaned and let his eyes fall shut. I lightly bit a peaked nipple and his groan turned to a growl.

In a hasty move, he shoved me onto my back, covered my body with his and nudged himself between my legs. He kissed me again, deep and passionate. I inhaled, taking his scent into me. Letting it tease my brain and spur my excitement. I spread my legs as wide as I could, feeling the glorious pressure of his cock against my opening as he pulled back from the kiss. His shimmering gaze held mine as he pushed that fat cock slightly inside me.

I arched back into the pillow. The stretching was more than I had anticipated. It wasn't going to work—there was just too much of him!

Kissing my neck and whispering reassuring words against my skin, he gently wrapped his arms under mine and gripped my shoulders, thrusting himself a little deeper. I felt the stretch, gripped his back and willed myself to relax. Tynan eyes were shut tightly. His golden brows were drawn together in strain. He was struggling to go slow, but I could feel his desires though our connection. He wanted to fuck me—and fuck me hard.

He pushed himself into me a little farther. I tensed again. *Relax, mon guerrier. I'll not hurt you, my love.* I could feel the love in his voice, feel it flow through me with each syllable he silently whispered. I took in an unsteady breath and willed myself to relax. He felt the tension ease and slipped the rest of the way in.

As he stilled for a moment, I could feel the pulsing of his engorged cock against the walls of my pussy. His hands gripped my shoulders a little tighter as he moaned his own pleasure. And then he started moving, oh-so slowly.

The pain disappeared, replaced with the ultimate bliss. With each stroke, my body responded eagerly to the feel of his cock, to the emotions he expressed with his touch. I thrust to meet him each time. I felt our magics start to mingle and the warmth from our joined bodies intensified to a point I hadn't imagined possible, filling my body, my mind with the surreal feeling of being enveloped in the combined powers, floating in a space not of this world, but one we shared only with each other.

I arched to him, pleading for more, grasping, clutching, loving the feel of his skin against mine and the friction of hot, sloppy sex.

I knew I loved him. And I could *feel* that he loved me. It was a completion I had never had in my life. I understood more in that moment about myself than I had from all the lessons and studying with Bevin, Doran or Manus. I felt it. I felt everything.

Tynan continued at his steady pace, making me tremble, making me beg. I was desperately clutching his arms and crying openly. He groaned in my ear and turned us over 'til I was looking down on him through my hair. Wiping the moisture from my face with a knowing grin, he didn't question the tears. He understood without explanation. We were open to each other and I could feel the mingled emotions we were sharing. He knew my desires, my fears, my power.

Take of me what you need.

I leaned back, pushing my hips forward, grinding him deeper inside me, further into my heart. Looking down on him, I felt as if part of me had been missing that I'd never realized was gone. His magic, his power poured over me and mingled with my own, giving back to me all I had lost during the battle, leaving me charged — and the sensation was divine. I could have drowned in his powers at that moment and not cared.

I lifted off his cock teasingly slowly for the first few strokes and watched as his face grew strained. His fingers dug into my hips. I could tell he was fighting his release. Leaning forward to brace myself with my hands on his chest, I accelerated my motions. A wildness came over me. I let myself go, opened myself to the power as Bevin had taught me to do. I felt the burn in my stomach rising and it echoed where we were joined. My pussy was on fire. It was as if we were engulfed in flames yet not being burned, the heat dancing around us.

I screamed as another shattering orgasm shook me. My nails dug into his chest, drawing blood. I felt him swell as he let himself come with me. Tynan shouted my name into the night, holding tight to my hips and pulling me hard onto his shaft.

The night exploded into white light and a tremendous clap of thunder. I didn't know if it was in my head or not — and at the moment I didn't care. I'd lost the strength to hold myself up and fell onto his chest, savoring the feel of his cock still throbbing inside me.

I lay there another moment, amazed, and then opened my eyes. I blinked twice to focus…

The huge plate-glass window was smashed into a thousand pieces. I turned to gaze at the other window that looked out over the back garden. That glass was also shattered, pieces of it gleaming in the moonlight on the lawn beyond. "I guess that thunder wasn't just in my head."

Tynan laughed. "No, my love. That thunder was born of your magic. I'm quite sure the entire island heard that."

I found the strength to sit up, still straddling Tynan. His eyes widened as he reached up toward my bellybutton. "Keena!" Hurriedly, he wrapped his arms around me and carried me to the mirror, setting me down facing away from it. He carefully brushed the tangled mass of hair from my face. He was grinning. I was amazed at the lightness of his eyes. He looked almost boyish.

"What are you doing?" I reached to kiss him but he abruptly spun me around to face myself.

The sight caught my breath in my throat.

I tried to talk but could only stare at my refection. My hair was falling in graceful waves all the way down my back, and around my face it feathered out like a lion's mane. The color had changed to a dark auburn, the shade of red oak leaves in the fall just before they drop from the tree. Golden streaks cut through it and shimmered so much they looked alive. My skin gleamed as brilliantly as the highlights. My hazel eyes were now a sparkling gold with flecks of black and green. Not a dark yellow but pure, glistening gold, like a piece of pirate's treasure.

"The spell," I whispered. I had come into my full powers and broken the remnants of Trevina's spell—and I was looking back at the face of the true Witch I had been born to be.

Looking farther down, I had to suck in a small gasp. On my stomach—from hipbone to hipbone and arching over my bellybutton—was a bold tattoo of the sun, seemingly rising from my womb. It was painted the same brilliant colors of fall, like my hair, and accentuated with golden streaks that shimmered in the candlelight. I touched it with the tips of my fingers. It was still warm from the heat of our bodies and magic.

The door flung open and Manus came barreling in with his sword drawn.

"No need for that." Tynan turned me to face Manus. I stepped in front of Tynan to block his nakedness but no one cared about the lack of clothes.

Manus saw the mark and fell to his knees, head bowed. Hogan came scurrying after him and as soon as he saw the mark, he did the same.

In unison, they looked up at me with identical expressions. Pride.

"My lady!" Hogan said, still out of breath from running after Manus.

"Get up, both of you." I turned back to look at myself in the mirror. I saw Tynan beside me in the reflection. Just looking at him made me weak in the knees. I let my gaze follow the line if his chest, down to his hips. "Oh! Tynan!"

He had a shadow of the tattoo as well. I turned and reached to touch his. It wasn't as bright or bold as mine, even on his light skin, but it was there. He looked down and saw it. His face filled with an emotion I didn't recognize as he ran his fingers over the mark.

"You have your full powers now," Manus proclaimed as he reached for my hand, placing a delicate kiss on my knuckles. When he released me, I placed both my hands on his shoulders to return the kiss—

He howled, jerking out of my grasp. Rubbing one of his shoulders, a smile crossed his face when he looked in the mirror. Where I had touched him, marks of the rising sun were left behind on my guardian.

Hogan shot to his feet to stand before me. "I wish to carry your mark as well, my lady!" He was practically spitting the words as he stood stiffly to appear formal. The look wasn't quite accomplished since, as usual, his mohawk fluttered back and forth from his abrupt movement.

Manus was still rubbing the burn. "You will be pledging your life for her and hers, Hogan."

"That, I have already pledged. It would be an honor to display the mark of her birthright for all to see." He stood as tall as he could with his chin tilted up.

I looked to Tynan and Manus, who both nodded. So I knelt before Hogan. I was worried. He wasn't as accustomed to pain as the rest of us were, and his blue-green skin and scales were so soft. I hesitated.

"I'm stronger than you think," he assured.

I nodded in apology and placed my hands on his shoulders. His jaw tightened and his eyes squeezed shut but Hogan remained silent. When I lifted my hands, dual symbols of the radiating autumn sun shimmered auburn-red on his tiny scales.

"Thank you for the honor." Hogan winked as I stoked his face with the back of my hand.

He looked up to Manus, crossing his arms over his chest. "*I* didn't cry out."

"*You* knew it was coming," Manus shot back, looking again at his shoulders in the mirror.

Chapter Five

෨

It was dark when I woke. With the windows covered, the only indication of morning was Tynan's cool and motionless body lying next to mine. His chest didn't move and his eyes didn't flutter at my touch. I guessed it was sleep. He wasn't dead. Well, not really, but I didn't want to know at that moment what happened when he slept.

I sighed. Thinking too much on our circumstances would drive me mad. We were now irrevocably connected. Dwelling on the distant future would only spoil the time we had together. We had years. I loved him and that had to be enough.

I snuggled up against Tynan's naked body, enjoying the quiet of the room. No Hogan, no Manus and none of the others fussing about to make sure I had everything I needed. Yet even with Tynan's luscious skin pressed next to mine, the pull of the forest became too strong to ignore.

I dragged myself away from him to prepare to go out and experience the wild with my new awareness. That's how it felt, the new power ignited within. Everything around me had new sharpness and clarity. It wasn't so much a visual thing as it was a new perceptual experience entirely.

As I soaked in the massive, claw-footed tub, I thought back over the events of the last month. So much had happened. So much had changed. I touched the mark of the priestess on my belly. It no longer burned but even under water the colorful streaks gleamed in the candlelit bathroom.

I felt guilty that I hadn't missed my old life, my human life, at all. I did worry about the parents who had raised me, wondered if they were okay. They believed I was dead, killed in the attack. It all seemed like a lifetime ago. But Doran had carefully explained that it was better they thought me dead. It would give them some closure. Doran was right—but how they must have suffered. I had to figure a way to do something for them. They couldn't know it was me, but I could do *something*.

I got out of the tub and dried off but realized that without Hogan there, I had no clothes. I wrapped myself in a towel so I could go search for the Gnome. Public nudity around my closest confidants was one thing, but traipsing around the manor in my birthday suit seemed inappropriate. I was quickly brushing my hair when I heard the chamber door open. *I can hear better?*

"Good morning, dear," Doran chirped as I met her in the bedroom. Grinning from ear to ear, Doran stopped to take a moment to admire the sleeping, naked Vampire in my bed.

"Oops," I said as I pulled the sheet from around his knees up to his waist.

The older Witch smiled and sat on the far side of the bed, not taking her eyes off Tynan. "I enjoyed the company of a Vampire Lord once, for about a month. He was a fabulous lover." Turning to me, her smile narrowed to a sly grin. "From the sounds of the sky last night, I assume you would say the same for Tynan."

A smiling, lighthearted and playful Doran was new. I watched her face as she savored her own memories. The softer look was becoming on her. She smiled again at the blush on my face. "I...the magic..." I really didn't know what to say, but she understood and didn't pry for details.

"I have seen Manus and Hogan this morning." She touched the tattoo on Tynan's stomach that peeked out above the edge of the sheet. "May I see your mark?"

I let the towel fall. I was proud of the mark and no longer ashamed of the body that carried it. In my human life, I would have died of embarrassment to stand naked before another woman. Now I was a Witch. I was Keena, Priestess of the

Wild, and my flesh was an embodiment of all that I was. I would never again feel the shame of a stifling, uptight society.

I *would* have walked naked through the manor looking for Hogan.

"The sign of the sun. It bodes well for you, my niece."

"Manus said that too. What did he mean?" I sat on the edge of the bed beside her. My hair was now long enough for me to sit on, so I had to push it back.

"You need not worry about that today. I feel the pull on you, the need to be out in the forest. Go and enjoy your domain, my niece." The soft lines etched into her face from the weight of her duties had practically disappeared. She looked so content.

"I feel it too, but I also know how much damage I've caused by not being as informed as I should be." I looked at Tynan. He was so peaceful, so gorgeous. We both just admired his form for a moment without talking.

"You're a wise one. I'll tell you some of what you need to know now but I want you to enjoy this day, Keena. You've earned it, and you have much to discover." She took a deep breath and got a faraway look in her eyes as she remembered. "When Feldema came into her powers it took us three days to get her out of the ocean." The memory seemed to stir feelings of regret. "She was a beautiful young woman. As she got older, the power-hungry woman you see now grew bolder. I all but encouraged her arrogance. I thought she needed the confidence as a young girl. As with most things though, Feldema took her confidence to the extreme. I'm ashamed, but much of her attitude can be laid at our feet. Since *you* didn't come into your powers as a teenager, Feldema, like the rest of us, assumed she would be my successor. I never would have dreamed she'd become such a mean woman."

"People are what they are." I ran my fingers over my mark. "What's her mark?"

"She is the Priestess of the Seas. Her mark is the crashing of the waves, the power of the sea. Yours is the rising of the autumn sun, the power of the harvest and giver of life."

Manus came through the door in his cat form, jumped on the bed and curled up at Tynan's feet. I wondered if Tynan was aware that we were all gathered around him. Manus' shoulders bore my mark even on his fur, two small auburn half suns stained into his gray. I rubbed his head out of habit.

"Long before Christianity, there were great kings in Ireland. The Kith coexisted with humans with little conflict, except an occasional tiff between men and the Slaugh or some of the Gremlins. The kings had the loyalty of all in their clans. Each king kept an Oracle as council and a Witch as a mistress. The arrangement created a political balance, leaving no reason for the supernatural to overthrow or undermine humanity."

She stood, walked to the table and poured a glass of water. "Then as Christianity started to spread throughout most of what is now Europe, fear and prejudice started to erode the peaceful coexistence.

"A young king who loathed the Kith came to the throne. He feared our power but couldn't resist the lure of magic or the touch of his Witch mistress. The Witch he chose, Agnus, served her role dutifully. She loved the king deeply. He took her affection and gave little more than lies in return. Since his queen bore no children to serve as heirs, he asked Agnus to carry his child. He told her the baby would be a child of love and not a political pawn. Agnus gave him twins, a girl and a boy.

"After their birth, he took the children from Agnus and exiled her to Thule, the island of the Slaugh, and deceived his followers into believing his queen had borne the children. In his lustful need for power, he mistakenly believed that the magic his children possessed would be overlooked by the very people he was trying to turn against the Kith.

"The king's plan backfired. In her anger, the queen threatened the king, telling him that she would expose him and his Kith children. He panicked at the thought of being seen as a sympathizer to the Kith. The queen convinced him that the children must be destroyed.

"With his plans to destroy the Kith in jeopardy, he staged an 'accident'. The girl survived, but the boy child was killed." Doran paused, and Keena could see the memories caused her pain just as fresh as if the events had unfolded yesterday.

Taking a deep breath, Doran continued, "Agnus had been betrayed. The King had used her body, he'd used her magic to gain power, he'd used her mind to gain information about the Kith and all the while, he had plotted behind her back to destroy them all.

"In her anger, she escaped the Slaugh—one of very few ever to do so. She returned to avenge her son and was able to save her daughter before any other 'accidents' could befall the girl child. She tried to stop the king's betrayal of the Kith but he had already set into motion things so grievous that we still bear that burden today. He went to the elders of the new churches and persuaded them that all Kith were pagan and evil, and that all species of magical power had derived their magic from the devil. Well, you probably know the rest."

I did. The burning times. "So what was the prophecy and how do I fit in?" I reached for Manus and snuggled him in my lap, watching Doran drain her glass as though her throat was suddenly parched.

"Agnus the Betrayed, as she'd become known to our kind, swore a curse on the king as she was burned at the stake. Her daughter was there in disguise to witness her mother's death. Agnus swore that the twenty-first Witch born to her blood would give birth to twins and that one of them would have the power and wisdom to reunite the Kith and humanity. Those twins would be born on Bloody Friday under the full moon. They would be very powerful—and would have to battle for birthright. One of them would be the salvation of the Kith."

Doran moved to refill her glass. "Your mother knew that her children would bear this burden, as did the rest of the

Kith—and many were plotting to prevent her from bearing her children at all. The Slaugh and some others have wanted to destroy or dominate the humans since we were relegated to the world of fairy tales and legend.

"My sister spent a good deal of her time fighting off attackers and carefully choosing consorts. She wasn't able to trust anyone. Hers was not a happy life. That's why she devised the spell to birth two very *different* Witches—two dissimilar women who would possess very different magics and very different personalities. In that way, Trevina knew her fulfillment of the prophecy would produce the strongest Witches possible to carry the burden of leadership.

"Then she hid the two of you away until your powers could help you protect yourselves. Few knew your locations or your identities. She lost her life being tortured by the Slaugh as they tried to find you both." Doran's expression grew pained once more at the thought of her sister. "But the brilliance of her plan kept you both safe."

I pondered a life knowing that my child would always be hunted. What would I have done to protect that child? "I wish I could have met her. She gave her life to protect me." Tears were running down my face.

"I feel, my dear, that the human blood you carry not only caused your powers to come to you late, but it will also provide the strength that will help you unite us all again."

"I have so much to learn." The joy of the morning had faded. "I have another question." Doran sat on the bed again, waiting. "Why the binding spell for my first lover?" I was running my fingers up Tynan's arm but he didn't move.

"It is also born of the Betrayal. You and Lord Tynan now share some magic. You may have his night vision or maybe some of his speed. You'll soon find out. And in return, he will share some of your magic. This is dangerous for us, as we are more vulnerable to our own magic than to that of others. The binding spell prevents those with the wrong motives from using the magic they've gained for betrayal or harm. You can choose whether or not to share your magic with other consorts, but with *la graine*, your magic is shared freely and instinctively. Thus the need for the spell."

I didn't like it any better but I understood the need for protection. I ran my hand through my still-damp hair. "What about his feelings, his ego?"

"Sharing yourself with others won't hurt him. It is part of who you are. You will have others for procreation, some for political reasons and maybe one or two just for pleasure. Tynan will expect it. His ego is well protected, my niece, since you chose him as your first and share your magic with him freely. You'll always have your thunder. Joining is different with all the Kith. They each have their own...special characteristics."

I lifted an eyebrow to her in question.

She let a little smile cross her lips. "The Vamps are powerful in bed," she touched his tattoo again, "but others have their own gifts. I would recommend if you meet up with a Troll that you have something to hold on to."

Manus lifted his head from the velvet. "My lady, don't frighten her."

She studied my face and then smiled. "She's not frightened. And I will warn that the Weres, with their animal nature mixed with your wild side...well, I would have some pain amulets available for afterward." She laughed at my open mouth and stood. I thought of Simon James and his long, lean body hiding under that fitted suit. Then winced with guilt over the thought and looked down at Tynan.

"But no one will ever bring the thunder for you like *he* will." She gently cupped my chin and raised my face. "That is why his ego will never suffer. No matter how different and how wonderful the others will be, Lord Tynan will be your favored and everyone will know that."

I knew *that* without being told.

"He has made a great sacrifice for you. I have no doubt that you will handle that and everything you face with grace and courage, Keena. And yes, there is much more for you to learn. But not today." Her thin lips curled into a knowing smile. "Today, you will go out and discover yourself. I will not ruin your first joining with all this." She turned to the door and said Hogan's name. He was there in less than a second. That never happened for me. "Please furnish Keena with appropriate attire for a romp in the woods." She turned back to me. "Go play with your magic."

* * * * *

I burst through the woods with a speed that amazed even me. I felt as if I could breathe through my skin. I had run and run and not tired, barely broken a sweat.

Hogan had dressed me in hiking boots, shorts, a green tank top—and a small blade on my side to appease Manus. It all moved with me as I flew through the trees and brush. The trees didn't exactly move for me, but I was able to bend and weave around them without really thinking about it. Even at high speed I was completely aware of everything. From the smallest to the largest living thing in the forest, I felt them all. I was part of the land and it warmed me. I understood why Feldema hadn't wanted to leave the ocean for days. If the water felt as good to her as the wild did to me, I understood well.

A gnarled old oak tree blocked the path, so I climbed it because I could. The view from the highest branch was amazing. I could see to the ocean in almost all directions. To the west a small gathering of large hills opened to grasslands that tapered to the ocean. In the east a set of small mountains tumbled down to the water's edge, making sharp cliffs and drops into the ocean. The air was crisp with no hint of pollution.

A large hawk swooped down and landed on a branch just out of my reach, screeching and flapping his wings as if agitated. He then took off, circled and landed again in a cloud of tussled feathers. I could *feel* his heart pounding as he worked those magnificent wings. His rich coffee-colored eyes darted about, unwilling to rest on one specific object. He screeched and blinked.

"Hello," I said.

He moved to a closer branch, so he was perched at eye level with me and only a few inches from the hand that was steadying my balance. I kept it still. He called out again and pecked lightly at my knuckles. I lifted my hand as slowly as I could so as not to startle the nervous bird, and held it out to him with my palm down. He ducked his head several times and took a step forward, ducking his head again and placing it under my hand.

As his feathers touched my skin, I felt my mark burning and the sizzle of magic in my hand. I pulled back immediately and lost my footing on the branch. Scrambling to gain my balance, I frightened him. He screeched and flew off.

Shit! I'd hurt him with my magic.

He made a lazy circle above the oak then landed back just where he had been. He lowered his head—and the symbol of the autumn sun was emblazoned on the gray and white feathers on and below his crest. He had taken my mark. More amazingly, he'd *known* to take my mark. I had to squint into the sun to watch him as he took off again, riding the currents above the ocean's edge.

Back on the trail, I slowed my pace. Occasionally I could feel the hawk's joy as he circled overhead. I had a new protector who would watch the skies for me.

The gurgling of a stream caught my attention. I followed the sound off the trail and to a small clearing. It was a beautiful sight. Stones and pebbles lined the banks and made little waterfalls, and at the edge of the clearing was a deep, clear, natural pool. The whole place hummed with life.

I couldn't resist. The day was warm and the water looked far too inviting to pass up. I pulled off my shoes and jumped in. The coolness of the water was shocking at first but as soon as I had made a lap the length of the pool, I had acclimated.

"Careful, my lady."

I had felt the presence of someone near, so the voice didn't startle me. Abbey came from the woods, naked and glowing. Following behind her was a fine-looking male Imp. He reminded me of a perfect doll, only the Imp was much more anatomically correct than any doll I'd ever seen. I didn't dare look away or I'd have insulted both of them.

"Abbey." I waded out of the water and sat on the bank next to where she had climbed up to sun herself on a rock. "Careful?"

"Feldema is the Priestess of the Seas." She leaned back against the stalk of a large, leafy plant I didn't recognize. The man sprawled on the grass at her feet. Male Imps were even more subservient to female Imps than Magicians were to Witches. He was lovingly stroking her leg. "Go on," she said, glancing down at him. "I need to talk to the priestess." He gracefully got up, smiled warmly and bowed to me then strode into the forest without looking back.

"She can affect the rivers and streams if she pleases," Abbey went on as I watched his perfect little ass disappear into the trees.

"I hadn't thought about that."

She gave me the look. The one you get from a friend who knows you stayed out too late the night before. "You had a good night. I heard it. How's your magic?"

All this time in the woods and magic hadn't really entered my mind. "I really don't know. I think I got some of Lord Tynan's grace and speed, but other than that..."

"You haven't tried any incantations yet?" She shook her head.

"I've been so wrapped up in the sensations of the forest... All right, I haven't even thought to try. Don't tell Bevin." Practical magic was the last thing I was thinking of. I was lost in the feel of the wild side of my magic.

She jumped to her feet. "Ditch the wet clothes and let's go have some fun."

I was so excited to have her help that I did just that. I stripped them all off and only put the blade back around my waist. "Now what?"

She giggled at me. I didn't care. I felt like giggling too. "Let's start with something simple. She picked up a pebble. "I'll toss it and you see if you can catch it," she said, letting the little rock fly.

I mumbled and the pebble stopped in midair and hung there. "First try!" She punched the air. "Now something harder." She pointed to a larger stone across the stream. "Bring it to you, and do it in your head—no words." I looked at her. I'd never even tried a silent spell. "Go on," she said with confidence. "Feel the power of the forest around you. Let it be a part of you, open to the sensations of it. Pull the substance of the spell from your womb. Most the time the words don't even matter."

I turned to the stream, concentrating on the essence of the spell, the soft earth beneath my bare feet, and felt the power moving in me. I thought the spell. The rock flew from its spot and straight at my forehead. I didn't even have time to catch it. It crashed into my head, knocking me back to the ground and cutting a gash in my eyebrow.

Abbey fell off her rock perch, laughing as she crawled over and checked my head. I couldn't help laughing with her as I wiped blood from my eye.

We spent the afternoon playing in the woods and trying different spells. With each one, I got more control. We laughed, joked and gossiped. As the sun started setting, we decided to make our way back to the manor. I marveled at the joy I felt in my heart and through my soul, the strength of the magic in my blood.

Abbey was riding on my shoulder as we made our way through an open clearing, following a path along the tree line. She was jabbering on about the antics of one of the other Imps in the kitchen when the hawk swooped low and screeched wildly. He landed in the clearing and flapped his wings violently toward the trees.

"Something's wrong," I said and instinctively put my hand on the handle of the blade at my waist.

A Slaugh swooped out of the woods, swiftly grabbing Abbey from my shoulder. He was about to take a bite from her tiny body when I lunged and kicked him hard in what should have been a stomach. My foot just met a bunch of dry, crusty bones.

It did enough damage to be a distraction and he dropped Abbey on the grass to turn on me. I crouched and held the blade out, waving it slowly. He lunged and after a short struggle with the blade, he got a grimy hand on my neck. I felt his black mist starting to gather around my face. I stabbed him twice but it did no good. I dropped the blade and plunged my hand inside the dried rib cage that was wrapped in rags and thought the spell for fire.

His dried bones and the fabric of the cloak burst into flames. The Slaugh howled and pulled away before evaporating.

I ran to Abbey, who was sitting up, staring at me. "You killed a Slaugh!"

"Yeah, so? I've seen Manus and Tynan do it enough times."

She lay back, putting her arm over her face. "But it took them years of training and practice. You...your powers shouldn't be..."

"Are you okay? Anything hurt or broken?" I didn't care about my powers right that minute. She pulled herself up and shook out like a dog. "I'm fine. Thanks to you."

I checked her over but found only a few scratches. "Race you to the manor," I said, still feeling the rush of the fight.

"Fine, but I get to use magic and you have to run."

"Deal." She was gone before I could even get the one word out.

I knew she would long beat me to the manor. I looked up to find the hawk that had alerted us to the danger. Had he not, the Slaugh might have been able to kill Abbey before I could do anything. "Thank you, my friend," I said, thinking that I needed a name for him.

Beyond the hawk, I realized the sun had set almost completely.

Tynan.

I ran with all I had over lumpy roots and through the thickest, darkest part of the forest. I was slightly winded and sweating. It was just full dark when I reached the edge of the back garden of the manor. My window was open and the candles were burning. I couldn't resist...

Keeping my pace, I leapt and dove in the window, tumbled head over heels and landed at the foot of the bed in a crouched position.

"Keena!" Bevin screeched. Manus and Tynan looked surprised for an instant then they both chuckled.

Tynan's smile didn't last once he realized I was nude and had blood on my forehead, shoulder and cheek. He grabbed me up quickly with one strong arm and with the other hand checked my face and head roughly. "You're hurt. What happened?"

I wrapped my legs around him without really thinking about it. I was so excited and felt so alive. I started babbling. "I was running like the wind...I could feel everything around me! I played with everything in the woods and a hawk took my mark...I have to give him a name...and Abbey played with me, helped me with my powers. I can spell without speaking...!"

Bevin gasped. My arms were rising and falling as I gestured wildly with my hands. Manus was still leaning against the wall with a smirk but Tynan looked as though he was going to burst with pride. "I climbed trees and swam in a pool and oh yeah, I killed a Slaugh! I really need to name the hawk—"

Tynan almost dropped me. If I hadn't had my legs locked around him I would have been on the ground. The glass of wine Bevin had been holding crashed on the floor.

They were all looking at me as if I was a maniac. I caught my reflection in the mirror and smirked at the maniac looking back. My hair was wild and tangled with leaves stuck in it. I was nude. My feet were filthy.

The door flung open and Doran came rushing in. "You killed a Slaugh." It wasn't a question. Tynan realized he had let go of me and put an arm around my back. Not that I really needed it, but it felt good to have his arms wrapped around me.

"I had to." I was still winded from the babbling and had to take a deep breath. "He was about to eat Abbey." I felt like I was apologizing.

"Abbey also told me that you can do silent spells." Also a statement but at least now she was smiling. I nodded and watched Bevin fall back into the chair, still looking very shocked.

"Abbey was pretty pleased with all of it. Why are you upset, Bevin?" I wiggled out of Tynan's arms.

"I'm not upset." She finally managed to get the horrified look off her face. I really hated that I kept upsetting her. I was trying so hard. "I just...it usually takes great practice to do silent spells. Most never can." I thought about that. She and Hogan both still mumbled their spells and incantations. She stood and tried to wipe the blood from my cheek but it was dried on hard. "It's fine, dear. I was only shocked. I have never heard of any who can do it the first day of their full powers." She looked at Doran. "I must thank Abbey for helping her. I would have never thought to have her try."

Hogan came in with a platter of cheeseburgers and fries. "From Abbey," he said, putting the plate on the table. "You're a horrible mess, my lady. I'll leave you some clothing in the bath." He headed to the bathing area.

Doran looked at the others. "Hogan's right. It is still her day." She turned to me. "We'll discuss the strength of your powers and how that may change things tomorrow. Have a nice evening, my niece." She looked over my shoulder to Tynan and smiled.

Still looking very amused, he pulled a leaf from my hair. "Bath or food first?"

I really couldn't decide. "I'm really hungry, but I shouldn't eat like this."

"And why not?" He pulled a chair around to the platter. "You are of the wild today. Eat like a wild woman and I'll get your bath ready." I sat and he poured the beer Hogan brought with the burgers. Not many others around the manor enjoyed beer but I still loved a cold brew. I was ravenous and ate twice as much as I usually would. Tynan watched me as if I was a meal myself. Even as filthy as I was, he was consumed with desire and I could sense it from him now more than ever.

When I finished, he conducted me to the bath and brushed out my hair before helping me step into the water. He bathed me gently but I could see the desire rising under the black leather pants he was wearing. I could tell he was trying to be patient as he worked but he was about to burst. I was as aroused as he was, maybe more. His excitement and the warm water had little quivers coursing through me with each teasing touch.

I couldn't stand much more. I wanted him. I wanted him wrapped around me, inside me. I stood without warning. "Lord Tynan, I didn't take you for a tease." He smiled up at me from his kneeling position by the tub. God, he was so hot with his sleeves damp, his smile revealing a tiny dimple on his left cheek and all that wavy, golden hair pushed out of his face and tucked behind his ears.

"I beg the lady's pardon." He stood, moving closer, so close that I could feel the heat from his chest on my bare nipples. I shivered, more from his heat than the cool night air. "I would never leave a lady wanting." He leaned down and kissed me, wrapping one arm around my waist and pulling my wet body to his. His other hand slid up into my wet hair. I could feel the full length of his aroused cock stressing the laces of his pants. He took his hand from my hair and lifted me up onto the bathroom counter, knocking over bottles and candles and pushing me against the black marble wall.

He pulled his shirt off over his head then buried his face under my hair, inhaling as his body pressed into mine. Wet kisses trailed down my neck. His fangs scraped across my heated skin. The intensity, the heat of his lips and the tingling from his teeth caused throaty moans from my body that I'd never heard. He peppered kisses and licks over my collarbone and down to my breasts.

I felt his magic and mine starting to mingle as our bodies touched. It was stronger than last night and I could barely stand it. I was wriggling, frantic with need, lifting my hips off the counter. When he leaned down and flicked his tongue over my mark, I lost all coherent thought. My muscles tightened, my breathing stopped and I burst into an exquisite, unexpected orgasm.

Tynan jerked back, his eyes wide with excitement and shock, his breathing erratic. He'd climaxed from the pulse of magic right along with me.

Feeling confident, I slid off the counter and went to my knees. I kissed his thighs and ran my hands up to his laces. I looked up, my gaze lingering over his clenched stomach and chest to watch his expression. His face was tight with anticipation. His hand grasped my hair, as if to hold me away from his body. I raised an eyebrow in question but my fingers kept working the laces.

"I… Women of the Victorian Era were not so fond of…" His voice was low, echoing with desire, longing.

"Lucky for you, I'm not a Victorian woman." He groaned low in his throat as I peeled the leather from his firm thighs and pushed the pants to the ground for him to step out of. He was still semi-hard after his release. Taking advantage of his smaller size, I sucked as much of him as I could into my mouth and worked some of my own magic.

He swallowed hard and rose onto his toes, his free hand gripping the counter for support. I took that lovely, curved cock as deep into my throat as I could and then pulled back, skimming my teeth along his shaft as I pulled away. He hardened under my continued efforts, grunting softly in a language I couldn't understand. I looked up and watched his beautiful hair move in the candlelight as he rolled his head from side to side, his face strained in bliss when he looked down and saw that I was watching him.

I felt the muscles of his ass tighten under my fingers. He was getting close and I quickened my movements but he stopped me, lifted me off my feet and carried me to the bed. He didn't put me in it, but lowered me slowly until I stood before him. He hesitated, leaning in for a kiss, stopping just before his lips touched mine. "I love you." A brush of his lips made me tremble. "I don't know how to say it so you can understand the way you overwhelm all my senses, so you'll know what's in my heart."

His face looked pained to think he couldn't convey his feelings in words. I felt cherished and superbly sexy in the presence of such true need. He'd already taken me to heights of pleasure and emotion I'd never experienced before, but these were raw, open feelings he was expressing.

I leaned forward. Pressing our bodies together again and pushing my hands roughly into his hair, I gave him a crushing, lip-bruising kiss. Delving into his mouth, I tried to convey my understanding with my tongue. His hands gripped my hips. I pulled back. "Show me, Tynan. What's in your heart?"

He looked into my eyes, his face creased with passion. He spun me away from him and ungraciously bent me over the bed. "As you wish." He brushed his fingers up the inside of my thigh with one hand, positioned my hips to the angle he wanted with the other. He groaned again, pleased that his fingers found me wet and ready for him. "Stretch your hands over your head. Keep your shoulders down on the bed." His voice was gruff and his commands further ignited my passion. I could only squeak out an acceptance of his orders.

After I complied, he bent over me, covering me with his body and holding my shoulders. He thrust inside. Not as slowly as the last time, not so gentle. I yelped at the initial invasion. His body kept me in place as he thrust again, not lessening the vigor, lifting me off my feet.

The wave of pleasure teased with a little pain was intense. His power was flowing over us, adding to my greedy need. I tried to answer his thrust, pushing back when I could, but he was talking with his body, showing me his passion and love. I could only hold on to the sheets and enjoy the feel of his smooth skin as his cock thrust inside me again and again. His breathing was heavy and in time with his thrusts.

Abruptly he pulled away, taking me upright with him. He spun me around and pushed me to the bed. "I want to see the gold in your eyes." He lifted my legs over his forearms and slammed back inside me without hesitation. His thrusts were so demanding that they would have sent me across the bed had he not been holding my legs. In this position, I could watch his face and it was etched with pure, passionate desire. His eyes were a lighter shade of blue than I'd ever seen them, still dark, but far more blue than black.

I teetered on the edge of orgasm, not able to do more than whimper and thrash on the sheets as he ground his hips into mine. His thrusting slowed, becoming very deliberate, pulling almost all the way out and then delving back in with a tender force. He watched my reaction to each movement. "You are the sun to my night, my love." I could feel his emotions as though they were my own.

The depth of our emotions, mixed with the feel of his cock inside me, pushed me over the edge. Thunder crashed. I felt my pussy start to tighten around him. His voice mingled with the slow, methodical rhythm of his fucking was so good. I tried to speak, to tell him I was coming again, but there was no additional breath to form sound. I could only lean up, clutch at his biceps and dig my nails into his skin as I heard the thunder.

Two, maybe three more thrusts were all it took for Tynan to groan and come with me.

No broken windows this time, just the triumphant thunder. He held still for a long, quiet moment and then gathered us both, breathing hard and sweat-covered, into the middle of the bed without separating our bodies. When I could breathe a little easier, I looked around at the open windows. "I do wish our orgasms weren't announced to the whole island every time."

"Doesn't bother me," he said.

I huffed. Men are men, even when they are the undead.

The island heard the crash of thunder two more times that night.

Chapter Six

ဢ

I felt the first hints of the sun and used a simple spell to close the drapes. "You're insatiable," Tynan said, leaning toward the nightstand next to the bed. "I've not spent such a night in all my years." His tone was soft and playful. I thought of all his years and considered it quite the compliment. Then again, I'd not enjoyed a night like that before either. I snuggled into the velvet of the comforter.

He fumbled with a bag on the table. "I have a gift for you." He sat beside me and held up a gold and silver chain. The twist of the contrasting metals was so delicately exquisite. There was a charm dangling from it. I took it in my hand.

"A bat?" The tiny bat was as intricate as the chain, his body fashioned from an emerald that glowed at my touch.

He smiled. "I thought you would find that amusing. It's an amulet I asked Bevin to make for us."

"Us?" I gave him a questioning look, having learned not to take anything at face value in this world.

"Put it on." He clasped the chain around my neck as I leaned forward. "I know you can hear me in your mind but I cannot hear you. With this," he ran his long fingers along the chain, "you can call to me anytime, and I can find you." He kissed me softly. "When I am away and you wish me near, you can call me and I will come. No matter the distance, no matter the time. I will come."

"You won't ever be that far away from me, Tynan, will you?"

"You will need your...space, Keena. Time with others. I will go about my life for days, maybe weeks or months at a time. When you want me or if you need me—"

I scrambled up to him, crawled into his lap and wrapped myself around him. "I don't want...space or others..." *Some great leader I'm to be, babbling like a teenaged girl.*

"You will, and I will understand. It's the way we are and the way we have always been. You're just not accustomed to it, but you will come to understand it and embrace it in time, just as you have the rest. You're going to do great things, *mon guerrier,* for our people and for mankind. You can't hide from who you are because of your feelings for me. No more than I can let my feelings for you intrude on your duties. It is all part of your birthright, Keena."

"I shouldn't have let you be bound to me. It was too much to ask, too much." We hadn't talked about it since it happened. I hadn't had an opportunity and really hadn't wanted to break the magic between us by bringing it up.

"I wouldn't go back and change that for my life, my love. You could send me away today and I would live my life content with these two nights with you. Do not grieve for me, because you grieve for nothing. My soul is filled with you and your magic. I will carry you with me forever no matter what."

I snuggled next to him when he lay back in the bed and closed his eyes and watched as sleep overtook him. I said his name in my mind, concentrating.

Yes, my love?

He had heard me even in his sleep. *Will you hear all my thoughts when I wear this amulet?*

Only what you wish me to hear. Bevin's insistence.

Then I want you to know I love you.

I knew that. He sounded like a cocky boy.

I grinned as I got up and went to dress.

* * * * *

I was wearing the black nightgown Hogan had left me the night before as I headed straight for the kitchen. Abbey was waiting for me with a huge grin on her face. She pushed a mug of coffee at me as I slid onto the stool.

"You narked on me yesterday," I said, pretending to scold.

"You kept me up half the night with your thunder," she spat back and we both laughed.

"Sorry."

"Can the man walk this morning?" She took a sip from her tiny cup.

"I didn't see him try." The coffee was perfect. I inhaled the scrumptious scent. "Abbey?" She caught the change in my tone. "How do you handle...I mean the..."

"Spit it out, girl." She crossed her legs as she sank back into a half-empty bag of sugar like it was a beanbag chair. Her lovely sea-green hair spilled over her shoulders.

"Do you have many different...lovers?" I watched her face change again.

"I thought you were going to ask me something hard. Yes, as many as I can." She smiled proudly and crossed her legs. "I just don't announce it with thunder."

"Doran says that will only be so loud with Lord Tynan." It was really a relief when she told me that. I couldn't stand the thought that everyone in WildLand would know every time I came. And what would happen on a stormy night? Would they think I was having an orgy?

"Keena, you were raised with the human ideal of monogamy. I swear it's the only culture that teaches women to completely suppress the sexual side of their nature as they grow into womanhood. Look around the forest. All the other male animals compete for the prize of a female. Sex is the *most* natural of things. Humans and even some of the Kith have somehow distorted that natural urge and made it dirty, almost evil. You are the Priestess of the Wild. Your true being is as beautiful and as wild as all nature. You'll see. It will come as naturally to you as the magic did yesterday."

"Thanks, Abbey."

She bowed her head and refilled the coffee with a flick of her wrist. I noticed she could also cast without speaking.

"Now, what else do you want to know?" she asked.

I thought about it for a moment. "I've heard a bunch about my mother, but no one seems to want to talk about my father."

She bobbed her head. "Well, he is half-Demon, born of an Incubus and a human somewhere in England. Your mother found him there. I think she wanted you to have some of his human blood."

"He *IS*?"

"Craples," she said, standing. "I thought you knew!"

"Is?" I asked again, almost whispering.

"I shouldn't be the one to tell you this. I have a big mouth." She started pacing the chopping-block table. "Doran may have my hide for this one." She kept pacing and muttering.

"Abbey, I won't tell her how I found out. Please, tell me about my father." I started to grab her to make her face me but I was afraid I'd accidentally hurt her. "Abbey, if she finds out I'll tell her I forced it from you, as your priestess."

"Of course, you're the heir, the priestess. I have to tell you what you ask." She stood with her hands on her hips. The shimmering bubble appeared again.

"You'll have to give me that spell," I said as she cast.

"Anytime. So you know how your mother died." I nodded my head. "Well, the Slaugh have your father too. Somewhere on their island."

"They still have him?"

"Yes. Thule isn't far. It's a very dark and disturbing place. The Slaugh are the hosts of the unforgiven and take the souls of the evil in humankind, but they also like to accumulate other things. Collectors, if you please…sometimes of the most hideous things. They fly out at night to go about their collecting and slumber by day."

It gave me a chill remembering that Bran created Vampires—and that the Vamps and the Slaugh shared that particular nocturnal trait. "Have you been there?"

"Caldrons no! I've heard of few who have ever escaped the Slaugh. And they're none the healthier for it when they return."

"Why do they have my father?"

"It's thought that they've held both yours and Feldema's fathers to use as bait. To use as leverage after one of you becomes High Priestess. But they also keep things just because they want them. It could be as simple as that. They like keeping secrets and souls, all things morbid." She shuddered. "Feldema's father died by their hands long ago."

"So King Bran has my father." I felt real hate brewing in me for the first time in my life. It smoldered in my stomach, burned through the mark.

She snorted. "The King is more of a figurehead, Keena. The real danger is from Nessum. He's actually a fallen angel, cast out from heaven. *Nessum* is the one who created the Vampires, trying to get stronger souls for Bran. The Dark Angel is also probably the one who left the island and captured your mother."

"Dark Angel... Do you believe in God, Abbey?" I was careful not to offend her.

She fell back onto the sugar bag. "Of course I do. Who doesn't?" She was very matter-of-fact. "We are all creatures of the God and Goddess, Keena. Otherwise we would have no power."

I was puzzled. "But I thought that the Christians were the reason for the fallout between the Kith and the humans?"

"Yes, but only because a king spread lies about us to one religious group—who steadfastly worshipped only *one* god. The poor, uneducated folks of that age went off half-cocked.

That doesn't mean we're not still God's children. That's why you have to reunite the Kith with the humans and bring peace to us all."

"Uh, no pressure or anything…"

"I mean that humans and the Kith are all God's creatures. If Bran and Nessum keep meddling in human affairs and causing troub—" She stopped short, stomped her little foot and cursed herself under her breath.

"Spit it out, little woman." I smiled at her.

"In for a penny…" she sighed. "The Slaugh have been trying to start wars for centuries. They stir up political turmoil, cause famine and plagues, whatever they can manage to cause chaos…mostly in third-world countries because they lack much of the modernization of the west. But if one of the plagues spreads…I don't want to think of the damage they could do."

"Shit." I picked up a spoon and began tapping the side of my mug. "Just when I think I can handle all this…" I tapped until Abbey raised an irritated eyebrow. "It's just one great big pig after another around here isn't it? So, I have to best my sister to claim the birthright then reunite the humans with the Kith and stop the Slaugh from killing off most of the human population?"

"Yes, yes and yes," she answered.

"That's all? No biggie. Have it done by lunch tomorrow."

"You want some whiskey in that coffee?"

I put my face in my hands and felt the amulet dangling around my neck. *Tynan.*

Yes, my love.

He startled me. *Oh — I'm sorry, I was just thinking of you.*

How sweet. He laughed just a little and the sound tickled my spine.

I'll be more careful. I didn't mean to disturb you.

Were you thinking of our lovemaking? His tone was light and playful.

I was blushing and Abbey saw it. She gave me questioning look. *Yes, I was...you?*

I'll never dream of anything else again.

Good night, Tynan, I thought with a laugh.

Abbey was still looking at me like I was crazy. I showed her the amulet. She took the charm in her fingers, admiring the work. "A communications charm," she murmured. "That Bevin is so good."

"Back to the point, Abbey. How do I get my father off that island?"

Manus' loud, booming voice sent us both screaming to our feet. "You'll do no such thing!"

Abbey almost lunged, steak knife in hand, before realizing it was him. He had been curled up just under the table at my feet.

Abbey shrieked at him, "Listen, you scraggly old pussy, if you don't quit lurking around my kitchen I'll sic a Werewolf on you!"

"I'm not lurking, it's warm in here and I haven't been able to sleep in my bed since...since it started thundering so often."

At least he had tried to be polite about it.

"Nonetheless, quit lurking." She was trying to straighten her frazzled hair. Manus changed to his man form, bursting the bubble as he did so. I should be used to seeing him change but it still gave me the jeevies. I had asked him once if it hurt. He said it stung.

Stung? To change from a ten-pound cat into a rather large man? I found it hard to believe. He said that his change wasn't as dramatic as a Were's because he was a natural Shapeshifter. That was all I got at the time since we were sparring and he wanted my attention on the fight. I'd never thought to ask him again.

He must have wandered in here in cat form because there were no clothes in sight and he faced us naked now. I found it hard to take him seriously. "Keena, Priestess of the Wild, you will *not*, under any circumstances, go to that island and you will *not* attempt to save your father."

"Awful pushy for a naked cat," I quipped.

"I am not making jokes, Keena. The island of Thule is off limits to you. You can't even begin to imagine the dark magic and nefarious things that reside there. It is most likely that Coyle is dead and not worth the risk. I ask your word!" He looked frightened. He had a strong grip on my shoulders and it was tightening more as he spoke.

"Okay, don't get so worked up." I was trying to pull away but he just held me tighter.

"I mean this, Keena."

I finally just stood and yanked myself back and he let go. "I *said* okay."

He huffed. "I know you, Keena. You forget I spent eighteen years at your side. I know what you like to eat, I know your favorite songs, your first love and when you lost your virginity as a human—"

"Eww," Abbey said. "How could you let him be around you that much?"

"I thought he was a *cat* for Christ's sake." I shot him my best shut-your-mouth look.

"What I'm saying is that I know you too well. You get an idea in your head and won't let it go. I know you'll dwell on it and plot on it and you will do something stupid."

"Uh!" I huffed. He was right and I hated that he knew me so well. As my loving pet, I had treated him as my confidant, held him to me when I cried. He had been there with me for everything as I grew up.

"You have too many important things to do to risk yourself with this."

"But he's my *faattherrrr!*" I was whining and I hated that too.

Abbey finally chimed in. "Keena, he's right. There are only very old rumors about Coyle and even if he *has* managed to stay alive in that place, he'll be…well, not a very sane man if he were to return."

"I give you my word," Manus said, taking me more gently by the shoulders this time. "Once you have succeeded Doran, I will help you negotiate for the return of your father, if he is still alive. Bran will want to be in your favor." He tried to smile. "If Coyle has made it this long, a little longer won't make a great deal of difference."

"I won't fight Feldema until the Autumn Equinox. That's months."

"He has been with the Slaugh for twenty-eight years. Six more months…that's all I ask, Keena. You must promise me."

"You need that time to get better with your spells for Feldema," Abbey said quietly. "She's had many years to practice and study. You're gifted but your spells will be unpredictable. You need all the time you have. She's very dangerous to you still."

I sat back on the stool. There was too much to think about, too much to worry about at once. Tynan being bound to me, Feldema, my father, the prophecy… "Maybe I do want that whiskey."

Chapter Seven

ɛᴑ

The pile of books in front of me was enormous. I'd been studying and practicing spells for weeks and was getting tired of the little library at the edge of the village. The open windows looked out over the forest and the smells and colors of late June crept in and distracted me, the spells and incantations I was supposed to be learning blurring on the pages.

Bevin was coming to collect me shortly to prepare for the latest council meet. Most were somewhat boring and tedious, much like a human city council meeting. Only occasionally was there a problem concerning misuse of magic rather than a civic concern. I made myself listen intently and saw how Doran handled each piece of business with the care and concern of a parent. She was a benevolent and strong leader, showing grace when needed and, on occasion, letting her ferocious side show through. Most of those occasions concerned the Slaugh or the Gremlins.

Tynan had been away on business for three days with Cliona, his second. The two of them were responsible for keeping rogue Vamps from deciding it was okay to terrorize and hurt humans, the ramifications of which endangered Vamps and humans alike. No one wanted Vampire hunters running around with wooden stakes and hatchets. It also seemed that the Slaugh were creating new Vamps, something they had not done in a very long time.

I missed him and spoke to him through the amulet a few times each day. During our last brief chat, he'd assured me he'd be home this afternoon.

A little black book dropped in front of me, taking my gaze away from the forest outside the window. "Check this out." Abbey climbed up the chair and onto the table. She shook, and a cloud of dust floated in the sunbeams. "Found it under the shelves in the back."

"What were you doing under the shelves?" I gave her an accusing glare. Something like that usually meant she was spying or prying. Over the last several weeks we had become the best of friends. The smart little woman helped me spar with spells and though she was better at defensive craft, it was still fun for both of us.

"Hogan and that sweet librarian are making eyes at each other in the stacks." One large stain was being difficult to remove from her knee. "He's almost babbling. It's cute."

The librarian was a very pretty little Gnome, and I knew Hogan only came with me here to get a chance to talk to her. I got up and peeked around the shelves Abbey had been hiding under. Hogan was dressed in a tunic that showed off the marks I had given him. He said something and the little Gnome batted her ungodly long eyelashes at him and giggled.

I returned to the table. "It's a shame *he's* not getting married this afternoon." Today's meet would actually be a ceremony to marry several Gnome couples. Gnomes were one of the few Kith species that took a single mate for life. The ceremonies were held only once a year and it was supposed to be a good party. "June weddings are always so pretty."

"Forget the weddings and Hogan." She kicked the book she had dropped on the table. "You'll be far more interested in this."

I turned it over and read the title on the front. *The Host*. It was a book about the Slaugh. There were others in the library but they hadn't told us much more about the creatures than we already knew. Abbey and I had been looking for clues about the island. Of course, Manus knew nothing of it.

I opened the cover and there was an ink rendering of the actual island across the inside cover and the first page. My jaw dropped.

"Must have been down there for decades, if not longer," Abbey said, leaning over the book. "I've never even heard of a map of the island."

I ran my hand over the book. It felt gross, slimy, but the pages were just parchment.

"What island?" Hogan said. I slammed the book shut and put my arm over it, trying not to be too obvious. "WildLand," I said with a smile to the librarian and all her eyelashes.

"My lady, there are many different maps of the island in our collection. I'll get as many of them as you like." She started to leave Hogan's side.

"That's not necessary. Abbey was just thinking out loud." We smiled at Hogan and his friend. Abbey started to play with her hair.

"Keena," he said, intentionally using my given name to impress his pretty friend. "I am taking Miss Laurel for a walk in the gardens." She blushed — or at least I think she blushed, it was hard to tell through the feathery scales and blue skin beneath. He went on. "That is, if you do not need me for the afternoon."

"I think I can manage for a few hours without you. Run along. Have fun." I shooed them with the hand that wasn't covering the book and winked at her, making her blush come on full and bright pink under the scales. Hogan led her away gracefully.

"What do you think of that?" Abbey said once they were out of earshot. "I always thought Hogan would be an eternal bachelor. Maybe he'll wed her next June."

"Why do they only marry in June?"

She plopped down on the table next to the book. "I think it's got something to do with their fertility cycles. Most of the weddings today will produce children in a matter of months.

They must only be fertile in the summer." She scooted herself closer. "Forget about Hogan's libido. Let's take a look at that map."

I'd been so taken with Hogan's public display of something close to affection that I had almost forgotten about the book. I started to open it and heard more footfalls behind me. "Bevin," Abbey whispered. I closed the book and tucked it inside the much bigger spell book I would be taking back to my chambers.

"Tomorrow morning, my room," I whispered back. Abbey gave me a nod of understanding.

Bevin swooped in and stood glaring down at us. "You two need to gossip less and cast more."

"Us?" Abbey cooed in protest. Bevin raised an eyebrow to reiterate her point.

"Gather your things. We have much to do to help prepare the meet room. Abbey, you must have a million things to do for the food preparations."

"I have everything in order but I guess I need to make sure the Imps haven't gone lax on me." She winked at me. "Terribly lazy, we are. It's amazing we get a thing done."

Every single meal I'd had at the manor had been decadent, delicious and superbly presented. "Lax" was the last adjective I'd use for Abbey's kitchen Imps.

"Off with you, lazy wench," I said with a voice that boomed through the quiet of the library. Abbey and I laughed aloud and only stopped at the heat from Bevin's glare. "Okay, okay, we're going. Loosen up, Bevin. It's a wedding, for cauldron's sake, not a political uprising."

"Every occasion is an opportunity for you to win over the loyalties of the Kith—even a wedding," she retorted.

"It's a party, Bevin, let her have some fun," Abbey huffed.

"We shall see," Bevin snorted and stomped away. We watched her hips and bun as they alternated side to side with each step she took.

I knew why she was concerned. Every time I'd been in the same room with the wicked half sister, we had nearly come to blows. I'd been lectured and scolded not to let the bickering happen at the wedding. I had agreed but insisted that Blondie be lectured as well. Doran had assured me she had given Feldema the same instructions and that she had agreed.

I wasn't buying a bit of it.

* * * * *

The meet room finally looked like it was being used for the purpose it had been designed. The light green walls and soft wood trim lavishly decorated with wild orchids, tiger lilies and freesia resembled a photo from a bride's magazine. The smell of the flowers drifted thick in the air. Music filled the room from an unknown source and mingled with the songs of the birds flitting around the open windows. Butterflies danced above my head as I took my place beside Doran. I made a conscious effort not to even look at Feldema.

We had greeted all the guests with Doran and Bevin between us, preventing any communication. Feldema appeared to be doing her best to ignore my presence as well. Maybe she had taken the warnings from Doran to heart. She was graceful and pleasant to the guests, even those I knew she disliked.

Shadowing Feldema were two new consorts. Both were very attractive, dark-haired men I took to be Magicians. I found all the Magicians pretty, of course, but wasn't drawn to them like I was to Vamps or Weres. Bevin explained they lacked the animal instincts that my body responded to.

I had found I had little control over those reactions, but I was still holding out on finding a second consort. I was in love with Tynan and just couldn't bring myself to cheat on him, even though he and everyone else insisted, over and over, it was *not* cheating. I suspected that was why he was starting to be needed out of town so much lately. I had asked him about it and, of course, he denied it. He just recited the same ol' song about listening to my body and all those other things I didn't really want to hear.

The ceremony was beautiful. Seven Gnome couples shared their vows with us and all of WildLand. Feldema anointed them with fresh waters and for the first time in centuries, a Priestess of the Wild would anoint them with the earth. As the priest said a prayer to the land, I knelt before each couple and rubbed the deep, rich earth of the island on the foreheads of the females, wishing them fertility and peace for all their years. They all cried and I had to bite my lip more than once not to do the same.

When I finished and stood, the whole room seemed to let out a collective breath. As I made my way back to my seat, I realized it was the first official act I had performed in public that didn't consist of beating the crap out of my sister. I made my curtsey to the line of colorfully dressed Gnome couples and sat, pleased with myself and my grace. I didn't trip and hadn't even looked at Feldema—but I could sure feel her leering at me.

After the ceremony the guests started mingling and talking and eating, and the music got a little louder to be heard over the conversation. There was laughter and even some dancing. I was amazed how much the nuptials mimicked human weddings. The Magician I was talking with told me that those types of ceremonies far predated modern religion. He was extremely chatty, and we discussed his life in Sacramento, California, where he led a small coven that seemed very excited about me. He gushed on and on about my coming to visit the coven and the plans they had made for assisting in my fulfillment of the prophecy. I found the compliments embarrassing and the flattery irritating.

I excused myself from the Magician and found Hogan and his date, the librarian. We sat at one of the elaborately decorated tables and watched the festivities. I chatted with them and some of the other guests who made their way over to introduce themselves. A palatable feeling of happiness was in the room and I couldn't help but wish that Tynan was there. He'd returned earlier that afternoon as promised but outside our bedroom, he found all things frilly and romantic both useless and tiring. In public, he held a serious and powerful image.

I smiled at the thought of him without communicating. I had gotten much better at that and no longer invoked the spell in the amulet every time he crossed my mind.

After I felt I had greeted and spoke to everyone, I headed off to the kitchen to find Abbey. I hadn't seen her since the ceremony and I figured she was coordinating the appearance of all the food and drink. I was happy as I walked through the hall toward the kitchen.

Happy, that is, until I walked around a corner and found Feldema and one of her new consorts standing in the hall, blocking my way. Intentionally, I suspected. The consort was bigger and looked more stern than most Magicians, but he was still prettier than me. He turned his back to me in insult. I really didn't care about such things, but I knew what he was trying to convey — *I don't like you and I'll hurt you if I can.*

"What is it, Feldema?" I sighed and crossed my arms. "Can't pick on anyone at the party?" Okay, so I started it this time. But it was coming either way.

She smiled her wicked, white-toothed smile at me. "Listen, old Witch." Her favorite affront was the constant reference to the age at which I came into my powers. "You're running out of time." She held her snide smile as she spoke.

"I know how much time I have," I replied.

"I underestimated you for the battle of might. I will not do so again. I owe you for the loss of my consort — and you will pay for that with your life!" she seethed.

"Kendrick was a slug, baby sister. I did you a favor." I stood with my arms still crossed, trying to appear bored. I saw the anger building in her. "So easily rattled," I said as a show of being her superior.

She mumbled and before I realized what she was doing, a ripping noise boomed from my side. A pipe burst through the wall and the spray of water threw me across the wide hall into the other wall.

Shit! I fought the spray and got to my knees to cast something back but Feldema and the Magician were gone.

Shit.

Chapter Eight

ဆ

The next morning, I made sure Tynan was covered before I let my voyeuristic friend in. She came bearing cherry-filled pastries and coffee. The tray floated before her and landed easily on the table. I was fixing my coffee as she headed to the bed.

"When do you sleep?" Abbey asked, climbing up onto the bed. "Yeoowies," she said before I turned to find her peering under the sheet. "I had fits all night thinking about men. No one was around for me," she pouted.

"Quit that."

"Why, he doesn't mind?" She dropped the sheet and headed toward the table.

"I'll never get used to the openness around here," I said as she plopped into a chair.

"We've had this conversation. You're the only one with the hang-up here," Abbey snorted before taking a bite of pastry.

"I just feel like Tynan made such a huge sacrifice..."

"He did it of his own free will, sister. He's lived this life for thousands of years. He'll start feeling guilty sooner or later if you don't at least consider taking another consort."

"I think he already does, at least from the way he's always talking about it and all the trips he's taking lately. But I can't seem to get that part of my upbringing out of my head just yet. I think I've accepted a whole hell of a lot in the last few months. Let me hold onto this for just a bit longer."

"Your loss," she said, filling my cup. She pushed her cup to the side. "So, is he out enough to talk about the B double-O K?"

"Yeah." I reached up to the amulet around my neck. "But I think I'll be safe." I took it gingerly over to the dresser and put it away. I rummaged through the stack of books I had brought back from the library until I found the small black book. The cover was still dusty and the feel of pages repulsed the nerves at my fingertips. Abbey had gotten all the way up on the table.

The worn parchment creaked as I tried to flatten the cover open enough to see the entire map across the fold in the middle. The map looked to have been drawn in ink. "This is a hand-drawn map." I flipped to the next page. There was no table of contents, no author's notes or reference information like most of the spell and potion books I'd seen.

No. On that page, printed in beautiful script, was a single sentence...

There be monsters here.

Abbey "oohed".

"They used to write that on ocean maps. I saw a really old one in a university library once," I said.

"The sailors must have come by *here* once or twice," Abbey joked, and I had to laugh. She was probably right.

I turned to the next page, and then the next—the rest was written in German. "You read German?" She shook her head. "Know anyone we can trust who might?" She pointed over to Tynan. "Very funny. He'd tie me down to the bed if he knew what we were up to."

"So all we have is the map," she said, turning back to it. "Why would the map be in English and the rest be in German?"

"I think someone added it later." I shrugged at my own guess and studied the map. Thule was an oblong-shaped island with a mountain range down the middle, similar to

WildLand. The side closest to WildLand was marked with the word ICE, the far side labeled FIRE. "If the land markers are right, it should be off the northwest side of WildLand."

Abbey looked up at me and nodded.

On the fire side, just beyond the mountain, was the word *Tutzlwarm*. I sounded it out and looked up at Abbey.

"Mythical creatures that burrow in the ground. That's all I know."

"That doesn't sound too bad." The words written atop the drawing of the mountains were faded doodles, but I could still make them out. "Valley of the Unforgiven. Guess that's where the Slaugh hang out." Abbey shuddered. At the far northwest corner was a faint drawing of a castle. "Bran's house?" She shuddered again. "Do these little boxes just below that look like other buildings to you?"

"I think so."

"I wouldn't imagine that Slaugh need shelter. That's where I need to go."

"Cauldrons, Keena, you'll have to cross the whole Island." Her face looked worried.

"Do I have another choice?"

She jumped up and clapped her hands. "Not really — but you *do* have help! I told you I had been trying to find the potion Bevin used to make that amulet for Tynan." I gave her a puzzled look. "Well," she continued, "my cousin was helping her Gnome friend clean up after Bevin did some particularly nasty potion. She makes some of the weirdest stuff for her healing. I would love to get a peek at her supply chest. God knows what that Witch has in there. Anyway, let's just say my cousin saw the recipe for your communications amulet…"

"So?"

"So? So I have it!"

"How does that help me with Thule?"

"Think, wild thing." Her tone was laughingly condescending. "If we change just one of the ingredients, it can let you share *sight* instead of thoughts." She held out her hands and cocked her head as it to say "Duh!"

"Howard!" I exclaimed, suddenly catching on.

"That's the most frivolous name I ever heard," she smirked. "But yes, Howard could do some scouting for you once on the island."

"Howard the Hawk is a great a name," I insisted. "And *you* are the smallest genius I know. What's in the potion?" I closed the slimy little book and slid put it back in the stack with the others while Abbey rattled off a list of fairly common ingredients and a few I hadn't heard of.

✳ ✳ ✳ ✳ ✳

"Where have you been?" Abbey demanded as I made my way into the kitchen late in the afternoon. It had been a month since the meeting at which she'd told me about finding Bevin's spell. We'd been slowly and secretly gathering everything we needed—and we would gather the last ingredient for the potion today.

"Bevin and Manus had me studying all morning, then sparring again." I showed her my burned shoulder. "Manus got me with a lightning spell. He's limited in his magic, but when he hits…" I touched the angry burn with a wince. Most of Manus' spells are offensive for his duties as a guardian, and he has to at least mumble his spells aloud, but he snuck up on me and struck me from behind before I could counterspell.

"You're still up to going, right?"

"Not much choice. Tomorrow night's the full moon and we won't have another chance for the amulet. But I swear, if Bevin doesn't relax with the practicing… I'm so worn out." I took the tea Abbey had made while I was talking. "Oh yeah, I got a boat arranged."

"How'd you manage that one?" She sounded as surprised as her big eyes looked.

"From one of the Trolls. I traded some gold buttons from one of my dresses. It wasn't much but it's the best I could do," I said.

"Hogan let you have gold buttons from one of his master creations?" She was mimicking his accent and tone as she spoke.

I laughed. "No. Remember when Feldema tossed me into the fountain?" I'd had a few more altercations with Feldema since the pipe incident. The first two, she'd gotten the best of me. Silly stuff really, spilling wine on me at a meal and once tangling my hair in knots from across the yard. During the most recent incident, though, I saw her lips start to move and could have stopped her before she used a blasting spell to knock me back into the fountain, but I allowed her to continue. I wanted her to go on thinking she could best me. It had worked once and I wanted that advantage again. "I took off the buttons before I gave the dress back to Hogan. He was furious that I 'lost' them. But we needed the gold. I only traded nine of them with the Troll, in case I need more later."

"And Hogan hasn't found the rest?"

"Nah, I put them in the pocket of the jeans Tynan bought me on his last trip. Hogan hates them so much he won't touch 'em."

Abbey cocked her head, "You're getting too good at this. So we have the boat, almost all the supplies and tomorrow night we'll have the amulet. Are you sure you're ready to do this?"

"I think. My casting has gotten fairly good. I'm as ready as I'm going to get."

"You know your spells won't help you with the Slaugh, you'll just have to fight them," she said as she stood to examine my face.

"I know. I'm not afraid."

She gave me a "yeah, right" look.

"Fine. I'm terrified—but I have to get him, Abbey. I'll fight the Slaugh. It'll be daylight and most of them can't be out then. I'm hoping good old-fashioned knives will help with whatever else is out there." I had been carefully asking questions of different beings on the island to get their impressions of Thule. Most shared outrageous rumors they had heard over the centuries, though everyone was adamant that Witch powers wouldn't work on the island. The bottom line was, I wouldn't know what was real and what was speculation until I got there.

"I'm more worried about Nessum. He's a *fallen angel*, Keena. I don't think he can be killed." She shivered and I did too.

"Let's just hope I don't have to worry about him." I changed the subject. "I'll go get my stuff and meet you at the tower so no one sees us heading to the water together."

* * * * *

The blood-of-the-dead coral grew off the south side of the island where the currents ran strong and the rocks were treacherous. Fog was rolling along the choppy water, making it look particularly eerie. The sight of the ocean was beautiful but I knew what it held. This was Feldema's world and I was not at all eager to enter, but it was the only way to get the coral. I had to dive for it and that meant going in. I stood at the edge of the water and took a deep breath. The cold air rushing into my lungs sent shivers through my body.

"You be careful. I don't know if Feldema has creatures that will alert her to your presence, but I don't want to find out the hard way," Abbey whispered, apparently trying not to alert anything herself.

I didn't know either. I strapped two small daggers onto my bare thighs and fastened a small bag to a strap of leather around my waist. "If you lose sight of me for too long, go get

Bevin and Manus." The surf was rough and she could easily lose sight of me in the churning waves.

She swallowed hard. "You make sure you get somewhere I can see you every few minutes."

"Okay, stay over there on those high rocks so you can see me easier over the surf. If anyone comes, you duck down." She nodded and headed to the boulders above the water. I stepped tentatively into the surf.

The water was freezing — not merely cool like the streams and river on the island. The cold waves seemed angry at my presence. I had a hard time getting past the breaks of the waves. In my mind, they were trying to push me back.

Swimming out the required hundred yards helped me adjust to the temperature. An Imp friend of Abbey's told her the coral was out about that far — and only Feldema was willing to dive in those dangerous waters. I was going to try. Looking around, I found Abbey sitting high up on the rocks. The sun was started its approach toward the horizon and her hair was gleaming in the brilliant rays.

She waved and pointed at her wrist to remind me to check in often. I took in a deep breath and dove under the water. When I opened my eyes, the salt stung but I adjusted quickly as I swam down. I was surprised at how well I could negotiate the waters. I had thought that, as a Witch of the land, I wouldn't do well in the ocean but I moved easily down to the reef.

The colors were dazzling. The reef was an entire world unto itself. Corals of all colors, growing one atop the other, looked like a giant painting. Some of them hard and luminescent, others soft and swaying with the currents in a ghostly dance to music I couldn't hear. Brightly colored fish darted to and fro, ignoring me as they went about their business of existing. I was running out of breath and hadn't seen any sign of the blood-red coral. I surfaced and looked to find Abbey, realizing the current had moved me down shore a bit. She waved as I found her on the rocks. I waved back, took in another breath and down again I went.

I saw a huge octopus under an overhang in the reef. It moved toward me to investigate. I contemplated attempting to kill it in case it could alert my sister. The creature drifted before me a moment then darted away. I decided if Feldema was aware of my presence, the octopus would have probably attacked.

I kept moving along the reef, using some of the smoother corals to pull myself along. I had to surface again. I had dived even deeper and had to struggle this time to get to the light of the surface. I splashed through with a gasp. I turned to look back to the rocky shore and once again found Abbey's hair shimmering in the evening sun.

I went under a third time. It seemed to be harder to hold my breath as long and the cold water was definitely starting to stiffen my joints. I moved along anyway, finally catching a glimpse of what I thought was the right coral. I quickly pushed myself toward it and broke off a piece with a dagger, tucking it in the bag.

On the way back to the surface my lungs were burning for air and my toes were numb. I watched as the surface came closer and closer. The setting sun was playing off the waves above. I hit the surface just before I thought I was going to bust, taking in large, labored breaths as I turned toward the shore.

Abbey was nowhere to be found.

I stopped just short of panicking when I realized I had drifted around a large outcropping of boulders. I tried to head back toward my starting point but the current, stronger now, would only let me head into shore.

By the time I got to the sandy shore I was exhausted from fighting the current. I sank to my knees to catch my breath then climbed around the outcropping to find Abbey.

She wasn't there.

I spun around, looking among the rocks for her, thinking perhaps she had somehow fallen. I found nothing. Maybe she had headed to get help since she lost sight of me...but her bag was still over by the trail. I was frightened and my heart was pounding—and not from the swim.

Running to her bag, I glimpsed movement on the water out of the corner of my eye.

A Slaugh!

He was standing on top of the ocean. *That makes no sense.* I stared harder and was able to make out the boat. It was the color of the ocean, making the small vessel near invisible if you didn't squint to see it. Then someone else came into focus—Feldema. She blended into the horizon almost as much as the boat.

The black-cloaked Slaugh turned slightly and I saw my best friend, Abbey, struggling in his grasp. They were heading away, neither of them looking back.

I had no way to help her. I couldn't swim to them, so I did what I did best—I ran. Ran with all I had, acid tears building behind my eyes, guilt pulsing through my veins instead of blood.

When I made it inside the manor I continued to run, darting from room to room, looking for Doran. Her chambers were empty. The meet room was empty. Finally, I skidded to a stop in a small dining room. Doran and Bevin were eating. They stopped, alarmed by the abrupt intrusion on the quiet meal. I was too winded to speak. I stood there shaking, hair dripping on the clean floor, mind frantic as to what to say, where to start, how to explain.

Doran ushered me to a chair and took my face in her hands. "What is it, child?" Her eyes filled with the fear I felt. "Tell me."

I couldn't stop the tears but managed to say, "The Slaugh have Abbey!" before my tears became a ranting, incoherent sob. Bevin gasped.

Doran knelt in front of me after issuing some orders to other house Imps who had gathered at the commotion. She brushed some hair tenderly from my face. "Slow down, Keena. Start from the beginning and tell me all of it." She handed me a glass of water but I pushed it away.

"I got her killed!" I wailed and started in with the hideous crying again. Tynan and Manus came rushing in. Seeing Tynan made me feel even worse and I fell into his arms as he took Doran's place at my feet. "Abbey!" I said to him as he lifted me up and sat, cradling me like a child. "They have Abbey! We have to go get her!"

He shushed me gently. "Tell us what happened, *mon guerrier*." He sat back in the chair and held me to his chest. "How did Abbey get hurt?"

Taking in a harsh breath, I told them the story—from finding the book to the long hours forming a plan. I watched their faces as I spoke. Doran looked mortified, Bevin was pacing frantically. When I got the part about the coral dive, Doran interrupted.

"So she fell into the sea?"

"No!" Anger took over and I stood up from Tynan's lap. "She wasn't even close to the water's edge while I was diving. I saw a Slaugh standing on the water. At least that where I *thought* he was. Then the light shifted and I could make out the boat. *Her* boat."

"What are you saying, Keena?" Doran asked carefully, already knowing exactly whom I was talking about. She was making sure I understood. Treachery was a punishable offense. *Physical* punishment.

"I'm saying that Feldema was on her boat with a Slaugh and they had Abbey. I saw it with my own eyes! I'm saying they were taking Abbey to Thule. Feldema gave the Slaugh your house Imp!" I shook with the words as I stuttered them out.

Doran sat back down. "We thought she was talking with them outside of the meets, but I never imagined—"

"Well imagine it!" I snapped, anger completely replacing my grief. "We have to get Abbey back before they hurt her!"

"What were you thinking?" Bevin asked. "Planning to go over there? You could have been killed or hurt yourself! I have told you time and time again you—"

"I'm too important to the Kith to be reckless." I finished the speech for her with a flippant tone. "I know. But I can't just leave my father there to be tortured! He's part of the Kith too. He deserves—"

"Bevin's right," Tynan said.

"Fine! I was stupid. I shouldn't have done it. Punish me, whatever—but we have to get Abbey!" No one said anything. "Tynan?" He gave me a supportive look but made no move to indicate he would go. "Doran, you can't mean we won't do *anything* for her?" I had come to them for help. They should be jumping into action—and instead they all just looked at me.

"I'm sorry, Keena," Doran said. "We can't go to the island. It is an ancient truce that I can't break—and neither can you."

"They've been *here*!" I shouted, starting to panic again. I knew the political implications of breaking a truce. It could cause an all-out war between the islands.

"Only when invited. I will talk to Bran, Keena, but—"

"What about my sister? She was with a Slaugh...she was part of the kidnapping!"

I moved to stand face-to-face with Doran. I continued, my voice shaking, "My priestess, what of her treachery?" If I couldn't do anything to the Slaugh then my *sister* would pay. "She has been conspiring with the Slaugh against me. Maybe even the ones who attacked us in Castle Dracula. What is to be done with her?" My tone was formal and in the manner of speaking that Doran would use. I was accusing Feldema of a horrible crime and Doran would deal with her as was decreed by our law. It would not be pretty.

A tiny smile started to curl one side of her lip. "I will deal with the traitor as should be done. If I can get any information on Abbey in the process, I will give it to you." She spun on her heels and started to leave but stopped before reaching the door, turning to me.

She stood silent for a moment, thinking. "Don't worry, Keena. I don't think they'll kill our Abbey. I will contact Bran and let him know she will be a valuable bargaining tool. But know this, Keena—Feldema and her supporters will be angry that you requested her punishment. When it is done, she will be even more likely to make the time between now and October difficult for everyone. It will be widely known that she is willingly aiding the Slaugh. There will be much division on WildLand, much for us all to manage politically.

"You are a smart Witch, as was your mother. I give you this one opportunity to change your mind."

Well, *that* was a hint if there ever was one. Obviously I needed to slow down and consider what it meant. I ran the possibilities through my mind, pacing as I did so. If Feldema used her punishment to sway those opposed to protecting the humans, it would be bad for the Kith *and* mankind. I could simply allow this to pass and deal with her myself. "It could be to my advantage to not expose her publicly." Doran straightened as I spoke. "It will bring less danger to the Kith and myself...and possibly Abbey?"

A slight nod showed that she was pleased that I understood.

"I won't accuse her now—*but,*" I went to my knee, "I request to make my claim for the next battle, Aunt."

She let a knowing smile curl her lips. "Yes, Keena?"

"I make my claim to choose the site of the All Hallow's battle. I wish to fight her in the forest. I choose blades and magic for the duel."

"Agreed." She started to leave again.

"I also request that the battle be for the vengeance of Abbey."

She stopped in the doorway, not turning to face me.

Tynan stood and Bevin did her usual gasp.

"No—" Manus began.

"She has made the request," Doran said, holding her hand up for silence. Still not turning, she asked, "Keena, are you sure? Do you think you have it in you to avenge Abbey? Can you kill your sister? Even with the knowledge of her treachery…you will have to kill her with your own hands."

I stood again. "If I leave her alive, her treachery will endanger all the Kith and humans as well. Her death will weaken the Gremlins and ensure the Slaugh have no favor with the council."

She turned to me finally but I couldn't read her face. "Then so be it, my niece. It is set." She bowed to me and took her leave, off to find my sister, no doubt.

Manus slammed his fist into the wall after Doran left. Plaster fell to the floor in a cloud of crumbled powder and dust and he cursed Feldema's title. Tynan was still standing, flabbergasted, at my side.

I went to Manus first. "Do you doubt me?" I asked sternly. "I have no choice, Manus, and I need your confidence now."

"I'm afraid for you, Keena. Feldema has always done whatever she wishes, with no regard for rules or honor…"

I tried to get him to look me in the eyes. He wouldn't. "Manus, you've pushed me when I've needed it, scolded me, even spoiled me. Now, I need you to support me. I need your faith in me. I need your bravery and your wisdom. Speak what you fear."

"I fear the prophecy is wrong."

Bevin flew at him, gripping his arms tightly. "*Wrong,* Manus! How could it be wrong?"

"It was created two and half centuries ago. It could be as wrong as any other!" he snapped back at her.

She was up on her toes, her wrinkled face so close to his she could have kissed him. "You chose as a young man to give your oath to Keena and her mother. If you haven't the stomach to be a guardian to a priestess then say so! And if you have truly lost faith in the prophecy we've held as hope for our people, then take your leave!"

Manus cringed at her seething words. "I can't watch her die," he said softly. "I have faith, Bevin, but I... The fate of many rests with Keena and the training we've given her. What if I've failed her? I fear—"

"You have failed *nothing*, Shifter." She called him by his species name to pinch at his pride. "You have helped to sculpt a fierce Witch warrior and she will prevail. She will claim her birthright."

"Manus." I pulled his shoulders until he had no choice but to look at me. "I will have my vengeance on Feldema. And with your help, I will have it well. You're the heart of my strength. Without your faith, that heart beats no more—and I *will* fail."

His face tightened at the thought. "I have faith, my lady. Forgive me. I just can't bear the thought of losing you." He looked at Tynan.

The hulking Greek soldier looked equally worried. I realized that the implications were even graver for him than Manus. I couldn't bear the anxiety in his face. I hated everything about my new life at that moment. Mostly, I hated Feldema. "I'm going to my chambers," I said and took Tynan's hand. "Manus, please have Hogan leave me alone this evening." I was still caught up in the formality that Doran always brought out in me. My language was abrupt and stern.

He nodded and ran his hand through his hair. "Keena, I only meant I would be devastated for death to come to you. I meant no lack of commitment."

I kissed him on the lips and left with a glance to Bevin.

* * * * *

Once back in my room, I got into the bath by myself, sat there and cried softly for Abbey, my mind imagining everything she might be enduring. I wept over the changes I'd experienced in the last few months. Has it really only been that long? I remembered my human life and how slowly time seemed to pass. Maybe that's why I would live so long, because things moved faster here. Maybe Witches needed a couple hundred years to live the equivalent of one normal human life.

In this world, joy came as quick as a clap of thunder and pain swooped down like a lightning bolt. Only this morning I believed I could become the leader that Doran and Manus believed me to be. Now I didn't know. I'd been stupid. Again. I'd risked my friend's life without thinking. I hadn't seen the depth of evil my sister held in her heart—and I took Abbey right to her.

I'd taken too many risks with those around me. Tynan was bound to me and would be miserable when I died, be it in the final showdown with the evil half sister or two centuries from now of old age. Either way, I had allowed him to sacrifice what was left of his soul to me, and I cried for him too.

I pulled my knees to my chest and stared into the water. It stilled and I could see my face in the soft golden reflection that the candles cast on the surface. My eyes were still bright as pure gold medallions. No redness or puffiness that would have accompanied the tears when I was more human. In those eyes, my eyes, I could see my past reflected on the surface of the bath water — my human parents, my friends and Manus in his cat form. I could see the joy of the Kith as they were made aware that my powers had awakened, could see the hope in their faces…

I hadn't been on WildLand for the announcement but I could see the reactions now, visions in the water. I could see the anger in Feldema. I could see her evil.

Then the vision shifted. I saw my mother — my *real* mother — desperately making potions, preparing to hide us. She was lifting a long blade over a cauldron in the process of casting. She turned it over me as I lay in a makeshift cradle in a cave. She tenderly made a tiny cut on the bottom of my foot with her blade. It was made of gold, the handle carved of wood and the blade decorated with Celtic symbols. She added the tiny drop of blood from my foot to the brew. She did the same with the blonde child that would grow into Feldema. Then she cast the spell, chanting the incantation over and over.

I could see the hope in her eyes for both of us. She'd known she was having twins according to the prophecy, and she had a plan. I had to accept it. I had learned quickly around here that nothing was as it seemed at first glance and there was a deeper meaning behind almost everything in this life.

Anger flared back as I thought of the events of this evening. I had to fix this problem I'd created with Abbey and still be what my mother, Doran and the Kith believed me to be. I didn't know how. I could only be myself and hold fast to the knowledge that I was more human than Feldema — and that was key. Leaving my father and Abbey on that island was not something I could do. If I was to be the salvation of the Kith, then I was going to have to do it the way I knew to be right in my heart.

If I left them to fate, to chance, I would fail them. If I failed those closest to me, how could I lead a large civilization and reunite it with humanity? No. There was no question what I had to do and why. I had to be true to my human nature, true to my honor, true to the birthright.

My face replaced the reflections of the past and I was looking only at myself in the watery mirror. Honor. I had to live my life with honor. Abbey would be counting on me. If my father was still alive, he needed me too. I couldn't leave them to become bargaining chips in a political arena.

I ran all sorts of scenarios through my head, trying to find the flaws, trying not to think of Abbey. The original plan would be harder now that the others knew most of it, but I had left out enough detail when I told the story earlier that I thought I could still get to Thule. But even with plotting and planning both the trip to the island and the battle to come with Feldema, my thoughts kept going back to Abbey. I would *not* cry again. I had to be stronger, smarter.

Keena. His voice almost sounded weak in my head. *Keena?*

I'm sorry, Tynan. I have to. I have to kill Feldema or die trying. There is no other way. I got out of the tub and started to dry to go to him.

You have never asked me what mon guerrier *means. Do you know?*

I emerged from the bathroom and headed to the bed where he was lying, fully clothed. "No. I know it's French. I like the way you say it. It makes me think you're proud of me." *I crawled up next to him and snuggled against his chest. It hurt to think he could ever be proud of the weakness I had shown with so many tears.*

He smiled. "Yes, that is what I mean to do. It means 'little warrior'." He was quiet for a moment. "That night at the castle, when you were standing in the moonlight, Keena... That moment I knew I would be bound to you forever. I knew you would bring me nothing but trouble and I knew you would have great responsibilities. I understood those responsibilities would bring you danger and would bring others to your bed. I gave you what was left of me as a man, knowing all this. Knowing that the shell of a man I had become could only be saved by you, not destroyed."

"I would break that spell if I could, Tynan, you know that. I let you give your oath too quickly. I wasn't fair to you. I was weak," I said into his chest.

"Our current situation makes me very happy, Keena. I will help you in any way that I'm able. I'm not asking to break my bond to you. But you must know this—if you go to Thule, I cannot help you."

Guess he knew me pretty well. "Reading my thoughts?"

"You could say so." He kissed the top of my head. "I need not read your mind to know you heart. You need to know that I can't go to Thule, even though I wish to help you. My soul is no longer pure since Nessum cursed us to feed on humans." I felt him tighten against me. "It caused us to lose the purity that saved us from him to begin with. If I go to Thule, Nessum would claim my soul at the sight of me." He kissed me again, brushing my hair with his hand. "I would move heaven and earth for you, give myself up to you for an eternity…but I can't set foot on Thule. I've spent centuries keeping my soul from him. I—"

"I understand. You don't have to go there." I meant it both literally and figuratively.

We lay quietly for a while with him holding me, the smell of the forest on his skin. *Tynan.* I kissed his skin with my lips and spoke his name with my heart.

Yes, my love?

I'm sorry to cause you such pain.

"It's not pain you give me, but I'll surely have gray hair before long."

Chapter Nine

❧

The following night, I packed everything I needed for the seeing potion and started off to the wishing well. The big stone structure was tucked away in a quiet clearing, deep in the heart of the forest. It was one of the places I felt connected most with my energy.

The sun had set an hour or so before and I stood with a small breeze to my face, taking in the cool evening air. The brightness of the full moon lit the forest in a mist of silver. I felt the life of all the living things around me, the force permeating my skin like a sweetly perfumed lotion. I loved this feeling, it called to me softly when I was indoors and I dreamt of it when I slept.

I started to ready all the tools for the sacred circle. I had done this plenty of times before but always with someone there to guide me. Tonight, for the first time, I was on my own. Candles flickered in the light breeze. Howard circled above and would warn me of any danger. The moonlight was so bright he cast a shadow as, every so often, his silhouette crossed directly in front of the moon. I had about an hour until the moon was high enough to become the last part of the power I needed to cast the spell and create the potion.

I needed Abbey. She should have been here to help with this one. It was complicated, and potions were the weakest of my skills. Not needing potions for fighting, Bevin had promised to work on them after the final battle. I would have to do the best I could and hope I didn't screw it up. Abbey had jotted everything down so she wouldn't forget anything. At least I had her notes.

The search for those notes in her room, however, had been agonizing. The place smelled of her. All her Abbey-sized things had reminded me of her funny nature, how she brimmed with life. I hadn't cried while I was in her personal space. I missed her more than I could have dreamed and I was drowning in guilt, but it was time to harden myself to my new life. I prayed she could stay alive long enough for me to get to her.

Hold on, little one.

I was just about to close the circle—keeping the power and positive energy in and the negativity out—when I heard footfalls heading toward me and pulled out my blade. I was still jumpy after yesterday and was taking no more chances.

Manus emerged from the woods, his face smug and strong as usual.

"I thought I'd find you here," he said, showing little concern for the collection of herbs and candles he would certainly recognize and, from which, surmise my plan.

"Manus, I have to do this tonight. I know your feelings on the matter. Please leave me to do what I have to," I said, turning back to the circle.

He stepped into it. "You can't do this alone."

I shot up straight. "You have so little faith in me that you don't think I can hold a circle?"

He cringed and I saw the pain that drained his color. Guilt over his outburst yesterday was etched in the lines of his face. I shouldn't have been so blunt but I needed him to be the strong one, the one who would punch me square in the gut without holding back.

He went to his knee, his head bowed low. "I have come to give what assistance I can, my lady."

I had figured that Doran would order him to keep me calm and as low key as possible. If he came to help me now, it was certainly against her orders. Against everything he believed. "You can't, Manus. You have Doran to follow."

He looked up at me. "I swore my oath to *you*. I will follow you to the end of your life or mine. I feared for you last night. I never lost faith in you. I'm sorry I expressed my fear so badly. I haven't felt that particular emotion before."

"Ever?" I sat cross-legged in front of him. Now that he'd mentioned it, I had seen worry from him, anger—but never true, deep-down, overtaking fear.

"Not real fear, the kind that turns your gut to snakes and your heart to pudding. I didn't handle it well." He let himself fall to the ground, sitting with one knee bent up and his arm resting on it, the color still gone from his face. "I couldn't think the unimaginable. The thought that Feldema might somehow trick you to your death... She knows as well as Tynan and I that you will go to that island to save your friend and your father. I fear it's a trap—and I fear if we're lucky enough to make it off that island, she will trick you again in the battle."

"You can't go with me, Manus. I can't ask you to disobey Doran's orders."

"She never ordered *me* not to go, Keena, she ordered *you* not to go."

He had a point. I didn't know what she'd do once she found out, but I had no choice. I had to follow my heart. "If I don't save them, what hope do I have for the rest of my duties? I'll lead the Kith with my heart, Manus. The heart that is Demon, Witch and human."

He smiled at me, reaching out to gently touch my face. His green eyes twinkled in the moonlight. "That is why I have to help you. I spent the night thinking about your life and your strength. You've faced all this with such fire. I realized that what is in your heart is precisely what will make you a great leader. I will follow you, Keena, and I will fight your battles with pride." He looked at the cauldron. "And I will help you set your circle so you don't turn that poor bird into a toad."

"What?"

"Your cauldron must be in the west side of the circle to invoke the spirit of knowing." Shaking his head, he moved the small copper bowl that served as my cauldron before setting it on a stand that would allow a candle to be lit beneath. He then rearranged some of the other tools. He stepped outside the circle and made himself comfortable sitting up against the well.

I stood in the center and swept the circle with a bundle of lavender, then closed my eyes. "Let this space be clear for my energies. Hold it secure from evil and discord." A golden bubble floated up around me and the candle flames burned straight, untouched by the breeze outside the circle. The light reflected off the bubble surrounding me. I could see Manus through it, the bubble making him look golden like the colors of the setting sun.

I took a burning candle and used it to light the purple candles at the points, invoking their powers. "I call to the Earth and to the North to strengthen my circle and the power within," I said, lighting the first one. "I call to the Air and the East to enliven the circle and the power within. I call to the South and the Fire to warm the circle." I lit the last with a bit of hesitation. "To the West and Water, I ask for the cleansing that will hold the circle pure."

A ripple ran over the bubble, leaving a charge of energy within. I dabbed my fingers in a bowl of oil and made the sign of the cross on my head to anoint my powers to each of the directions. The ripple coursed through the circle again. It was closed and it would be a place for me to come and meditate and practice my skills from then on. The ground was singed along the bottom where I had drawn the circle. I had one just like it in the cellar at the manor. This one felt stronger. The wild was working with me, through me.

I gathered the ingredients on the ground as I sat in front of the cauldron. The hair on my arms and the back of my neck danced with the energy of the circle. I felt alive. I poured the rest of the anointing oil into the copper cauldron and lit a candle under it. I waited for it to heat to the warmth of a lover's touch. In the case of my recent love life, that was pretty warm. I thought of Tynan, who would be wondering where I was when he woke. I couldn't rush through this though. He would wait.

I faced the western horizon and prayed to the invisible sun. "I ask of the sun to invoke the power of light magic into my circle." I added the first of the ingredients to the cauldron. "Allspice from the Orient for positive energy." I crumbled the spice into the oil. "Comfrey, from the island of WildLand, please grant me safe travel." I tore off a piece of it a dropped it in, the smells already starting to mingle.

"Cinnamon, grant Howard the psychic energy to communicate with my eyes." It sizzled as it hit the oil.

I turned to the east and looked to the shadows of the night. "I ask of the shadows to invoke the power of dark magic in my circle." I continued with more ingredients. "Juniper berries, to extend Howard's vision. Balsam tree, for spirit communication, to spread wide with the wings of the hawk."

I opened a vial that Abbey had gotten me. I have no idea where she got it, but she was nothing if not resourceful. I hoped silently that resourcefulness was helping her now. "Dragon's blood, for the binding of me to the wings of the hawk." Then I dropped in a feather from Howard's head, plucked from my mark, brown and white at the base with an orange tip.

I took up a mortar and pestle and ground the blood-of-the-dead coral—the ingredient that caused me to lose my friend. I tilted it to Manus. "More," he said. I continued grinding until it was dust and tilted the pestle to him again. He strained to see through the circle and then nodded his head.

Kneeling over the cauldron and facing north, I chanted, "Coral, from the dead of the sea, block unwanted thoughts and project the hawk's vision solely to me."

Manus coughed to get my attention before I poured the dust into the potion. "Tears," he said. I didn't understand. "You need to add part of your vision. It needs your tears so you can see."

"Oh." Tears would be easy, I just thought of Abbey and my father and they came easily.

"Just a couple," he said. I leaned over the cauldron and let two tears fall into the mixture. They sizzled as they splashed into the heated oil.

I stood and invoked the goddess to bring her powers to me and infuse them in my potion. Finally, I dumped in the blood-of-the-dead coral to prevent unwanted thoughts. That would protect Howard from others using his powers and spying on me through him.

The potion flared at the addition of the coral. It gurgled and boiled for a few seconds then glowed a vibrant green. I took out a small amulet and dipped it into the shimmering green liquid. It flared suddenly with an orange flame and hissed as it enveloped the amulet. The power of the potion in the cauldron fizzled and died when the amulet was sealed. Now it just looked like oil and herbs. The magic was cast.

I had hung the amulet from a small strap of leather, which I dipped into the oil to seal the flexible material.

I doused each candle with the proper thanks to the directions and spirits then stepped through the circle to break it. "Thanks," I said to Manus. "I almost forgot the tears."

"No problem, that's why I'm here. Want to try it out?"

I called to Howard. He immediately swooped down, barely missing Manus' head as he landed on my arm. He was huge for a hawk—and heavy. Manus took the amulet and tied it to the hawk's right leg. Howard raised his wings and made a sharp call of protest to the attachment, but settled down once Manus quit fiddling with the ties. I bounced him on my arm to get him moving again and he obliged, sailing out of the clearing.

I didn't see anything.

"You have to invoke, Keena, otherwise the spell is incomplete."

Duh, I thought and closed my eyes and called to him in my mind. It was blurry at first, but soon the brightness of the moon and the beauty of his sight came into the sharpest vision I had every experienced. He could see far better than I could and even in the dark, everything was crystal clear. Howard shook his head a couple times. "Is it hurting him?"

"Nah, it's just that he can feel you there with him, like you can when you communicate with Tynan."

Howard took a deep dive toward the ocean and plunged in his talons in an attempt to snag a fish near the surface. I gave a gasp at the quickness of it, the speed of his movements. I felt a rush from the sensation of traveling with him, the feeling of freedom as he circled the prey he had missed on the first try. I could see half of WildLand from this height. It was a breathtaking, moonlight-silver landscape from his point of view.

I opened my eyes to see Manus looking at me. "That was incredible."

"I'll bet. We'll have to try it for me someday."

"We need to get back, I told the others we would be training. But I think Tynan knows better. No need to make him worry yet."

Of course, Tynan knew exactly what I intended to do—he just didn't know when.

* * * * *

That evening Doran had a meet for the Demons, as they didn't care much to mingle with other species. Outside of Doran, Feldema and myself, there were a few Gremlins—whom the Demons insisted attend as witnesses—and our consorts and guardians.

Doran was trying to determine where the tricky beasts' allegiances fell. We filed into the room with the usual entourage and took our seats with the very small audience of Gremlins. Doran then went to the center of the room and cast a circle, staying outside of it. Then she uttered the chant to summon the first Demon.

The circle surged black and filled with smoke. In the smoke stood a huge, bat-winged creature that held the air of death around him. I felt it and shuddered. Tynan put his hand over mine for support. I should be used to all this spooky crap by now, but every now and then...

I glanced over to Feldema. She looked more bored than anything else. The Demon greeted Doran and waited to be invited out of the circle. At her request, he gave an oath to behave himself and stepped out before the circled filled with smoke again. Before long there were four of the most powerful Demons from other realms in the meet room. They made the air heavy with death and magic.

Doran asked them her carefully planned questions and they answered, mostly with other questions. It all seemed very futile to me. They were vague but polite for Demons. When she finished they moved around the room to greet and talk to the Gremlins. I left Tynan talking to Doran and strolled to the nearest open window — the Demons' presence was so stifling that I needed fresh, clean air.

Karackos, who was rumored to be an Atlantean Demon, came to my side. My skin crawled at his nearness. He looked back over his shoulder at Feldema and I saw a wash of longing cross his face. *Interesting.*

In contrast, the look he gave me was one of pure disgust.

"Priestess, I have something you might want." He was watching my expression. I tried to keep it blank. "Something you may want very much."

"I have no need of anything you may wish to barter, Karackos." Demons barter everything. It's their very existence.

Summon a Demon to do your dirty work and you owed him something. If you didn't negotiate the terms properly it was *your* problem—possibly endangering your soul.

"I beg to differ with the lady. It has to do with your mother and your friends on Thule."

I gaped at him.

Damn. I had shown a sign of interest. He wouldn't let it go now.

He had turned to watch Feldema as she stood talking with a Gremlin. I could see the yearning in those disgusting eyes. Maybe this wouldn't be so bad. I still tried to keep my face steady.

He brought his gaze back to me. "Can we talk alone, my lady?"

"Yes," I said. And before I knew it, I was being drawn from the room and spinning into blackness.

Damn! I forgot to set the boundaries. I was in trouble *again.*

I was jarred from the darkness as I landed in an open wheat field. Off in the distance was an old Southern antebellum home. The warmth that the bright sun should have provided wasn't there. "Where are we?" I demanded.

"This place is an illusion for your benefit, since the actual place of my existence would be…uncomfortable for you." He waddled rather than walked closer, huge wings stretched wide from his body. They were the color of an old bruise, black and blue and yellowish, and his talons made those on the Slaugh look like thumbtacks. With a face like old, loose leather hanging from his bones and red eyes, he was the stuff that childhood nightmares are made of. It was hard not to step back from him or let him see how much he disgusted me.

"What do you have to barter, Karackos, and what do I have that you want?" I folded my arms and tried to look unimpressed. It was sickening to watch his loose skin swing from his chin as he talked.

He pointed a talon to the side and an image of Feldema shimmered into view. Somehow I managed to keep the poker face. "I can't barter my sister. She's not mine to give."

"I can help you get your father and that Imp off Thule." He watched me carefully for a reaction. I didn't give him one. "They are both alive." It was a token he offered, a gesture of good faith. I knew bargaining with Demons was dangerous. You had to be very specific or they would use any loophole you left them.

"Knowledge I already have." I tried to sound bored again.

"Knowledge you *suspected*—but I tell you it is true." He was watching my face carefully.

"Fine. So what do you want with my sister? I've told you I have no right to pass her to you. What are you asking for?"

His faced changed into what I suspected was his best attempt at a smile. "You are to kill her, are you not? You asked for vengeance for your Imp friend."

He shouldn't know that already. It wouldn't be asked or granted publicly until the battle. How did he know so much? Keeping my poker face was getting harder by the minute.

"Killing my sister is far different from turning her over to be consort to the likes of you, Karackos." I was guessing that was what he wanted, from the way he looked at Feldema. I was going to kill her whether I liked it or not. I had to. But turning her over to a Demon? That was something else.

"She would make that deal with me, would she not?" he spat. He had a point. She'd trade me to the first Demon who asked—but I was not her. I couldn't do such a thing. He leaned in a little closer and I could smell the death. "I do not need her as consort," he said as he looked longingly at her image, still shimmering in the air. "I wouldn't deny her if that was what she wanted, of course, but my need of her is much different."

"Has she made such a deal with you? That she would turn me over to you if she gets the chance?"

He made the almost-smile again. "No, priestess, you are not to my taste. The smell of you…your *honor*. It reeks like that of your mother. I could hardly bear you as a familiar." His face changed to obvious disgust.

"Familiar?"

"Yes, red Witch. You are too noble for me to be around for too long. But the white Witch is much more appealing…"

"Like to like, evil to evil. I get it."

"I cannot get my powers from the earth like you can, red Witch. I have to gather energy from the ley lines that exist throughout the realms. I need the filter of a familiar to channel and strengthen that power. A Witch of Feldema's ability would be very valuable to me." I could swear he was about to start drooling.

"But I'm still not able to give her over to you. And what would you have that is so valuable I would even consider it?" I was really doing a good job of appearing as though having a conversation about turning my sister into a battery charger for a Demon was no big deal. Who'd have thought?

"I know how to kill the fallen angel."

He said it softly, as if he didn't want anyone to hear. I lost my poker face.

"That's right, red Witch. Think on that. Two birds with one stone. Your lover's tormentor dead and your Imp and father back."

"Karackos," I raised my eyebrows mockingly, "that's information I might figure out on my own. You ask too high a price for it. If you think me so noble, then you know I wouldn't trade a life for it—even Feldema's." I had regained some composure.

But even I wasn't sure if I wouldn't trade her over for that information.

I guess I was about to find out.

"I thought you might feel that way, red Witch, so I offer you this. At the moment you are about to kill her, summon me. I will give her the choice of death — or life as my familiar."

I turned away from him to think. The deal would help me with my plans to rescue Abbey and Coyle and I wouldn't have to kill Feldema. She would still pay for her treachery by spending the rest of her life as a Demon's familiar. Hmmm.

I turned back to him and tried to study his face. There was nothing there. "May I question the details?" He nodded his head. "Why would I give her the opportunity to bind herself to you so she can gain your powers and use them against me later?"

He straightened his torso a bit and tilted his head. "You have my word that while she is bound to me she will have no power to hurt you or yours." He wrapped his big, yucky wings around his body and crouched, waiting for the next question. He looked like he was squatting to pee.

"And if I'm unsuccessful on Thule or at battle with her, and *I* die, then you get what, Karackos?"

He actually laughed. A booming, eerie laugh that echoed through the realm. "You are your mother's daughter, Keena, Priestess of the Wild. You have missed little." He stood and waddled close to me again. "Then I have underestimated you and I have made a bad deal."

"That's it? No 'I own your soul'? No 'you will spend eternity in servitude to me'? Nothing?"

"I simply ask that if you are victorious, you offer the white Witch the choice. Your soul will remain clean and your conscience may remain clear." His chin wiggled at me.

I didn't trust him as far as I could launch his massive, disgusting body. "I don't know."

He moved around me and past Feldema's image, lingering to take a long look at it. "Nessum tortured your mother for months trying to find you. Doing unimaginable things."

He was trying to play on my emotions—and it was working. I saw her from the vision, tenderly taking the drops of blood from our feet and then gently kissing each little wound.

"She was brave and took it well, even as he had her for himself time and time again." I was grinding my teeth, hard. "She never divulged to him where she hid you. The Dark Angel killed her himself when he thought her useless."

That did it. The rage was too great. The pictures I'd created in my head as he spoke were too much to bear.

I would have vengeance for my mother as well.

"Remove your garment, Karackos," I said without emotion.

"My lady, I told you I have no interest in you." He looked positively repulsed.

"Nor I, you. Trust me. I want to see if you're wearing Feldema's mark. You would lie to me if you've already bound yourself to Feldema. I know that's the only thing that would allow you to do so."

I gasped as his garment disappeared. The rest of his skin was just as dark and discolored and saggy as his face, and he stretched out his wings so I could see he carried two phalli. "Not for your taste, I'm sure," he said, baring his fangs in what seemed a mocking grin. "I bear no mark of the Priestess of the Sea or any other." He turned to show all of himself and then stopped, once more facing me. He waggled his dual dicks and watched my expression. "There are many who would appreciate such endowments." Looking down at himself, he laughed at my discomfort.

"Fine," I said as his garment reappeared, none too soon in my opinion. "I have one final item."

"Say it."

"I am offering you a very strong familiar—you've offered me only information that may or may not help me. I request a blood favor from you to use in the future as well as the information."

"Done," he chirped. "I was wrong—you are even better at this than your mother was." He made that face that came close to an evil grin again.

I tried to think of any other outs I may have missed. Nothing came to mind. I was sure I would live to regret this at some point, but at least I would now have an advantage on Thule. "Done."

Before I could say anything else, I was being pulled through the dark and stink again and we were back in the meet room. No one seemed to realize we had even left.

"You will have your information back in your chambers when you get there," Karackos said, turning to leer at Feldema. I almost felt sorry for her—but she would have a choice, so I really didn't feel bad at all.

I watched him waddle to Doran, bid his goodbyes—if Demons say goodbyes—and disappear into a cloud of smoke in the circle. I took in a lungful of the fresh air from the window. The stink of Karackos lingered, as if on my skin, in my hair, and I wanted it off me.

Manus approached and gave me a questioning look. Had he been watching? "Are you all right, Keena? You look..." As if I'd been to another realm? As if I had traded my sister into the servitude of a major Demon? "Like you've had a fright."

"I'm going to my chambers. You need to come with me."

"What have you done *now*?"

Now he looked as though *he'd* had a fright.

* * * * *

We snuck away without Tynan even noticing. By the time we opened the door to my chambers, I had finished telling Manus the story. He was fuming.

"Keena, dealings with a Demon...!" On the table was a simple, black wooden box, smaller than a shoebox. I opened it immediately. Inside was a scroll. The writing on it looked to be Arabic. I cursed Karackos aloud and the text changed to English. *Cool.*

"See? His word is good," I said. Manus just kept frowning.

The scroll looked ancient and the parchment was more worn than the pages of the old book about Thule. I read most of it and found nothing useful. I was sitting in one of the velvet-covered chairs. Manus was pacing and watching to see if anyone was coming. I got through the story of the fallen angels but there was nothing of interest there. I didn't much care how Nessum got here. I wanted to know how to get rid of him.

The last line told me, and I read it out loud. "And the death of the Dark Angel can be brought by the wielding of the sword of an innocent he hath slain."

Manus stopped short in his pacing. "How is that useful?" He snatched the box off the table and found another slip of newer paper that I would swear wasn't there before. "The blade of Trevina is still in her skull on display in the Castle Bran."

"So," I said, putting the scroll back in the box, trying not to think about my mother's skull on display in a trophy room. I would have to deal with that later. "Karackos kept up his end of the bargain. All I have to do is slay a fallen angel, rescue my father and Abbey, beat Feldema in the battle and then honor my end of the deal."

Manus scowled. I smiled at him and rose to kiss his forehead. "Take this." I handed him the box. "Hide it. Or better yet, destroy it."

"Keena, you've made a good bargain by the skin of it. But Demons are seldom only skin-deep. When you summon him, be very wary. We can't release you from him easily if he's tricked you in some way."

"I know."

"Feldema will probably choose death, Keena. Being the familiar to a Demon is not a pleasant existence."

He almost shivered. Not quite, but it was close enough to pique my curiosity. I had to ask. If I damned her to that existence, I should be strong enough to know what it would be. "And?"

"Witches can draw their magic from the earth but Demons can't. They have to draw energy directly from ley lines. It's like using raw electricity. Karackos will filter that energy through Feldema. After some time, she may lose her own powers, maybe even her mind. I've seen humans used like that and they only lasted a few months. They just weren't able to filter it through their minds and not be affected. He wants Feldema because she'll be able to do it better and longer. Since her powers are so strong, she may even be able to do it as long as she lives."

"Wow. That would really suck."

The loud chuckle I loved so much echoed in the room. "Yes, it would. That's why I'm worried that either Karackos or Feldema have plotted against you in this. You realize that you'll need to summon him into a circle to protect yourself?"

More magic I couldn't do well yet. "This just keeps getting better and better."

Chapter Ten

ဆ

I was pulling a silk nightgown out of a drawer when Tynan came in. I felt his presence as a featherlight touch as he entered.

Hogan had finally given up and let me have some clothes in my room. With Tynan around so much, I hadn't wanted the Gnome there as often. His cute little librarian kept him occupied, so it worked out well. For major events and dinners he was still dressing me, but he left me what he called "those play clothes" for day-to-day wear around the manor. I had shorts and T-shirts for running and training, and a few nightgowns and teddies for the evenings. I didn't need the latter much but I had them if I chose. I was going to put one on until Tynan got there.

He was behind me before I could turn to acknowledge him. His smell surrounded me, his breath warm on my neck. I hadn't seen him move closer. He was just there. I turned to him, my face at his collarbone. He eased back a little and I looked up, surprised. He rarely moved away from me if he didn't have to.

"You left with the Demon." It was a statement, not a question, so I didn't say anything. I saw something in his face I didn't recognize and it made me anxious. I didn't want to tell him about my deal with Karackos. I didn't want him to worry about me any more than he already did, or try to talk me out of going to Thule.

"I—" He kissed me tenderly before I could say anything more, his hand sliding into my hair, tilting my head. I let myself fall against his tight abdomen and wrapped my hands around his back and pulled him closer. The kiss was melting my will.

"I see you won't tell me what happened. So be it." His dark brows were drawn tightly together. I wanted to soothe him, to tell him everything would be okay. But I had figured out yesterday there was a good chance that nothing would ever be okay or normal in my life ever again.

"I'll have many things to deal with, Tynan, not all of them you'll need to know about." I tried to make it sound like it was just another council meet issue or something.

"I know you're going soon." His cheek was so close to my lips I could taste him.

I let out my breath in defeat but he kissed me again with all the emotion and tenderness he could muster. I felt every bit of it and I tried to say something else, but he stopped me, putting his masculine fingers over my lips.

He moved behind me and started to undo the little buttons down the back of the scarlet gown Hogan had fashioned for the evening. As the last one came loose, the gown fell to the floor. Featherlight kisses and gentle touches caressed my shoulders, sending goose bumps down my back. His hands moved slowly around my waist and shivers ran through my body. My knees were coming close to not doing their job.

His fingers made their way to my clit and he let his index finger dance lightly back and forth, stroking my passion as surely as he was stroking my clit. I was wet already. His skin, his smell, always turned me on well before his touch had the chance. I loved the way his body felt against mine. He sizzled with passionate heat that went straight to my pussy when he was near.

I was deep into wanting to feel his cock in me when Tynan's head jerked up suddenly. "Cliona," he said, his voice harsh.

Cliona was his second-in-command. She was also older than dirt but looked no more than twenty-five. He bent to get my dress for me and helped me partially button it up. The knock at the door came just as he finished. At least she had the decorum to knock. Most of my friends here didn't. Tynan opened the door for her and invited her in for a drink. She came in, but I felt the same coldness from her as usual.

Where Tynan had adopted a mixture of old and new, Cliona had embraced everything about the modern world. Her clothing, gadgets and demeanor all screamed high-tech female. She wore shiny, tight leather pants and a long, dark coat at all time, regardless of the temperature. The Vamp stood close to six feet, her dark brown hair straight and sleek and cut in a very hip bob that added to her youthful appearance. Her eyes were the darkest green I had ever seen. They turned black when she was riled up.

Nessum turned Cliona during the Witch Hunts in the early part of the Inquisition—another soul that got away. She'd been accused of witchcraft, tortured and killed. Many real Witches *did* lose their lives in those times, but she was just a servant woman accused by the jealous lady of the house. Hence, she didn't care much for Witches, so I didn't have to be a psychologist to know she thought I was unworthy of the sacrifice Tynan had made for me. I didn't disagree with her, but I didn't much care for being treated as if I were second-class, either.

Then again, to her, I *was* second-class. She also thought his affection for me showed a weakness in him. I'm sure there was more, but I didn't care enough to find out.

I tried to excuse myself from the room so they could talk but Tynan insisted I stay. Cliona spoke directly to him, all but ignoring my presence. I left only to have Hogan bring us some food and more wine. They didn't eat but I was starving, so I had a nice meal of chicken and dumplings with fresh snap peas. My eating also seemed to bother her. Maybe she missed the food. Tynan always enjoyed watching me eat. I caught her glancing over at me and she made a disgusted face.

She left after a couple hours of discussion over some rogue band of new Vamps and her plans to stop them. She had help from others and I had no doubt that she could handle the situation, but to be polite, I asked Tynan after she left, "You need to go to Russia?"

"Not at all. Now." He spun me around and started on my buttons. "I believe I was trying to seduce you."

"A fine job you were doing," I said as the dress hit the floor for the second time this evening.

"Really? How so?" His breath was hot on my neck as he spoke.

"I think making you wait has wound up your motor, Lord Tynan." I turned, only to be swept off my feet and taken to the bed.

"You think so?" He was peeling his shirt off. His movements were slow, deliberate.

I watched his fabulous skin appear a little at a time. His attention was on my face as I enjoyed him. The ripple of a true warrior's muscles — muscles that had spent days at a time marching and carrying supplies — was a glory to behold. He was packed tight from top to bottom. What a sight it must have been to see him in his armor, the sun golden in his hair. It made my mark — and everything south of there — burn for him as he stripped oh-so slowly.

A gentle breeze made its way through the open windows. He reclined beside me, placing one elbow above my head and lying on his side. I started to say that I loved him but he stopped the words with an amazing, tender brush of his soft lips.

The moonlight was dazzling on his pearly skin. His warm fingers trailed down over my collarbone, over my naked breast. My nipples peaked as if to beg for more attention. He repeated the trail on the other side of my body. He lingered over my stomach, tracing the muscles, teasing my navel, stoking my fire and making me squirm.

I wanted to close my eyes, to experience the sensation of touch alone, to isolate the sweet torments that were raising gooseflesh. But the greedy nature of the Witch wanted it all. She wanted the sight of his sparking midnight-blue eyes, to memorize the rise and fall of his chest as he took in air, the twitch of heavy shoulder muscles as his arm made its journey. This Witch wanted to see his wrists flex as he made tiny little swirls at my hip with his nails.

Such luxurious attention made every synapse in my body start to fire. My whole body was alive and wanting. When he traced the curve of my ankle, my toes curled and he gave me a knowing smile, only encouraging my pussy to clench tighter in anticipation of where his teasing fingers might move next. The whole experience was intense and relaxed at the same time. He was in no rush. I was on the slow track to an intense orgasm with no hand on the controls.

The combination of the fabric of the bed, the smell of jasmine on the breeze and the tickle of his breath on my skin was the strongest potion that had ever been mixed in the manor. I was drunk with it. How long had he lingered, touching, nibbling and kissing? I had no idea and no care. I only knew that I wanted him. I no longer cared about Thule or the Slaugh. I only wanted to be wrapped in the strength of his arms, to have his thick legs pressing on the insides of my thighs, to feel his shaft caressing the walls of my pussy.

My slow, relaxed breathing steadily increased as his touch firmed, reflecting his own need, which increased with each stroke of his hand. He rubbed the inside of one leg and then the other, stopping just before touching my aching pussy lips. The teasing made me arch with the need to bridge the distance he'd intentionally left between his hands and my wet lips. I worked hard not to speak, not to break the natural magic that came from two people truly enjoying the energy of each other.

His breathing was becoming deeper and more erratic. He dug his fingers into my hipbone and turned me onto my side, facing away from his body. His cock pressed into my lower back, demanding what his fingers had been enjoying for what seemed like hours.

Tynan nudged his knee between my legs, making me open for him. The head of his thick cock slid along my opening, teasing, promising.

I finally gave up the silence to moan a quite plea. "Tynan, please."

"Please what, my beautiful lover?"

I had started to wriggle. My body was pleading. My hips rotated in circles, urging him, begging him. "Love me. Fuck me."

His grip tightened and he slid inside. "Keena, your body fits mine so completely. My hands were sculpted to caress your skin. Your pussy is heaven wrapped around me."

I was stretched and full of him. It felt better than just fitting together. It felt as though his body was taking over mine and making me stronger, better, happier. I wanted this feeling to last forever and used a hard thrust to push away the reality that lay just outside this sanctuary.

His fingers tightened on my hip and he quickened his thrusts. The heat generated between our bodies was enough to fuel the fires of every house on the island. Each sure thrust drove the flames higher, pushed my magic to call to his. I tried to hold it back, to let the natural feel of flesh on flesh bring us to that beautiful plateau.

He pushed me away, turning me into the sheets, spreading my legs farther as he arranged me flat on my stomach. His movements were sure. His usual quiet, strong demeanor felt more looming then ever. When he reentered me, his length pushed deeply inside me. My toes curled. Tynan gripped my hips again and drove his cock even farther.

Then he started a wonderful, slow grind. I could feel his thighs against mine as he ground his hips against my ass. His thick cock was rhythmically circling inside me and stroking spots that I had no idea were so sensitive. He didn't pull back. No thrusting was needed. He simply lay flush atop my body and stroked over and over.

My eyes were watering from the pleasure. "Tynan!" I moaned into the sheets as I clung to the mattress for purchase against his pressure. This was surely the end. Nothing would ever feel this good again.

There would be no way to recreate the magic of this moment. Everything about this moment was perfect, the intensity of his lovemaking and the honesty in his emotions. If I lived through tomorrow, this would still be as close to a perfect union as possible. I strained to imprint the moment on my brain before the orgasm overtook my body and shattered the moment in my mind.

When it hit, I pushed back against his body, trying to take more of him. I wanted to be a part of his flesh, of his being. His grip tightened on my hips and he groaned something in a language I didn't recognize as I felt him swell and pulse against the straining muscles in my pussy. We stayed locked in that position for a long time, breathing hard before he released my hips and eased us between the sinfully soft sheets.

I lay on my side, curled in his arms. I knew why he had gone so slow, been so loving with me. He was thinking it might be our last night together. He knew that I was going and it frightened him. I ached at the thought—ached with the knowledge that we would go through these emotions every time I had to face something dangerous. My life would be filled with danger. I had little choice.

I could fight now and take the path the fates had set for me—or I could let Feldema win and take Doran's place as High priestess. That I couldn't do.

The slow and tender lovemaking lasted throughout the night. He took his time, making sure not to miss touching or kissing a single inch of me. I thought he was trying to memorize every curve, every angle. I returned the favor.

The thunder was low and rumbling throughout the night, like the beginning of a far-off, distant summer storm.

* * * * *

Tynan had taken his sleeping position before I woke up. He was on his back, arms softly at his sides. I dressed in my black jeans and the leather shirt I wore for my training sessions with Manus. I strapped two small blades to my legs, while at my waist were two matching daggers. I also wore my biggest knife—a saber with a thick blade and large, heavy grip—in a harness that held it on my back where I could reach it over my shoulder. I tucked another small switchblade into my boot. I wished Witches used guns, but then again, nothing on Thule would die from a bullet.

I pulled the soft, emerald-green sheet over Tynan and then kissed him gently on the forehead. I heard his voice in my head.

Come back to me, mon guerrier. *I'm not ready to give you up.*

I almost cried again but caught myself. I was about to go fight the Slaugh on their turf and try to kill a fallen angel, so somehow crying now would be ludicrous.

I will, my love. I kissed him again on those perfect, soft lips. I started toward the door and took off the necklace that held the amulet. I held it and rubbed the bat between my fingers. The gleaming emerald sparkled in the candlelight. I slid it down into the front pocket of my jeans. If things went badly today, I would not call out to him in pain or fear, tempting him to Thule or torturing him with the knowledge that he couldn't save me.

I wouldn't have him in my head if I died.

I ran from that thought, ran through the forest toward the beach—toward the island of Thule. I used my fear and uncertainty as a motivator to gather some much-needed strength, to pull from the woods and from WildLand what I needed for the journey ahead.

Manus was pacing along the beach when I made it to the far side of the island. "You're late," he snapped.

"I got here as fast as I—" I stopped abruptly when I saw the boat over his shoulder. "Is *that* it?"

The damn thing was small. *Very* small. With one tiny sail. The wood looked half-rotted, as if it hadn't been in the water in years. I made my way to it and kicked the side, unsure if it would get us to Thule, much less get us all back. Manus looked angry again. "*You* made the trade—you tell *me*."

"I guess nine gold buttons doesn't buy much around here. You got everything?" He was still scowling at me. "What? You got a better idea? Want to go ask Doran for one of hers?"

He snorted as he tossed a bag into the rickety vessel and handed me a backpack. It was really heavy. "Giving me the light one, huh?"

"It's got cold-iron chains in it." You can't bind Slaugh with ropes or other metal, they would just slip out—but cold iron holds them tight. I wasn't planning to hold any of them anyway. I was planning on taking out as many as possible, if I ran into them at all. We were going during the day, and few of them could do much in the daylight.

Secretly, I was hoping that meant Nessum and Bran as well, but couldn't be sure. The tales of creatures and protectors and traps on the island worried me more than sleeping Slaugh.

But my first worry was the ocean—and we had to cross a lot of it in this little boat. I was hoping Feldema wasn't as good at reading me for my plans as Manus and Tynan. It did look choppy out there, but no more than usual.

I held my breath and stepped onto the tiny sailboat, the wood groaning beneath my feet. Manus made a groan of his own. "I hope this thing holds us for the trip back," he said.

Trying to be an optimist, I was encouraged that he thought we would *need* it for a trip back. He shoved off, climbed in, pulled the sail in the right direction—and we started moving. The breakers threatened the vessel and it creaked and groaned, and we both released a sigh of relief when the little boat made it past. The waters on the other side of the reef were choppy but not strong enough to overturn us.

I held tight to the side as Manus maneuvered us toward Thule. Salt spray and cold gusts hit my face—and my stomach started to disagree with the rhythm of the boat's motion. I decided not to fight it and just let go. I vomited over the side violently, more than once.

"You okay?" Manus was trying not to laugh.

"Go ahead and laugh. I deserve it." After all, I was a warrior Witch who couldn't even hold her cookies on a boat. I had forgotten about my seasickness in planning this dubious adventure. Dumb again. "We all have our weaknesses."

"Here." He held out a small leather band with a tiger's eye bead tied to the center of it. "Tie it around your wrist. Pirates used pearls, but that should help. Put the bead on your pulse point but not too tight."

I followed his instructions. After a few minutes, my stomach started to calm some. "Hmm. It's helping." He looked back to the direction of the island while I kept my eyes peeled on the waters around us. I could only imagine the creatures Feldema could call from the depths of the dark ocean to stop us in this tiny boat. I didn't want to dwell enough to frighten myself, but I wanted to be prepared.

The boat lurched hard. I braced myself but my stomach only made a small protest. I would make it.

It was cold and I was glad for the sun beating on my skin. The sounds of the wind and the flapping, tattered sail were comforting. I tried to concentrate on that and not the rocking of the boat and the water just under the worn wood of the floorboards. "How long?" I asked.

"A couple hours at least. Relax. We'll need our energy." Manus crawled over the bags and around the pole that was acting as a mast and sat beside me. The wooden plank I was using for a seat bowed at our combined weight. He didn't try to hold me.

We sat silently as time seemed to pass at a crawl. Manus eventually stirred and from the depths of one of the bags, found an apple, which he handed to me. It felt warm and real in my hand. I didn't eat it. I just held it, as if it was a piece of WildLand I could carry with me.

The sail snapped suddenly — and the mast bent in the stress of the wind, splintering.

Manus cursed an oath under his breath as he used one of the chains to do what he could to secure the mast back into place. He leaned back to see if it was going to hold but another blast of wind came and it started to bend again.

I quickly cast a binding spell and it held. I prayed it would hold for the remainder of the trip.

"I shouldn't have brought you," I said, putting my hand on his shoulder. "Turn us around. I'll come back on my own." He ignored the comment completely by adjusting the sails. "I mean it, Manus. I put Abbey in danger and now I've done the same thing to you. I'll never forgive myself."

"Too late." He didn't even look up. "I would just follow you when you came back and I wouldn't get to enjoy this wonderful yacht." I barked out a little laugh and watched as he fumbled with some rope.

We saw the island come up out of the horizon. I figured from the position of the sun it was well after noon. After getting a late start, I was worried about the time. I didn't want to be on that island when the sun went down. It looked like a pile of rocks from the distance but I knew better.

Manus stayed silent as we watched the island get bigger.

When we reached the shore, stepping out of the boat took my breath away — and with it, my power. It drained away from me like a fading shadow. I could neither stop it nor call it back. The earth under my feet was utterly lifeless. I knelt and put my hands to the dead soil. The black, crusted earth beneath my hands was totally without life. The energy that I always felt in the soil of WildLand was missing.

I looked across the cold, bleak landscape. From the ocean to the base of the mountains was a frozen forest. The stumps and trunks of a thousand dead trees stood out against the sky. They weren't just dead. The circle of life and death is a part of every forest's essence. These trees were like stark, blackened bones, lost to some unearthly battle long ago. It hurt to see them still standing, unable to be saved or taken back to the earth that had borne them.

That very earth was as dead as the trees, so they would stand frozen for an eternity.

"You'll be okay," Manus said, dropping the backpack next to me. A cloud of dusty earth rose in an unnatural protest of the disturbance. "It'll be similar when you go into a big city. All the steel and metal will drain you but in a city, you'll adjust. Here, our magic isn't really gone, just too weak to help us."

I had a hard time standing back up on my own. Once I got over the feel of the dead forest, I realized just how cold it was. Not cold enough to freeze us to death, but enough to make us ache if we stood still too long.

Then it dawned on me that we were indeed on the mythical island of Thule.

I was suddenly terrified.

If we were going to make it off this island, I had better speed things up a bit. Since getting off the boat, my actions had felt dulled. I watched Manus moving to the boat to tie it. He seemed to creep along like a motion picture that was running at the wrong speed. "Must be a trap. We're moving too slowly." I concentrated and moved toward him. My speed resumed to normal. "Just think about it and it goes away."

He looked over his shoulder at me as he knelt, jerkily securing the boat. He closed his eyes for a second and then resumed at a normal pace. "That was weird."

"Hint of things to come?" I grabbed the backpack and headed toward the mountain.

He grabbed me. "Keena, at least *try* to let me protect you." His eyes were pleading. "It *is* my job."

"I will. You've done a smashing job so far." I punched him on the shoulder and headed into the dead forest.

On Thule, the trees didn't welcome me. I couldn't move through them as I could those at home. Instead, the dead branches seemed to reach and grab, roots rising to trip us as we walked. I knew they weren't, but it was hard not to believe. Disturbing, but I tried to ignore it, afraid if I thought about it too much it would slow us back down to the unreal speed we'd felt at the shore.

Manus was just off to my side, making his own path. We didn't want to walk single file. It would have left one of us with an obstructed view and slowed us in the event of an attack. We moved ahead steadily, eyes darting and aware of everything around us.

Howard made his appearance above us, the only life around. Manus looked up to watch him gliding and circling. I concentrated and opened my eyes to Howard's view. He drifted about fifty feet above us. He searched the ground in short, quick movements of his eyes and head. Howard was as confused by the lack of life as I was. Through his eyes I was more dead woods, no signs of anything moving. "Nothing," I said, as I brought my vision back to my own. Howard shrieked as I left his head.

"I don't like this at all," Manus said in a low voice, his cat eyes darting back behind us. "Too quiet. Too easy." He hadn't slowed his forward movement and neither had I—but my hands searched out each of my weapons. It wasn't a conscious action, just an impulsive need to know they were all where I'd left them. The only real fights I had been involved in so far were against my sister and a single Slaugh, so I wasn't sure of myself. How would my body react without my magic? Manus had spent hours upon hours trying to emulate various battle scenarios, but I had always known it was him on the other end of the weapons. There's security in that.

What lay in wait out here was starting to wash over my skin like unseen water and I had no way to know what to expect.

Patches of ice started to appear among the thinning trees, making the footing more and more treacherous. The land was slightly sloping upward, and the dead soil gave way to loose rocks in between the ice. The air was polluted with something wretched I couldn't identify. We moved on, glancing at each other and around us frequently. I tried to push out my powers to feel something, anything. "I just can't feel anything here."

He nodded. "Me either. Makes my skin is crawl."

I gave him a knowing look, glad it wasn't just my own fear that I felt.

Chapter Eleven

80

The forest of permanently petrified trees had thinned to little more than dead sticks when I suddenly stumbled on some ice and went to my knees, catching myself with my palms. I didn't scream, but the sudden loss of control sent adrenaline surging through my system.

Manus rushed to help me up. "I got it. Just tripped." But my eyes focused on what at first looked like a bleached-out piece of wood. It wasn't the same wood of the blackened forest...

Another scream lodged in my throat. It was a bone—and not large enough to belong to an adult. It was a tiny femur...a child's femur.

"Bones!" I said as I stood as fast as I could without falling backward. After gathering some balance, I took a step back. The sound that rose from my boots—now that I knew what was on the ground—was a spine-rattling crunch.

The simple act of turning to Manus made me feel weak, as if my blood was draining away from my brain. "They're everywhere." The air felt heavy. I had to struggle for a breath as I scanned every direction.

Bones.

"Keena." His voice was steady and calm, his green eyes locking with mine. "Take a breath. They're just bones." He gripped my shoulders, the softness of his expression holding my attention away from the tiny femur at my feet. "We need to figure out what left them here. Steady. You can do this."

"What ate all the meat off them? That's what you're saying, isn't it?" He nodded his head. I didn't want to know what ate this much. I scanned the area again, using the motion to loosen the grip of fear that had clenched my nervous system and was holding me stuck to the spot. Manus was right. I had to get control, remind myself what I doing here. My father…Abbey. I pictured her little face over and over in my mind. I took a deep breath and looked around, studying the terrain a little closer.

The bones were all dry and bleached. None looked as though they'd recently made their way here. Either that or whatever brought them was damn good at stripping them clean. "They're either old or…"

"Yeah. You feel any life around us at all?" We had instinctively moved until we stood back to back.

I took one of the daggers off my waist. "Nothing really alive except Howard, but something knows we're here." He didn't answer but he didn't really need to. We started moving toward the mountain again, slowly, trying to step precisely so as not to alert anything to our presence by crunching the smaller bones under our feet. There was still no sound around us other than our own footfalls on the bones and rocks as we moved.

I felt the brush of something against me. Nothing physical…but I had a bad feeling, an unnatural caressing of something unwanted and unseen on my face.

There were mounds and piles of rocks and large stones all around us, the foothills to the small mountain, but nothing large enough for us to hide behind. Nothing for whatever was heading toward us to hide behind either.

I scanned the rocks on the side of the mountain—then I felt the same presence behind me. I spun, letting Manus come around to cover our front. Behind me there were only more rocks but the feeling was getting stronger. Still, I saw nothing but the gray and black of the rocks and shadows. My heart was beating so fast I heard my pulse roaring in my ears. I tried to steady my now-splintering nerves. I spun the daggers in my hands several times for something to do and to keep from gripping the handles so tightly.

I caught a small movement just under my foot. I looked down quickly — and saw another shift from the pile of bones to my left.

Two bones were moving toward each other. A third bone joined them.

I held my breath as the bones assembled right before my eyes. "Manus! They're rebuilding!" I jumped back.

"I see that." He sounded almost causal but when I could draw my gaze away from the skeleton forming in front of me, I saw his face was tight with concentration. We backed up only to find other little piles of bones were also moving, sliding together, some already together enough to begin pulling themselves from the ground.

The boneyard was coming to life.

I backed against the largest boulder I could find to protect my back. I could hear the scraping and grinding of the bones as they stood. The bony carcasses seemed confused as they started to move about and search for us.

"Now what?" I asked. One of the skeletons moved toward the sound of my voice.

"Kill it," he said, as he stumbled backward beside me, moving up onto a large rock pile. A skeleton, not fully formed, grabbed him around the ankle. Manus raised his foot and smashed the remnants of bones.

Kill it? *Right.* "Um — already dead!"

"Got a better idea? I'm all ears."

I didn't have one. A fully formed creature came at me. As it stumbled, I decided it was best to replace the dagger with my saber. I pulled it over my shoulder and swung it through the torso of the zombie skeleton in one smooth motion. The jarring of steel colliding with bone radiated through my arm. The shattering bones sent a ripple of disgust through my stomach, which hadn't fully recovered from the seasickness.

The top half of the body fell at my feet. It dragged itself forward, bony fingers reaching out, legs pushing the bottom half in the wrong direction. I swung at another, catching it through the ribs. The blow and inertia sent it to the ground. Kicking at its head, I managed to knock the skull off.

They weren't held together too well, but they were tenacious creatures.

The thing just pulled its head back on, looked up at me with empty eye sockets and started to get up. I kicked out again as it reached full height, breaking the bones at the knee. It stumbled and fell at my feet but managed to grab my ankle with a strength I couldn't have imagined from fleshless, unmuscled bones. "Shit!"

I brought the sword down on its wrist and the bones shattered. My ankle was bleeding, but nothing major.

Manus, meanwhile, was in trouble. I tried to work my way closer, hacking through more skeletons as I moved toward him. He was fighting three at once. One of the skeletons had reached over the boulder behind Manus and grabbed him by the neck. Yet even while holding it by the forearm, trying to stop it from choking him, Manus continued to fight off a smaller one from the front and a larger one from the left.

The two I had sliced apart to get closer to Manus were looking for their heads, which I had kicked off in the process. I climbed up the rocks and brought the sword down on the skeleton latched onto Manus' neck. It fell to pieces as I sliced downward, shattering its spine and ribs. Once free, Manus took out the other two with large, sweeping swings of his blade. I swung at several more that were clawing at the rocks.

Another grabbed my shin. I brought the saber down on its wrist. Bones shattered—and so did my blade. Shocked, I stood there for a second and looked at the broken weapon.

More were heading toward us from the field of bones, and the closest was trying to climb the rocks after me. It skidded and slid back down, the dry, stiff bones too uncoordinated to grip the stone. "Up! They can't climb!"

The Shifter tucked away his sword and dagger and we scampered up as fast as we could. We needed to go up anyway. This was as good a place as any. We alternated pulling and pushing each other up the steeper inclines, ascending as fast as we could.

We stopped a ways up to check each other's wounds. "That ankle's going to bruise," he said as I poured water over the scratches on his shoulder and back. "There's a pass over there." He pointed in the direction we'd been heading before the attack of the skeletons. "The bones were a trick for misdirection. On the way back we'll have to take the pass. Let's not forget our new friends when we come back by."

"Forgetting won't be a problem. Zombie skeletons." I rubbed my forehead. "That's another first." He spit his water as he chuckled.

When we finally crested the top of the mountain, the wind had changed from icy cold to scorching hot in the distance of a footstep. After being cold for so long, the heat was drowning. It wasn't a dry heat. It carried the moisture of the ocean, and walking through it was like walking through a sweltering fog. At least it was downhill. Not that down was easier than up, but it made me feel like we were making good progress.

Halfway down the other side, we stopped to rest. While sitting on a ledge, I cast the spell to invoke Howard's vision. I didn't want to get dizzy and fall down the mountain while looking over the island through his eyes, so I leaned against the rock wall to steady myself.

There were a dozen or so small shanty-looking buildings standing in clusters off to the northwest. Wood, just as rotted and decayed as the rest of the trees on the island, made up the three-sided shacks, which faced away from us. Strips of fabric from makeshift windows danced in the ungodly hot breeze. Nothing else moved around them. The entire side of the island looked deserted. But then again, so had the last...

Just a short distance past the buildings stood the Castle Bran. From the hawk's perspective, it didn't look too large or sinister. I was willing to bet that from the ground, sinister wouldn't even begin to describe it.

The compound was oblong and wrapped around the single tower that jetted skyward at the back of the walled courtyard. The keep was attached to the tower and the open yard was cluttered. The big gate was down at the front center of the wall and the drawbridge lay open over a dry, empty moat. Maybe they were expecting us. Who could tell?

I couldn't control where Howard flew, so my view remained well above the island. He didn't seem to want to come too close to the ground. I didn't blame him.

In between the base of the mountain and the shacks was a whole lot of nothing. Sand, random boulders and waves of heat rippling up from the ground.

"Where are all the Slaugh during the day?" I asked as I slipped getting up from the ledge.

Manus held out his arm for me to balance myself. "Under your feet."

I yelped despite myself. There were too many shadows in those cracks and crevices. "I could have lived without that information," I said, trying to get my nerves under control.

Manus shrugged. "You asked."

I told him about the layout as we moved down the mountain. Try as I might, I couldn't help thinking about the Slaugh under my feet. I knew it was hours until dark, but I really didn't want something to jump out and grab me.

Manus must have seen it on my face. "You've been walking on them for hours and *now* you're worried about it?"

"I'd have been worried about it before if I knew. Besides, it keeps me from worrying about that little desert in front of us. I feel something alive in there. I'm guessing it's the *Tutzlwarms*. How much you know about them?"

"About the same as you," he said, his expression flat, but I could see the tension in the taut muscles of his neck. "I'd sure like you to still have that saber." We moved down the rocks, the steepness giving way to gentler hills.

We stood at the edge of the sand. It wasn't exactly black, but it wasn't the golden sand I'd seen in Arizona on family vacations as a child either. Small boulders protruded here and there. Inwardly, I wished we could leapfrog from one rock to the other to avoid walking on it. It might look like harmless sand but it was another trap, and danger lurked just beneath the surface. It crawled over me like ants...I mean *Tutzlwarms*. I knew anything with that name was going to be trouble.

"Burning daylight, little lady," Manus said in his best John Wayne voice, which was woefully bad in the best situations. Now, it wasn't funny at all. But the fact he was trying to make me laugh helped ease the growing tension we both felt.

Reaching out my hand to his face, I said, "I needed that."

He covered my hand with his. "We're not halfway through this yet, Keena. Are you okay?"

I really didn't know. I could see the shacks, small in the distance, and wondered if Abbey or my father was in one of them. It hurt to think so. Out here exposed to the heat and the winds. I really hoped they were in the castle, but that thought wasn't any better. My stomach tightened at the burning from under my mark, surprising me—it was the strongest my energy had been since arriving. My altered powers were churning, wanting to fight the offishness of Thule. "No choice. They're here somewhere, Manus. I have to be okay—so *they* can be."

He kissed my palm before I pulled it away from his face. "You know there's a very real chance that both Coyle and Abbey..." He trailed off. He didn't want to speak the words aloud and I didn't want to hear them.

"I know. If that's so…I'm sorry to have dragged you out here, Manus."

"My honor." He smiled and took a step onto the sand, his foot only sinking about an inch into the granular, sooty-looking substance. I followed. In the grand tradition of sand, it was hard to walk through — or trot, as we were doing. Neither one of us wanted to spend any more time than necessary in the island desert. I had walked in deserts before, and plenty of beaches, but never with the fear that the sand itself might swallow me whole. My heart was pounding and sweat ran down my face and neck. The leather tank top was stuck to me and my palms were sweaty. The sand was blowing around, sticking to my skin and stinging my eyes.

I managed to get close to a large boulder and some smaller rocks around the midway point. I jumped atop the smaller pile as if it were second base. Manus followed. He was panting from the exertion of running in the sand. We took drinks from a canteen and he stuffed it into the pack on my back before hopping off the safety of the base.

Before his feet hit the ground, I was hit in the side and knocked off, landing hard on my shoulder. My head spun from the force of the blow and with the added weight of the pack, I couldn't right myself fast enough.

As I struggled to my knees, another gut-wrenching blow came from the other side. I gagged and fell as fire spread through my torso, ribs giving way under the pressure of the hit. Doing my best to roll, I landed in a crouching position, my toes and one hand on the ground, while the other hand held pressure on my screaming ribs.

It made it easy to see Manus struggling with a giant lizard-snake thing.

The mammoth light-gray beast, with dark splotches that matched the sand, jerked hard to remove itself from Manus' blade. Fitting its name, it had the general shape of a worm but the belly of a snake, the legs of a lizard and a head that looked like a snapping turtle. Manus brought his saber down in the middle of the thing's skull. The blow was hard enough that I heard the blade scrape as it hit bone.

I didn't have time to see what affect the blow had on the *Tutzlwarm* or Manus because of the movement of sand in front of me. I drew a blade from my side just as another *Tutzlwarm* emerged from the sand as easily as a fish would jump from water. I rolled out of its way this time, barely, and plunged the dagger into its soft underbelly, splitting it open as it dove past. The unearthly wailing sound it made as it flopped around with its insides spilling onto the ground hurt my ears.

Hunched down, trying to hold my ribs and ears at the same time, I saw Manus still struggling. "The underbelly!" He drew one of his daggers and made an uppercut movement, slicing the *Tutzlwarm's* throat from underneath. It died gargling on blood that disappeared into the sand. It was absorbed by the dry earth almost immediately.

The sand directly under me began to soften and move. I tried to stand but sank faster than I could move my weight forward.

Sand swallowed me from feet to knees. It happened so quickly I couldn't move against it. When I struggled, it softened more and sucked me farther. Manus reached out but the sand was moving all around me, not letting him get close enough to pull me out.

"The iron! In your pack!" Manus got himself up on the pile of rocks as I struggled to pull the pack off. I swung the pack around and my ribs screamed in pain, making me release my hold and send the bag flying into the shifting sand. It was sinking. I leaned forward, fighting the pain. I missed the shoulder strap.

"Cauldrons!" Angry and on the verge of panic, I bent even farther, the dirty sand now up to my thighs, and somehow managed to stretch far enough to grab the bottom of the strap before it disappeared in the churning granules.

I tossed Manus one end of a heavy chain and he pulled. I stopped sinking, but the suction created by the sand that was now at my hips wouldn't release me. He wrapped the chain around a large boulder for leverage and pulled again. "It's no use," I shouted. I wasn't budging and the iron chain was digging into my forearm. The force pulling me down was winning.

Another of the worms launched out of the sand, flying at my face. I couldn't get out of the way. I heard Manus cursing and the clattering of the chain as he wound the remaining length of his end around the rock. I leaned forward as far as I dared without putting my upper body on the sand and shoved the dagger upward at the bottom of the worm, only nicking it as it dove back into the sand behind me. The movement shifted the sands again, pulling me down past my hips.

I closed my eyes and concentrated hard. *Thrust*, I thought. *Thrust!* I felt the power surging in my abdomen and it burned as much as my battered ribs. I pushed it outward, screaming with the pain of the magic leaving my body, sending power into the sand as I cast.

THRUST!

The sand exploded out from around me, letting me move my feet. But the hole I had made with the spell was too large and I started to sink back in. Like water returning to the sea after a wave, the grungy sand was slipping back in around the cavity faster than I could climb. I was sliding farther in instead of getting out.

I grabbed for the last link of the iron chain. I almost lost my tenuous grip but held on and gritted my teach as I pulled myself tortuously away from the hole. By the time I reached the sanctuary of the rock pile, all had gone deathly quiet again. Even the sweltering breeze had stopped.

"Your magic worked here!" Twenty feet away from the rocks, Manus lay on his back, panting. I was holding my side and trying to stand.

"I guess it did," I huffed and cringed at the pain.

He lifted himself to one elbow and looked at me. "That was Demon power."

"It hurt." I was still winded and trying to breathe shallow. "Demon power?"

"We didn't know if you had inherited any of the Demon power from Coyle. I guess you did. He must feel your presence here, perhaps even did something to help."

He grabbed his pack and rummaged to find a pain amulet, handing it to me when I approached and kneeled next to him. I slipped it over my head. "Bevin's magic doesn't work, though."

"I figured. But I brought a few just in case." He ran his hands through his hair and pushed it from his face, then pressed at my side to try to see how bad my ribs were. I cringed at each touch. "Sorry. Feels like only two are broken. Can you manage?"

"Yeah, just need a breath. We should probably move on before they come back."

"I wouldn't if I were them." He shook his head. "You about threw me off the island. I think I was ten feet in the air. Were you directing that my way?"

"Uh-uh, I was pushing down," I replied, trying to get all my hair behind my ears. The band had broken.

"Damn. You're *really* that strong, even when it hurts?" He was shaking his head.

"Everything seems to be strongest when I need it to be."

Translation—when I'm terrified.

"Maybe *you* should be *my* guardian." I saw a change of expression cross his eyes.

"Who'll sleep on my feet?" I laughed.

He didn't. I had too much to worry about right now to soothe his ego. Evil sisters, fallen angles, the fate of the Kith and lovesick Vampires were enough. He looked off toward the shacks.

"Manus," I said softly. "I'll always need you." He looked back at me with some uncertainty but managed to smile.

"On we go. What's the plan?" He stood and offered me his hand.

Pain shot through my side as I stood. I stretched and made an effort to see how much I could move. The screaming pain subsided to a sharp tightness as I shifted and moved around.

"Let's check the shacks first...then we'll get to the castle."

"We're running out of daylight. Should we split up?"

I was shocked that he even suggested it. I hadn't thought he would ever allow it. But I guess my little show of power gave him a bit more confidence in me. "Not yet. We still don't know what else it out here, and I want you at my side."

Chapter Twelve

ဢ

Nothing else jumped us from the sand. Manus moved through it as though he didn't expect anything to. I was a little more hesitant, watching for any movement or shifting in the smooth texture of the little desert. Nothing moved.

The shacks were larger than they had appeared through Howard's vision. They stood fifteen feet or more high. There were twelve of them, standing in groups of four, each cluster arranged in a U-shape. They all faced the other direction — we were walking up to them blind.

I felt the salt spray from the ocean. We had made it almost all the way across the island. It was late afternoon and I knew we wouldn't be getting out of here before dark, no matter what happened from here on out. The thought of a night here with the Slaugh made my gut tighten. I had no idea what would happen to us after dark.

We moved quickly but cautiously, knees bent and ready for any attack. I had a dagger in each hand. We hit the backside of the first shack and put the wall to our backs. Manus used a hand signal to tell me to stay while he rounded the first corner.

I went right after him, bending lower.

He kept moving and I followed, making as little noise as possible. When we neared the front, he motioned that he was going around. I waited this time. He swung around with his sword up, ready to engage.

I stayed a heartbeat and heard nothing from him so I followed. We stood in front of the first group of shacks, and could see into all four at once. There were torn bits of faded, old fabric that may have covered the openings once upon a time, but now they stood open to our eyes...

The stench hit me, violent cramping twisted my stomach and I spun, falling away from the sight, holding my breath against the smell. I landed on my knees, sucking in hot air, fighting the urge to vomit.

Manus was backing away as well. "Collectors," he whispered. "Remember, they're collectors." He gripped my shoulder strap and yanked me from the ground. "Come on, we're too late here." He dragged me, moving as fast as he could to get past the sight, his strong jaw quivering.

I stood and tried to walk past without looking again—but I couldn't bring myself not to. Before we passed the last of the four shacks, I turned back.

The shacks were stacked from floor to ceiling with bones. Not clean, old, dry bones, like those on the other side of the island. Most of these still had some meat that used to be someone's flesh. Each of the structures held different types of bones, well sorted and stacked with great care. The skulls in the last one were arranged by size. The ones nearest the top were the tiny remains of babies or little animals. My gaze was drawn to one at my eye level, a skull that would be about the same size as mine. There was a tuft of blonde hair still attached and bits of skin clung to the side of one cheek.

I held my breath in fear, not able to walk past it. These people deserved better. The rotting smell was overwhelming in the heat and my stomach threatened again.

"My lady," Manus said in his formal voice to get my attention. "We have to move on." He was able to keep his head turned away. Maybe he had seen something this awful before—his face said that perhaps he had. I hoped it wasn't more than once.

He finally pulled me in the direction of the next set of shacks. I found it hard to move my feet. I didn't want to see what was in the next. He rubbed his hand down my back to comfort me as we moved but I could only think of Abbey. Had they done this to her?

The thought panicked me and I ran ahead of him and around the nearest shack without even bothering to hold my blades up for protection.

Manus slid up next to where I'd stopped, his sword out and ready. I *did* still need my guardian. He looked relieved when we realized it was a collection of a different sort.

There was an eon's worth of garage-sale stuff. Pottery that looked like it had Egyptian markings, bicycle tires, radios, ship parts, kitchen stuff, tools—all manner of day-to-day objects of life through the ages. Even a computer monitor was thrown on top of one of the piles. This junk wasn't as carefully sorted or cared for as the bones had been. *Not as precious?*

I took in a deep breath in relief. We only had one groups of shacks left to go.

I let Manus take the lead but I was counting on another unprotected collection. Goddess help us, what would this one hold?

He swung himself around the side of the shack and I watched his face as he gazed over the contents. He looked surprised, even amazed, but not frightened.

I stepped around and my mouth fell open to match his astonished look.

These four shacks were in the same U-shape. They too were filled floor to ceiling and from side to side—but these held all things shiny and glimmering.

There were chests and baskets of jewels, reams of silk, stacks of gold and silver bars as high as me and every gold-covered thing you could imagine. On one shelf there were Aztec masks, more Egyptian trinkets and a golden bowl the size of a large pizza—filled to overflowing with gold teeth.

The afternoon sun was hitting all the gold, making it twinkle and shine. It was hard to see as we made our way to the far side of the treasure to end all treasures. I spied a stack of gold, silver and ornamental swords, daggers and a variety of weapons. "Manus, hang on."

I stepped to the pile and pulled out a blade, holding it up for inspection. It looked like an old pirate sword. I swung it back and forth. Too heavy. I dropped it back on the pile and pulled out another that wasn't as ornate and looked Asian. It felt good in my hand, and was well balanced. I tucked my blades back into their sheaths and grabbed another dagger from the pile and stuck it in my waistband. Manus let out a little laugh as I grabbed one more.

"I saw those bones back there. I need all the help I can get." He made a face in agreement and grabbed one more dagger for himself.

Howard screeched loudly. It wasn't his normal call—it sounded panicked and alarmed. I couldn't tell which direction it had come from. I froze and cast the spell to see through his eyes.

Everything was black. I held my breath as my heart started pumping too fast.

"What is it?" Manus asked, turning slowly with his sword and the new dagger pulled.

"Just blackness." I heard the panic in my own voice.

The blackness lightened to reveal a man tied to a large, wooden crucifix up against a stone wall. His face was gaunt and pale, bruised from abuse, cheekbones narrowed from hunger. Something hit him from the side and he opened his eyes, ever so slowly.

They were *my* eyes—golden and brilliant against the ashen skin.

"Father!" I looked around frantically although I only saw what Howard saw. I spun in my spot.

Manus shook me. "Tell me, Keena! What was it?" I opened my eyes as the scene before me went black again.

"They know we're here. They have Howard and my father. I saw him." I turned back to the pile of weapons and pulled out one more dagger, shoving it into my boot. "If he's alive, maybe Abbey is too."

"I'll go around the back of the keep, you head up the side wall."

"I'm going in the front door, Manus. They know we're here. No use sneaking around. I'll face Bran on *my* terms. He doesn't frighten me anymore. One of us isn't living past today." I turned toward the castle.

Manus looked away, knowing there was no arguing. "I'll go around the back side just in case." I gave him a nod and walked away. I saw my father in my head again and knew if I didn't face Bran head-on, I had no chance of getting him out. Bran wanted a face-to-face fight and he was going to get it.

I just hoped I was up to it.

The drawbridge was down and the high stone walls *did* look sinister as I stood at the edge of the bridge. It was bigger and scarier than it had looked from Howard's high point of view. I stood tense at the bridge to give Manus a moment to get around the back and to gather my nerve. I thought of my mother and how she was tortured here.

Were any of those bones in the shacks hers? I had to swallow hard to get past that thought. So many had sacrificed so much for me over my life and most of them I wasn't even aware of until they were gone. Today I would do my best not to get killed and make their sacrifices in vain, but I had to follow what my heart knew to be right. I had to put a stop to Bran and his manipulation of my family. They had all suffered, my Witch family and my human family, at the hands of the devil inside these walls. I wasn't backing down.

I channeled my fear into anger and stepped onto the ancient wood of the drawbridge.

The soft smacking sound of my boots echoed over the dry moat as I crossed. My heart was in overload mode again. I took several deep breaths as I walked at a very steady and controlled pace. If Bran was to see me coming, he would see me coming with confidence.

I made it off the bridge and into the courtyard unaccosted. I felt the presence of life within my reach, but there was also the presence of something...*other*. I kept moving, only drawing the newly acquired sword when I reached the main door of the keep.

Inside it was empty, too quiet. The main entrance led to a large room just inside, and opened onto two smaller rooms to either side. I stood and listened. Still nothing.

Manus came through one of the side doors. We drew down on each other, and then relaxed. "I came from the big room and circled to the side." He pointed to the far side with his sword. I walked to the other side room only to find it empty, except for a table and some scattered, dusty chairs.

"Nothing," I said. "Where would the trophy room be?"

He gave me a questioning look. "I need Trevina's blade. Best to have it before we find company," I explained.

"Up one or two floors, I would guess. I think there's only five from looking at the windows. Prisoners will be down. Hurry," he said, ushering me to the stairs. "They'll know something's up if we don't go to them soon."

We went up the steps two at a time to the second floor. It looked almost as abandoned as the lower level. Dust and sand covered any remaining furniture, and there was little of that.

As we hit the top of the stairs at the third floor, things changed. A tapestry on the wall opposite the stairs was clean and the gray walls weren't coated with dust. Someone or something used this area often and recently. I stopped on the top step and let Manus take the lead. He swung around the corner and kept moving. I peeked around and then followed.

The first room was a bedchamber that looked much like Tynan's at Castle Dracula. Gray, carved-stone walls held huge portraits, and heavy drapes in dark maroon matched the rumpled bedding. The bed had been slept in but was now empty. Somehow the bed didn't look like Bran's style.

Something on a side table caught my eye. I walked to it, traced my fingers over the delicately engraved dolphins covering a brush handle. The hair in the brush was fine, long and white. "Feldema." Even I said it, I still couldn't believe it. Who was she sleeping with, Bran or Nessum? Even *she* wasn't capable of sleeping with a Slaugh, was she?

Manus saw the brush and shook his head in disgust before motioning me forward.

The next room was a living area that seemed to second as a trophy parlor. It took up the rest of the floor. There was a modern-looking bar set up at the far end and the rest of the decor was new. Persian carpets graced the floor and plush leather furniture was arranged in two different seating areas.

Along the two longest walls were the spoils of plundering and battles, more personal than the junk tossed in the shacks outside. These items had been handpicked and well taken care of. Skulls, treasures and trinkets were precisely lined up within bookshelves and hung purposefully on the walls. I didn't see Trevina's blade along the walls. There were others, but I would recognize my mother's sword from my vision. I didn't need to study the others to know hers wasn't on the wall. I scanned the bar area in the back — not there either.

I turned to ask Manus a question but the words were lost before they left my mouth. My stomach knotted and I felt as if all the air in the room had suddenly vanished.

In one of the seating areas — protruding from her own skull — was my mother's sword.

A wooden platform held the skull, the blade sticking out of the top of what was once my mother's forehead. Too weak to stand, images from that vision floating in my mind's eye, I fell to my knees.

The display—obviously made for the purpose—held the skull at an angle, the jaw dropping to make it look as though she were perpetually screaming.

I couldn't help it. Silent tears started to fall. I sucked in a ragged breath, the pain reached my chest and I started screaming. Rage and sorrow over the death of a woman I couldn't remember overcame me. Images of my sister sitting in the leather chair next to our own mother's skull, sipping wine and laughing with her lover, were more than I could bear.

Manus had turned from the wall he'd been searching and was at my side instantly. He stood looking at me before taking a step forward and kneeling, reaching out for me. I shoved his hands away and stood.

After gaining a bit of composure, I pulled the sword gently from the skull then sliced a large swatch of material from one of the fancy drapes. I wrapped my mother's remains gently in the maroon velvet. Still sucking in air and crying hard, I tucked it inside the backpack.

My mother's blade felt like it had been made for my hand as I tossed and spun it, swinging my arm from side to side to get the feel of it. Perfectly balanced, it fit my hand better than the custom blades I had back on WildLand.

I didn't bother to say anything to Manus before turning and heading back down the stairs. He followed silently. Keena, Priestess of the Wild, was now a warrior with a very clear mission—and I needed no pep talk or advice from my guardian to be ready for battle.

We met two of the Slaugh on the landing to the main floor. I sliced through both of them without slowing my pace. They disintegrated into the fine sand that made up the lifeless island. I felt my power surging as I hit the stairs that led to the basement. It was the Demon power and very unfamiliar to me. I had to contain it if I was going to get through this without blasting everyone in the basement. I turned at the bottom of the stairs.

A basement is wasn't — a dungeon it was.

The thing looked like it had come straight from a Hollywood movie set. Large sconces with burning candles adorned the walls, lending an eerie yellow light to the room. There were shackles and torture devices scattered on the walls and floors. The placed reeked of the dead. There were several large crucifixes — and one small one.

Abbey was tied to the smaller one in the far left corner and looked to be unconscious. I prayed she was passed out. My father was hanging from nails in his hands and a chain around his neck. Every bit of exposed flesh was scarred or open and bleeding. The horror of the sight was overwhelming. I felt the bile of true hate in the back of my throat. I thought I had felt hate before, but now I understood. I was baptized by it.

My father tried to crane his head up to see me as I barged in. It was a struggle, but he managed to open his eyes, to focus. The tiniest of smiles showed on his parched lips. I swallowed hard. His body couldn't have weighed more than seventy-five or eighty pounds.

"Look, Coyle, I told you she was coming to join you." Bran stepped from behind a large column to my left. His voice wasn't much more than a whisper. I turned to face him, the blade of Trevina in my right hand and the one from his treasure trove in the left. "Keena, Priestess of the Wild...welcome to my humble abode." His grungy face was actually smiling under the cape. I could see the glow of his red eyes. The stink of him reached my nose, making me sneer even more.

"Humble is a generous adjective for this, Bran." I kept eye contact with him but heard Abbey moan. I was afraid to look at her again and draw attention to her.

"You have broken a truce by coming here, priestess." He stepped closer to me. I didn't back up.

"I believe that my sister has been breaking that truce for a while, Bran. Would you like me to talk to Doran for you?" He didn't flinch as I stepped slowly over to the right to try to put myself between Abbey and the King of the Slaugh. He circled with me, never breaking eye contact.

"Dark comes soon, Keena."

I stepped toward him. "I won't be long. I'll just have these two and be on my way."

"I think not, Witch. You may join them, but you won't be leaving my little oasis." He stepped toward me. We were close enough to draw blood. The stench from his decaying form filled my nostrils, caused my weak stomach to tighten. I fought the nausea as I felt the Demon power surge again.

He felt it too. He backed up a couple steps.

His red eyes flared from under the cape. "You have no power here, Keena."

"Try telling yourself that over and over, Bran. See if it helps." He was frightened. I could feel it. I stepped forward again. "Where's your master, Bran?"

The red in his eyes flared bright as he shouted, "I serve no one!"

"I don't believe you, Bran. Nessum pulls your chain. Everyone knows that. They *laugh* at you." He was shaking. "Easily rattled too." He was almost at the stairs, backing away.

"Enough!" The voice rolled over me like a cold fog. I knew who it was, I just wasn't happy he was at my back now. He must have materialized behind me in the room. Looking around, I also realized that Manus wasn't there. He had been behind me coming down the stairs…

I backed farther to the right, toward the nearest wall, trying to keep them both in my view. I dropped Trevina's blade to the side of my leg so Nessum couldn't see it. Little miracles, he was on my left, so my body hid it from his view. I still had the other blade out in front of me.

"Keena, nice to see you. I am pleased that you have come to us. Saves me the trouble of sending any more of Bran's pets after you. I will gain so much more pleasure this way." Nessum was beautiful. Tall with broad shoulders and a thin midsection, he looked more like the modern concept of a Vampire than any of the real Vampires did. The veins marbling his face and pale skin were the only thing that took away from his appearance. Surely, Feldema was sleeping with him and not Bran.

"Sorry, Nessum. I don't play as well with the evil and undead as my sister does," I said, still trying to keep them both in sight.

"I had a different impression. Lord Tynan, after all, is just as undead."

"Not really." Where the hell was Manus?

"Your father has sustained me over the years so well, I'm sure you'll do the same. Now, I will let him and your little friend go—if *you* stay in their place." His voice was serene. I got the impression of a calm morning looking over the still waters of a mountain lake.

"Yeah, right. They just leave, and right before sundown. How nice of you. The Slaugh will slaughter them. No deal, Dark Angel. How about you just let us all go and I'll forget this happened." I knew it was corny, but I was trying to appear cocky, whether I felt that sure or not.

As his laughter thundered throughout the entire castle, I saw something gray move out of the corner of my eye on the stairs—and hoped it was who I thought it was. Nessum still had his head tilted back in laughter.

"Not that funny." As I said it, Manus jumped on Bran's back in his cat form, sending him forward, toward me.

I bent and swung my right hand toward him, striking his chest with my mother's blade. *Thrust,* I chanted. Burning pain pushed up through my abdomen.

The power of the spell and the blade exploded into the King of the Slaugh. Bits of sand and dust shot outward. Manus flew across the room and into the wall, hitting hard and falling to the floor. Nessum stumbled back into the crucifix holding my father, knocking it down and breaking it. Coyle's hands were ripped from the spikes. I felt the thrust push back against me as it bounced off the walls. I didn't go down, but I had to struggle to steady myself.

Nessum came up fast and flew toward me with his hands raised to start a silent spell. I knew better then to let him finish. I lifted my mother's blade and steadied it to plunge into his chest.

He stopped cold, his gaze locked onto my eyes, searching to discover if I knew what power I held over him. When he found his answer, he started to back away. I gave him a tiny smile and thrust forward.

Nessum disappeared, vanishing completely out of the room. I stood there a second, sword gleaming in the torchlight.

Manus made a small noise, shifting back to his human form. "You okay?"

I nodded. "Get dressed, get Abbey and find Howard." I knelt at my father's side. He fought to open his eyes again. He was alive, but just barely.

"About damn time!" Abbey said as she approached my side looking none the worse for wear. I picked her up and kissed her on the head.

"I thought you were hurt." I was so happy to see her.

"I told them all kinds of bull to get them to leave me alone. Then I pretended to pass out so they'd wait 'til I was awake to torture me." Those big blue eyes looked past me to my father. "He's not good. Nessum has been feeding off him regularly." She bent over him and touched his head. "Coyle, we'll get you outta here, baby, just hold on." His eyes darted back and forth between us while Abbey tenderly rubbed his forehead.

I looked up at Manus—who cradled Howard's broken, lifeless body in his hands.

Chapter Thirteen

ဢ

"Try not to yank on the hair, little woman." Abbey obligingly adjusted her perch on my backpack as we moved along the sand. I had sent another thrust spell through the sand in the hopes that it would keep the *Tutzlwarms* away. So far, so good. Manus held Coyle with his right arm. I had him under my left. The going was slow, but we were going. The mountain pass we had seen on the way in was just ahead of us but the sun was creeping down the horizon and the shadows of the evening were stretching their long fingers toward us.

"We're never going to make it, Keena," Abbey said as she held on to my shoulder sheath. Her weight wasn't much on my back. We'd walked through the forest on WildLand like this many times. I was one of the few people she, or any Imp, for that matter, would let carry them. It felt wonderful just to have her there.

I had grown very aware of when the sun was coming and going during all the time spent with Tynan. I had gotten used to his cycles and I could feel the darkness creeping up around us. Manus moved faster and I did my best to keep up. My father didn't weigh much but it was dead weight nonetheless. He moaned a bit here and there, but mostly he was out.

We were at the end of the rocky pass through the mountain when the darkness overcame us. I heard the calling and flapping of the awakening Slaugh all around. They would locate us soon if we didn't find somewhere to hide.

"Manus," I said, stopping before we headed out of the pass. "We should find a cave or something in these rocks. The boat is too far away. Then we'd be stuck on the open ocean." He agreed and went ahead of us to find some cover. I tucked

Coyle and Abbey into a small gap in the rocks and stood guard.

It wasn't long until the closest Slaughs sniffed us out. Fresh blood, so close to home, stirred them and brought them quickly to our location.

I stood in front of Abbey and Coyle and slashed at the creatures. I could smell the rot of them, just as I had with Bran.

I hunched over and tried not to vomit. My weak stomach was going to be the death of me.

Straightening to swing between dry heaves, I managed to spear one of them and it disintegrated, showering us with dust and sand.

Abbey levitated a small rock and smashed it into a Slaugh attempting to take advantage of my bent position. It jerked back and hit the side of a hill.

"Your magic works?" I shouted. "Keep going!" I was slashing and jabbing and she was pounding them with rocks. The pass was narrow, and they got tangled in each other, sending one to the ground and others off into the air in frustration.

Several went higher, over the rocks and cliffs of the passageway and came at us from the opposite direction. Abbey was still helping me fend them off when Manus fought his way back to us. "Found one. I'll get Coyle, you go in front. Abbey, stay in the back and keep at it."

We made it out of the pass and the short distance to the cave Manus had found. He placed Coyle on the ground and backed into a small opening, pulling my father behind him. Abbey ran in without even ducking. One last Slaugh tried to follow us in and I stuck it in the face with the golden blade of my mother's sword. I backed in, warding the opening behind me.

Bran was dead, Nessum was AWOL and our magic was working. The night might be survivable.

We made our way about twenty feet into the mountain and braced against the back wall of the cave. I cast a second ward over the opening. I really didn't need to. The Slaugh were too big and bulky to get in and they seemed uncoordinated, unable to work as a group or continue to attack if they couldn't see us. But it made me feel better.

It was freezing in the cave. "Manus, do you still have those amulets?"

"Yeah, why?"

"Our magic is working, maybe they do too." He dug through his bag, pulled out three glowing amulets and handed them to me. I sat behind my father and put his head in my lap after hanging the amulets around his neck. "Water?" Manus handed me the canteen. There wasn't much left. I poured some on my father's lips. His tenseness eased a bit but he was starting to shiver.

Abbey found some stones and spelled them to heat up. We arranged them around his narrow sides. I rubbed his hands in mine. His bones were almost as fragile as the skeletons in the boneyard.

"Bran must have been blocking the magic." Manus handed me another of the warm stones. "We're dead if Nessum finds us in here. He'll just make the mountain fall on us."

"Either that or Nessum was blocking the magic and is gone. He really freaked when he realized I knew how to kill him." I rubbed my father's hands gently as we talked. The sounds of the attacking Slaugh lessened as they gave up their futile attempts to penetrate the wards.

"Nothing like mortality to scare the crap out of an immortal Dark Angel," Abbey added as she hovered over a warm stone.

"You fought with heart today, Keena." Manus touched my shoulder.

"Howard died," I said, looking away. I remembered the image of his little body broken in Manus' hands.

"He gave his life honorably, Keena," Abbey said softly. "That's a good way to die for any Kith creature."

"We're not out of this yet. We still have the ocean to cross tomorrow and I'm guessing the wicked half sister knows we're here by now." I told Abbey about the brush. She was sufficiently grossed out by the thought of Feldema with either Bran or Nessum. The boat ride home was going to be difficult at best. I was so thrilled by the thought that my stomach turned in anticipation of the waves.

We sat quietly for a while and I thought of Tynan, knowing he must be worrying. I wouldn't call to him until tomorrow, until I was safe. I didn't want him to come for us tonight. I felt the familiar pangs of guilt mixed with love.

Coyle moved on my lap. He opened his eyes—*my* eyes—and looked up at me. He tried to speak but only croaking noises came from his throat. I brushed his cheek and he leaned his face against my hand and closed his eyes again. "I've got you, Daddy, don't worry. I'll get you home. You rest. I'll get you home." His shoulders relaxed and his breathing leveled.

I traced shaky fingers gently over a large scar that ran from his neck across his chest and ended just under his right arm. It was thick and stiff to my touch. Most of his body was now wrapped in tattered fabric we'd taken from one of the shacks, but the exposed parts were all damaged. They had left little of him unscathed. His light-gray hair was thin, his face even thinner. His hands looked to have once been large and strong, but now were ravaged from abuse. We had wrapped the gaping wounds from the nails tightly in more fabric.

I cried inside as I touched every badge of courage etched into his flesh. He had endured almost thirty years of hell because of me. I couldn't bear the guilt. I felt my body trembling.

He moved and struggled to look into my eyes again. I felt a tiny bit of energy from him. His magic. I felt it in my mark and opened myself to it. Opened myself to magic that felt so close to my own. I let it crawl into my heart and wrap around me. He was holding me the only way he could. The man lay dying and even in his pain he was trying to comfort me. I leaned down and kissed his forehead, touched his cheek with mine. We were linked by our magic in a way I knew would be there forever. I felt him gain strength from the magic I wrapped around him. It wasn't healing him, but it was strengthening him.

Manus kept watch over the door for a while. "They went off to collect. I think we can get some sleep in shifts."

"I've slept a bunch hanging around in that dungeon," Abbey said. "You two sleep. I'll keep watch."

"You sure?" Manus asked.

"I could use some coffee but I can manage it. Besides, I need to keep warming those stones or we'll all freeze to death."

Manus moved behind me to put himself between the rough wall and my back. He was warm and solid. "This is a change. You usually sleep on *me*." I laughed and he gave me a small shake. I was asleep much faster than I thought I would be.

* * * * *

Abbey woke us as dawn was pushing its way through the darkness. We gave Coyle the last bit of fresh water and headed through the boneyard. The bones started pulling themselves together but they were no match for us now that our magic had returned.

The boat was still where we left it. Manus tentatively set Coyle on the floor in the center, while Abbey and I crawled onto the makeshift seat. As Manus shoved off, I held my breath. I could feel Feldema's power rising from the splashing of the waves. It lapped at me as the water hit the side of the tiny boat.

I felt the full surge of my powers as soon as we were away from the desolate island, which now just looked like a pile of rocks in the water. Nothing more than an obstacle for ships and boats to avoid. We sailed easily into the open waters. As the tiny boat carried us on the winds toward WildLand, we looked uneasily out over the rough waters, watching, waiting for Feldema's fury.

"She's toying with us," Manus said, looking out over the bow.

Abbey heated another stone and placed it up against Coyle's chest. He was starting to shiver again. I sent him a warm rush of my power. His magic responded to mine like a brush of a kiss on my cheek. I couldn't believe the tenderness of the unseen caress, it warmed me in return from the inside out.

We sailed in silence for about an hour. Maybe more—it was hard to tell. I started to see the barest tinge of green on the horizon. I let out a deep breath at the sight of it.

As soon as I felt the wave of relief rush over me, the wind came to a stop. The ocean smoothed to glass as the sail fell empty and quiet. "Shit."

"Look alive!" Manus said.

I took a piece of the rope that was holding the sail and cut it, tying one end to my arm, just above the elbow. Manus looked at me with one eyebrow raised. I pulled my mother's sword from my back and tied the other end of the rope to the hilt. "I'm not losing this to the sea for her to have." I stood to see how far the rope let the blade fall. I had tied it just out of my reach, but it wouldn't be lost to the sea.

There was a lurch in the water off the port side. "Here we go, guys," I said. "Brace yourselves." Abbey put herself down in the bottom of the boat with Coyle. Manus and I stood with our legs apart and our swords out.

Nothing happened, the water was still and black in the noontime sun.

"There be monsters here," Abbey whispered from her place at Coyle's side.

Something in the water raised its head, now off the starboard side but at least a good twenty feet away.

Okay, so the Loch Ness monster may be real too. This thing looked like Nessy on steroids. Its head rose—and rose and rose—out of the water, at least fifteen feet, and I glimpsed three humps behind it as the beast moved toward the tiny boat fast. It ducked down and smashed the boat hard with its head.

The vessel didn't stand a chance. Wood split and the wake of the creature pushed the broken pieces apart. Manus fell forward into the water. The rest of us flipped backward and half the boat landed over us, leaving us in a pocket of air between the water and the boat.

Abbey was kicking frantically and holding on to the seat, which was now above our heads. I had Coyle under one arm and held us both out of the water, gripping the same piece of tattered wood.

"Abbey, swim out from under here and get on top. I'll bring him." She followed my instructions and went under the water.

It was dark and murky as I pulled Coyle with me under the remnants of the boat. Abbey was already on the floating fragment when we surfaced. I flung Coyle up and he groaned, my ribs crying out from the effort. She pulled his shoulders as best she could. When we got him safely out of the water, I pushed them as far way from me as I could. I turned in the water to find Manus.

Only the movement of the broken pieces of the boat disturbed the smooth surface of the water. I went under and tried to look around, but it was too black. I surfaced to find Manus and the monster struggling some distance off to my right. The huge sea dragon had him in his bite. He tossed the

Shifter, catching him again across the middle, trying to get a better grip. Manus was trying to stab at it even as he was bitten repeatedly.

I pulled one of the daggers and flung it at the side of the dragon, not too close to its head to keep from hitting Manus. The dagger hit home, plunging deep into the side of its neck. The dragon jerked. It dropped Manus as soon as it saw me and came at me with great speed.

The sword was dangling just past the reach of my fingertips. I dived under the surface and the creature surged past me. Massive turbulence from its wake sent me tumbling backward through the water.

I kicked and struggled for air, fighting to find the direction of the surface, breaking through just long enough to get a lungful of air before the thing clamped its toothy mouth on my leg. It pulled me down, fast and with little effort. I brought the sword down hard, stabbing into one ugly green eye. The sea dragon jerked against the force of the blow. I twisted the blade and the dragon abandoned my leg to swim off, dragging me behind him until I could pull the sword loose.

Back on the surface, I got to Manus. He was struggling to get back to the piece of floating boat. I helped him up onto it. My leg was burning from the cuts made by the dragon's sharp teeth. Manus was cut severely in more than one place across his stomach and back. He was bleeding badly. I tried to hold pressure on the worst wound on his stomach but the cut was larger than my hands. "Manus, can you shift?" He didn't respond. "Manus! Can you shift?"

He looked at me, not understanding. "If you shift I can cover the wounds and stop the bleeding. They're too big now." He rested his head back and closed his eyes, his face tight, his breathing shallow, his skin losing color. He took in a big breath and started a slow and painful shift. Before he could completely change I saw more movement coming toward us from behind him.

Fins. Sharks.

I got the sword in my hand again and ducked under the remains of the boat to meet the sharks head-on. The first reached me before I made it all the way under the boat. He came close but didn't attack. I reached out and tried to slice it with the blade but missed. The second, right behind him, wasn't so lucky. I cut open a large wound on his side. Two others that were following went into a frenzy and attacked the injured shark. I had to surface and get more air. They were busy, but at the rate they were tearing through the flesh of the injured shark, it wouldn't be long until their attention came back to me.

I searched the horizon to find the touch of green. It was in the opposite direction of the feasting sharks. Thank God for small favors. "How's he doing?" I asked Abbey. She was holding the soaked cat with both hands, holding the blood back as best she could.

She looked at me with pleading eyes, blood seeping through her tiny fingers. "I can't stop it." The winds were picking up again, making the sea choppy. I couldn't swim them to shore. The sharks would be back at me too soon. Coyle was still out and hanging with a leg in the water. I pushed it up onto what was left of the boat.

I had no choice. I held on with one hand and pushed my hand deep into my pocket and found the delicate twist of silver and gold tangled in the wet denim. *Tynan*, I thought as I pulled it out and held it tight.

Where the hell are you? His voice was fraught with worry and anger.

In the water. I'm okay. Manus is hurt bad and — I was hit in the side by one of the sharks and spun underwater.

Keena?! he roared in my head, but I couldn't answer. The shark was coming back at me. I could barely make it out in the churning water but it moved with a lethal grace and speed I couldn't miss. No time to fish for the sword, so I drew a smaller dagger. The shark pushed against my side, knocking against my broken ribs. I screamed underwater and stabbed at the shark.

The hit to my side made me drop the necklace. I watched it sink out of my reach, unable to move fast enough to reach for it.

I had to surface and couldn't go for the necklace. I pushed up, found the air and took in a forced gulp, along with some water. I choked and coughed at the intrusion of the salty water in my lungs. Turning, I saw a shark heading for me. I put my hand out and said the thrusting spell in my head. Water shot high into the air and the shark spun and shot off. The others followed.

I hadn't even thought to use my magic before that moment. That wasn't good. Manus was hurt, I was hurt and my magic hadn't even come into my head. I swam back toward the others, cursing.

When I reached them, Abbey was talking in a slow, steady voice to Manus. "You stubborn, mangy cat! Hold on!" I felt another wave of guilt hit as I tread water, not really caring if anything else was coming up from the depths below. I could only watch her struggle with the cat that was almost her size. I reached out to feel for Manus' magic, to try to touch it with mine. I felt it, weak and struggling to respond. I rested my head on the floating debris that served as our own little island.

Something grabbed me by the sheath around my shoulders and pulled me from the water. I struggled violently against it.

"Keena!" It was Doran's angry voice. I turned my head enough to see that Marcus, one of her consorts, had me by the saber sheath and I relaxed so he could get me into her boat. Two other Magicians started to get Manus, Abbey and Coyle. I was tired and weak and fell into Doran's lap when Marcus put me beside her on the floor of the boat.

We were safe.

Chapter Fourteen

ഇ

I woke to wonderful warmth and the sounds of lots of people talking. I was in a small bed I didn't recognize. I saw Coyle first. He was in the bed next to mine, propped up, watching me and trying to wrap his magic around me.

I smiled at him. He tried to do the same but one of the newer wounds on his face prevented his lips from moving that far. I clambered into his bed, kissed his head and brushed what was left of his gray hair from his face. He was home. I was happy to lie next to him and feel his energy mingle with mine.

Bevin appeared, pulling back the sheet hanging around our beds. She touched Coyle's forehead. "It's a miracle he survived at all." I watched her as she put some healing herbs on his face and tucked the shimmering blanket in around his sides. I looked at her and didn't have to ask out loud before she started talking. "It's healing his insides, he'll get stronger. His mind is strong, though I don't know how. They split his tongue, years ago it looks like. But I think we can get that back with some time." As she talked, I felt the push of tears behind my eyes. "His legs are going to need a modern healer though, so I've called for a Witch in Florida who's an orthopedic surgeon. She'll be here in a week or so." Bevin smiled.

"Manus?" I asked.

"Fine. Those Shifters heal amazingly fast. He's prowling around somewhere." She was in her element, whizzing around, making Coyle comfortable. My leg was miraculously healed and my ribs felt sore, but otherwise fine. I stood once more to test my steadiness. The amulets around my neck swayed and took care of any remaining pain. I looked down at Coyle again and felt grounded though weak.

I had managed the impossible and gotten them all back alive.

Cliona strode into the small healing room. "May I see you?"

"I figured Tynan would be here," I said.

"I put him to sleep this morning." Her face was pinched. "After two nights and days of pacing and worrying, I thought he needed to sleep."

"Two days? We were only gone one night," I responded, confused.

"No," Bevin said. "This morning began the third day of your absence. Doran and Tynan and the rest of us have been going out of our minds with worry. Time moves differently on Thule, Keena."

I thought about how slow things seemed when we'd first arrived. It made sense. I looked back to Cliona. Her displeasure was written across her perfect, angular face. "I would have touched based with him sooner if I'd known that."

Her anger didn't seem to lessen with my explanation. "I had to *put* him to sleep, Keena. It wasn't pretty. I usually can only do that if he's hurt. He fought me—and he'll be very angry when he wakes."

I was surprised she could do it all. Tynan had eased me to sleep before. I knew he could do it to someone else. I couldn't imagine what it would take for her to put him to sleep against his will. "I'll bet. I'll take the blame, Cliona," I said, but she didn't look any happier.

I walked past her and started down the hall toward my chambers. Bevin stopped me and handed me an extra pain amulet. I was still in my torn jeans and tattered tank top, but I didn't have any of my weapons. Doran must have taken them. Hogan met me in the hall and started to scold me. His big eyes were wide and I could tell he had been worried sick. I bent down, took his shoulders in my hands and pressed my forehead to his. "I'm okay, Hogan. I'm okay. Bran is dead and Nessum took off. I'm okay." I kissed his nose. The touch of others is soothing to Gnomes when they're upset. It's part of their existence to take reassurance with touch. My hands on his shoulders assured him and his tension eased.

Cliona made a noise as she backed against the wall, her face whiter than usual, as were her eyes — not a bit of color to them at all.

"What is it?" I asked, straightening.

"You saw...*him*?" Her voice almost didn't hold.

She looked terrified. I didn't think that big, bad Cliona could be terrified by anything. "Yeah, I saw him. I almost killed him."

The color came back to her as she scoffed at me. "No one can kill him." She was so matter-of-fact. I opened my mouth to argue and then closed it. I decided not to tell her about my mother's sword. The less people with that particular piece of information the better. Maybe she would go after Nessum herself. Tynan would never recover if something happened to her. They had been together for centuries — and he would need her when the time came that I would leave him.

I hurt for him again at the thought of it. If I told her my mother's sword could kill Nessum, she would surely try. If she failed...I couldn't bear for him to lose both of us. I kept my mouth shut.

I started toward my room again, Hogan babbling after me. Cliona was following behind him, also asking about Nessum. I just wanted out of the dirty clothes and to fall into the bed next to Tynan.

"What did he look like?" Cliona asked. I stopped and studied her. "Not many have faced Nessum and lived to tell of it." She was so tall and beautiful.

"He's as beautiful as the rest of you, only not. He was pure alabaster. He was marbled with the life of others running in his veins instead of blood, making him appear black under his skin. His eyes were dark like yours, but completely dead." She took in every word, as if to memorize it. "You'd know him by sight if you saw him. You won't need my description."

She shivered. "I hope I *never* see him." I nodded and started walking again. Cliona stumbled over Hogan, his shorter legs moving much slower.

I opened the door to my chambers, chuckling as Cliona chided Hogan about his pace.

I turned away from the pair—only to find Feldema straddling Tynan's thighs.

Her skinny, naked body was bent over his, her wet hair dangling around them like a cape. A thin trail of blood was running off his hip.

Our necklace was wrapped around her hand, Feldema pressing it against a cut on Tynan's lower stomach. The twisted silver and gold of the chain was covered in blood. Tynan's arms were spread wide and Feldema was chanting.

The Witch had recovered my necklace from the sea and was using it to spell him.

Reacting to the rage and hate in my heart, I lunged at her, knocking her off the far side of the bed as she finished her chant. Cliona was there instantly and she grabbed Feldema by the throat, lifting her to the wall. Feldema's head made a satisfying crunching sound as it bounced from the force, sending her white hair across her face.

"*What did you do to him?*" Cliona roared. Feldema tried to speak but couldn't. Cliona's hold on her throat was too strong. Feldema tried to cast, but Cliona just tightened her grip. Feldema's feet started kicking out at the Vamp.

"Hogan, go get Bevin! Now!" I shouted at the stunned Gnome, sending him running out of the room. I turned to Tynan. In the center of his mark, bisecting the sun, was what looked to be an insignificant cut. From it trickled the precious blood that kept him alive.

I watched as the mark started to fade before my eyes...

"What have you done?" Cliona demanded, but Feldema's face was red from lack of oxygen. Cliona's fingers easily tightened on her neck, digging in, cutting at her flesh. Blood trickled down Feldema's porcelain skin.

I felt a tightening on my own neck. Air started to become harder to take in. I tried to take a breath, only to find my throat tight and pain enveloping me. Blackness started to dance at the periphery of my vision.

I felt the world slipping away. Shadows crossed my vision. I was a baby again and Mother appeared in the dingy cave, chanting over the two of us, Feldema and me. I was focused on the blood dripping from the point of her blade into the cauldron between us. Her voice was musical, soothing, sending waves of her magic over us.

I remembered the feeling of warmth and love spreading over me, over my sister, binding our lives together...

"Cliona!" Doran's shrill voice barely pierced the vision. I was watching my mother's tender face as she chanted, head titled to the heavens...

"Cliona, you're killing them both!" Doran's panic pulled me from the vision. I struggled to breathe, writhing on the floor, holding my neck, digging and scratching at the invisible hand that held my throat.

I felt the hand loosen on my neck, Feldema's neck, and air rushed into my burning lungs. I was coughing, gagging. Feldema was doing same, still held to the wall.

Cliona didn't let go of her or let her down. She just held her less tightly so we could take in breaths. The pain eased from my throat. I tried to get up but could only make it to my knees, dizzy and weak from the lack of air, tired beyond belief from the time spent on Thule.

Through her gasps, Feldema actually started to laugh.

Bevin was unloading a bag of stuff onto the table. Doran moved closer, kneeling at my side. "You only felt Feldema's pain as her death was coming?" she asked as her hand stroked my back. I nodded.

I tied to clear my thoughts, none of them making any sense. "I saw another vision of Trevina. She was binding us together."

Bevin let out a small gasp. Doran's face held certain fear. I was still dizzy and confused.

Feldema's laugh got more cynical as she cried, "You can't kill me!" She kicked again, trying to get loose from the grip Cliona still had on her. "You have no power over me! I have taken the strongest to my bed and I have his strength in me!"

The memory of the brush with strands of her white, silky hair danced through my mind.

"Nessum is going to ensure that you *never* take Doran's place! He will not allow it. And through me, he will be able to rule the Kith. Through me, he will!"

Doran stood and paced to the far side of the room, her face tight. "What's going on?" I asked hoarsely. Doran looked tentatively between Bevin and me. I struggled to stand, anger taking over from my pain and tiredness. "No more smoke and mirrors, Doran! Tell me what this all about! None of it seems to be a great surprise to you. What the hell is going on here?" She didn't say a word. "Doran — *tell me the damn truth*!"

I was seething.

Bevin put her head down. "Your mother had two children to fulfill the prophecy…to ensure that one of you would be our salvation. Once you were born, she clearly couldn't bear the thought that her children might have to battle to the death. She must have cast the spell to bind you, to prevent either's destruction."

"Can you break that spell?" I asked.

She didn't look at me. "No. It's old and has been with you both your entire lives."

I felt my knees getting weak again. I really didn't know if I could have killed Feldema anyway. I had killed some of the

Slaugh, but they were soulless monsters. I hated my sister for her betrayal, but I had truly hoped she would choose to serve Karackos over death. "Can you strip her powers and put her away?"

Doran answered, "We can lock her up and keep her here, but..." She trailed off, looked over my shoulder to the window. "The Battle of Birthright can no longer be to the death. If she dies, you die too."

Feldema tried to pull herself away from Cliona again. The Vamp tightened down. "You can lock me up if you wish, Doran. You are losing your hold on the Kith! Nessum and Bran have been busy building loyalties, and they will have me as High Priestess. You will *die* and Keena will be a prisoner to the Slaugh as her father was!"

"What have you done to Tynan, Feldema?" I was tired. This new information was not sinking in at all. I needed to get Tynan healed from her poisonous spell and I needed to rest.

"Your precious love is yours no more, old Witch," she spat at me. "He will not remember you. He will not long for you." She was proud of what she had done. Even through the hoarseness from being choked, I could hear it. "He will find you unworthy of his attentions."

Bevin put some healing herbs on his stomach. It was a small wound but she did it anyway. I helplessly watched as my mark continued to fade, all but gone now. Doran strode to Cliona, taking Feldema by the arm and flinging her at Manus. "Take her and lock her up!"

Manus did as she said, dragging Feldema, still laughing hysterically, from the room.

Doran pulled me to her side, sliding her arm around my waist for support. "Bevin, can you break Feldema's spell?" she asked.

Bevin straightened. "I should be able to. He may be confused at first, but he'll get all his memories back eventually." She started gathering up her tools from the bag she'd brought in. While she placed her potions and casting tools on the table, I crawled on the bed and touched Tynan's face. He was so perfect in his daytime slumber.

"Doran?" I could hardly get my voice to work.

"Yes, my niece?" She came to sit by me on the bed.

I looked from her to Bevin. "If he doesn't remember making his pledge to me...or his place with me..." My heart started pounding so hard in my chest I thought it was going to explode. I placed my hand over his mark as the last of the color faded from the setting sun. I saw Doran's face start to follow my line of thinking.

"Keena, you can't mean...?" She stood and turned away from me.

"If he doesn't remember the pledge or bringing me to my powers..." I still couldn't get the rest out of my mouth.

"He will no longer be bound to you, Keena." She turned back to me, her face as pained as mine. "He'll not be bound."

The room became still. I looked back to Tynan, my heart breaking. "Bevin, don't break the spell." It was little more than a whisper.

"Are you sure, Keena?" Doran put her hand on my shoulder. "He won't remember your time together or have you in his heart. You'll not be able to try to rekindle your relationship. He may even be unkind to you, depending on the depth of the spell."

No. I wasn't sure. Could I live without him? Could I sleep without him wrapped around me? I didn't think so—but I had wished and hoped for a way to release him. I had hoped it wouldn't mean losing him altogether, but I had no other choice. "But...after I'm gone, he won't spend centuries missing me. He may even find someone else." I looked up at Cliona. Her face held a softness I'd never seen. "Will he find another to love?"

I had only ever seen contempt for me in her eyes, but the look she gave me now was pity. I couldn't bear it. "Keena, he hadn't had a relationship that I was aware of in a very long time. I wasn't happy with his decision to bind himself to you, but he *does* love you." She looked at his sleeping form and then back to me. "I hadn't even seen him smile much in the last hundred years. I'd hate for him to lose that."

I stood and took her arm. "But if he found someone to love him?"

"He found you. I suppose it could happen again."

I turned away from them. "Hogan, take Lord Tynan's things to a guest room. Clean all his clothing so there is no trace of me on them."

He rushed to my side. "My lady, you cannot!" Huge tears threatened to fall from his eyes.

"Do it." I was losing my resolve fast. "Doran, will you call someone to take him to the room?"

"I'll take him," Cliona said.

I kept my face to the wall. "What about the last few months? What will he remember about that if not the time with me?" Hogan was rushing through the room and gathering his things. Abbey came in. She didn't say anything. I felt her presence and dropped to the floor, too weak to stand any longer, too afraid to look back. She came to me and crawled into my lap. Bevin came to me as well.

Feldema had given me an out for Tynan, and I was holding fast to the strength to let him go. I *had* to let him go. Every fiber of my being was screaming — but I had to.

Cliona had to clear her throat before speaking. "I'll tell him he was injured badly when hunting rogues. It's happened before. We always come here if it's bad. He'll still be confused, but…"

"What about the rest of the Kith? If they see he's no longer with me?"

Doran spoke. "They'll think you've let him go. Like Feldema did her first."

"So they'll think I'm a bitch. I can live with that. I'll have to. This is the only way out for Tynan." I was still trying to convince myself that I had the courage to do it. What did I care if the Kith thought me cruel?

Abbey stood. "They won't think that at all, Keena. You forget who's the root of all the grapevines around here." He hands were on her tiny hips. "I'll make sure everyone knows the truth. Don't you worry about that. Leave it to me, wild child." She gently kissed my forehead.

I had to keep myself from smiling. It would have hurt to smile. I saw my communication amulet on the floor. I pushed the beautiful twists of gold and silver toward Bevin, my heart breaking again.

"Bevin, take that with you. I have the resolve not to try to use it to make him remember at the moment." I looked back at the bed, at his face briefly. "But tonight, maybe tomorrow…I may lose that resolve."

Cliona picked Tynan up, carefully, like a child. Her strength amazed me as she cradled him. I stood and touched my lips to his cheek, my tears flowing freely. I felt sick. "Take him." She turned and strode to the door.

Cliona hesitated and looked back over her shoulder at me. She nodded once. "My lady," she said with deep respect and turned, not looking back again.

"Bevin, take that and go. Doran, make sure that he's okay and that he believes whatever tale Cliona gives him. Make sure the household is aware that no one talks to Lord Tynan about me unless it's official business of some kind. As soon as you're sure he isn't permanently injured by Feldema's spell…have him go back to his life." I stood as tall and strong as I could. I balled my fists at my side to keep my trembling hands from showing.

"Keena…we need to discuss what happened here today." She still wouldn't meet my eyes.

"I'm tired. Leave me alone." I was holding out as best I could. She turned and left without another word.

Abbey touched my hand. "I'll give you some time to clean up and rest. I'll bring you some food later." She walked out and pulled the door closed behind her. The silence in the room thundered in my ears. I could smell Tynan all around me, feel his presence in the room. I wanted to run to him, to shake him and make him remember. I wanted him to take me in his strong arms and tell me everything would be all right. I wanted to undo the last hour.

I fell to the floor, unable to stand against this world a second longer. It was too hard.

At some point, I felt Manus come in and lift me. I heard Hogan milling about the bathroom. I was vaguely aware when they put me in the tub. I felt them pamper and fuss with my hair and dress me in silky green pajamas, but it all seemed a far-off dream. I was not there with them. Numbness was all I felt.

"I want to go back," I whispered against Manus' shoulder as he placed me on the bed. "I want my human life back. This is too hard. I can't do it. I'm not strong enough. I want to wake up tomorrow in my old house, with my old boring job." I felt like I weighed a thousand pounds as I lay in the bed. "I want to wake up from this nightmare and be back where Vampires, Witches and Trolls are things of myth and there is nothing hiding in the dark. Back where a bad day meant my car ran out of gas or my computer crashed." His tender green eyes sparkled as he looked down on me. It hurt to look at them. It hurt to lie there. "Can you send me back, Manus? Can you make it all go away?"

"I wouldn't if I could, Keena." One corner of his mouth curled up into the smallest of smiles. "You are so much stronger than you know. Your heart is pure and your soul untouched by evil. You gave up the one you love most because it was the right thing to do. You are our salvation."

I turned away from him. "I can't bear it, Manus. I can't!" My stomach tightened again.

"You will, because you love him. I have faith in you. We all have faith in you. Someday you will find your way back to Lord Tynan. A love that strong will always find its way. In time, Keena. You have to find the faith and the strength to be ready when the time comes.

"You have much to worry over. Focus yourself on the challenges ahead. You spent your human life overcoming so much. You lived in a world of humans where you didn't belong and you survived against all odds." He tilted my face to look into my eyes. "Your father needs you now. Our people need you. You will be High Priestess. Find your power, Keena. Your heart belongs to all the Kith and theirs to you. Let the wild heal your heart, let the Kith bring you the same strength they feel from you." He kissed me gently on the head and brushed his hand over my hair.

He stood back and shifted to his cat form. And my favorite gray cat crawled into my arms. The same cat that had snuggled with me most of my life. His soft, gray fur, which smelled so familiar, eased my pain with just a touch. He purred and rubbed his head across my chin.

Chapter Fifteen

℘

The morning greeted me with a warm breeze through the open windows. Hogan and Manus had redecorated my room in one day, trying to get as many reminders of Tynan as possible out of sight. The light-blocking curtains covering the windows had been replaced by large French doors on opposite sides of the room, with sheer drapes that danced the breeze. The heavy, dark velvet bedding had been replaced by amazingly soft cotton sheets and a bedspread with bold ivy patterns intertwined with delicate gold accents. Large plants had been brought in, and with the doors open, it was as if my room was part of the garden. Butterflies and birds came and went freely.

The only other things helping me get over the loss of Tynan were sitting at the table. Proud and smiling at the pretty Imp, Coyle nibbled cherry turnovers out of Abbey's little fingers. The two were laughing and making a huge mess with the pastries.

This is how I had awakened the last several weeks, Coyle and Abbey having a grand breakfast while waiting for me to get up.

"If you two get any more of that cherry filling stuck on my floor, I'm going to ban you from my room," I said as I crawled out of the bed. A breeze blew through the room and I inhaled the air, taking in the life around me, letting it fill me and stir the magic as it did each time I woke up.

Abbey poured my coffee and slid the cup toward me on the table. "I clean up my messes, priestess—and *yours*, for that matter. Have a seat." I crawled into a chair next to my father.

"Good morn," he said through his tortured mouth. All his most recent wounds had closed and were healing nicely. The myriad scars would forever remain, but he had gained some weight and his mind somehow had managed to survive the years of torment. He had started telling me about my mother and the love they had for one another, but we had not talked about his hell on Thule. He would tell that tale in time, if he wanted to. I admired his will to survive and took strength from his courage as I watched him heal.

How could I give up my life over a broken heart when he had held on for me through years of unspeakable pain and sorrow? After allowing myself a couple days to pout, mourn and generally act like a jilted teenager, I realized I had gotten what I wanted all along. Tynan was free. I would have preferred that it happened much later in my life, but he was free. Bigger problems needed my mind clear. I would love Tynan forever, but I couldn't have him. I needed to honor his courage by gathering my own.

"Chewwy, youwa favowite." Coyle handed me a turnover and took another bite of his own. I had to smile. The speech impediment the torture had caused made him sound like a three-year-old. When I teased him, he threatened to spank me.

Doran rounded the corner in the hall with Manus and Cliona. They all had somber looks and walked with a purpose that said something was wrong. My heart raced.

"What's wrong? Is Tynan hurt?" I shot to my feet.

Doran gave me a sympathetic look. "No, my niece. He's fine. I didn't mean for us to frighten you. Cliona wished to speak to you formally. Manus and I are here to witness."

I looked at Cliona. Her stern, serious face gave me no hint as to the reason for the visit. I felt Coyle stiffen beside me.

"If I had known you were coming on an official visit, I would have dressed." I looked at my father. He took my hand.

"Your attire is fine, my lady. I have to be back to Castle Dracula soon. But I needed to do this first."

"Cliona, what's the matter?"

She glanced around the room and took in a breath. "I'd like you to give me your mark, Keena, Priestess of the Wild." She went to one knee so smoothly she seemed made of rubber. "I pledge my life to yours. Your honor to mine."

Fainting seemed to be the wrong response, but I couldn't have been more shocked. "You have, have you? What's happened, Cliona? Why is my life suddenly so valuable to you? I thought you'd be glad to get me out of Tynan's life. Then you could keep him as far from me as possible."

Her cold expression never changed. "There are those, and I was one of them, who thought you too human to be able to guide our council into the future. Those who believed you wouldn't be strong enough. We've watched Tynan over these last many weeks, Keena. He's dark and unfeeling." I felt my stomach cringe at her words. I could tell she saw the anguish in my face. "Like he was before you came into his life. I realized that we have, over the years, lost that part of us that was once human. Tynan had found it again in you, and had spread that hope to the elders of our kind once again. Vamps are still living in the shadows. We move mostly in the night, but we had all started to feel somewhat human again during his time with you."

She took my hands in hers. "It is your human heart, along with the strength of the Kith, which will make you the very strength of what the council is intended to be. Your unselfish act of setting Tynan free, even though it cost you, made me see the great value of your heart. Honor me with your mark, Keena. Call on me and mine, and we will fight with or for you."

I felt the burning start deep in my stomach. My magic was coming alive, responding to the sincerity of her words. Her conviction and her hope wrapped around me. She was able to project her feelings over me the same as Tynan had projected his to wrap me in his love. She pulled her long leather coat off and let it fall to the floor, exposing her bare shoulders. "Does Tynan know what you're doing here?"

"Yes, I told him of my intentions. I had to tell him a different reason, of course, but it had the same message. He reluctantly agreed that we should support you."

"You honor me with your belief in me, Cliona. The Kith will be in a lot of danger in the coming years and I would be proud to have you as one of my warriors. I pledge to you as you have to me. To respect and honor." I placed my left hand on her right shoulder. She didn't flinch at the burn. I removed my hand and a shadow of the brilliant sun on my stomach shown on her pale skin.

Doran broke the silence in the room. "Thank you, Cliona."

"You have Keena to thank. It would be better for her if *you* would trust her as much," she replied.

Doran turned and left without a response. I had always known Doran was leaving things out in her teaching with me. I also knew I would get everything from her eventually—but I didn't realize others knew as well. I gave Cliona a questioning look.

"I hope it'll come in time, Keena," she said. "I don't know what she hides, but I can feel it all the same. I just can't tell if it's to protect you or to alter future events. Be wary."

"I've learned that lesson the hard way." I offered her a seat. "Tell me how he is."

"As I said, he's just like he was before. Sometimes he looks like he's trying to piece something together, deep in thoughts he can't identify. I even found myself hoping he would figure it out."

"No, Cliona. If he remembers even some of it—"

She reached for me, putting a supportive hand on my arm. "I know. You are dealing with this better that I thought you would."

"I've had a lot of support."

Abbey, who had been suspiciously quiet, butted in. "And a lot of food and a lot of wine." Cliona gave her a small smile.

"He wouldn't want me pining away and crying and hating everything," I said. "I really wanted to."

Cliona nodded. "The same fate you saved him from is now your prison. You'll live again, Witch. You'll love again. You'll have to. Your body will insist before too long."

"Everyone keeps saying that."

She stood. "They really *have* left you in the dark, haven't they?" She looked at Abbey. "You haven't told her?"

Abbey slunk back in the big chair and rolled her eyes. "In the past, but I didn't think she'd want to hear so soon after..."

"What?" I said.

Coyle reached for me and tried to speak slow and clear. "As a Witch, youwa body has gweata needs than you had before. Trevina loved many of us. She had such a wondahful heart." I could see he still loved her. It was in his golden eyes as he struggled to speak clearly. "It will come," he said. "When youwa ready. It will come and you won't be able to stop it."

I knew all this, had been told many times—but I still couldn't imagine opening my heart again.

"Well said." Cliona gathered her coat and rummaged through her pocket then held out her hand. "I have a gift for you." She opened her hand. The twisted gold and silver chain sparkled in the sun. I backed up. "No need to fear it, Keena. I had Bevin make some alterations." I hesitantly took it from her hand, afraid of communicating with Tynan. "Now it speaks to me," she said.

I held it up. Bevin had encased the bat charm in an emerald the size of a dime. Next to the bat dangled a silver teardrop, a glowing ruby at its center.

She touched the teardrop. "You don't have to wear it all the time. I know for a while it'll bring you pain to even be near it. But have it close so you can speak to me when you need to." She started to the door and turned back. "When you need me, Keena, I will be there for you."

"And I for you."

She nodded and left the room.

* * * * *

Leaving Coyle and Abbey giggling and carrying on about some Gremlins' antics at a nightclub, I made my way down to the prison chambers that held my sister. Down here, the light, homey feel of the upper floors faded to stark cold. The walls in the lower levels were smooth concrete and left bare of decoration. I felt my powers weaken as I neared the cells.

Approaching the observation area, I could make out the voices of two guards talking casually about shifts. I stood silently behind them long before they sensed or saw me. The one sitting at a monitor jumped as I cleared my throat to let them know I was there.

"Sorry, priestess. No one told me you were coming." His face looked pale and immovable as he checked a list to see if he'd missed something. "No. Not on the list."

"I want to see her for a minute." I tried my best smile and watched his face soften. This might work.

"The High priestess said no visitors. With...without her permission." He tried to get his face straight again. The other officer, obviously his subordinate, had moved to stand at attention against the far wall of the cave-like room.

"Really? I thought Doran knew I was coming. I'll just go up and interrupt her. I'll see if she'll pop down here and..."

I watched for the moment when the words finally sank in. "Interrupt the High Priestess? That won't be necessary." He rummaged through some amulets and handed me one, still shaking his head, unsure if he was doing the right thing. "Her powers are being held at bay by wards, spells and the restraints of the cell itself. You'll need this to ensure yours

230

remain intact. Do not touch the bars or the prisoner. You have five minutes." He turned and led me down the hallway off the observation room. It was lined on either side with cells. All those we passed were empty. Not much crime on WildLand, I guessed.

He walked me about halfway down the dank corridor. "She's in the last on the left. Holler if you need me. We'll be watching." He turned and headed back to the observation room.

I calmly waked the remaining length of the hall to her cell, my boots making soft squishing sounds on the concrete floor. The cell looked like every cell from every TV cop show I'd ever seen—stark and uninviting. She was sitting on the edge of the bed against the far wall. Her head hung low, her once-gleaming hair was dull and frazzled. Her usual shining skin was ashen. She didn't look up.

"I knew you'd come, old Witch," she hissed without looking up. "Does my appearance amuse you? See what happens if you neglect your body's demands, what happens when your powers are stripped from you?" I remembered what it felt like on Thule, to be without my witchcraft for a short period of time. She had been in here for almost six weeks. I shuddered involuntarily at the thought.

"Why do you hate me so much? What have I done to cause such hate?"

She laughed, sounding more than a bit psycho. "Nessum had told me for years you would show up and try to claim my birthright. The only thing he was wrong about was how strong you would be. He told me your human blood would weaken you." She tilted her head up just enough to look at me. Her ice-blue eyes were dull and red-rimmed.

"Nessum pulls your chain, Feldema?" I tried not to sound too taunting.

"I have no need to have my chain pulled, old Witch. I have his powers in me. I have no need of him. He is only a means to an end." She still sat, glaring at me, hands gripped tightly to the edge of the bed. I felt her anger boiling across the short distance that separated us.

Her absolute hate for me hurt. I wanted to hate her in return, to have the real desire to end her life. But those feelings had all come in moments of anger. I didn't hate her. I didn't want to kill her.

My face must have betrayed my thoughts. "Have no pity for me!" She flung herself forward, stopping just in front of my face. She held tight to the cold-iron bars. "I will kill you as soon as I have a chance! I should have done it before now!" she spat.

The venom in her words and the speed at which she hit the bars made me stumble a step back. Still only feeling compassion for her, I gathered myself. "You die if I die. Mother bound us together." I said it soft and slow, not in anger, just as a matter of fact.

She started laughing hysterically, the sound echoing in my head, causing a sharp pain. "You don't know who you're fighting, Keena, Priestess of the Wild! You are so ignorant of the world around you. There are other ways to live besides *life!*" She was shouting and laughing as she moved back into the cell.

I felt the screaming laughter on my skin like pins. I had to back away, to run away from the echoing sound in my head. The guard was heading toward me as I ran past him to the upper floors, toward the sanctity of the forest.

I hit the outside and took a deep breath, feeling my power, my light, coming back to me. Her voice and laughter were parlor tricks, but they had worked. I fell into the trance and lost the resolve to question her further. Even through all the protective wards in the area, she had managed to push me with her mind.

A Vamp trick.

I pulled off my boots and socks, needing to feel the soil under my feet. I started to jog, seeking the comfort of the forest, the very earth itself. I felt it under me, strengthening me. No leaves were damaged by my step, no insects crushed as I made my way through the bending and winding paths I'd followed so many times before.

I slowed to a walk to think about what Feldema had said. She still intended to kill me even if it brought about her own death. How could I fight that? How do you fight hate so strong? She thought she would live even after my death.

Other ways to live besides life…

Doran. I needed to talk to Doran. There was something to Feldema's words, something that was just out of my reach. I knew it.

* * * * *

Doran's office door stood open. It looked like any executive's office, except for the soft lines of the stucco walls of the manor. There were gentle touches of life from the plants and the brightness of the open window. Her desk sat empty. Behind it was another door that I hadn't paid much attention to before. It was slightly open.

I approached it and pushed it open a little farther. "Doran?"

"Geez!" A man sitting at a desk in front of a computer yelped, standing quickly as a coffee cup hit his lap and dropped to the floor. His face was stern and angry, and he had to be at least six-foot-six. A white tank top clung to every rippling muscle of his abdomen. He was built, but not like someone who lifted weights alone. No, this guy was chiseled from years of military training. Every muscle honed to perfection. A blade hung under each arm, ready for a crossdraw. On each hip was an automatic weapon of some sort.

Guns. The first I had seen on the island.

"Priestess?" His big body straightened and his tone changed, anger over the interruption and the spilled coffee now gone. "I'm Jordan…"

He kept talking, but I could only watch the muscles of his taut stomach move as he spoke. My body reacted wildly to him. I couldn't get air in my lungs.

"Doran's not here…"

I heard part of it, but as he continued to speak, I was blatantly looking at those hips. They were angled perfectly and tucked into dark, military cargo pants that also showed off his long, thick legs. I managed to get my gaze back up to his stomach.

"Priestess?"

I glanced back to his face and then back to his stomach as the muscles tightened again. *Stop it*, I said silently to those muscles, trying desperately to get my gaze back to his face.

"Sorry," he said, sighing.

I finally found his steel-gray eyes. I was lost. My nipples tightened, heat rose from all the wrong places. His eyes drifted briefly down the length of my body. I could tell he was trying not to look at me as obviously as I was looking over him. We were both failing at subtlety. I felt a blush creep over my skin. His body was reacting to mine as strongly as mine was to his.

Stop it! I was talking to myself this time. Trying to get myself under control.

"Sorry," he said again. He straightened, standing at attention and trying to look over my head, off into space.

My mind was frantic with desire. My imagination was running wild with it. Visions of being naked and draped over his big, tight chest ran through my head. I watched a small smile start on his lips.

"You must block your mind from mine, priestess."

"Mind?" was all I managed to croak out. I was still trying to get my eyes to stay away from his middle.

"My lady, I am half-Demon, just as your father. One of my abilities is to read minds." He was still looking over my head, holding himself stern. The man was definitely a soldier of some sort...

Then I realized what he was saying. He was reading my thoughts — thoughts that were running out of control. Thoughts of taking him here and now on the floor...

"Oh God!" I said, covering my eyes.

"Take a deep breath and feel for me in your head. Then put up a wall, my lady." He was fighting not to smile, fighting to keep his hard, stern look. I took a step back from him, mortified and blushing madly. I felt his gentle touch in my head — actually *felt* it. It was a weird kind of tickle. I concentrated and pushed it out and put up a mental barrier.

"Very good, my lady." No apology, just business this one. "Very good. First try." He was still looking over my head. It was easy for him, being so tall, but I felt the overwhelming need to turn and run. I took a deep breath.

"You were looking for Doran?"

"Yeah. Doran. She's not..." Once I'd stopped looking at this abs, I was able to take in more than just this hulk of a man in a tight tank top. The room was covered wall to wall with computers, videos monitors...displaying events all over the world. Radios and walkie-talkies lined a shelf and stacks of newspapers were scattered about a small table off to the right. All the equipment seemed to be the latest and greatest in electronics.

"Wow," I said. Technology was my element, my previous work...that part of my human life that always made sense. People and relationships were always a mess, but computers and electronics were easy to understand. "Jordan, was it?" He nodded, still watching the wall behind my head. "What is all this?"

"This is the surveillance center for the Kith, my lady. I'm the head of our security force." I looked back at him and my body forgot all about the computers and monitors and started to demand I have him. Again. He was so tall, so muscular in a hard, proportioned, powerful way...

I took in a deep breath. I had to get out. I stepped back again.

His brows drew together. "You shouldn't have gone to Thule, my lady. It was careless."

This guy took his job very seriously. "I did what I had to do for my father." I was still backing away.

"I admire your determination and strength, priestess." He let his eyes glide up and down my body as he spoke and I felt it like a stroke of his hand. "Next time you intend to 'do what you have to do', I insist that you come to me for assistance." His body was reacting to me as he spoke. I couldn't help but notice his own hard-on pressing against his black fatigues as he spoke, so hard the buttons holding him in place were straining.

"Okay." I couldn't say anything else. Embarrassed, I turned and darted out of the room and rushed to my chambers. My heart wasn't ready, but my body was demanding release. Release with the hulk of a military man named Jordan.

I took a long, cold bath to ease the yearning and desire. It almost worked.

Chapter Sixteen

&

"He's a complete soldier," Coyle said. "And I believe he was born of the Incubus Foras, one of the oldest and stwongest Demons in the upper realms. I knew Jordan as a vewy young man. He had alweady served as two diffewent men in the U.S. service. He aged out once and changed his name and reenlisted," Coyle explained as Abbey nodded her head.

"*And* he's downright *hot*, Keena. Go with it!" She had that look in her eye.

"Please, I can control myself and not act like some sex-starved kitten." I was really beginning to wonder if I could or not. The demands my body was starting to make were getting harder and harder to ignore. I was still unsure, but my body was not at all concerned with my heart.

"Not for long," Coyle said as he took a drink. "We keep twying to tell you. You are as wild and sexual as nature, Keena. You need the touch and release of sharing magic. Youwa power will start to drain from the struggle. It's a fact."

"What. Ever." I was intentionally teasing. "I have to go. Manus changed our workout to the afternoon today."

I left them in my room, laughing after me. I thought of what my father said about Jordan as I navigated the manor's halls and made my way to the gym.

The room was full of others working out. Usually, Manus and I were there very early and I guess I had arrogantly assumed that the facilities would be reserved and private. There were several Weres on the weight machines and two Magicians sparring on the open floor.

I headed for Manus. He was standing at the back wall talking to a Magician I had seen once or twice before. Manus looked up and acknowledged me as the Magician headed away. As I reached Manus, the Magicians on the sparring floor cleared off and began to do other exercises or stretching.

I was in my black leather pants and top, two blades at my hips and two strapped to my thighs. Manus didn't speak before heading to the middle of the floor. I followed him.

Spinning, he struck at me before I realized we were starting.

I was used to his tactics by now and reacted quickly, completely avoiding his touch. I returned the advance, slamming him hard to the ground and forcing an elbow into his side. Placing his feet to my stomach, he thrust me up but I landed on top of him in a fluid move, coming down hard on my right shoulder. We struggled apart, both gaining our feet and starting the dance again. I was much faster than I used to be. Tynan's Vampire speed was with me.

After a few minutes, he stopped pulling his punches. So, he wanted to work on stamina and endurance. Fine with me. The exertion felt good, cooling some of the other needs my body had been fighting. Thinking of those desires and the Demon at the heart of them, I lost concentration for just a second. Manus took advantage and connected, crashing his forearm into my jaw, sending me back several feet to the floor.

Shaken for only a second, I gathered my energy and flipped to my feet, using the forward motion to cartwheel toward him and wrap my legs around his neck. My forward momentum sent us both to the mats. We landed with his face in my crotch, my thighs strangling him.

He started to turn blue and mouthed "uncle" at me. I loosened my thighs to let him breathe, but only when he repeated the word out loud did I loosen my grip enough for him to move his head.

It was then I realized the others had all quit their own workouts and were clapping. Manus was still between my legs, breathing hard. Then I saw Jordan directly in front of us, standing at ease, smiling down at me. He was wearing a tight SEALS T-shirt that said "When you absolutely, positively need it destroyed overnight".

Urgent and deep need slammed through me. This was not a simple infatuation or desire. I felt uncontrollable lust. I stumbled trying to remove myself from straddling my friend and guardian — who quickly realized I was reacting to Jordan. I saw the amused twinkle in his eyes.

"You haven't slowed in all these years, Manus," Jordan said, extending a hand.

Manus took his outstretched hand and shook it hard. "Good to see you, man. Hard to tell with Keena, she's become a good fighter." He nodded in my direction. "You two should give it go sometime."

"Manus!" I felt the blush run through my whole body.

They both eyed me, Jordan's right eyebrow raised. "A *spar*, Keena," Manus clarified. He was almost laughing, as was Jordan. Thankfully, most of the others had gone back to their own workouts.

I could have just slunk away but I tried to recover. "I might hurt him," I said.

"That you might, my lady," Jordan said with his smug little smile.

I couldn't help looking down as he tightened his stomach muscles intentionally. I gasped. Manus gave me a questioning look. Jordan's self-confidence hung around him like a cool fog. Saying nothing else, he winked at me, bowed slightly and turned to walk away, proving his backside was just as perfect as his front. The black cotton shorts he was wearing were tight and left little to the imagination.

Manus gave me a strange look. "Have you two already met?" I nodded my head, still not trusting my voice completely. "And?"

"And nothing," I said, picking up a blade I had lost in the sparring.

"I wish somebody would look at *me* with nothing in her eyes like that," he said teasingly.

"Shut up."

"Whatever you say, my lady." He bowed and left me there. I could swear he was giggling as he left. I stomped out of the gym and stormed back to my chambers.

Abbey was still there but my father was gone. "What are you wearing tonight," she asked as I came in.

"Tonight?"

"You promised to go out with us tonight. Keena, you're not backing out again. You need to get out, have a little fun." Her tiny hands were on her hips. I had promised to go after she and Manus had worn me down over the last few days. I had agreed, but really had no intention of going at the time. But she looked so cute standing there waiting for my answer. I needed to get out of the room. I was restless.

"I don't remember a promise, little woman." I wiped my blades clean and put them in their cabinet.

"You said you would and that's your word. You always do what you say you will. That's as good as a promise."

"Fine. I'll go. But! I'm not having any fun. You got that?" I snarled at her.

"Cool. Hogan will be here in a couple hours to dress you."

"I can—"

She was gone before I could argue.

* * * * *

We all walked together to the backside of the village, chatting like old friends, Manus, Abbey and I. It felt comfortable. I had not been on this side of town before. Quaint shops and housing took up the main streets and most of the east side of the village. The west side was more a proper business district—and behind *that* was the party district. We passed several nightclubs. Different kinds of music flowed out into the cobblestone street. Jazz, hard rock and soft, soothing oldies mixed and mingled with the night and the voices of other WildLanders walking the street.

No one stopped us to acknowledge me, as often happened when we were out during the day. I was just another partygoer out for the night. It was freeing, and lent itself to a lighter attitude. It felt like I was walking along Bourbon Street in New Orleans.

The night was perfect. Not too cold, just enough breeze to announce that autumn was firmly in our midst. I was wearing a pair of black leather pants with a pair of low-heeled boots and a sequined tank top. Hogan and I had fought for an hour about what to wear. He had started with a gold catsuit that matched my eyes and left little to the imagination.

Grumbling as he left, he thought I might as well have worn my sparring clothes. The sequins served to save his reputation from utter ruination. He also added some diamond earrings and twisted the front of my hair up into a fancy braid with diamond barrettes, letting the rest fall down my back.

We stopped in front of a rather plain-looking building with a line out front. Manus and Abbey went straight for the door. The door attendant motioned for a hostess and a beautiful Gremlin led us inside. She wasn't hard to follow — her brilliant orange-and-yellow-scaled skin shimmered brightly in the darkened club.

A blaring techno beat had Abbey bouncing with the rhythm as she moved. Manus led me through the crowd, holding my hand. I had never been good at clubs in my human life and right now I was even less sure of myself. My body was acting of its own accord. I was nervous. As I passed all the beings in the bar, I could feel some of their powers reaching, testing, a hint here and there. I slowed to pay attention to one or two with unusual vibrations just a heartbeat longer than others.

A large, green Gremlin turned to recognize me, toasting me with his drink over a big, toothy grin. The air was thick with the press of the crowd and heat generated by the dancers on the floor. Manus pulled on my hand.

We made it to a long, tall bar table near the side of the dance floor. It was one of those that you had to crawl up into the chairs, but it gave you a good view of the dancers and the rest of the bar. The crowd wasn't as tight by the table and there were several people already gathered that I knew. Michael, one of Abbey's favorite Magicians, was a funny man, always cracking jokes—mostly at Abbey's expense. I smiled at a few of the other Witches from the manor and some of the other kitchen staff.

As Manus moved from in front of me, he pulled out a chair at the big table.

Jordan was sitting on the chair next to it.

I froze in my spot. Manus pushed me into the seat and headed to one of the Witches, dragging her directly to the dance floor. I started to say something to him as he left me sitting next to Jordan but my words were lost in the loud music.

The others left for the dance floor. *All* the others. They peeled off in couples as if it had been choreographed. I was left sitting next to Jordan at the big table. "I think we've been set up." He leaned in to yell over the music. I managed to close my mouth. "Would you like a drink?" he asked. I nodded my head.

He came back with two bottled beers, no glasses. "Beer okay? I should have asked."

Beer was perfect. "Fine." I took a really long drink, maybe half the bottle. He huffed out a small laugh.

I watched Manus and the others dance. Manus was a master on the floor, dancing with two of the Witches at once and managing to pay them equal attention. His cat-like movements were smooth and alluring. He had both the women enthralled.

"Dance?" Jordan asked. He had to lean in close again to be heard. His breath tickled my ear. My desire shot into overdrive. I shook my head no, too fast, too hard. "You don't dance? Not at all?"

"Always had two left feet." I also had to yell to be heard. He shook his head that he couldn't hear. I couldn't bring myself to get any closer. I huffed and gave up and cast the spell for the privacy bubble around us. The noise from the bar faded away. He looked around at it and smiled.

"I have two left feet. I was never a good dancer." My voice was almost normal again.

"You've changed since then. I saw you spar today." The look he gave me was primal. "Now that you aren't stuck in the human world, a world out of sorts for you, you move like a dream." His face still held the edge of the professional security man but his eyes danced with that dark yearning that men get when they think they have a sure thing.

Even with that arrogance in his eyes, I was at a loss for words. I blinked and tried to ignore the wetness growing between my legs. I wasn't sure I wanted to be so close to his powerful shoulders or the manly smell that came off him like heavy cologne. It wasn't cologne, it was just him—but it was working on my senses either way.

He looked off to the dance floor. "I spent over forty years trying to fit in with the human world. I used my powers as best I could, to fight, but once I found the rest of the Kith..." He trailed off.

"How'd you find them?" The change of subject was a good thing. It gave me something else to think about. And with the privacy bubble, I could watch the dancers and listen to him without concentrating on the way his lips moved when he spoke.

"I was on a mission with the Navy and got shot up in some remote Indonesian hellhole. I got hit in the chest and fell into a muddy river. Another half-Demon felt me using my telepathy to hide from the enemy, found me and pulled me to safety. He did what he could to heal me then brought me here. I've never left."

"Ever?" My body had eased back just enough that I could at least carry on an adult conversation.

"I go out on missions, but I live here. I don't have to hide who or what I am." He turned and looked into my eyes. "You don't either."

I blushed again. His eyes were mesmerizing, all that silver so welcoming, so hot.

He winked again. "Okay, Keena. Time to dance." He held out a hand. I looked at it.

"I really can't." I felt the heat rising in me again at the thought of touching the big, strong hand before me. I wasn't sure I could control my body if it got much closer to his.

"Trust me." He took my hand off my beer and stood, pulling me to the floor. Just enough room for us opened up. The music blared again after he'd stood and broken the bubble. The current song had a beat that was slow and churning. Jordan pulled me up against his body and wrapped one arm around my waist. He bent his knees enough that our hips met, one of his thick legs slipping between mine. I put one hand on his chest and let the other fall to my side to match his free arm. His hips started to sway with the music. He was looking down, watching the way our bodies moved together. His attention was completely on where our bodies met. I was watching his face in an attempt to lesson the effect his swaying hips were having on my senses.

I slowly let my gaze move down. He was wearing a black silk shirt tucked into tight black jeans. We were a melding of black on black, moving as one.

The heat started to rise in the club and in my mind. He moved us together so perfectly. I could feel his growing erection against my crotch and the tenseness of his thighs as he crouched low to fit his leg between mine. He pulled me tighter against him.

My head fell back at the feel of our bodies so connected. I closed my eyes and let the sound of the bass thumping through the air move through me. The rocking got more intense, sending my head swaying back and forth in time with his arousing movements. His right hand covered the entire expanse of my back and was softly kneading my skin. He put his free hand on my middle, fingers splayed across my stomach, and I felt his magic come through his touch. It lit me up. My magic responded immediately. I was wet and wanton, my pulse too strong. I distantly realized several songs must have passed but I heard nothing, felt nothing but his touch…

I pushed against him to get some distance from his cock. My body was screaming to stay close, to take him. My mind was running scared in the night. I used both hands this time, trying to push away.

He leaned close and stopped dancing. "Keena, are you frightened of me?" I could easily see the distress etched on his jaw. "I didn't mean to scare you." He let me pull away from him and wrapped his arm around mine to lead me back to the table.

The coolness of the beer was not helping. The pounding thump of the bass vibrated through me. He was too close. I couldn't fight the surging need that I was experiencing, the wetness in places that were screaming for his touch. All of it was out of my control.

"I'm really sorry, Keena. I feel your need. Why are you playing hard to get, teasing?" He had leaned in close to my ear, touched my hand.

I couldn't stand it anymore. I hopped from the high bar stool and fought through the pressing crowd. The bodies all touching mine only inflamed the need.

Once outside, I kicked off the boots and did the only thing I knew to douse the fire Jordon's heat had stoked to an absolute inferno. I headed to the woods and ran back to the manor, taking the long way through the forest and into my chambers through the open French doors.

I fell onto the bed. My body was still burning with the need. The run did nothing to sate the demands my powers were making of me. I stripped off my clothes to fulfill myself. I ran my fingers over the swollen flesh of my pussy. Hard, determined strokes did nothing to ease the rampant lust. My clit was throbbing, my nipples tight and warm, and nothing but Jordan's touch would quench this. My own touches were doing nothing to take the edge off. I saw Jordan in my mind, pictured him with me, on me, touching me, fucking me. The aching intensified.

I rolled myself in the down spread and felt my body quiver with need. I had never felt so alone, so out of control.

"Keena?" Jordan's voice was low and beckoning. I sprang up to my knees and made sure I was covered.

"What do you want?" I *hated* being so out of control. I always had, and this was the most out of control I had ever been. My own body was running rampant with no inclination to respond to what my head had to say.

"I…you called to me. In my mind." His stern face looked angry in the moonlight. I had been fantasizing about him. I must have dropped my barrier to his mind reading.

"Arrgg," I growled. "I *hate* being this out of control." I fell back on the bed staring at the ceiling.

I heard a thump. "I brought your boots. I'll go." He started to leave. "Keena, you'll have to follow your nature at some point."

"I just wish I had more control over this crap." I was still staring at the ceiling, clinging to the covers for comfort.

"You have all the control you want over it." He stood motionless in the doorway, trying not to be so big, so overpowering and doing a very bad job of it. His silk shirt shimmered in the moonlight and highlighted the shape of his shoulders and his chest. I had to look away.

"Just how is this supposed to be control? I turn into a fire-eating dragon every time I'm around you."

His eyebrows rose. "Dragon?" He shook his head. "Do you have this reaction to all men?"

I thought about that. It wasn't all men. Not Manus or any of the other men in the gym today. None of the men in the bar had sent me into overdrive the way the huge half-Demon did. "No."

"Then it's only men you're attracted to. Isn't that control?"

"Not conceited at all, are you?" I rolled away from him, fighting the urge to grab him and pull him to me.

"Close your thoughts to me, Keena, before I lose my mind to your fantasies. I can only restrain myself so much."

God. I was driving him crazy along with myself. I fought to build the mental block back up. "I'm so sorry, Jordan. I just…"

"I'll leave."

"No. Don't." I had to sate this need. He was right. They were all right. It was a part of who I truly was and I had to accept it.

"Keena, you're not ready. Call to me when you are and I'll come to you. I'm not such a beast that I'd take you unwillingly. I don't want you to hate yourself *or* me for this."

He was gone before I could turn over and run to the open door. Damn. Damn. Damn.

I ran another cold bath and plunged myself into it. He was right. I had to face this attraction when I was calm and decide what to do about it. The coolness of the water helped. Sliding completely under, I let it cool my whole body. I had to have more control over myself. I had been raised white-bread middle-American. Church on Sundays. Good little girls don't just fling themselves at men and hop into bed. My body wanted it so badly, but how could I just let go? I didn't even know his last name.

I can't just flop into bed. I just can't.

"Keena." It was Abbey's timid voice at the door Jordan had left through.

"You set me up, you little bitch." I tried to sound angry but it didn't happen.

She poked her head around the door of the bathroom. "I'm sorry. Manus told me about him this afternoon. We thought if you just had some time out with him you'd—"

"What? Climb into bed with him? I can't do it, Abbey! I know I'm not exactly who I was months ago, but I'm still somewhat that person. Casual sex was never for me." She had come all the way into the bathroom and tilted her head at me, questioning. "I can't explain it to you other than to say it's just not me."

She climbed up to the edge of the huge tub, straightening her little silver skirt as she crossed her legs. "You're right, I don't understand. But I'm not so stupid that I can't see that it's important to you. I'll try. I don't know how to help you. Your body is going to keep upping the stakes, wild one. Your power needs the exchange with others. We're going to have to figure out something."

She was right and I knew it. I started to agree—but heard my bedroom door crashing open and then Hogan came rushing in.

"Keena, get out! Get dressed!" He was panting, his eyes bulging. "Manus was attacked. He's hurt!"

I was out of the tub and he had me dressed in record time. We rushed to the healing room. Jasmine and the scent of healing herbs filled the waiting area. It was quiet except for the chanting from the far room down the hall.

Doran met us before we went in to see Manus. "Looks like a Gremlin attack, but it's hard to tell."

"How bad is he?" I was starting to walk around her to go to him, but Doran stopped me.

"Had to be several of them." She was trying to keep the worry off her face. Her expression was blank but I saw everything in her eyes. I felt my heart sink looking into those eyes. "Keena." She looked down. Abbey grabbed my hand and gave it a squeeze, a show of support. "He's been cut up...badly. Bevin is with him right now, let her do her magic."

I realized I was holding my breath and had to exhale before speaking. "*How* badly?" She didn't answer. "We left him less than an hour ago. How badly?"

She wouldn't raise her head. "It's bad, Keena."

The room started to spin and I felt weak. I tried to focus on something. Anything. The chair in the corner seemed to be perfect. Neutral, plain and unemotional. I took in a deep breath. "What happened?" I was surprised it came out.

She put her hand on my arm to steady me. "We're not sure. Jordan is looking into it. Looks like he was attacked on his way home from the club. We'll figure that out. You need to sit."

Yeah. Sit. I didn't think I could stand anymore. She ushered me to the neutral chair in the corner that I had suddenly found a great fondness for. I admired that chair as we moved to it.

Manus was just beyond a slightly opened door. I heard the chanting coming from the room. I heard Bevin's soothing voice mingled with a couple others. The scent of the herbs drifted from the little room into the hall.

I was numb. I couldn't lose Manus. He was my rock, my friend. He'd held me together as I accepted this new life. He'd held me together through my human life when he was my cat. Manus had been my sanity, my joy and my strength for so long. I'd loved him most of my life.

Abbey got up in my lap and I held her. We rocked together with the rhythm of Bevin's chanting and just held each other. We didn't need to say anything, didn't want to break the healing power of the Witches in the other room. Doran paced back and forth along the far side of the open waiting area. Her steps made no noise. Her face was blank, showing no expression. I held tight to my friend.

The chanting had drifted into a low, melodious tone, and the aroma of the herbs and incense so strong it was choking. I couldn't keep thinking about how hurt he must be. I had to do something, anything. "It would have had to be a planned attack," I said softly to Doran. She stopped pacing and turned to me. "A couple troublemakers out to start trouble at a bar wouldn't have taken him down." She shook her head once at me. "How do we know it's Gremlins?"

"Bites."

"Bites?"

"There are several stab wounds, but the bites are definitely Gremlin." She started to pace again. "Jordan will give me a full report later. I'd ask you to join us…"

"I can manage this, Doran. I have to be part of this."

"I can't have this investigation fumbled because you can't control your—" She took in a deep breath. I looked down, embarrassed that she knew about it already as well. I hated the fact that everybody knew my life so well at that moment.

"How does everybody know about this?" No one answered. It didn't matter. "I'll control it, Doran. I can't sit back and let this go. I have to be a part of it. I have to help Manus."

"You *can't* control it, Keena." She held my gaze. "You'll help Manus by being at his side. I'll take care of the investigation. You are not to go off and take this into your own hands. I'll not have you endangering anyone else like you did on your little trip to Thule."

"He's hurt because of me, Doran," I said.

She spun and stepped closer, the blank gaze gone, replaced with anger, maybe disappointment. I couldn't tell. "He's hurt because he left your side in public. He's hurt because he was trying to placate your sensibilities to sex." She turned away again.

I was stunned. He should have left the club with me. He didn't because he thought Jordan and I had left together. *God.* Abbey hugged me tighter. Her face was buried in my shoulder and I felt her start to shake. I rubbed her back, more for my comfort than hers.

Doran turned back to me. "I'm sorry, Keena. That wasn't fair."

"But it's true." I leaned back in the uncomfortable chair and closed my eyes. "I'll figure out what to do about my...sensibilities." I didn't exactly know what. I couldn't continue this way either. My body running my mind was unacceptable. Things were too messed up. Feldema and I still had to fight on All Hallow's. I had to deal with the fact that I couldn't fulfill my bargain with Karackos and the Slaugh were getting restless without their king or Nessum. All this—and all my brain could concentrate on was my libido. I had to get myself through this.

We were all quiet again, listening to the soothing chants of Bevin and her coven.

I thought back to my human life, to my old job. I led a large group of computer geeks through impossible deadlines and months of overtime and stress. I was the organizer, the motivation for the group. I was the one who held everyone else together. Why was it that now I felt like *I* was the one who needed to be held together? I had lost my ability to manage and control.

Here, things were life and death instead of the threat of a loss in the stock market, but the situations called for the same leadership and skills. Stop and analyze the situation and put together a plan of action. I could do that. I had to have the same faith in myself here, as Keena, as I had in Mary Hughes in the business world.

I had to…for Manus and for myself. I had to take control.

Chapter Seventeen

❧

The door to Manus' room opened slightly and Bevin shuffled out. Her huge gray bun was tussled and hanging low to one side. Tendrils of hair fell to the other side of her face. She looked up at us and gave the smallest of smiles. Not a happy one that would have made her eyes sparkle, but a tiny twist at the edges of her lips. I let out a big breath.

Doran went to her. They embraced hands. "He'll live." Her voice was soft and tired. "He got cut from chin to belly. More on the back...but I think he'll live. If he'd gotten here much later..." Doran shushed her gently. "He lost a lot of blood."

"The bites, Bevin?" Doran was still being gentle. Bevin was tired and it showed. I'd never seen her look as old or fragile as she did at that moment. I had thought the old Witch invincible. Then again, I'd thought Manus was invincible.

Before she could answer, Jordan came through the door, buttoning up the black silk shirt. It was untucked and he had a hat pulled low on his head. Doran gave him a questioning look and then shot a quick glance my way. She rolled her eyes back to Bevin. I just sat there cradling Abbey. Her small hand gripped my arm when Jordan arrived.

"There's one big bite on his shoulder. It's definitely Gremlin."

Jordan turned to face Doran, leaving his back to me as much as possible. He was trying unsuccessfully to be as unappealing as he could. It was cute. My body wasn't responding through the grief and concern over Manus. Thankfully. "Deirdre was taken to the holding area." His tone was soft as he spoke to Bevin. Deirdre was one of Bevin's apprentice Witches. I heard Bevin take in a lot of air and Abbey dug her nails into the skin on my arm. "Someone saw some of the Slaugh just before the attack, but no one saw the actual ambush."

Doran took hold of Bevin so she could stand. Jordan continued in a very formal way. "Manus was walking Deirdre home because he'd thought she'd had too much to drink. The attackers must have thought she was lady Keena."

I started putting the pieces together as he spoke. The holding area must be the morgue. Deirdre must be dead. I felt my stomach lurch.

"I've had extra security put on the manor and there's a unit searching the area for any Gremlins who were seen in or around the club who can't account for their whereabouts tonight." He was all business and held the posture of the head of security, tall and straight.

He turned to me. "No more runs alone in the woods far a while, lady Keena. I've put guards outside your room and you need an escort when you leave the manor for any reason. I have to assume this was meant for you, not Deirdre." He was looking at my feet and not my face, still trying not to upset me. "I mean it." His eyes darted up to meet mine. "No impulsive actions. Stay armed as much as possible."

I was starting to get offended. But then again, I *had* run off to Thule without asking for any help or backup. I had earned his mistrust on this matter. I thought of Manus and just shook my head. I wondered how mad Jordan would be if he knew about Karackos…

His face changed dramatically after that thought. *Shit.* He was reading my mind. I slammed up the wall that blocked my thoughts. He started to say something but I interrupted him. "Bevin, may I see Manus?"

"Not tonight, my niece," Doran answered. "Both he and Bevin need their rest. You as well. Take Abbey to her chambers then try to rest. I think the next few weeks are going to be…"

"Hell," Jordan offered when she couldn't find the right word. He was looking directly at me. Doran nodded at him as she looked back to me.

She ushered Bevin past me. "Go on, Keena, get some rest. We'll talk tomorrow and you can see Manus." I still hesitated.

Bevin reached out and touched my arm, still holding Abbey. "He will live, Keena. He will be irritating you again in no time." I got a real smile from her that time and the tension in my stomach eased a tiny bit.

Abbey's coffee helped me calm down some. Bevin had only said Manus would live. She'd not been very specific. But for tonight, having him alive was enough. I'd worry about anything else later. Abbey was on the chopping-block table swirling her spoon in her mug. I sat in my usual stool and we were talking over the events of the night. "If I could have just held myself together..."

"Then you'd have been killed," she said.

"None of us were armed." Jordan's voice came from behind me, making me spill my coffee on my lap. He laughed. "Turnabout is fair play." I almost laughed too, but my body wasn't as occupied with Manus anymore and it lurched to attention at his appearance, even looking as disheveled as he did.

I can do this, I told myself, making sure my mental wall was up and taking in a deep breath. "If I hadn't run out, we would have all probably left together and that woman wouldn't be dead." There. I managed to think over the need rising in the middle of my stomach.

"We'd have all left together and we could all be dead, Keena. Don't blame yourself." He took a step closer. Too close. My walls came crashing down as well as my will to overcome. I was breathing way too fast. How could I be thinking about sex when Manus was hurt and Deirdre dead? I was swimming in lust and could do nothing about it. I stood up and backed away from him.

Jordan's head dropped. He took in a deep breath. "Keena, your wall. I can't think when I can feel all that from you." His hands were in fists, his pulse pounding hard against his thick neck. I waned to run my tongue over it. I tried to block him and managed for just a moment, but couldn't maintain. He took in another deep breath.

"Think baseball!" Abbey shouted. "Both of you!" I looked at her, stunned for a second, and her diversion allowed me to hold the walls up. How embarrassing. I could feel the blush running up my face.

"Priestess, there are guards at your doors. You'll have to keep them closed." I drew in a breath. I loved my doors being open. "I know this will be limiting for you to have all the necessary precautions, but it's a must. Doors closed. No runs." He raised an eyebrow. "And I want to know about Karackos."

"I…I have to go." It was too much to deal with, too much sensory input—worry, fear, anger and desire. I stumbled sideways and darted past him and out of the kitchen.

He called down the hall after me. "Keena. Priestess!" I heard him curse. "Listen to me!" His arrogance and control rolled down the hall after me like his voice.

True to his word, Jordan had a Magician outside my chambers. I approached slowly, hoping my urges didn't extend to him. He was tall, thin and attractive, and was standing in the usual bodyguard stance. Up against the wall, one hand crossed over another. He saw me and nodded his head as I passed and went in. Evidently, my mandar didn't put him in the have-to-have category, which was currently only occupied with Jordan, King of the Arrogant.

Both French doors were closed and the thin sheers pulled to block out the night. The room seemed smaller. Thanks to lights that had been set up outside, I could see the silhouettes of other guards standing outside each door. It was dark and lonely in the room all of a sudden. I sat on the bed watching the silhouette of a guard move back and forth across one door.

Suddenly an eerie cold came over me. I stood and looked around the dark room. I felt something odd and used my magic to light the candles.

One lone Slaugh stood next to the door in the far corner. He was next to the cabinet that held all my weapons, pushed into the corner. I almost yelled out to the guards before noticing a small puddle of something that looked like blood on the floor at his feet. The blood wasn't crimson but dark and sticky, like blood that had been exposed to the air for a while. I stood and watched another dark, sticky drop splat into the puddle.

He said something faint. Since the Slaugh only whisper at their best, injured, I couldn't make out the words.

I started to make move toward him. He shook his head and the hood fell back, revealing a head that was little more than a skull with taut, decrepit flesh straining across the bone structure. Deep-seated eyes glowed red, distant and weak. "I am Dannaiva," he said, struggling to speak. "I was second to Bran."

I took one more tentative step. If he'd wanted to jump me, he could have as soon as I entered the room and I'd be dead. No more running around unarmed for this Witch, even inside the manor. Jordan was right about that.

He took another raspy breath. "Nessum has not returned to us. Most of the others are planning…" He had to make a concentrated effort to take in air. "The humans. Chaos."

"Why?"

"They want to walk free again. Even if you are what the prophecy says, the Slaugh will never walk free, priestess." He seemed to be doing a bit better. "Humans will never accept the Grim Reaper roaming among them." I pulled one of the chairs away from the dining table and pushed it toward him. He didn't move to take it. "They do not realize if they start the destruction of humanity, they are destroying their own food source."

"Food?" I felt like I should ask more.

"We feed off souls, priestess. If my people start wars and famine and disease to tempt souls to the dark, then eventually there will be little left. They feel the overpopulation of humans will leave plenty after some of them destroy themselves and each other. But *you* know modern humanity. Modern technology fuels mass destruction…

"Feldema's entrapment and Nessum's fear of you have left us without leadership. I and others have tried to talk sense to the masses, but…" He faltered, the puddle at his feet growing fast.

"You're hurt. I'll get some help." I started toward the door.

"No!" It was the loudest word I had ever heard from a Slaugh. "I am dead already. He held up his arms and let the sleeves on the robe fall back to his elbows. His hands had both been cut off above the wrists. "They will kill me no matter what now. The rest of the upper ranks are already dead. Feldema must call Nessum back to her or the others will destroy everything. They are joining ranks with the Gremlins who have sided with us for centuries. A war comes."

"Feldema can call to Nessum?"

"She is irrevocably connected to him. Nessum took her at a very early age, after she came fully into her powers, and she has been with no other since. He controls her completely."

He tried to steady himself then took a step to the side, away from the cabinet. "You must stop this, priestess."

"How am I supposed to stop it?" I retreated and sank back onto the bed. "If Feldema has shared herself with Nessum, doesn't she have much of his power?"

"He holds back from her. He has used her, drained her almost completely and given her only the impression of power. He will continue to use her to exact his revenge on humanity. I know not what he fears in you, but you must use that fear to destroy what cannot be destroyed." His voice faltered again. He drew in a long, gurgling breath. The black blood came faster and dribbled along the entire front of his robe. I hadn't realized the dry creatures could even bleed. "You must, priestess…" His eyes slowly looked down.

"I'll do what I can, Dannaiva." His eyes burned a bit brighter for an instant.

"I have but one last request of you, priestess." He looked up into my eyes with his red ones. "Please put me out of my misery. They have taken my hands and most of my insides."

I looked down at the puddle where he stood. He had risked himself and others to warn us. I went to the cabinet and pulled out my mother's blade.

"I bid you rest, Dannaiva." He tilted his head into a nod and I plunged the blade through his chest. I heard the ribs give way. He didn't close his eyes but the glowing red faded to black, his last breath escaping with a real yell—and he shattered into dust. All that remained was the pool of black on the floor coated in the dust.

The doors all burst open at the sound of his final cry. The guards swept the room with guns and magic. I felt it on my skin. I stood still, not wanting to distract them from their search. The guard from the hall straightened first and mumbled something into a microphone hanging over his mouth. He stepped toward me. The others turned to face the outside to watch for anything else.

"I'm okay," I said. He only nodded and moved to examine the puddle. I sat back on the bed with the blade dangling between my knees. A spot of the dark blood not covered in dust glimmered in the moonlight. I had thought of the Slaugh as soulless creatures and had not held any respect for them, or remorse at their deaths. Now I did. They weren't honorless, just a different species. I felt guilt over those I had killed on Thule. I had told myself they deserved to die. They had earned it.

But they were soldiers, as Jordan is a soldier, and doing what they felt right for their race. I respected Dannaiva. And felt a sad pride for ending his life in a noble way.

"What happened?" Jordan shouted at the guards, not me. He had tucked in his shirt and removed the hat. I moved to put the bed between us, the most distance I could get in the room. The need started to boil as soon as he'd arrived. I held back my magic as it tried to call to him and checked to make sure the wall was protecting him from my thoughts. All was intact. I was getting better. He needed to work and not be distracted by my weakness. Doran and Bevin rushed in after him.

"I don't know, sir," the guard said. "We checked the room and no one was here. We have been standing guard at the doors."

"How did it get in then?" His face was red, the veins in his neck pulsing.

I spoke up to stop him. "Jordan, the Slaugh was here to give us a warning. He meant no harm to me." Doran was by my side instantly. I told them the rest. "Nessum has had Feldema since her maturity. She hasn't been with anyone else since." All movement in the room stopped. Everyone looked shocked. I quickly explained the rest of what Dannaiva had told me.

I was fighting my needs hard. My legs were trembling as if I would swoon. I felt my pants getting wetter from having Jordan so close. Bevin slipped another amulet in my hand while they talked about the intruder. "It will take the edge off the need, Keena, but it won't work forever. I hope it buys you some time."

As soon as the chain was in my hand, I found some relief. The desire was still there, lingering like a mysterious fog around me, but the urgent need receded. I slipped it over my head and let the opal stones fall against my heart. It cooled the fire considerably. I squeezed her hand. "Thank you." Even exhausted from working on Manus, she had managed to make me an amulet.

"It will not last long. Use it to make the decision your own." She smiled, but her face was pained and weary.

Doran looked at me. "What is it that Nessum fears from you?" Her gaze was hard, searching. If I told her, I would have to tell her how I knew and about the deal with Karackos. I wasn't ready to do that.

"I'm not sure I know." I kept my face as bland as I could. She tilted her head, skeptical. "Really. I don't know why he's left his minions." That was the truth, anyway.

She made an exasperated huff and glided out of the room. Bevin squeezed my hand again and followed her. That left me alone with Jordan and his guards.

"You're okay?" His tone hadn't softened and he didn't try to come any closer. I nodded and held up the amulet. He gave the slightest of nods to the guards and they returned to their positions. "*Are* you?" he asked again.

"I'm able to maintain the illusion of control right this minute, yes." I knew it was just a spell to make me feel less of the tension, but I'd take it. If I took off the necklace, need for him would envelop me.

"Go out with me then." It sounded like a command he would give his guards. He never took his eyes off me. His confidence was so appealing.

"Date? Me? I hardly think I'm capable of dating anymore. This thing," I lifted the amulet off my chest and dropped it again, "may give me some peace, but it's all still there. I'm still trapped by what my body wants no matter what my heart or mind says."

He took another step toward me and then, obviously thinking better of it, backed up. "Keena, I would really like to get to know you. Remember, I was raised human too. I know what your mind wants. It wants courtship and respect before you give your body. I understand." His face softened just slightly, despite the hard lines of masculinity.

He did understand and was willing to give me the time I needed. Somehow, that was more attractive than his incredible body and Alpha persona. "I appreciate that, Jordan. But the reality is that with all this going on, we can't really date. Can we?"

"Fine. I'll meet you in the gym in the morning and I'll be your sparring partner until Manus is back up to it."

Maybe I couldn't date him, but I could spar him. The thought of hitting the conceited man had its appeal.

Chapter Eighteen

ဆာ

I entered the gym, leaving my guard outside the door. I liked it empty like this, quiet and smelling of sweat, with the energy of other beings lingering in the still air. I went to the mirror and started a stretching exercise designed to bring my energy to my core and relax the mind. I felt the tension of yesterday seeping away with the Zen-like movements. Manus had taught them to me early in my training and the centered feeling only got deeper and stronger as time went by.

I felt Jordan's presence as he came out of the locker room. I didn't need to turn to see him. I felt where he was even with my eyes closed. I could sense him as he moved, his magic hinting at his intended direction. Concentrating on the magic, I could interpret each of his actions as he gathered his weapons and did his own stretching. I felt his every move as if I could see him while I stretched my mind, body and magic.

I had never done this precise kind of sensing before. I turned to face him, eyes still closed, standing on one foot with the other held up to my hips. He moved slowly in the other direction and I followed, eyes still closed, twisting my body on one foot to match his direction.

He stopped and so did I. "You have found the ley-line magic." He was very matter-of-fact.

I opened my eyes and felt the now-familiar surge of desire but was able to squelch it easily. "Others have mentioned it, but I don't think I know exactly what you mean." I slowly lowered my leg to the floor and continued to the next movement of the stretching dance.

"Open your eyes to the world as you did when you followed my magic. The line has gotten stronger here since you came to us. The ley is seeking you."

I tried to open myself but I only saw his perfect, masculine lines in the room around me. "I don't see anything."

He smiled. "Just me?"

I stepped out of the stretch. "I *mean*, I only see the room and you in it, you arrogant—"

"Easy, girl. It will come. You're close. When you can see it, you can draw strength and power from it. The ley lines weave around the earth. You'll see them when you're ready."

"If I hear one more person say 'when you're ready', I'm going to scream," I huffed somewhat childishly.

"Keena, power comes in bits and pieces to everyone. If it hit you all at once, it'd be like driving your car into a wall. All of us have gone through this. Most of us did it as we matured through puberty, so it was easier. You want it all now and want to control it all now. I understand your need for control. It comes from facing the human world alone and misunderstood, even by your own mind. You managed in that world by staying in control of everything and everyone around you. But this world is not so easily controlled. Let it come in a trickle, or the wave will destroy you."

His arrogance was annoying. "How do know all that?"

"I did the same thing. I grew up without any guidance for my powers. The powers scared me and I had no control over them, so I controlled everything else I could."

I found myself even more attracted to him for sharing that bit of himself, but I wouldn't let *him* know that. "Fine. We here to fight or have a therapy session?"

He laughed. "Bring it on, little girl." Giving me an evil smile, he crouched and drew his wooden sword from his side. We had decided to use the practice weapons and pull punches since we had never fought each other before. We circled for a moment, looking for the "tell" that would clue one of us into the other's intentions. I realized he wasn't going to lunge first — so I did.

I fell to the floor and swung my leg at his calves, knocking his feet out from under him. He landed hard on his ass but rolled over and got to his feet before I did. The Demon was fast for such a big man. He caught me midway up, landing a kick to my side. Since he hadn't used full force, I was able to let the momentum push me over sideways and roll away before he could pounce on me.

Our practiced dance continued for some time, each getting the better of the other from moment to moment. The half-Demon moved far differently from Manus. His stride and motions were harsher, stronger. Manus moved like a cat, all sleek and flowing. Jordan moved like a force of nature, each effort big and dangerous. He was holding back and I still had to strain to keep the upper hand. It was a good reminder that I had grown accustomed to Manus and his fighting style. I wouldn't always face the same opponent.

I finally spun on him unexpectedly, pinning him to the wall, mock blade at his throat, body pressed hard against his. The smell of him, masculine, with no perfumes, no hint of anything but his skin, assaulted my senses. I jerked and turned away, taking a few steps to clear my nose of his scent. He stayed at the wall.

"Close your eyes and use the ley to follow me," he ordered, voice hard. I turned back to him. His eyes were closed. "Channel that feeling, the pent-up energy, to find the ley lines, Keena. Close your eyes and use the frustration, enhance it."

I did as he said. Crouching low, I closed my eyes and concentrated. He moved silently around my right side. I felt him move farther away and then try to come in closer on the left. I turned to him, eyes still closed. He lunged, dropping to the ground to hit me below the waist. I felt it all and easily jumped over him. He spun back up on his feet and continued his assault. I blocked three more attempts before he landed on me and pressed me to the floor.

"Keep them closed. Feel for the power with your mind. Search the room for it." He was pressed hard to me. I felt my desire for him start to grow even with the amulet.

"Use it to see the line." He uttered the command softly into my neck. I could feel the heat of his breath on the little hairs behind my ear.

It burned slightly as I channeled the frustration to my abdomen where I most felt control over my magic—then I opened my mind, letting down all the walls.

I could see spider webs in hues of blue under my eyelids. As I opened them, I found the room glowing a mild blue. Running through the center of the workout area was a deep-cobalt-blue line, almost purple. It hovered, glowed and hummed. The power in it was a living, breathing thing and was beckoning to me.

Absentmindedly, I pushed at his shoulder. When he realized I saw the line, he slowly rolled off me. I stood, almost afraid to touch it, afraid to break the trance and lose sight of it. Power hung in the air.

A strong magic lived within the shimmering blue. I felt it, smelled it, and reached out without taking another step. It arced back to me as a lightning strike, single threads joining with me through the tips of my fingers. The lights dimmed in the gym and I felt the power surge through every cell of my body. I felt the thrust of my Demon power welling inside me. It burned, consuming my mind and making it hard to think. The feeling was too much. I had to release it. I needed to thrust it out. I was full, overloaded and starting to panic as it threatened to overcome me.

Jordan's voice came softly through the air from everywhere. "Channel it back to the line." Feeling anchored to his voice, I imagined the thrust going back to the line, back through my fingers. The blueness of the ley line expanded with the power, looking like a snake that just had a big meal. The brightness intensified and all the lights in the gym went black for a second.

The door flew open with a loud smack and the guard rushed in. Jordan stopped him with a hand signal. I felt the power leaving me and dissipating into the line. I was no longer tired from the exercise. For the first time in a very long time, I was content and confident with everything. I had everything I needed. There was no fear, no sense of dread or worry. I was filled.

"You can close it out the same as you found it. Close your mind to it and it will wait for you."

I closed my mind in much the same way I closed my mind to Jordan's psychic abilities, building a little wall in my brain to shut it out. I turned to Jordan, who was still lying on the floor.

He smiled. "You have more Demon blood than I thought, priestess. It's rare to be able to share with the line. Most can draw little bits from it, but few can build on its power and share it back. It is the gateway to other realms and it has welcomed you. You are a remarkable woman."

I blushed, still feeling very content. He got up. "Grab a shower and we'll have lunch." He walked away and I watched him, his confidence still hanging around him as sure as his power.

I shook my head and opened my mind to the ley line again. Just in case I had imagined it. It still hung there, shimmering with the blue of darkest sapphire. I reached for it again and it came to me quickly. Power filling me. I was aware of Jordan removing his clothes at the lockers, the guard shifting uneasily from the energy in the hall. I could feel others moving about above me, on the next floor. I took a step forward.

"Don't walk through it, Keena," Jordan called out from the locker room. "Slow down. Remember, you don't have to control everything at once." His voice seemed to surround me, filtered and echoed by the power of the ley line. I pulled away from the line, backing up and pulling my hand back.

It released me with a small swooshing noise. I closed my mind back down. I still felt that sense of wonder from it, gained understanding from it. I sat on the floor for a moment to contemplate the experience.

I had fought so hard for control over everything, holding myself back and endangering others in the process. I was struggling to hold on to my humanity. I had controlled everything and everyone around me in my human life and I couldn't here. It was time to accept I wasn't just human anymore. I was something else that held a piece of humanity, but I wasn't human. The time had come to accept myself — and those around me — completely. To embrace all aspects of my being and use that human part of me that I *did* have confidence in to understand the rest. Easier said than done — but I knew where to start.

I pushed through the door of the locker room and silently walked past several rows of lockers, following the sound of running water to stand just at the end of a row and watch Jordan. He soaped the top of his head and the tiny bit of hair that had not been shaved off.

I wondered what color it would be if he let it grow out. It looked very dark. The soap slipped off his head and dribbled down the center of his muscled back. Those back muscles rippled as he worked the shampoo over his head. The bubbles trailed farther, over the curve of his hip and down his tight butt muscles. I released a breath I hadn't known I was holding. Every bit of him was tanned, tight and wholly masculine. Hard and deadly, he was a machine made for one purpose.

"Not *one* purpose," he said and turned to me. I had to make myself not gasp at the sight of his stomach, rippling and shimmering with water and soap. "Have you come to drive me insane? I want you to have the control you need...but I can only stand so much. You do realize you affect me the same way I affect you?" His face was still hard and I could see he was losing his patience with me. I had to think for a moment to realize why I had come.

"I...I..." The amulet was still working. I had come on my own. I had made the choice and had the control over the situation that I needed. I had come to him because I wanted to. He understood me, wanted to be with me. Not for the power of the priestess, but for me. He could have taken advantage after the club. He could have—but he'd waited for me to make up my mind. Even though he tried to hide it behind arrogance, the alpha male had given me control.

I was ready now and he still wanted to make sure it was what I wanted. I raised my hand to the amulet and jerked it from my neck. Need rushed over me and I watched his eyes roll back just from the feel of my magic reaching for his.

His whole body tensed from it. Water was still running over him, leaving his skin shiny and slick. He reached out his hand to me and I went to him without hesitation. His mouth found mine and his lips took possession of me. Wrapping his wet arms around my waist, he pulled me closer, the full length of our bodies pressed together.

His was so tall he had to bend down to reach my lips with his. He pulled his face from mine and turned us so I was under the water. The coolness of it shocked my skin, the intense change of temperature adding to the onslaught of sensations. "Cold shower?" I had just enough voice to get it out.

"I didn't have the help of an amulet," he said against my skin, his hot breath teasing as he kissed his way across my shoulder. His hands were working at pulling off the sheaths that had held the sparring blades. Big, nimble fingers found the bottom of the tank top and lifted it off easily.

He kissed my chest, moving ever so slowly to my pointed nipples. I arched my back, giving him better access. He nibbled at them through the fabric of the little sports bra I was wearing today. I wanted to watch his hands as he explored me. I was shaky, needful and open. Cool water was running over my face and body. I waited for the steam to rise from my heated skin.

My bra fell to the tiles. I heard a small moan escape from my mouth as his lips caught one of my breasts and sucked it hard into his mouth. I let out a louder moan from the sheer ecstasy of his tiny bites, my knees starting to feel weak as I held his head to my chest. I used his body to steady mine as his bite increased in intensity. The sensation echoed the cascade of the shower, sending waves of pleasure down my spine. He treated each nipple with equal zest. He bit hard then let his tongue lightly circle and ease the sharpness of his bite, the treatment making them sore and even more sensitive. I clawed at his back to hold myself upright.

He held me up with one arm and moved his free hand to unzip my leathers. His mouth was moving slowly and deliberately across me. My pants fell to the floor but were still around my ankles as he lifted me with no effort and carried me out of the locker room and into the gym.

He stopped long enough to ward the door to prevent any interruption. Gently, he placed me on a pile of blue vinyl exercise mats. The wetness of my skin made me slip a little but he rearranged them to hold us steady. He pulled the leathers free of my feet. For a few moments he stopped and let his hungry gaze follow the lines of my body.

He moved to hold himself above me, his eyes gliding up and down, the Demon silver of them swirling like molten liquid. His knees were on the mats on either side of my thighs. "You're sure you want this?"

I let my gaze run the full length of his chest and down to his proud erection. His face was rough and strong, shoulders bulging from holding his weight above me, thighs long and taut. As I eyed his cock, it jerked in anticipation of my answer.

I let my gaze rest squarely on his groin. "Yes, I want this." He didn't hesitate again. His lips moved gracefully over my skin, lingering when he sensed it was particularly arousing for me. He bit and kissed and sucked and I could only writhe beneath him and respond as best I could to touch and tease. Jordan's attentions left me a puddle of yearning need. He touched all the right places, using a rough grasp when needed or a soft, loving stroke in contrast as he explored. He felt like a longtime lover, one that knew my body well.

"I have seen some of your fantasies, Keena. I know exactly what you want from me." He ran his tongue around my bellybutton. I gasped and raised my hips in a begging gesture, my body urging him to move lower of its own accord. He did, settling himself between my legs and teasing me with kisses, nips and licks along the insides of my thighs. He parted me and worked that talented tongue on my clit. I was amazed at the precision of his movements. His tongue flicked in firm, quick strokes across my clit. My toes curled, my heart was about to beat out of my chest. The room spun. He groaned, pressing harder with his tongue and slipping one of his thick fingers into my pussy.

I shattered into a wonderfully painful orgasm. Weeks of denial fractured in a moment of perfect pleasure. My magic reached for his, responded to it and his emotions. I felt his pleasure mingled with mine. My muscles tightened, back arched, and screaming his name, I came. It swept over me and brought a grunt of pleasure from him. He got up on his knees and pulled my legs around him.

He hesitated only slightly to take a good look at me as I was splayed in front of him, then urged slightly inside me, testing my eagerness. I wiggled and tried to press myself over the length of his beautiful cock. He held my hips tightly so I couldn't. Deliberate in movement, he was not rushing but not intentionally teasing. "Not yet. Let it come to us slowly. Let it build."

The intense feeling of him stretching me brought another wave of pleasure to flow over me, my muscles fluttering around the tip of his cock as he held it just inside my pussy. He growled as he felt me tighten on the tip and obviously could stand the pleasurable torture no longer. He thrust hard and deep. His fingers dug into my hips as he pushed his way in so deeply that I needed to pull back, but he started the withdrawal on his own, again painfully slowly.

I wiggled again to encourage him to move faster. My own impatience was driving me insane. His eyes were watching my reactions, the muscles of his arms and stomach tensing to control how much I could move.

Several more times he thrust in and out, so slowly I was whimpering. "What do you want, Keena? Tell me."

"Please, Jordan." I couldn't get enough air. "Please…"

"Not until you say it, Witch."

I knew he could see the things I wanted in my mind. He wanted to hear me, to have that consent. "Fuck me, Jordan. Please!"

He responded with a faster pace, relinquishing his grip on my hips so I could mirror his rhythm. My hips arched to meet him, forcing us closer together and bringing another deep growl from him.

"You want it harder, Keena?" He'd read the desire in my mind but once again I could feel the need to hear the words.

"Yes! Harder…harder!" The words enhanced the feeling of being naughty. We were fucking like teenagers in the high school gym and the teacher was just outside the door. The smells of the gym and the echo of my moans and his growls in the big room also made me feel a little dirty. It was hot, and telling him what I wanted only made it hotter. I had a feeling Jordan liked public sex.

I gripped his arms and arched into him. I was getting close to another orgasm when he lowered himself so he could kiss me again. His mouth trailed from my lips to my breasts and his cock slid out. I whimpered and wiggled to try to maneuver us back together. He gave a small, satisfied chuckle. He took a nipple into his mouth, sucking hard enough to pull half my breast between his lips. His tongue made lazy circles around the nipple as he rubbed his cock against my thigh, teasing me.

"Jordan," I pleaded. "I want you inside me."

He bit hard on the tender flesh in his mouth. He let that nipple slide free and took the other in his teeth. The tease of pain caused me to arch against him, and added to the desire to have the feel of his cock back inside me. I dug my fingers into his arms and braced for the intensity of his penetration.

It didn't come. He continued to tease my breast. His hands were roaming my torso, stopping occasionally to squeeze and torment. I was writhing in need on the mats.

"I want you inside me, Jordan. For cauldron's sake, Demon, fuck me!"

The groan that came from the half-Demon was so fucking sexy. It was as if I was fulfilling his deepest fantasy. Maybe I was. He *had* said he wanted me as much as I wanted him. Now he'd heard from my own lips how much I wanted him.

He watched my eyes as he pushed back into my aching pussy. No longer did I feel as though my body was reacting without the consent of my mind. I wanted him. I wanted this for *us*. His lips, his kisses were for *me* and not the wanton Witch alone. I felt his emotions in his touch as his hands traced the outline of my body as he loved me. "Oh! Jordon!" I felt another orgasm building.

He threw his head back when I shattered, my muscles tightening around him, milking him. He slowed his thrusts to enjoy the sensation. I watched his face tighten and his eyes roll back from the feel of my pleasure. When my last pulse passed, he built up speed again, pounding into me, reaching for his own release. I felt him swell and heard the vinyl under his hands give way, ripping from the force of his fingers digging in. I groaned, tore at his chest with my hands to control the surge in myself as he reached his peak and shouted loudly, not caring who heard us.

He continued to grind as I wiggled and moaned, reaching, grasping, gasping. The urgency in his movements had pushed me over the edge one more time.

My breathing was erratic, as was my heart rate as he slowed. Whispering teasing words in my ear and dusting my body with gentle touches, he tried to calm the wild Witch. "You are *so* beautiful, Keena."

When my breathing was closer to normal, he rolled us over so I was draped over his chest. "Did I live up to the fantasies, my lady?" I could only manage a shy laugh. I was swimming in the afterglow as he continued, "Next time I will show you how we can add our Demon magic to it."

I thought about that for a moment. "If it gets better with the magic, I don't think I'll survive it."

"Don't underestimate yourself." We remained still for a few quiet moments. The only sound in the room was our hearts trying to get back to a normal speed. He kissed my head. "I have watched you grow, Keena. Longed for you from a distance for years. I wouldn't have survived if you had rejected me."

I didn't look at him but I felt his sincerity, his relief. The sudden softness of his voice touched me. "How?"

"I was the one who found you. You were around twelve, I think. You were so cute then."

"I'm not now?"

He chuckled. "No, you are outstanding, beautiful…sinful even. But you outgrew cute at about fifteen."

I liked this softer side of him, but knew he shielded it well on purpose and I would never betray it. "At fifteen I was tall and gangly."

"We always saw the beauty that you have only recently seen. I have dreamed of holding you in my arms for years."

"Why weren't you my guardian instead of Manus, then?"

"Can you be in love with your guardian?"

Manus had made his pledge to protect me always, but he couldn't be a consort. "Oh."

"I *did* handpick Manus from the volunteers. I felt your need of companionship and gave you a friend and a guardian." He kissed me again softly on the head and ran his hand over my hair.

Again I was humbled and at a loss for words as I thought of all those who had spent years protecting me, waiting for me to come into my power. I knew Jordan must have had lovers over the years, but he had waited for me. I was glad I had been drawn to him, happy to be in his arms. I twirled my fingers around his chest.

"Thank you," I said and kissed his nipple.

"For?"

"Making sure I had a friend, making sure I had Manus." *And for showing me your softer side.* I didn't say it, but it meant more to me than he would ever know.

A knock came at the door Jordan had warded and one of the guards called out, "Sir, others will be arriving soon."

Jordan made a scowling face at the closed door. I should have been embarrassed but I wasn't. He rose to a sitting position, bringing me with him, and kissed me on the forehead tenderly. "We should get you dressed and go see Manus." I gave him a questioning look. "I knew you'd want to, so I checked with Bevin. She said we could see him around lunchtime."

I rested my head against his chest and it felt good. Right. Why did I have to fight everything so hard? Why did he accept who I was and I couldn't? Would he accept all of my life? "Jordan..." I began softly.

"You have not closed your mind to me, Keena. I know who you are and I understand your responsibilities. My human, possessive side will not like you in the arms of another, but I will accept it. I've had relationships with Witches before."

"Is it the Witch in me that makes these demands?" I nuzzled closer.

He tightened his hold on me. "The Witch makes the demands, the Demon makes them urgent. If I'm able to regularly satisfy those demands, urgency won't overtake you so badly. Your magic abruptly lost its connection to Lord Tynan, which heightened the need. It won't be so bad again. The shock from his loss only made the rest of it worse for you." He lifted me to my feet with a sure-of-himself smile. "Let's go see your overstuffed kitty cat, priestess."

* * * * *

After returning to my room to clean up, Jordan escorted me to the healing rooms. I walked confidently next to him. He towered over me but his presence no longer intimidating me. I heard Doran and Bevin before we got the waiting area, no tension in their voices. That was a good sign.

When we came around the corner they both stopped talking and looked at us. I fished the amulet out of my pocket and handed to Bevin. "Thanks for the time," I said without letting any embarrassment into my voice.

"That wasn't much time." The old Witch wriggled her eyebrows.

"All I needed." I glanced back at Jordan to see he was blushing. Doran was doing her best not to laugh. She coughed into her hand. Jordan blushed even more. It was too cute to see the hulk who had forced me to talk dirty to him embarrassed.

Doran looked back to me. "I feel a change in you, my niece. I like it. What is it?"

I went to Manus' door without saying anything. He came first. Then I was going to have a talk with Doran. They all followed me in.

He was sitting up and conscious. His bright green cat eyes met mine with a small smile, the movement tugging on the cut and making him cringe. The nasty gash started at the bottom of his chin and wound itself into a big, grotesque question mark that stopped at his navel. Bevin had it coated in herbs but I could see under the treatment—and it was bad. I felt hot tears at the backs of my eyes.

"Don't, Keena. I'll be okay. Bevin is sure I'll be able to shift again." He talked by moving his mouth as little as possible.

I looked back at Bevin as I sat on the side of his bed. "Was there a question of that?"

"The cut was deep and went through a great deal of muscle tissue. If that tissue was too damaged, he couldn't shift. We are healing it from the inside out to insure he won't have that problem. The stabs in the back weren't so bad. They'll heal fine. This one," she motioned to the huge question mark, "it's almost as though they put some sort of poison on the blade to make sure the tissue died."

"So they *wanted* to make sure he couldn't shift if he survived." I glanced from Jordan to Doran. "And the Witch, Deirdre? Was there anything specific about her injuries?"

Doran nodded to Bevin as if giving her permission to tell me. Bevin took in a deep breath. "She was decapitated, probably with the same blade."

"Jesus Christ!" I had to close my eyes. "And you think that was meant for me?"

"Especially after your visit from Dannaiva last night. We are going to have to intervene soon," Doran said. "I have contacted the one who is claiming leadership on Thule now. He is coming tomorrow evening. A formal meet, Keena. You will be there to assist me. Something has them very frightened of you." She waited for me to say something but I held my knowledge as well as her gaze and offered nothing in return.

Manus broke the stare-down. "Can I talk to Keena alone for a minute?" Doran just turned and left. She knew I was hiding something. Too bad. She did the same often enough. When the others were gone, Manus took my hand.

"I'm so sorry," I said, kissing his knuckles. "This is my fault. I should have stayed with you."

"Stop it. I failed in my duty. If you had been with me...I just..."

"Now *you* stop it. We're both alive. I'm very sorry about your friend." I kissed his knuckles again.

Manus pulled his hand away. "You have to tell them, Keena. You have to tell them about the deal with Karackos."

I thought quickly to make sure my wall was up to block Jordan but it was too late. He had been there and gotten part of the memory, part of the worry brought to the forefront of my mind. Jordan flew around the corner. His strong face looked harsher than usual. He was red-faced again—but this was not a blush.

"What deal did you make with that monster, Keena?" His voice was as unforgiving as his look. Doran and Bevin had followed him back in.

"Damn it," I said.

"Keena, not funny. Karackos is ruthless and he plays games. You should not have summoned a greater Demon." He started to say something else but stopped himself.

Doran put her hand on my shoulder. "Keena, what was the deal?"

I stood and felt the anger rushing into me. "First of all, I didn't summon him, he came to *me*. Second, it was a really good deal at the time."

I was going to have to spill the beans. So I did. I told the story, all of it. About the deal to trade Feldema or kill her, about Nessum disappearing when I confronted him with Trevina's blade. Doran's eyes grew large as she stared at the blade she hadn't noticed hanging at my side. I touched the hilt of it when I told them about finding it in my mother's skull. I'd spent many nights dreaming of it since. In the dreams, it wasn't just a skull. It was her face, strained in pain. I left out the part about the dreams and told them how I had lost the skull to the sea on the way back from Thule. Bevin almost swooned.

"You poor dear, poor dear," she crooned, over and over.

Jordan was positively oozing anger. His fists balled so tightly I thought his knuckles would break. "But you can't offer Feldema the choice anymore, can you? And you didn't think it necessary to tell me this?"

I stood up as tall as possible and faced him. "I told *Manus*. He's my guardian. I had no obligation to tell you anything at the time. Hell..." I swung around to face Doran. "I didn't even know we *had* a security force at the time! No one seems to think I need to know anything around here until something's bit me on the ass! I need to be better informed. Then, and only then, can I make the right decisions on what I need to tell others! If I learned nothing else from my human parents, it was how to assess a situation and make good choices. But I can't make good choices without all the information!"

I stepped even closer to Doran, tired of all the guessing games, tired of them thinking I couldn't handle the truth. "If I'm to be this great leader you want me to be, Doran, I think it's time that you stop treating me like a child and fill me in on exactly what's going on around here. I can only make decisions based on the information I have. So far, that's been *shit*."

Doran looked like she was going to take a step back from me, but didn't. "Until now, I didn't think you could or would truly accept this life. I didn't want to drown you in all the sudden changes." Her voice sounded a bit defeated, realizing she'd been wrong. Being wrong was something Doran was not accustomed to. "Can you understand that? There is so much for you to learn about our world. We tried to give you the basics, to let it all sink in. I see now you have decided to accept who you are and I apologize if my trying to make the adjustment easier was interpreted as a lack of trust. I assure you, it was not. Your coming to us so late is new for us. I didn't know how to..."

She did take the step back then, her tone becoming more serious. "If I pushed too much on you all at once, I would have chosen what I thought was important for you to know, swaying your opinions of the things and species of our world. You have to form your own opinions based on the events that unfold before you. You have to decide what you feel is important and make your own decisions, one way or another. I wanted you to find your way to us through your own heart, Keena, your own strength." She sat down in a small chair, which made her look bigger than she really was, and made a small huffing sound. "Again, I apologize if I've offended you. I will tell you anything you wish to know, from this day forward."

"No more trying to shield me? No more games?"

"There *were* no games. But you're correct, my niece. You have every right to be a part of your own destiny. I should not have taken that choice from you."

Jordan stepped in between us, his face still taut, fists still bunched. "That still doesn't change the fact that she made a bargain with Karackos that she can't fulfill." He turned to me. "You do understand that if you can't offer him Feldema, *you* will be obligated to take her place, be bound to him, to serve him in any way he sees fit?"

I reached up to touch his face. He calmed a bit but I could see he was truly worried about me and not just because he was head of security. His silver eyes were swirling. I felt his love and began to understand that my heart knew his already. My powers chose the Demon, for more than just his physical presence and his ability to protect. His heart was part of the package and my magic was drawn to him for love as well as lust.

"Yes, I know what that means. I'll have to deal with that when the time comes. First, we have to deal with the Slaugh. If they decide to declare war, then the deal with Karackos won't matter, will it?"

"I was right," Doran said. "You *have* come to understand your destiny. I am pleased."

"So glad you approve," I said. "What's the plan for the meet?"

Chapter Nineteen

ℰℛ

"This is getting us nowhere." Jordan dropped the pile of papers to the table. I'd made him bring me everything the security force had on the Slaugh and we'd spent the afternoon making sure I understood all of it. There were four different stacks, and while I had made it through three of them myself, he and Abbey were trying to give me bits of information from the last. "I've been through all this intel before." He strode across the room to the open door to look out again. He had grumbled when I insisted I needed at least one of them open.

"They seem to run much like the military. I mean, they have a very strict hierarchy." Jordan gave me a "duh" look. He was so arrogant and so handsome at the same time. "So this Trammel guy who's taken over was way down on the list of flunkies. Maybe fifth or six in command."

"And?"

"And…you were in the military, right?" I asked, standing to pace as I spoke. It seemed to help me think.

"A couple times. Army. Navy."

"So…when you were a grunt, did you understand the politics?"

"Not really. The lower-ranking officers follow orders. The politics wouldn't matter to them."

"So Trammel would have to be a badass to take on the upper members of Bran's command, but he probably isn't the most politically attuned member of the ranks."

"That should help some, but—" He looked pleased with me but his face hardened and he stopped speaking abruptly as

Cliona came through the door. I had felt her presence as she came close but didn't think to mention it.

"My lady." She knelt. Jordan turned his back to her.

"Cliona, good to see you—and quit with the formal crap around me, would ya?" I dropped the folder on the table and reached out a hand to her. "Back so soon?"

"Doran called. I'm to stand as your guardian for the little party this evening. You should have called me yourself when Manus was taken out of commission." She turned toward Jordan's back. "Or your head of security should have."

Jordan turned to acknowledge her for the first time. "I'll be her guardian until Manus is healed." He was slow and deliberate with his words.

"You're the new boy toy. You can't be both." She was intentionally teasing him.

Jordan growled. "I'm no one's boy toy, *fang*." They had started to head toward one another. I felt power start to fill the room—Jordan's power. Like nothing I'd ever felt, it touched us all. Abbey gasped. Cliona hissed at him, showing her fangs. I'd never seen the Vamp so angry. Her skin faded to almost pure white, her eyes went dark with red rims.

"Hold on you two!" I stepped between them. "I don't know what the hell *this* is all about, but I don't have time to deal with it." They stood several feet from each other and held eye contact over my head. I felt Jordan's power start to fade. It left my skin cold as it dissipated. I had to take in a small breath. "You think we can play nice, kids?"

"I always play nice," Cliona said, walking back to the table and flopping herself into a chair. Jordan huffed. Cliona made a tiny, smug smile and rolled her eyes. "If you think the half-Demon is up to the task of consort, who am I to argue?"

Jordan yanked his T-shirt off to expose the scratches I had left on his shoulders and chest. "I think I'm up for it." Cliona laughed out loud. He made that growling noise again. "I heard no complaints from the priestess."

"You." I pointed to Jordan and then the door. "Go get dressed." I turned to Cliona. "And *you*...back off." Jordan left without another word, the door slamming behind him. Cliona laughed again.

"What the hell was all that about?" Abbey asked, her eyes wide. Cliona just shrugged, still looking very satisfied with herself.

I sat across from her. "Really, Cliona, I don't need another problem right now. You two have an old relationship I need to know about?"

She laughed again. "Don't worry, my lady, I've had no relationship with your warrior. He's just an easy target with his enlarged ego. I push his buttons when I can. We've worked together before." She straightened. "I'll behave."

"That sure looked like something close to lust and hate to me," Abbey piped in. I had to agree.

Cliona huffed this time. "The Sarge and I have long pushed each other's buttons, and never once did that turn to anything sexual. It's more of a power struggle. He can't stand the thought of a woman as his equal in a fight. His human ego can't process it. But we don't let it interfere with a job. We have a healthy respect for each other." She leaned toward me with a sly smile. "That was more fun for him than you realize. Keena, know this about him—he's more fun when he's pissed. It brings out the best in him. I would love to have had a chance at that power, but it would have ruined the fun of tormenting him. You do have good taste in men." She winked. "But if you tell him I said any of this, I'll bleed ya dry." She was smiling happily.

I couldn't believe the change in her from the time I was with Tynan. The grumpy, all-business Vampire was lighthearted and fun. "I think I like this side of you better."

"Than what?"

"Than the ice-queen Vamp I used to see when you came to talk to Tynan."

She looked down. "I'm sorry, my lady. I was not happy about his being bound to you. I was only concerned for him."

"As you should have been. I understand, Cliona. I wouldn't have ever allowed it if I understood everything I do now." I watched her face lighten again. She was truly beautiful when she didn't look so stern.

"I know that. So what are we up against now?" She picked up the paperwork. "Do you think Nessum will show at this little party?"

A rush of fear ran over me. "Can he take your soul if he does?"

"No, we're safe as long as we don't go to the island seeking him. Doran debriefed me as to why he just disappeared. I do wish you had passed the information about the blade of an innocent to me."

I gave her a long look. "And you or Tynan would have taken off and tried to destroy him." She didn't try to argue. "He hasn't been killed with one yet. I still don't know if what Karackos says is true. Nessum may not know for sure either. I couldn't risk either of you with something I didn't know as fact."

She leaned back. "You're smarter than you look—and you sure did scare the crap out of Nessum."

"That I did." I smiled slightly at the memory. "So no, I don't think he'll show up. If he does, keep your mouth shut and let me handle it. I don't want you pushing his buttons like you did Jordan's. I don't want Nessum that mad."

* * * * *

Hogan waved his hands and what was a pile of leather on the floor danced around me and landed perfectly in place. The buttercream color highlighted the gold tints in my hair and the gold of my eyes. The top wrapped around my torso, barely covering the tops of my breast. The sheaths for the blades on my hips were made from a golden fiber, twisted with black into intricate designs. I was not dressed to look pretty, but confident and powerful instead.

The shoes were three-inch heels made from the same material as the sheaths. I would have preferred a lower shoe, or even a boot, but the spike heels really made the look of dominance complete. Hogan left my hair loose and flowing around my face like a lion's mane. The look of a wild predator. It was effective.

Jordan came in. He was dressed in a head-to-toe black security uniform. It consisted of an exquisitely tight, sleeveless T-shirt and even tighter leather pants. His guns were tucked neatly under each arm in holsters and he wore a blade on each thigh. His power—not his magical power but the power of his confidence—radiated from him. The scratches I had made on his shoulders showed as well.

If his face hadn't melted to that of a smitten child when he saw me, I would have thought him made of stone. I enjoyed that soft look on him.

So did Cliona. "Put your tongue back in, Sarge. You can play slap and tickle later."

He growled again but didn't take his eyes off me to acknowledge her. His face *did* return to its usual stony hardness. "Doran said they were ready, my lady. Are you?" He held out his arm to escort me.

"For you two? No. For the Slaugh? Yes."

We walked in silence toward the meet room. Doran was waiting at the door. It opened when we got there and we entered in a very formal manner. First Doran, followed by her guardian and her two consorts, then I followed a few steps behind with Cliona, with Jordan bringing up the rear. The rest of the court came behind us.

There were six of the Slaugh over to one side. They made the faintest bow as we passed and took our seats on the raised dais. Again, this was an all-out show of power and dominance.

Jordan seemed uncomfortable as he lowered himself to his place by my side. Cliona mumbled "boy toy" under her breath and he made that angry growling sound again. I was really starting to like that sound.

The Slaugh filed into the open area before the court. Trammel looked angered by the fact that we towered over him. His tiny red eyes were glowing brightly under the black hood. His entourage moved in behind him but not too closely. They spread out to his sides, looking more like bodyguards than officers.

I stood back up and walked down the steps to face him. He was a good five inches taller than me, so I didn't get too close. I didn't want to have to look up at him. I heard Doran and the others shift at my movement. I was breaking protocol, but Trammel wouldn't know.

"Trammel." I didn't use a title because he didn't have one yet. "We'll forgo the ceremony of this occasion because I doubt you're smart enough to know what it is." He took a step back and his eyes flashed, but he didn't reply as I continued. "Let's just get down to business." I walked around him and eyed the two Slaugh on his right side. I passed them and went around to his back. He didn't turn, not wanting to show fear. The smell of death lingered on him as I passed around his left side to stop right in front of him again. "What plans of war do you have against the humans? And remember—my guardian will know if you speak the truth or not."

"Why has Nessum not returned to us, priestess?"

"I don't know, Trammel." It was the truth. I knew why he had left, but not the reason he hadn't come back. "Are you not leader enough to run the island without your Dark Angel?"

He swung so hard and so fast that I almost didn't see it coming and didn't have time to set myself well. I spun around as he made contact with my face. Jordan and Cliona were both halfway down the steps before I could hold up my hand to motion them back. Cliona immediately stopped but Jordan kept coming. "Back off," I told him. He gave me a stern look, but slowly backed up and took his seat. Cliona put her hand on his shoulder.

I turned back. I had expected it and could have remained facing him if I hadn't worn the damn heels—but I got the reaction I wanted. He had expected me to let my guards have at him. He was backing away as I turned to him. I felt the trickle of blood from my lip. I wiped the drop and licked it off my finger. A tease.

"You're a soldier, Trammel." He was watching my mouth as I spoke. "You have proven that by slaying your upper ranks—but what do you know of humanity?" I stepped back in close to show I had no fear of him.

"I know what I need to, priestess. We will destroy their governments and lower their numbers so that we, and the rest of the Kith, can walk among them again without fear. Nessum and Bran had centuries to do such and didn't. You killed Bran and Nessum has left us. I will carry on and do what we have planned for centuries."

"When was the last time you were among humans?" I asked coldly, and with a hint of superiority.

"What matter is that?"

"Answer me, Trammel. When was the last time you or your guards here have walked among the humans? What do you understand of the modern world outside Thule?"

"Centuries."

I huffed and waved a hand and an image of New York City appeared in a shimmering mist in the air. Bevin made a pleased-sounding hum behind me. The image changed to downtown London. "The modern human world is different, Trammel. They are connected by technology, educated in the arts and medicine." Each time I spoke, an image appeared to illustrate. "They have modern weaponry, some of which I saw on your island, tossed away like junk. You have no clue what will happen if you start a war in the modern world, do you?"

"Only a weak human would try to frighten a Slaugh, *Keena*."

This time he *had* insulted me. I spun around and kicked him square in the jaw. I had to jump to do so but I connected with the brittle bones of his face. He hit the ground. Again Jordan stood as Trammel's guards came to his side to get him to his feet. He waved them off and laughed as he got up. "We understand one another, priestess. Go on."

I changed the image to a shot of a huge explosion. "Trammel...this is a nuclear explosion. Do you know this kind of weapon?"

"I've heard of such a thing."

"Then you understand that the frail, corrupt human governments wield enough power to use such weapons. They will panic when resources are short and blame other governments and they will attack one another. They are not open-minded enough to do anything else."

"So?" He crossed his arms.

"These weapons will destroy *all* humanity, Trammel. Not reduce the population, not kill off a percentage of them. These weapons destroy land, people, animals, oceans—everything for hundreds of miles, and leave the earth poisoned for centuries to come." I saw understanding start to show on his black, wrinkled face. "There are enough of these weapons to destroy the world several times over."

"That is ridiculous! Why would a government have them if they will destroy themselves by using them?"

I had to laugh. He was right. "I never said it was smart. I simply give you a situation to consider. If you start meddling with the humans the way you have in centuries past, the human governments will panic and they will destroy the planet itself. I would hazard to guess that's why Nessum and Bran did not do so, wouldn't you?" I walked around him again. He studied the image of the nuclear explosion for a moment.

"I'm not sure I believe you," he finally said.

"Fine. Don't." He turned his head but not his body to face me at his side, eyes glowing again. "It is two weeks until All Hallow's. I will be facing Feldema."

"Still? Even though you have held her prisoner?"

"I still have to follow our laws to succeed Doran. We will still fight. Take the next two weeks to study modern humans. See for yourself if I speak the truth. Return for All Hallow's and we'll discuss."

"If you release Feldema, Nessum may come back to us." He sounded almost excited.

"You take the next two weeks and study, understand? You may find you no longer need the oppression of Nessum."

"Nessum has protected and led the Slaugh for all times, priestess. The turmoil since he left has been…difficult." He almost spilled something but he was following the path I wanted him to, so I didn't push to find out what it was. "If he returned, we would welcome his leadership."

"I think you're strong enough to lead on your own. You've taken out the entire upper ranks of your society and managed to control the lower. You have managed that by might, Trammel. Take some time to learn to lead them with wits as well."

"I accept the compliment, priestess, and return it." He looked back at the image of the explosion. "I suppose we have let those who led us keep us uninformed. I accept. At All Hallow's, we will return for your festivities."

"Trammel," I said, as Doran and the others stood and made their show of a bow. "I would request a truce until then. No more assassination attempts against me or mine."

"I assure you, priestess, I have ordered no such attempts. If some of mine have done so, I will stop it for the truce." The Slaugh returned the bows and filed out of the room.

I turned around to face the platform. All of them were staring at me in stunned silence. "Can we eat now? I'm starving."

Doran raised an eyebrow. "By all means."

* * * * *

We all sat around a large oval table in one of the dining rooms. Abbey had joined us and there were several other house Imps fussing with the meal. I was famished, so I had already finished my salad as the others regaled her with tales of my performance at the meet.

"Keena," Bevin said from across the table. "When did your magic get so…"

"Good?" I supplied for her. "A while back." I took another bite of steak. Cliona sat next to her, twirling a wineglass and looking amused.

Abbey piped up. "She can do much better than just a picture show, Bevin."

Doran leaned over her plate and put her elbows on either side of it. "Then why do you not display it more often, niece?"

"I didn't realize I needed to." It was an honest answer.

"What do you mean?" She really looked perplexed.

"I don't know. I see Witches do almost everything with magic or spells. I'm just not used to doing things that way. If I need to close a door, I get up and close it. It just doesn't occur to me to use magic unless I *really* don't want to get up and close the damn door."

"But," Doran argued, "it would show others your powers if you used them more often."

"I don't feel the need to show off. Using my magic for every little thing would be showing off." She still looked perplexed, and so did most everybody else.

Jordan said, "It's part of you, Keena. It wouldn't be showing off." He put more potatoes on my plate without even realizing what he had done. Cliona laughed. He shot her an evil look.

"*Part* of me, yes." I wasn't sure I could explain it to them. "I was stronger and faster than most human kids in school. But I was clumsy too, so that strength and speed could backfire on me sometimes. My father, my human father, taught me that flaunting things that I was better at would only make others resent me. So I didn't flaunt. It's the same now. I can use magic, but I choose to do so only when I must. Abbey and I practice in the woods often, but it's more like playtime."

Bevin looked at Abbey. "How good is she now?"

Abbey looked to me and I shrugged.

She looked around at the others. "If you leave out potions…in my opinion? Better than Doran."

Cliona spilled her wine and Jordan coughed. Bevin and Doran exchanged a quick glance. Doran tilted her head and gave Abbey a look that said *you work for me*. "When were you going to let us in on that little secret?"

Abbey straightened. "No one asked *my* opinion and I didn't feel it my place to report on Keena. She shows everyone around her respect and friendship. I wished to return that. If you'd asked about her progress, I would have told you."

"So you don't gossip about our priestess?" Bevin asked jokingly.

"Only if it's something she wishes gossiped about." She took a drink from her little wineglass.

"It's another of my secret weapons," I mused—and used my magic to lift the wine bottle and refill my glass and Jordan's. Bevin watched with wide eyes. "Now back to business. Nessum is the wild card." The bottle moved up the table to Doran's glass as I spoke.

Bevin said "oh my" as she followed its progress.

"You think he'll show for All Hallow's?" Cliona asked.

"I think he may show before then."

I was looking at Cliona, not the bottle. Jordan and the rest were still watching as it moved smoothly from one glass to another around the table. "Remarkable," Bevin muttered as it filled hers and came to rest beside her glass.

Being able to cast and hold a spell while talking and thinking about other things was becoming second nature. These days I had to hold up walls to Jordan at the same time as well. It was still sometimes difficult, but it was coming faster and faster.

"Is that enough showing off for you, Doran?" Abbey said.

"It'll do. Keena, I must really apologize yet again. I had no idea you had grown so much over these last few weeks. I was worried about your heartbreak and your…"

"Human sensibilities?"

"Yes." She looked ashamed as she held her hands up, clearly unnerved that she'd not paid more attention to my progress.

"Let's just say I threw myself into my work to avoid the personal issues. Coyle and Abbey have been helping. Now you know. So let's get back to Nessum." I kept my poker face but inside I wanted to laugh, pleased I had surpassed their expectations.

"You think he'll show before All Hallow's?" Jordan asked again.

I looked at him. "You don't? How many guards were on Feldema before my midnight visit from Dannaiva?"

"Two."

"And now?" I asked.

Jordan looked as surprised at my question as the others. Seems *he* didn't know me as well as he thought either. "Six. Two in the observation room and four in the cell corridor."

"So *you* think he's likely to come for her too."

"I'm not sure we can stop him if he does. I'm really only hoping they have time for someone to notify me if he shows."

He didn't look happy about leaving his men in such a situation.

I turned back to Doran. "Where would he go and why?"

"He's a Dark Angel, Keena. He can go anywhere he wants, on this earth or any of the realms of the Demons. I wouldn't even be able to guess."

"Okay, then let's stick to the why," I said.

"Why?"

"*Why* hasn't he already retrieved Feldema, if she's what he really wants? If she's not what he really wants, than that would explain why he hasn't come for her—but *why* abandon her, and the Slaugh? Why leave Thule in such a mess?"

They all looked around, waiting for someone to answer. When no one ventured a guess, I continued. "If we figure out the whys, then we'll know what he's planning. How do we find out the why?"

Doran pushed her plate away. "I'll see if I can talk to Feldema again."

Jordan chimed in. "Maybe we can find another Slaugh who'll talk. They may not know the where, but they may have a clue about the why. I've got a few informants in the Gremlins. They haven't given up anything yet, but I'll push 'em a little harder."

Chapter Twenty

ℬ

The rest of the evening, the group traded ideas about why Nessum might have left. Not one of the theories any better than another. The exercise left us all frustrated. Frustration and several glasses of wine made me a little restless. We all said our good nights and headed back to our rooms to turn in. "I really need a run," I said to Jordan, taking his hand.

"Not a chance, little girl." He kept walking toward my chambers.

Tilting my head to look up at his face, I gave him the best pout I could through the wine buzz. He drew his eyebrows together and shook his head. "Not going to work, I can't keep up with you." He was right. The man was built for power and strength, not speed.

"Fine, a walk then. I really need to be outside for a while. I want to feel the forest around me. Please?"

He huffed. "Okay, but just a walk."

We headed into the forest and I dropped the high heels at the edge of the woods. He picked them up and took my hand to keep me at his pace. Inhaling deeply, I let the night cleanse my lungs. Bats fluttered their wings in the distance as they did their midair dance to catch insects. A raccoon led her kits through the undergrowth ahead to get them out of our way. I felt alive and free, even walking. I fought the urge to take off and run.

"No you don't," Jordan interrupted. I'd had my wall up to his thoughts so he must have felt the tension in my body.

"Just a walk," I said, heading in the direction of the clearing by the well. It was nice, almost like a real date or something, but the entire time my legs were itching to go.

We meandered, not talking, simply walking and enjoying each other's company. He even tried to help me through the thicker part of the woods, lifting me over a downed tree and holding my hand to cross a creek. Jordan was domineering and overbearing where my protection was concerned, but he was also trying to be a gentle lover. Cute.

"I've seen you change so much," he said as we met almost nose to nose as he lifted me.

"You have?" I asked, looking at him. His face softened for just a moment, that tender look I knew was just for me.

"I've seen you through much of your life, just like Manus. I witnessed your graduation from college, your jobs. When I couldn't be there for the bigger things, Manus reported to me."

"I never saw you." He sat on a massive downed tree and it brought him about to my eye level.

He laughed that arrogant laugh of his. "If you had seen me, I'd have not done my job, would I?"

"If you were such an admirer, how come I've been here for months and only recently met you?" I started walking. These emotions were making me uneasy. He had known me for years and I had just met him. He didn't answer. "Well?"

I looked back at his chiseled profile and saw something on his face I couldn't read. The mountain of a man sat still and looked like he would shatter if I touched him. But he said nothing. He started walking again, pulling me along with him.

"I'm not sure of the sensitive side of you, Jordan. I think I prefer the bossy, arrogant grump. At least then I know what to expect."

We hit the clearing and walked to the far end of it. "I think we should head back, Keena. It's late and you need some rest." He tried to sound stern but I had him figured out now. He was just as drawn to me as I was to him, maybe more so. I wouldn't see this side often and I could tell it made him uneasy. That was to my benefit.

He stepped into the circle I had made to create the potion for Howard the hawk's amulet. I swiftly closed the circle from the outside, trapping him in. Circles were used to call Demons and hold them, so when Jordan tried to leave the circle, he couldn't.

He looked shocked. "You closed a circle without ritual magic?"

I walked around the circle that held my own personal Demon. "I said I'd been practicing. You're the chief of WildLand security, Sarge, you should have known all this." I was teasing.

"Very funny, Keena. My people said you and the Imp were playing around in the woods."

I came right up to the edge of the circle and pressed a finger into it. The glowing bubble gave just a little. "Well, I guess your people had better learn the difference between girls playing in the woods and Witches practicing. We made it fun but we definitely had an agenda." I circled him again. "I guess I can go for a run now, can't I?"

The little vein in his temple started to pulse. "Keena, this is not funny. I can't protect you from in here. Now break the circle."

"I don't think so." I moved into the woods and started running. He was shouting all sorts of obscenities at me. I stayed close and only ran enough to feel the earth give beneath my feet and the woods come alive to me, the colors expanding and brightening. I don't know why running made it all seem so much more alive, but it did and I drank it all in.

The volume of his cursing let me know how far I was from the huge man in my circle. I also didn't know how far away I could be and still hold the circle closed, so I ran through the trees surrounding the clearing a couple times to stretch my legs. It wasn't all I wanted, but it was enough.

I made my way back to the clearing and broke the circle before I got all the way back to Jordan. He was seething and marched over to grab my arms below the shoulders and lift me off my feet. "Do not *ever* leave yourself unprotected like that again. Do you understand me?"

I should have been mad but I wasn't. After all, I had pissed him off and Cliona was right. It was kinda fun.

"Protecting me isn't your job anymore, Sarge." I wrapped my legs around his waist and used them to pull myself closer to him. His power rushed over me, sending shivers down my spine, and I purred at the feel of it. His hard, muscled body and his magic turned my body into an instant raging fire.

He raised his eyebrows and let go of my arms. I held myself in place with my legs tight around his waist, clenching my abs hard. I wrapped one arm around his neck and ran my other hand over his chest. He growled.

"The Vamp queen isn't here, is she? So it is still my job." His breath ran cold over the heat his power was pushing through me. I relaxed my legs, sliding intentionally slowly down his body, making him close his eyes as my mound passed over the bulge in his leather pants before dropping to my feet.

"Like that, do you?" I let my hand trail the length of his stomach and stop just above the top of his pants. He opened his eyes and looked down at me. I smiled sweetly. "Then catch me if you can."

And I took off running toward the manor.

"Temptress," he growled and came after me.

I kept it to a jogging pace to stay within sight of him. I was laughing freely, taking in the sounds and the essence of the night. I didn't think I would ever feel this free again after Tynan. But having Jordan grumbling behind me and the wind in my face was freeing. Joyful.

I felt a warning presence in the woods. A nearby squirrel jumped in alarm so I stopped suddenly and tried to listen over Jordan's footsteps. When he realized what I was doing, he stopped, immediately silent. "What is it?" he whispered and moved noiselessly up behind me, covering my body with his.

I turned my head just a bit to the left to listen. "Someone coming, quarter of a mile maybe."

Jordan lifted the earpiece he had taken out when we were talking and put it back in his ear. He mumbled a command and waited for responses. "One of mine." He had moved his arms possessively around my waist. I turned inside them and got up on my tiptoes to kiss his chin. He looked down and frowned at me. I pulled his head to mine and insisted on a full kiss. Obliging, he took the last moment of our time alone to try to convey his feeling in that kiss. His lips were warm, his tongue insistent in my mouth. I pulled away and turned as the incoming guard burst through the trees.

"Sir, there's another crime scene."

"Detail, Charles." Another guard came in from the left.

He had been closer to us. I knew it instinctively.

"Jordan!" I said, with a large hunk of anger attached to it.

He turned his attention to me, not happy that I'd interrupted his work, and gave me his terse look. "My lady?"

"Have your men been following us all evening?" My hands were on my hips.

"Of course. We have to keep you under surveillance at all times now. You understood that."

I did understand and I tried to keep myself calm. I had to get over the feeling of being trapped and realize the need for security. I thought of Manus in the bed with the huge scar. But I was still angry about my sudden lack of privacy and his casual attitude about it. "And if we had decided to play priestess and her boy toy?"

The two guards dressed like SWAT members were turning red-faced, trying not to laugh.

Jordan frowned deeply but didn't flinch. "Then they would have been in for a good show, my lady." He turned back to the red-faced men and gave them a look that evidently they had seen before. They went straight-backed and completely blank-faced. "Report, Charles," Jordan repeated in a smooth, stern voice.

"Another Witch. Sector two. Same M.O."

"How long?" he barked.

Charles answered with quick words. "Less than an hour, sir."

Jordan stood still for just an instant and then started barking orders into the small radio in his ear before pausing and turning back to his men. "Charles, Tomson, escort the priestess back to the manor," he ordered the guards as he started off in a different direction.

"I'm going with you," I argued.

"No. You are to go to your chambers. Cliona will meet you on the way."

He kept moving away from me and Charles nodded toward the manor. "My lady."

I walked beside Charles as he headed for the manor. Tomson trotted behind me. They were both Magicians, both beautiful though not as frail looking as many Magicians. Maybe Doran had a taste for the delicate-looking men. Either that, or Jordan had recruited all the bigger, more robust of the species on this island for his guards.

I felt to see if either had drawn a ward to keep me with them. None.

So they couldn't hold me...

I yanked the clear wiring from the radios in their vests before they'd even realized I had moved—and ran. I could hear them yelling and arguing back and forth with each other, but I kept running in the direction Jordan had gone. I didn't know where sector two was, but I was betting that Mister Efficient had taken the most direct path. Even running, his trail wasn't too difficult to follow. All I needed was a bent branch here, a disturbed bit of ground there.

Once in the open at the edge of town I lost his trail, but opened my mind to feel for others. Not far off to the south I felt the emotions and presence of several beings. Rounding the back of a small cottage, I saw Jordan just making it to the scene. I came up behind him quietly. One of his guards was bending over the body on the ground, holding the Witch, and when he looked up at Jordan, I saw the heat of anger and repressed tears in his eyes.

A second guard stood from his squatting position next to the distraught man. "Allen," Jordon said with all his authority. "Let go of the body."

The second man looked past Jordan to me. "He was her only consort." Jordan followed his gaze and growled at me then turned back to Allen, who was still holding the remains of his lover.

Jordan lowered his voice but didn't take the command out of it. "Allen, release her."

He started to say something else but I passed him and stood behind the guard, placing my hand on his shoulder. He looked from me to the body and then reluctantly let her go, gently placing her on the ground before standing and taking my hand. I walked him away from the others and pulled him into a hug. He dropped his gun and it clattered at my feet. Falling against me, the young man wrapped his arms around my waist and let his head drop to my shoulder. He was heavy, but not enough to knock me off balance. His pent-up tears quickly roared into loud, hard sobs.

I heard the other guard informing Jordan who the Witch was, and explain that she and Allen had been together for four years. Fortunately, Allen couldn't hear through his sobs. I ran my hands up and down his back as he cried, not offering any words. Nothing I could say was going to help.

Jordan shook his head and looked back toward us. I saw him stiffen at the sight of the man in my arms, but he went back to business without a word. I felt the horrible pain in the Magician's cries. He had obviously loved the Witch deeply. I couldn't help but think of Tynan. Would he have felt this kind of grief had I died on Thule? The thought made me even more relieved that I'd had a chance to let him go. I was lucky, he was lucky and a twist of fate turned a disaster into an opportunity.

An older Witch approached from behind. Allen was still weeping softly on my shoulder. She gave me a meek smile and put her hand on Allen's shoulder. He turned to her and his sobs slowed even more. She took his hand and led him away, giving me another meek smile and mouthing the words "thank you" as she left. I watched them until they rounded a corner and moved out of sight.

I stared for a moment at the corner of the cottage they had gone around and anger flowed over me. Had that poor Witch been killed because of me? I tromped over to Jordan, determined to help any way I could. That man's grief would not go unavenged, I promised myself. I grew madder with each step, hands fisting until my nails were drawing blood. Jordan was leaning over the body, trying to undo her shirt so he could look at the wound in her shoulder.

She was a tiny woman. Really much smaller than me. "She was only thirty-five," one of the other guards reported to Jordan.

He hadn't noticed me yet. His mind was intent. "A mere babe," he replied. I started to refute the statement since she was actually five years older than me, but I held my tongue.

Unfortunately, that was when my gaze found the top of her torso—and the pool of dark red blood just under the stump that was once her neck. Her lover had held her so tightly I hadn't noticed. Muscles and bones that were never intended to see light glistened in the moonbeams.

I looked down to see some of the blood that had transferred to the guard now staining my leather top. I felt my knees go weak.

Needing to move, I followed the thick trail of blood across a patch of glossy grass that had the same eerie red and found the missing part of the Witch. Her face permanently etched in a silent scream, her eyes glazed with terror. Another large pool of blood had soaked into her blonde hair, making the strands look like angry serpents.

I had to put my hand out to steady myself. Jordan had appeared beside me and I found his shoulder without looking away from the silent scream. He put his hand on mine and squeezed. I looked away from her face to his. He had that soft look I was learning to crave.

My stomach lurched and I turned and ran to the spot I had held Allen. I fell to my knees and let my stomach go. I hurled until there was nothing but bile. Jordan held my hair away from my face and rubbed my back, not saying a word. I tried to remind myself to thank him for that later.

Cliona came out of the woods and rushed to me. Jordan helped me up and pushed me into her embrace. She felt every bit as strong as he did. "Take her home." His tone was soft. I looked at him. He touched my cheek. "Go on. I'll take care of her, Keena. Go home."

I turned back to Cliona and she pulled me off toward the manor.

When we hit the yard, I ran past the guard at the door and into my bathroom. I washed my face and brushed my teeth. I looked in the mirror and saw only that poor Witch's face. I didn't even get her name. I stepped out as Abbey came into the room with all the necessary ingredients to make margaritas. "I didn't hear what her name was. She died because of me…and I don't even know her name."

Cliona made herself a drink and flopped into one of the chairs. "I don't think this is about you." She took a slow sip. "This one didn't even resemble you. You weren't in the area. The killings are unrelated."

"She was small and blonde but…" I was still standing by the bed, holding on to the large wooden post. The shadow of a guard passed by outside the door.

"There was another killing a while back," Cliona divulged. "The Witch was out in the woods. It looked like an animal attack. Her throat was gone but her head was still attached. I'm guessing we have a serial killer on the island. Manus and his friend were attacked not because of you, but because they were in the wrong place at the wrong time. Jordan will probably agree when he gets back."

"Great. A serial killer on top of everything else. He'll never let me out of the room again." I quickly changed into my trusty leathers and a tank then went to the table and poured the tequila straight into one of the margarita glasses, taking down about half in one drink. When I closed my eyes to let the burn of the alcohol slide down my throat, I saw the poor Witch's face.

"Damn," Abbey said. "At least you can hole up in here with the hulk."

I huffed.

Cliona took a big drink of hers to match mine. "First time you've seen so much blood?"

"Blood? No. It's not the blood. The…" I couldn't think of what to say.

"Body?" she finished.

"Yeah, I still see it when I close my eyes." I raised the glass and finished the drink. Cliona refilled it.

Abbey started to say something but Cliona gave her a stern look. "Drinking's good right now, Abbey. Really good."

Abbey raised her own glass. "To numbness."

Cliona and I lifted our glasses and we all took healthy swigs.

"To Tynan," I said. "I miss the dark Vamp."

Cliona and Abbey lifted their glasses. "To Tynan," Cliona echoed loudly. Then she continue, softer, "Not to worry, Witch. A connection that strong cannot be severed for eternity."

I smiled at the thought but drowned that childish kind of wishful thinking away with another shot.

We made several other toasts before the effects of the tequila eased my anxiety. Abbey started to share some of her favorite gossip as we slowly slipped into a wonderful state of drunkenness.

"You know," Cliona slurred. "You get under the Sarge's skin even more than I do."

I took another long drink, no longer affected by the burn of the tequila. "If I didn't know better, Cliona, I'd say you were jealous." Abbey looked to her for a huge denial. There was a moment of silence then we all laughed heartily.

"I am. Well...I *was*." She lifted her glass. "To Sarge!" We joined her. Then she said, "I could have done him, you know. There aren't many men who can stir this cold blood. Jordan was one of them."

Abbey had crawled up on the table and pulled herself upright enough to prop against the upside-down ice bucket. "Why didn't you? You can have damn near any man you want."

Cliona waved her off, knocking over her empty glass. She proceeded to set it upright. It only took two tries before she could pour more tequila into it. "I can't stand wimpy guys. They have to be at least as strong as me or..." She made a raspberry sound like a child.

We laughed at her. "That doesn't leave many...except for other Vamps," Abbey said.

"Tell me. Vamps are all medieval though. They want to take you on forever. Well...unless you're just a human snack. But with the few of us female Vamps, they want some kind of lifetime bond. They get all...*you* know, Keena."

"I do!" I managed to laugh out.

Abbey started to slip off her bucket. "Then why not Jordan?"

"He was in love with the pretty priestess here." I gawked at her. "Plus, we work together too much. I wouldn't be able to trust him as backup if I thought he was looking at my ass instead of the bad guys. You know what I mean?"

"No. Whadda ya mean he was in love wiff me?" I slurred.

"He talked about you way before you came into your powers. I saw it in his big silver eyes. He's been waiting for you. Yes he has. And now he's mad at you."

I sat up as straight as I could and took another big swig. "Why the hell is he mad at me?"

"You don't love him back. And Mister Big Ol' Ego can't stand it!" She laughed riotously and put her head down on the table.

"How can I love some guy I just met? He's yummy and all, but geez." I waved my hand to push her away even though I didn't come close to touching her. "And anyway, how do you know I don't love him?"

She lifted her head off the table. "You didn't mark him, Keena. Your joining didn't mark him. He's gotta be upset. Your body marked Tynan at your first joining, but you didn't mark Jordan. He thinks you've made him a onesie."

"A *what*?"

"A onetimer. Someone you don't really want as a real consort." She laughed out loud. "That's why I called him a boy toy. I was just egging him on, but—"

"Oh my God!" I tied to stand, to move, but only succeeded in falling to the floor. We all laughed. From the floor, I tried to talk through my laugher. "I called him a boy toy in the woods." I was still laughing and had to catch my breath before continuing. "And two of his men heard!" I kept laughing—but they didn't. "Oops."

"*Keena*! You didn't!" Abbey's eyes were huge.

"I didn't know! How can I tell my body who to mark and who not to?"

Cliona helped me up, all of sudden looking much more sober than she had before. "Subjects can formally request the mark, like I did. But your *body* will also mark those you love. You marked Tynan because you loved him."

"He had just pledged an eternity to save my stupid life. Of *course* I loved him, for that if nothing else."

She cocked her head to the side and rolled her eyes. She was considering the facts. "Either way, you didn't mark Jordan—and you made it clear to him and his men that you have no intention to. He will certainly think you mean him to be a onesie."

With all the Latin and serious names for everything around here, that was such a childish name for a one-night stand. It made me giggle even more. Until I realized that I had hurt Jordan unintentionally. I felt bad but could still feel laughter coming over me. "Maybe it'll curb his arrogance," I laughed, and they laughed with me once more.

"That wouldn't hurt any, but really, Keena," Abbey said. "You don't want to leave things like this."

Cliona poured me another glass, emptying the second bottle of tequila. "The man *does* really love you. I think if you look inside your heart, the Witch part of your heart, you'll know that you wouldn't have been attracted to him if you didn't have true affection for him."

I sat there a minute and thought it over. They were quiet and a little wobbly as they watched me work out my own emotions. I *did* have feelings for the overbearing hulk of a man. How was that?

"See," Cliona explained, "your heart is that of a Witch, your blood burns for men you love. You'll feel that burn many times in your life. Take advantage of it. Many of us envy that in Witches. Makes life much more—"

"Sexy!" Abbey blurted. "Let's get out of here, Vamp. I think she has some apologizing to do." She tried to start gathering the remains of the evening and dropped or spilled more than she got on the tray.

While I watched her, I opened my mind to Jordan and called to him. "Leave it, Abbey," I said. "We'll get it later."

Abbey left. Cliona lounged across the bed. Jordan didn't come.

We sat for a while longer. He still didn't come.

"I guess he *is* mad," I said, slumping down in my chair.

"Go to him," she said very matter-of-factly.

I slung open one of the French doors and Charles spun to attention and then relaxed when he realized it was me. "Take me to your leader!" I demanded. Cliona laughed behind me.

"Ma'am?"

"Geez, lighten up, Charles. Is that your last name or first?"

"Ma'am?" He stood stiff with his weapon at the ready.

"Nevermind. Take me to Jordan." He still looked at me, puzzled. "*Now*, Charles."

"Yes, ma'am!"

I started to follow but I couldn't keep my feet from trying to run off by themselves. He took my arm and escorted me around the garden and down the main drive. Cliona was giggling behind me and making comments about Charles' butt. I was trying to keep a straight face but kept slipping into stupid giggles.

Jordan opened the door to his home with a huff. "Sir," Charles said meekly. "The priestess insisted on seeing you."

Jordan's gaze found its way to Charles' arm, slung around my waist. Charles pulled his arm away as if burned and I almost fell, but Jordan caught me as I stumbled forward, my hands falling on the pythons he called arms.

"Oooh!" I said with glee, squeezing them.

"Dismissed," Jordan said to the guard standing in his doorway.

"Sir?" he questioned.

He groaned again. I swear I made that man growl and groan constantly. "I'll watch over the priestess tonight. The killings are not related to her." His voice got more rigid as he explained.

Cliona caught Charles around the shoulders and started to walk him away. "You off for the night, sailor?" she asked.

I laughed against Jordan's chest muscles. He had removed his shirt and evidently showered. I was captured in the feel and scent of his skin, clean and spicy, all male. I looked up at his face. He still looked displeased and I remembered why I was there. I straightened myself as best I could while swaying. "I came to apologize to you, sir." I hiccupped.

"You're smashed."

Not a question, so I kept going, trying to ignore his rippling stomach muscles. His lip did a little quiver thing that usually meant he was trying not to laugh at me. I put my little wall back up as best as possible. "I have been informed that I inad... inaddve... That I insulted you. I am truly sorry. I had no intent...of making you a onesie."

He cringed at that last part. He started to talk but I put my hand up. "No. I mucked this up. I have to fix it. I don't know why, because we fight like angry badgers, but I want you all time. Over there on that couch would be a good place to start."

He just stood there looking at me. I couldn't read either of his faces. They were both a little fuzzy. "I accept," he finally said.

I took a second to let that sink in. The time didn't help. "The apology or the couch?"

"The apology. You're too drunk to take advantage of on the couch."

I pouted and tried to get closer to him. I attempted a sultry walk but managed only an awkward stumble and fell against him instead. "How about we finish that dance then?" I asked. "Music?"

After giving me a frustrated sigh, he held me steady to make sure I wasn't going to fall. Watching me as he moved away, he started music that was much like that in the club, just not as loud. He moved himself back into position and started swaying us together to the beat. Slow. Steady. And sexy. His thick, muscled leg was rubbing very nicely between mine. The feel of it went a long way toward breaking up the tequila haze in my head. He put his hand on my stomach as he had in the club and let his Demon power spread and move over me. It was hot, like tiny little fires dancing on my skin. I let myself lean back and feel his magic move through me. Every nerve jumped as the power stroked them.

The beat slowed even further and he moved our hips in a delicious, churning, circular motion. I felt my body heating up. Burning for him. The feel of his magic coursing over me, the rolling of his hips, brought life back to me. The tequila was gone, replaced by his power pulsing through my veins. I managed to drag my gaze from where our bodies met to his eyes. The silver swirling in them was like molten metal, his pupils tiny and his expression filled with hunger.

I leaned as far back as I could and pressed myself harder to his erection. He groaned. I opened the place where I had found my own Demon power and let it free. It thrust out abruptly but I quickly pulled back. He gasped as it hit him full force then rolled gently, as his had done. I had no idea how my power would feel for him, but hoped it had the same effect his had on me. To make him burn.

It must have, since he pulled me back up and took me into a hard, possessive kiss. His tongue demanded entrance to my mouth. His hand moved through my hair, pulling my head back, making his access to my mouth easier. The kiss sizzled. I had to pull back to catch my breath. He gave me only a second and kissed me again.

His hands roamed across my back, leaving streaks of heat as they left one place and found another. He pulled back this time and moved to my collarbone and started trailing kisses over my exposed shoulder. I started to remove my tank. He stopped me. "Not this time, Keena. We rushed last time. This time, I get to play a little."

I couldn't get any words to form, to either argue *or* agree. He lifted me and carried me toward the bedroom. I got a good look around his place. It wasn't that big, much like a two-bedroom apartment. But it was immaculately clean, not a thing out of place. All the furniture was bland, sturdy and sensible. It fit him perfectly.

That was, until we made it through the bedroom door. The music was also piped into the bedroom — in this case, more bed than room. The darn thing was bigger than mine, bigger than any bed I'd ever seen.

The room was dark navy. Hell, maybe it was pitch-black. The walls, the floor, the bed...everything was dark. There was a neat ebony dresser one either side of the bed and fanciful paintings of Demons on the walls. The paintings were in brilliant colors that stood out on the dark paint. The bedspread also had an image of a ferocious Demon in the same bold colors. A soft light glowed from a source I couldn't find, making his tanned skin glow and the swirl of his eyes look incandescent.

He watched my face as I looked around, still in his arms. "The true nature of a Demon is in his lair," he said with his arrogant tone.

"What does this say about your nature?" I asked, suddenly caught up in the swirling of his silver eyes.

"You can tell me that when you get to leave here." He smiled a genuine smile that gave away his thoughts. "I remember your fantasies, my lady. Don't forget that." With that, he threw me on the bed. He stood on the foot of it. Not on the floor, but on the bed, the ceiling more than high enough to accommodate his six-foot-six-inch height. He undid the button on his pants. I crawled over and took the zipper from his hand and pulled it down, watching his face as I pulled the opening apart to find he'd not bothered with underwear after his shower.

"Commando!"

"Yes," he said and let the pants fall from his hips. I gave a greedy gawk at the sight before me. The ridge of muscles just above his hips was too enticing not to touch. I ran my fingers along them and followed the journey down his lower stomach to the treasure below. I took that beautiful cock in my hand and he dropped to his knees so he could kiss me again as I moved my hands over his tight skin. Rock-hard and satiny smooth all at the same time—and not just his cock. His whole body was taut. He moved against the rhythm of my hand, reacting to the slightest touch, thrusting into my fist. The responsiveness was such an aphrodisiac. His stomach muscles tightened as he made low, grunting noises. Cauldrons, I loved that stomach.

I kissed my way down his chest, lingering over his tight nipples and nibbling them. I kept up the stoking and he gave no sign that he would take control. I ran my tongue along the line of each of those stomach muscles that I had fantasized over so many times, weaving a path to the small indentation of his bellybutton. He moved us around, putting his back to the headboard without breaking the motion of my hand or his thrusting. Then he purposefully fell backward, leaving me between his muscled thighs.

He was completely naked and I was still fully dressed. I was there for his pleasure at that moment and I didn't mind at all. After all, this was an apology, wasn't it?

I looked into his eyes as I took as much of that hungry cock as I could into my mouth. I couldn't take all of it. But he growled that throaty growl in appreciation of my efforts to do so. I *really* loved the sound of that growl. I pulled back, little bits at a time, stopping to run the tip of my tongue around his head. When I reached the end I let his head linger on my lips, his juices dripping from my lips. I moaned at the feel of his taut skin.

I was still watching his reaction and noted his face was now completely relaxed and blissful. I ran my lips along the side of his shaft and watched his eyes roll back from the sensation. I took as much of him as I could again, loving to watch him watching me. I felt the first hint of him losing control to the pleasure I was giving him. His hips arched and his stomach clenched.

He reached down and pulled me up to straddle his waist. "*I'm* in control tonight. Remember, little girl?" he said. He was a wide man and my legs were stretched around his stomach, the leather of my pants straining. "Strip for me, princess."

The order caught me off guard for just a moment. But I was still apologizing, so I stood on the end of the bed. I moved to the music and erotically removed my outfit. I dropped each piece on his stomach as he watched me with those hungry eyes. He took time to gave over every part of me. Each spot his gaze landed tingled from the power of his eyes. It was the boldest, most erotic thing I'd every experienced.

Once all my clothes were piled on his stomach, I continued to move with the music. He didn't move to stop me. He watched with that wanting look on his powerful face and enjoyed. I didn't feel insecure or awkward. For once I felt graceful, beautiful, even exotic. I let the feeling take me and moved to dance over him, dipping myself low, teasing, taunting.

He pushed the clothes to the floor and raised one hand to lightly trail up the inside of one of my thighs. His power surged from his fingertips, sending fire straight to my pussy. Heating me to a state of arousal I couldn't have ever imagined. I dipped down hard, making his big hand move closer to the part of me that wanted his touch the most. I felt his knuckle glance off my clit.

"Not yet," he whispered. "Let your power go, Keena. Let the Demon power consume you." I took in a deep breath and let the rhythm of the sensual music take control of the movements of my body. I opened myself again, found that spot down in my belly where the Demon power lived and called it. It surged, forcing Jordan to take in a raspy breath. The only place we were touching was where my ankles touched his sides. I was dancing above his stomach, facing him, watching him. Trying to see what my newfound freedom did to him, *for* him.

I pulled the energy back and let it roll out in waves over him, until I could feel my own power moving across my skin. I dipped down, letting my head fall forward and my long hair dangle across his chest.

My power was warm like his as it drifted between us, but different. More like electricity, it had a blue aura to it, a light, shimmering blue. It felt wonderful as it rolled over and off me and then across his skin. He was writhing in it, thrusting his pelvis into the air. Eyes closed, head pushed back on the black pillows, he looked like he was going to come just from fucking my power.

"Your magic feels like the ley lines. Cauldrons, Keena!" His voice was low and throaty. He sat up and pulled me down over him, sliding his hand between my legs and through the small nest of auburn hair. He groaned again in pleasure as he felt my wetness. He lifted me by the waist and lowered me ever so slowly onto that cock.

I sent another wave of power over him just as the tip of it was inside me. He dug his fingers into my waist. "Careful, woman, or this won't be so gentle."

"Who said I wanted gentle?" I asked and let it flow again. It was met by his surge of fire over my skin. I sat myself hard on him, pushing his shaft all the way inside me. His eyes rolled completely back and his head fell backward, hands releasing my hips. I leaned down and ran my tongue over his left nipple and then started to ride him.

With a rhythm that matched the music, I slowly ground in circles. His cock mirrored that motion inside me. The slow torture was good, but I wanted all his Demon strength tonight. I lifted myself up and slid back down. Tightening my pussy over his shaft as I sank onto him. His head swung from one side to the other with each stoke. I gained speed and increased the force each time I lowered myself on his cock.

It didn't take long for him to start thrusting upward to meet me, our magics rolling over each other each time we plunged together. I was near screaming, gasping for breath, clawing at his chest as I held on to him. The combination of our natural chemistry and the magic was exquisite.

I couldn't hold on any longer and let my orgasm wash over both of us. He growled again and rolled us on the huge bed. He took control and went back to a steady grinding that outpaced the music and felt divine. I heard myself crying out each time he plunged into me, filling me completely. He took in a deep breath, slowed and let his power roll over me. I felt the waves of another orgasm and I dropped my wall to his mind to let him feel what I felt.

He cried out my name as he felt the walls come down and his sensations mixed with mine. He tried to hold back, lifting his head and cursing, but I felt him expand inside me, his whole body tense. He groaned loudly, sending even more chills through my body as he came.

"That was the most intense thing I've ever felt!" he breathed out between deep, fast breaths.

"You've been in others' heads during sex, haven't you?" I was just as breathless.

He nodded, still breathing hard on my neck. "Yeah, but no one ever had the... They didn't..."

"Enjoy you as much as I did?" I finished for him. My body started to remember how to breathe again.

"That's it," he half-laughed, half-coughed as he pulled out of me slowly and sat back on his haunches, looming over me.

"Good." I ran my fingers down his stomach, lightly tickling. "Well, lookey there."

He looked down to see the shadow of my sun tattoo across his hips and over his abdomen. He touched it timidly, as if it would disappear if he rubbed it.

Then he graced me with the biggest smile I had ever seen on his face, and let his body fall to the side. I fell asleep on his chest, Jordan softly rubbing my side with his rough hand. Completely sated and completely happy with the big, arrogant oaf.

Chapter Twenty-One

ဆ

"Great cauldrons, Keena, if you destroy any more amulets, the shop in town will be on backorder. Now concentrate!" Bevin sounded amused as she chastised me. Manus laughed that furball laugh from my bed. He had healed almost completely in the last couple weeks and was back to prowling around my room and being my guardian. Cliona had gone back to Romania to arrange for her band of Vamps to be here for All Hallow's, and the rest of the island was deep in preparations for the festivities.

"I don't understand. I've read and reread all the potions. I've gone out, found old grimoires and studied. I just can't get the magic to do the right things." I dropped the split amulet on the table that had been turned into a makeshift altar to the goddess. "Geez, this is frustrating."

"Relax, honey," she sighed. "It's a good thing you're not battling Feldema with potions though."

"Funny." I started to clean up the mess, again.

"Keena, really," Manus said. "Your powers and your magic are so strong since you and Jordan started...um...."

"Yes?" I said over Bevin's head. "Manus, what would you like to say?"

He lowered his head. "I'm just saying that you don't really need potions when you can levitate a boulder or thrust lightning out of your fingers. I wouldn't worry about it."

Bevin blushed. "He's right, child. I would like to see you have a better appreciation for the art, but you have gained so much from Jordan that I am continually amazed each day when we find something new."

"I would have rather not found out about the lightning by scalding Jordon's ass," I huffed and flopped into the chair.

"He goads you so. He deserved it. I don't get why you two have to fight like, well...cats and dogs." Manus licked his paw and rubbed his ear.

Bevin giggled. I had to stop and make sure I heard it correctly. She didn't giggle often. "You two do have fire. I had a man like that once, Keena. Keep hold. He'll keep you young, that one will."

"He'll be the death of me is what he'll be. I swear, he is the most arrogant man I've ever known." I packed a few more things into the bag I keep for potions. The leather was stained green from accidentally turning a sleeping potion into some foul goo, and the side had a large burn from turning a healing salve into some sort of living acid.

"He's a good match for your wits, girl, and you know it or you would have tossed him out long before now. You like his fire as much as he likes yours. Hot sex, I presume?" Bevin asked with a completely serious look.

Manus hacked up a real furball trying to laugh. I just let my mouth fall open as the little old Witch waited for an answer. "Yes" was all I could say.

"All is well then," she said and took her things and left. Manus was rolling on the bed.

I let my mind drift to the hot sex part and opened my mind to Jordan, just enough for him to see what I was thinking. I pictured myself bent over his work desk, with him behind me. Then I closed my mind to him again. And smiled.

"At least things aren't dull around you, priestess," Manus said and stretched out to take a nap.

Within moments the door was flung open and Jordan stood there, his face clouded with desire. Manus jumped up. "I'm outta here." He dashed off the bed and headed out the open door.

"I asked you *not* to do that to me while I'm working, woman." He had that sexy growl in his voice.

"You're done early then?" I asked, getting up and heading toward the open door, trying to make a show of escaping him. I had truly tortured him a couple times while he was on duty by letting him see my little daydreams. He repaid me with the fulfillment of those daydreams. He stomped up behind me and wrapped one of his huge arms around my chest as the other undid my jeans and pushed them to my knees. I kicked them off as he dropped his pants to the ground and removed his boots. He ripped my shirt off, then his own. Lifting me against his chest, he carried me over to the nearest wall and bent me forward, bracing himself against me.

"I left a little early. Things were quiet. But you didn't know that." He slid his free hand over my rear and between my legs, finding me wet and ready. He growled again. Cauldrons, I loved the feel of that sound rumbling over me. "You're such a little prick-tease." He pushed inside me as he said it. Not slow and easy but hard and dominating.

I closed my eyes and had to suck in a great deal of air. I felt his power rush over me and mine responded automatically. He groaned at it. I opened my mind to him, to let him feel how I loved to have him inside me, to let my pleasure mix with his.

He pushed harder and harder to find the right rhythm and thrusts to maximize my experience, reading my mind to twist or tilt to meet my needs. It was wonderful. His skin was heated, his scent filled the room.

I opened my eyes and glanced out the open door to my right. The ley line was drifting just outside. Recently it seemed to be attracted to our magic as we enjoyed each other. It drew closer and closer. I reached out to it and it drifted into the room…to my fingers…

Jordan yelled at the pop of electricity as my magic mixed with the power of the ley line. Things went black for a second and then we were spinning and drifting through nothingness.

He managed to pull out of me and hold me to his chest as we landed in a strange place.

We were standing in a small, cold, ankle-deep creek. The air around us was fuzzy with the silvery blue of the ley. The terrain on either side of the creek was barren, covered in jagged rocks as far as the eye could see—a huge field of gray desolation and stale air. The sand in the creek was soft but if we had to negotiate the rocks we wouldn't be able to on bare feet.

"You've pulled us into another realm," Jordan whispered, as we stood and looked around.

"Realm?" My heart started pounding. "Okay. That sounds bad."

"A Demon realm, Keena." He turned me to him. He looked down at me and kissed my head.

"How'd I do *that*? I thought half-Demons couldn't go to other realms? Hell, I'm one-quarter at most!"

"You keep changing the rules on us."

"Okay...how do we get back? What realm is it?"

He ran his hand through his buzzed hair and shook his head. "You've got me there. This is a first for me."

The rocks behind us rumbled and he spun, putting his naked body in front of mine in a protective stance. "Maybe Karackos pulled us here. I *did* touch the line."

"Not good either."

A booming voice came from all around us. "Jordan of Foras, I have summoned thee!"

"It's for you, dear," I said, trying to trace the direction of the voice. Hearing him being referred to by his full Demon name did nothing to calm my nerves. He straightened and his shoulders seemed to spread even wider.

Man, he was sexy when he went all warrior.

"Your walls, lover," he groaned.

"Sorry, but we *are* naked." I was trying very hard not to be frightened and the sight of his muscled back had provided a bit of a distraction.

The voice came clearly from in front of us this time, with a hint of laughter in it. "You are most definitely of my lineage, Jordan of Foras." A huge creature moved up from out of the rock, as though he had been a part of it. We had probably looked directly at him and didn't even see him. He was the same texture as the jagged limestone, but he took the shape of a very big man. His form was very similar to Jordan's but taller, bigger and covered in rock. Jordan looked back to make sure I was hidden from view.

"Your father?" I guessed from behind his back.

"My mother's Incubus. My father died years ago," Jordan said defiantly. "Why have you summoned me, Foras?"

The Demon growled. That sounded very familiar too. I suddenly had a toga-like garment on and so did Jordan. "I meant no disrespect to you," Foras said. I stepped around Jordan to get a better look. "Would you prefer a human form?" He changed as he said it, morphing into an eerie reflection of Jordan, only bigger and just a hint older, with longer hair. I heard Jordan take in a breath at the sight. "You have never summoned me, Jordan. All others of my lineage have done so at least once, yet you have never called."

"I've had no need of you." Jordan stood still, tall and sure of himself.

The Demon did laugh then, the sound echoing through the rocky terrain. "You have not, my boy, you have not. You have made me very proud. Others speak of you highly in the realms. And now," he gestured toward me. "Your woman —"

"Don't even *look* at her! As gatekeeper of the Underworld you don't have the privilege to look upon such beauty and goodness. Having come from such evil seed, I'm surprised I've been blessed enough to belong to her. Why have you brought us here? I will not bargain with you."

The Demon Lord actually looked down to avoid seeing me. I held tight to Jordan's hand. "I respect your wishes, son. I have nothing to bargain. I have merely brought you here for a warning. I owe you that since you have never summoned me. I also offer a gift for the priestess."

He held out his palm and a skull appeared in it. I recognized it immediately.

"You offer a gift of death, Foras? It's out of character for a Demon who is known for his superior logic." Jordon tried to move me back behind him.

"Jordan, no," I said, pushing past him. I stumbled trying to take the few steps through the water to get to the edge of the creek. Foras made no move to come closer.

Jordan growled and grabbed my arm. "Keena."

"It's my mother's skull. I lost it in the ocean on my way back from Thule." I looked at the skull with the split in the forehead and felt the pain of her death pour over me again. I reached a timid finger out to touch it. "How did you get it?"

Foras leaned toward me just enough to let me take the skull, while Jordan tightened his grip so he could pull me away if necessary. Foras nodded slightly for me to take it. "Another of my gifts is the ability to find treasure and lost items. You lost it, I am simply returning it."

"Thank you," I said as I took it carefully off his huge hand. The skull looked impossibly small in it. He nodded again and glanced up.

"And the warning?" Jordan's voice sounded wary.

Foras took his gaze from me and back to the ground. "The power she wields, especially when you are fuc—*joined*. It touches the ley and moves within it. I have felt it and recognized it as yours and that of the priestess. It is an intoxicating mix you two make." He sounded joyful again but barely looked up to see Jordan's expression. I saw pride in the face of the Demon Lord.

"I don't need *you* to tell me that, Foras." The Demon Lord lowered his glance at Jordan's words. That in itself showed a great respect to Jordan, but my half-Demon didn't relax a bit.

"I would imagine not, my son. But others feel it was well. They may be tempted to do as I have done and not have the same intentions. You must teach her to shield that power from the ley when you are joining. Her mind is far too open. She wields much power, but as she is a youngster, she is easy prey for other gatekeepers. I suspect she will be able to handle Karackos easily — but another lord or gatekeeper may be more trouble."

"You have proven that you mean no harm, Incubus," Jordan said.

Foras raised his head. His silver eyes perfectly matched Jordan's. My power reached for his unintentionally. I pulled it back but it was too late, he had felt it. His gaze met mine for just a split second and then flashed back to Jordan, trying to keep his word.

"Find her help, my boy, or she will be the wench of a Demon Lord not long after All Hallow's. The balance of power will not withstand such. If you have need of me, I would consider it an honor to teach the priestess to block out the mind of a Demon Lord." He raised a hand and we went spinning back to the unreal state of being between things. I looked around to try to see anything specific, but there was nothing there to see, just hints of things, of places and feelings.

We found ourselves back in my room, Jordan holding tight to me and me clutching the skull to my chest. I shivered. "It's okay, lover, we'll figure this out too."

"Um…how is that? I have two days until All Hallow's, the battle with Feldema, Nessum is still out there, Karackos, the Slaugh and now *this*. I'm running out of time and ideas."

"I know," he said, rubbing my head.

"One thing at a time, right?" That had become my mantra.

"Right." Then he cringed. "Maybe we should take Foras up on his offer to help. It's the quickest and easiest thing on the list."

I turned back to him. "That's not what you really want is it?"

He gave me that soft face I usually only see after a long, wonderful session of tremendous sex. "We can't just summon any of the Demon Lords for this. Some are the keepers of the gateways to Hell. None of them are to be trusted. I don't know any other Demons with that kind of power whom I trust any more than Foras right now, do you?

"Point."

"Let's go to the well for this."

"Now?" I'm not sure why I was shocked. Once Jordan made up his mind, he acted.

"We've got the banquet later, and tomorrow and All Hallow's are full of other official functions. It's now or never."

* * * * *

We went to the well after changing and gathering my tool kit for ritual magic. Jordan had insisted on doing the summoning. That way, if Foras had ulterior motives for me, they would be useless. I instructed him on the ceremony of making and sealing the circle. His magic snapped in place a tight, glowing, yellowish bubble around the circle. The feel of his magic stirred mine.

He growled as mine reacted to it. "There are more reasons than one for you to be able to control your reactions to my power. I couldn't fight for you and have your magic touching mine at the same time. I'd be too distracted."

"Finish this up. I'm getting nervous."

He started the summoning. Black smoke filled the circle and then Foras appeared out of the smoke before it faded into the ground. He was so tall that he had to hunch down not to touch the top of the bubble.

"That was quick, my son. I'm pleased you use your logic as well as your muscle."

"Foras, gatekeeper of the Underworld, answer me true. Have you freely offered your assistance to the Priestess of the Wild, with no foul intentions?"

Being in the circle of the summoner, he had to tell the truth. Maybe not all of it, but the base of his statements had to be true. "Jordan of Foras, I have spoken the truth. The motive is to assist the priestess in fulfilling the prophecy, as well as preventing an imbalance of powers between the gatekeepers."

"Explain that," Jordan demanded gruffly.

"If one of the stronger gatekeepers were to pull your woman through the ley and keep her bound to him, the gatekeeper would be much stronger than my Master had intended."

"That would upset the balance of the gatekeepers?" I asked.

"You are correct, my lady. It would not be good if a gatekeeper became stronger than the Master."

Jordan released the circle and Foras stretched and took in a deep breath. He strode to where I was sitting on the edge of the well and raised a hand to my head.

Jordan leapt on him immediately.

I jumped and shrieked as they started to fight. That was, until I realized that they used no magic or any of the fatal blows that I knew they both could use. I sat myself back on the well and watched as the two egotistical males rolled on the ground, punching and shoving like high school boys. It looked like a primal male-bonding ritual.

It was interesting in that aspect—but then Jordan managed to throw Foras into a tree, rattling the huge oak to its roots before he hit the ground. Foras was grabbing Jordan again when I shouted, "Boys! Play he-men all you like, but do *not* destroy my forest!"

They stood frozen in complementary headlocks. Jordan actually started smiling. Foras let him loose and Jordan followed suit, actually slapping the enormous Demon on the back. Foras looked at me then Jordan. "I can I touch your woman now? I need to be in her mind for a short time to assess her abilities."

I snorted. "You should ask *my* permission, Lord Foras, not his."

Foras looked back to his Demon son and Jordan nodded. "I told you, I belong to her, not the other way around."

Foras gave his son a questioning look. "And this does not bother you?"

Jordan gestured to me. "Would it you?"

Foras shook his head and came to face me. "May I?"

I nodded. He placed one hand on the top of my head. His hand was so large his palm sat over my forehead and the ends of his fingers almost came down to the back of my skull. I felt his power roll over me, through me. I felt his touch in my mind, soft, gentle, seeking. I was uneasy at the feeling of intrusion.

"I am merely seeking the boundaries you have created for yourself. I will not invade your private thoughts or memories, my lady." He was looking over my head and off into the depths of the forest. "Try to block my entry this time." He retreated from my mind. I thought and put up the walls I pictured in my mind. His mental embrace returned. I felt it moving along the walls, searching, looking for a weakness. He found it easily by simply trying to push through the wall.

"It is adequate protection for most but try to make it stronger. Maybe not using the visual of a wall, but the visualization of your power instead."

"I don't know how to visualize my power."

"You do. How do you see Jordan's power when you are making love?"

Now that was easy. "Fire."

He smiled again. "Yes, I suppose you would. Use your power to push me away from you, and try to see it in your mind as you do it."

I did as he asked, and as usual my push started as a giant shove and he stumbled backward. I had closed my eyes and saw the push in my mind. It was blue and as glimmery as the ley line itself. "It looks like the ley line," I said.

"That's why the ley is so attracted to you, and someday you will be able to use the lines much like a full Demon. Maybe even travel within it. Your power being so close to the earth's own magic is what makes you so strong, priestess. It will also make you a target, always. The sooner you can manage this power, the easier it will be for you protect yourself."

I saw the look on Jordan's face. He looked positively white. "What?" I asked.

Foras looked from Jordan back to me. "Do you have a familiar?"

"Not really," I said, still watching Jordan.

"You have Manus," he interjected.

"He's my guardian, not a familiar."

Foras asked Jordan, "Will this Manus act as familiar until she finds a suitable one?"

Jordan nodded.

"Fetch him." Jordan left without a look back. I had the feeling he needed a minute alone, but I wasn't sure why.

Foras looked back at me. "Use that visual to block this attempt." He reached his hand to my forehead and I felt his push on my mind. This time I made a bubble that looked like my circle and made a barrier in my mind. He pushed and moved around it with his attempts to filter in. I felt my head start to hurt and sweat forming under his hot, heavy hand. I was starting to feel weak. He lifted his hand and the coolness that followed in my head was immediate. I had been holding my breath and took in a deep gulp of air.

"Much better. You should be able to block the most powerful with that. It will be easier with the familiar."

"I can't have Manus around every time we…make love, Foras."

"That's not necessary. The familiar is to be with you when you confront any other Demons or the Dark One. Nessum will return to you soon. He cannot let you live."

"You know about that? Karackos tell you?"

"No, priestess. I am the finder of treasure and lost things, remember. I know the power of that blade of yours. It was not hard to figure out once I heard you had found it. As for the problem with Jordan, simply block him from your mind at those times. It is the combination of his power and yours that sweeps the ley and lets others know you're vulnerable. If you are using the ley intentionally, you cannot be pulled through."

"He's not going to like that much."

"I suspect not," he agreed.

"Why did he look so concerned that my magic is close to the ley magic?"

"Like I said, there will be many who will want to," he hesitated, "*exploit* that power. You will become more of a Demon than even he is, even with so little Demon blood in your veins. Mix that with the power I have heard you carry with your Witch blood, priestess, and you will become a target of those who oppose your views. And also a great leader for those who will follow."

"Great," I sighed.

"You seem unsure. Do you not believe my prediction?"

I got up off the well and started pacing. "No, I believe it, Foras. I've heard it over and over for the last several months. I just...I don't know how to deal with it. I was just a plain human less than a year ago. Since I've been here, I've stumbled over traditions, endangered many others and made a great many bad decisions. I'm afraid that I will not be this great leader everyone expects. I don't want to fail the Kith. Let's face it, historically, I fail most everything."

"There are perspectives other than your own, my lady," he said, moving to squat in front of me so he could look up at me. His eyes swirled with the same liquid silver as Jordan's. "Yes, you have much history and tradition to learn, but you show strong character, good logic and a very big heart. The power does not draw you to corruption. That says much. Trust yourself. You are bound to stumble." He stood and put his hand on my shoulder. "Hear this well—you have *everything* you need to get through All Hallow's in your mind already. Use it."

I smiled at him.

"I am very proud of Jordan. I was before he found you, but even more so now. Know this also, Keena, Priestess of the Wild. I will not sully this night or Jordan's trust by ever using my knowledge against you or yours. Call me when you have need. No bargains, no trading. Call and I will come."

"What are you two looking so serious about?" Jordan asked as he and Manus came through the woods into the clearing.

"Trust," I said. Manus stopped in his tracks as the looked back and forth between Foras and Jordan.

"You have summoned a Demon Lord now? Keena, *what* is the *matter* with you?"

Jordan broke in and explained it to Manus in his stern soldier tone. Manus readily agreed to try to be a familiar until I could get a proper one, and we practiced channeling the ley magic through him. The experiment worked well, other than Manus feeling very dizzy afterward.

We decided it was all worth it to prevent ether Karackos, Nessum or any other strong Demon Lord from being able to get into my head at any time. I certainly didn't want some big nasty pulling me unwillingly into another realm. We thanked Foras and sent him back to his realm.

Tonight, the All Hallow's festivities started.

Chapter Twenty-Two

∞

The next two days flew by in a crowded blur. Hundreds of supernatural beings had gathered from every corner of the world to be part of the All Hallow's celebration and to witness the Battle of Birthright that Agnus the Betrayed had prophesied as she'd burned, twenty-one generations past.

The spectrum of power gathered on WildLand was extraordinary and not lost on me as I was introduced and presented.

Feldema was still remanded to her warded cell. I wondered more than once if she could hear the festivities, and felt bad for her. She had waited for this day most of her life, secure in her belief that she would take her rightful place as the High Priestess. Then I show myself and in less than a year, her world falls to pieces. How she must have felt, I wondered, as she sat alone in a warded cell instead of indulging in all the feasts and grandeur of an All Hallow's to match no other in the history of WildLand. I had tried to speak to her again but she sat with her back to me and ignored my presence. I can't say I truly blame her.

All the pomp and circumstance brought me a complete understanding of Foras' statements about corrupt power. I personally was uncomfortable being ushered around and praised for greatness I hadn't yet proved, but if one was drawn to this kind of power, it would be easy to take advantage of and misuse. I tried to be gracious, and take the compliments and praise as humbly as possible.

More than once I had to lean on Jordan and let him navigate me to more neutral ground among my allies. Abbey ever gleamed and interceded to relate the tale of the trip to

Thule, which had come to be called Coyle's Return. Of course my father was there, and almost back to normal health. He beamed and found old acquaintances and friends among those gathered.

I'd had a couple of close calls by getting too close to Tynan, but Cliona managed to get in the way and distract him. It was as if everyone around me was afraid the spell would be easily broken by a word or accidental touch between us.

I fought heartache over seeing him. Tynan still held a place within me, his own magic part of me, but I remained convinced it was for the best that he not be bound eternally. I missed my beautiful lover. Jordan did his best not to act jealous of Tynan, and his extra attention when Tynan was near was more comforting than he would ever know.

I felt unworthy of the gushing appreciation from beings who had spent sometimes centuries building power and making others safe from humans or other rivals. Trying to keep it all in some sort of perspective, I spent most of my time trying to figure out what I was going to do about all the things that could come to pass during the battle. Doran and Bevin had quit giving advice and opinions, but their silence didn't help either. I was still sure the battle, now just hours away, would be a disaster.

Doran's last bit of advice was to follow my instincts. "They are all you have when it comes down to it," she'd said. What the hell was that supposed to mean?

Foras' comment that I had all I needed in my head also echoed over and over again, even in unsettled dreams.

* * * * *

We sat at the last formal dinner on All Hallow's. Abbey's Imps had produced a fabulous feast of candied pheasant. The meet room was wonderfully decorated in purple and gold and illuminated with candles floating gracefully in the air. Somehow the room looked bigger than it ever had, but even so, tables extended out of the room and well into the formal courtyard beyond. I was having a hard time concentrating on the polite conversation.

A coven leader out of London was speaking to me from across the table, her pretty round face lighting up as she spoke of all the Witches and the new emergence of Wicca in London. "It's getting close to a time when we will be accepted, my lady. There are shops of all kinds that line a particular area in the city of London proper and they specialize in the magical and the occult." She dabbed her chin with a vibrant purple napkin. "There is one in particular that even caters to Voodoo. They carry such things as dead men's ashes and Witches' voices. I'm sure it's all nonsense…"

She kept talking but I had stopped listening once those words left her mouth. *Witches' voices* hung in a fog in my head.

I touched Jordan's thigh to interrupt a conversation he was having with a Werewolf on his left. I whispered in his ear, "Did the dead Witches have their tongues missing?"

He gave me a strange look I couldn't read. "One was missing part of her larynx, but the others were too damaged to know if something was missing. But tongues — I don't think so. Why?"

"Nothing."

He squeezed my thigh in return, left his hand there and went back to his discussion of some type of weaponry.

What did that mean? Witches' voices. I knew it was important. I just couldn't put it together. The pretty Witch kept talking and Doran seemed to be listening to her, but she was watching me.

I hadn't eaten, I couldn't. I could only move things around on my plate and worry. By now, they would have brought Feldema up and started to get her ready. Her powers would be restored once she left the warded cell and I was nervous about that. Would Nessum give her all his powers for the battle? And what about Karackos? And Nessum himself?

The dinner seemed to last for hours. As the full moon settled high in the night sky, Jordan escorted me back to my chambers to prepare for the fight.

How things had changed, I thought. I looked in the mirror and saw the old version of myself. I no longer recognized the mousy hair and sad eyes that were all part of that old life. I had been alone.

I blinked and was back to Keena in the mirror, with the wild red and gold hair, the gleaming golden eyes. The fighting leathers, now familiar in fit and form, like a comfortable set of pajamas, clung to me in representation of the battle. The black leather rig strapped over my shoulder and around my waist was part of who I had become. My birthright was the warrior Witch, defender of the Kith, protector of humanity and conduit to bring those two worlds together. My power flared slightly, warming me.

I closed my eyes and tried to back away from the situation and put all the pieces of information floating in my head together. There had to be a bigger picture.

Nothing.

I visualized my powers and felt that familiar fire in my belly. It was comforting, that spot, the place that brought forth my powers, the place where I was both Witch and Demon, that part of me that made me who I was.

"Your weapons are ready," Jordan said from the door.

"I need a moment alone with him, Hogan." Hogan finished braiding my hair back and left the bathroom. Jordan came in and closed the door behind him to shut us out of earshot of the others who waited in my bedchamber.

He took my face in his big hands and kissed me, letting his lips lightly brush mine. "God speed," he whispered.

I put my hands over his. "I love you, Jordan," I said, looking him in the eyes. "I know I've never said it to you, but—"

"I know," he said with his usual gruff arrogance and opened the door. "Time to go."

I followed him out and let him put on my blades, checking and rechecking the sheaths and harnesses. When he finished, he stood straight, hands on his hips. Then we headed out of the manor to the main courtyard where everyone was gathered around the perimeter of the open area designated for the battle.

"Bevin," I leaned down and whispered. "What would Witches' voices be used for?"

"Not the best time to be studying potions, Keena."

I smiled at her. "You never know."

Bevin looked frightened but she managed a meager smile. "Old, old mimicking spells. Foul-smelling stuff too. It requires a blood sacrifice, so we no longer use it in earnest."

Doran's voice announced the beginning of the ceremony. We filed out to the center of the courtyard with Feldema and her group doing the same just to our left. She looked tired and weak, but held her head high, a look of confidence on her face. Did she really feel that confidence or was it a mask?

Doran spoke of the prophecy and the rules of the Battle of Birthright. I let my attention wander through the crowd who'd gathered to witness such an occasion. Most were listening to Doran but some watched Feldema and me. I caught Jordan's worried look. He changed it as soon as he realized I saw him. Manus was at the ready. Cliona also watched me and not Doran.

Others were gathered around by their species in neat little cliques. Witches were gathered by the stand that held Doran, Bevin and others members of the council. The Slaugh were off to one side of the garden-turned-battleground. They hadn't come to any of the other festivities, but I made eye contact with Trammel and he gave me a respectful nod.

Then I looked over at Feldema. Her hands were trembling just slightly. It was a mask. How much power did she have without Nessum? I let my power reach toward hers. It barely sparked in return. She jumped and glared at me.

He had drained her…

Why? What was his plan?

"So let the battle to prove birthright and the vengeance of Agnus the Betrayed show us the true holder of the seat of High Priestess!" Doran shouted, and the crowd went wild. "The victor resides over the council of the Kith in a year and one day!" There was another great cheer from the crowd. All attention moved to the two of us. We bowed to Doran.

Feldema turned to me and made her formal bow, which I returned. I tried to meet her gaze as we straightened. She wouldn't, and I could see she was still trembling. She took her stance and made a hasty lunge for me, a small blade drawn. I was able to get out of the way easily and she tumbled to the ground.

The crowed all gasped at her weakness. I turned and walked toward the trees. She was weak and without power. I couldn't fight her. I could easily kill her *and* myself in the process.

She lunged again and I just spun out of her way. She fell again and got to her knees. "Just do it and get it over with, old Witch! Kill me and put me out of the misery of *this* life!" She screamed it at me. More gasps and lots of conversation rippled through the watching throng. *This life?* In the cell she had said something about other ways of living. Had Nessum promised to make her a Vamp after she died? He wasn't here.

"She is too weak!" came a shout from a Gremlin among his group. "You have held her and drained her power, Doran!"

Doran started to explain that the cell wards only prevented her from using her power while contained — when smoke and an odor that turned my stomach replaced the usual jasmine smell of the forest. Feldema smiled. Something was about to happen and I didn't like the sense that I had no control over it.

The foul smell filled my nostrils. *Old spells...* Bevin's explanation of Witches' voices floated through my mind. I thought back to the old grimoires I had studied over the past and remembered a spell in one of them, a spell that would cast the voice of another to the wind.

As I made the connection, I heard my voice—not coming from me, but the woods.

The Witches had been killed to steal my voice!

I searched the woods beside us for any sign of another but found nothing. Feldema was still yelling at me to finish it all. I looked to her face. Her eyes were dancing with delight. She was far too happy to be begging for death. She knew I could no more kill her than she could me.

Through the fine smoke that came from just inside the woods, I started to hear my own voice cast a deadly fireball spell. I quickly grabbed up some of the earth from beneath me. I could destroy a potion like no other and I needed to now. I spat on the dirt and flung it into the woods toward the smoke. It disappeared with a sizzle.

"No!" Feldema shouted. "You will kill me or I will kill you! Ether way, we die!"

She lunged from her kneeling position and managed to slide the blade into my side, near the same place she had the first time we fought. She drew it out. Some shouts and jeers came from the crowd. I stumbled and put my hand to the wound. It stung and took my breath away, making it a few seconds before I could thrust her away using my Demon power.

The thrust pushed my twin backward and she landed against a tall pine tree. I cast again and wisteria vines wrapped around her, holding her to the tree and keeping her immobilized.

I felt dizzy. Not from the wound, which wasn't bleeding that badly. I felt a gentle push on my mind. It wasn't Feldema's power. It was too strong for that. I stumbled again and closed my eyes to find the source of the power. I reached for the ley and pushed it through Manus to filter and close my mind. My bubble went up inside my head as Foras had taught me, making it easier to find the silvery streak of unusual power trying to touch me.

The silver of it was wondrous—angel magic. But it was blotched with blackness that looked like tar floating in a clean river.

Nessum.

I held the bubble in my mind and turned around to try to find him. He wasn't in the crowd that was now loud with arguments and words of encouragement and condemnation.

I concentrated even more on what was happening in my mind. It was taking a great deal of power to hold back the surge of magic trying to invade. I felt blood start to pour out of my wound now. My efforts were making me sweat. Holding the spell to keep Feldema pinned to the tree, holding the bubble against Nessum's prodding and the blood loss were all wearing on me quickly.

I looked at Feldema. She was bleeding in the same spot I was. Bleeding hard.

I felt for my wound and the blood running over my hip and down my thigh. She wouldn't be bleeding too if I weren't dying. I saw Jordan. Cliona was holding him back and when I looked at him, he dropped to his knees. I was not going to let them down.

I needed Nessum out in the open. I took a deep breath, feeling the pain of it in my side. I held my hand over the wound and reached the other toward the ley and found it close to the trees. I walked directly into the line.

The pain from the wound subsided. I felt the touch of another unfamiliar magic on my skin, silky and gentle. I had never felt such a soft touch of magic. It wasn't Nessum's, Feldema's or mine. I kept my body in the ley line, gaining strength from it.

I followed the trail of the new magic to the crowd. The aura matched one of the UnSeelie Court Elves in attendance. Elfin magic. That's why I didn't recognize it. He was producing a glamour.

I used the extra strength of the ley to break the link of the spell from the Elf, watching his face as it snapped and broke. He stumbled and fell backward. One of the guards reached him before he could make his way from the crowd. The blood slowed to a trickle at my side. I wasn't dying and neither was Feldema. The glamour was to frighten me, distract.

Nessum's magic was still trying to find a way into my mind. He needed something from inside my head. I couldn't imagine what. Why not face me and fight? Why not just take Feldema and run to another realm? The strain of fighting his probing was wearing on me. In my mind, I pictured myself grabbing that silver line of power still prodding at me and yanking on it like a rope.

Nessum appeared just in front of me. The surprise of the gathered beings echoed in a communal inhale of the cool night hair.

"Nessum!" Feldema screeched as he turned to me. He held out his hand and I found my feet moving, my body rocking forward, dragging me out of the ley. Nessum was controlling my feet, moving me away from the power of the line. I fought to keep each foot in place, watching his calm, beautiful face. Those eyes. Joy and love filled my being, pulled me toward him. I was lost in his sparkling, perfect Vampire eyes. It was the thrall. If I kept the eye contact, I would be lost to him.

I managed a blink then fought to hold my eyes closed. The sounds of the crowd echoed through my ears as the pull of Nessum's power was shattered. I looked down, keeping my eyes from his as I worked back into the line. But my head started to rise just as my feet had started to move. I shut my eyes to block the effect of those eyes before we made direct contact. I felt the magic of the ley line leave me. It hurt to be pulled away from the magic and it left me with a popping sound that echoed through the forest.

"Nessum," Feldema pleaded again with weariness. "Why haven't you come for me? Why did you leave me to rot in that cell?" She was sobbing hard. I opened my eyes and looked at her face, at the tears streaming down her cheeks. Love, disappointment and grief all showed in her eyes as she sobbed.

He turned and stepped toward her, his magic not releasing me in the least. "It appears I chose the wrong sister." His tone was smug and uncaring as he glanced toward me and then turned his attention back to the crying Witch tied to the tree.

"But...I *love* you! You love me! You promised we would be together forever. You promised!" Her utter loyalty and loss reverberated in the air. Her body hung limp with her pain.

"Pity too," he said, running a finger along the side of one of her breasts. She tried to arch into his touch through the bindings.

I felt the presence of two more Vampires moving close from the forest. They emerged and stood to my sides, just behind me. I could just make them out in my peripheral vision. I saw Cliona and Tynan stiffen. They wouldn't dare move while Nessum was there. Jordan had returned to his feet and stood stiff. No one could help me. The Dark Angel was too powerful.

Nessum took his gaze from Feldema and back to me. His features were so perfect, so beautiful. Alabaster skin covered a perfect bone structure, long golden hair graced his shoulders. He wore a Roman-style tunic with golden trim and a belt that held a small dagger only. I closed my eyes quickly so as not to get caught up in his beauty. His charm could move me against my will.

"I made the same mistake most of the Kith had, my love." He was still talking to Feldema. "Little Miss Mary's human blood didn't weaken her as we all suspected it would."

"But Nessum! I did everything you asked. I took no others. I gave you powers and asked for nothing in return. Please, Nessum!" She was sounding frantic. I opened my eyes and let her loose from her wisteria bindings. She ran at him and draped herself in his arms.

He gave me a disgusted look and waved his hand, and she was flung right back to the tree, again surrounded by the vines. At least I had let go of the spell holding her and only had to concentrate on blocking him from my mind. His power was still there, still probing for a way in.

"What is it you're looking for in there, Nessum?" I tried not to betray the fear that was filling me.

"Weakness, Keena. We all have one. You found mine. I'm looking for yours." He stepped to my right, still trying to probe.

I was being drained. My body felt as if the very blood was being slowly drained from it. A bead of sweat ran down my back and my knees were getting weak. "What do you want with me, with Feldema?"

"Power."

I kept my eyes down but my chin was still held up by his magic. "You have more power than anyone here. Why more?" I was fighting to keep standing.

He stepped behind me. He was between me and the two Vamps who were his backup. "It appears to me that you have great power. You are standing to fight me, are you not?"

I didn't know how to answer. I caught him out of the corner of my eye on the left as he started back around. His feet were so close to a circle I had drawn in practice weeks before. I could see the outline of it in the grass...

Could I close him in it? I looked forward, desperate not to draw it to his attention. It was only a slight disturbance in the grass but I wasn't taking any chances.

"I had it planned, Keena. Feldema. The prophecy. Never did I dream that the Creator would grace one with as much mixed blood as you with such power. Though it is obvious that I have never understood His intentions."

If he would just back up one more step I could try to trap him. I would have to drop the bubble blocking my mind from his and reach for the power of the ley line to maintain the circle. I was too weak at this point to hold both. It was worth the shot.

I looked back to the crowd. Tynan was itching to attack, as was Cliona. Jordan was crouching, ready to strike. If the circle didn't hold, what weakness would Nessum find in my mind and how would he use it? He took another step away from the circle. If I was going to try, it had to be now.

I started the spell for closing the circle in my mind, leaving the last few words for just the right moment. Then I took in a long, cleansing breath and held my head to the moon, making a small prayer.

As I dropped the bubble in my mind, I felt his surge on my memory. The burning of his invasion made me fall to my knees as I called on the Demon power from my belly and thrust. I felt the energy of it leave my body.

I hadn't the strength direct it, so it spread through the courtyard. I heard gasps and cries from the crowd but I only watched Nessum.

He stumbled back a step. Not enough. I thrust again as I felt his power surge through my mind harder. He stumbled back again and I started the last words of the spell to close the circle as his second foot fell within it.

Nessum's hold on my mind ripped away and pain shot through my head, tears pushing at my eyes. I fell to the ground.

He roared and pushed at the bubble of magic that now surrounded him, trapping him in my circle. The shimmering blue of the circle gave at the strength of his power. I lunged for the ley line and the clean, smooth feel of that power as Manus channeled it for me. The energy responded immediately.

I felt the joining of other powers in the line. Doran, Bevin and several of the coven leaders had come to the line. The strongest Witches in the world were feeding me power through it. My magic, joined by theirs, turned the bubble to a luminescent violet. Nessum roared again. Feldema fell to the ground out of her bindings, still pleading, crying to me to release him — to him not to forsake her.

The two Vamps had tried to attack me in the process but Tynan and Cliona stopped them before they could touch me, and I heard the turmoil of the fight off behind me. I felt sore from head to toe. Jordan knelt beside me. I sank into him for the feel of his warmth.

"You've accomplished nothing, red Witch!" Nessum spat, his beautiful, calm face now contorted. The glittering blue of his eyes was replaced with red, glowing hatred. He made a summoning chant and a woman appeared, hanging loosely in his arm. He held her around the waist with one arm and she hung like a wet towel at his side. She slowly raised her head.

"Mother?" I panted, heart lurching. She gave me a pleading look. My human mother in the hands of this beast was about the last thing I could bear this night. Jordan tried to lift me but I struggled free and shoved him back as I crawled toward her. "Mother!" I got as close as I could, still holding the spell that kept Nessum imprisoned, the ley magic moving with me.

"Mary? Where am I? You...you are..." She tried to look around but being held in the awkward position she could only look at me. I studied her face, realizing how much I missed her gentle tones and prodding nature.

I stood, energized by my anger, and drew my real mother's blade, Trevina's Blade, from the sheath on my back. "Nessum. Release her or die."

"You can't hold me in your pathetic circle for long, Keena. Let me out now and maybe I won't kill your human mother as punishment for entrapping me." He took the dagger from his belt and held it to her throat.

"Damn it, Mary!" my mother cried out as he put the dagger to her throat. "Let him out."

I took a deep breath — and looked at her face again. Seconds ticked by. "Kill her then," I said, stepping back from the circle and spinning the blade of Trevina in my hand. There were more gasps from the crowd.

"Keena…" Jordan began, putting his hand on my shoulder. I held a hand up to him. He stepped back.

Nessum grumbled, "You would have me kill the woman who nurtured you?"

"That's not my mother." More gasps. The woman vanished as quickly as she had appeared. "Parlor tricks, Nessum? I would have thought better of you."

He growled, and it was not the sexy growl that I had grown to love from Jordan, but an earth-moving growl that built to a screeching howl.

"He's called the Slaugh," Jordan said.

Trammel and his followers didn't flinch or make any sign of answering Nessum's call. They simply watched intently, waiting. The Witches were still doing their best, pouring their magic into the ley line. I could see the toll on a couple of them. I felt it too, but was too frightened to think of what to do next. I had to kill him. Yet, if I killed him, his supporters and followers could send the Kith into war.

Red Witch. He'd called me red Witch…

Karackos had been the only other one to call me that.

I stepped back and used Trevina's blade to draw another circle beside the first. Jordan gave me a concerned look. I winked, teasing with a slight smile. Another growl of anger ripped from Nessum's beautifully evil face.

I loved it when a plan came together. And finally, I knew what to do.

I summoned Foras.

"Well, Keena, Priestess of the Wild," he said, bowing first to me then to Jordan. Jordan returned the greeting and Foras looked around him, offering a shocked look at the fallen angel in my circle. "I see you've had a busy evening. How may I be of service to you, my lady?"

"Lord Foras, I request only that you answer a question."

He looked around again. "And for that answer, lady Keena?" I realized in public he must bargain. In private he had promised help, but in public he had to remain an Upper Demon Lord who would never give anything—or any deed—for free.

I thought for moment. "I think the question alone will be payment for the answer."

He tilted his head at me. The same look came from Jordan. Foras considered it. "I will accept the terms."

"Thank You, Lord Foras. Previously, you and I had discussed a bargain that I struck with Karackos." Foras nodded. "If I change the payment of that agreement...exchange it, so to speak, with Nessum, would that upset the balance of the gatekeepers?"

I saw all the onlookers exchanging glances and heard the murmurs as they tried to understand the question. Foras understood perfectly. He rubbed his chin and looked from Jordan back to me. "No, no it would not. The Demon in question would not be able to make use of the prize in such a way. He will think so...but he will not." He bowed deeply. "And I do appreciate the warning. I consider this a more than fair bargain." He rose. "I would request to remain and see the show, Keena?"

"Thank you again, Foras. But I don't believe I can hold three circles." I nodded beside me to the rather angry Dark Angel.

"I will summon you after she releases, if you would like," Jordan offered. Foras bowed again. I broke the circle and let Jordan summon his Incubus father. He did and released Foras. Some backed away for him, others moved closer to get a better look. Gatekeepers rarely moved about among the earthbound, and surely not at a function such as this.

A hush fell over the crowd as I drew and closed the circle again and summoned Karackos. He appeared immediately, looked around and saw Feldema crying, head hanging. He saw Nessum caught in the other circle. "Lady Keena. We have an agreement and I fulfilled my part. Has she agreed to come to me?"

"I have not given her the choice. I wanted you to know her condition before you thought I had misused our bargain." I was getting weaker. The energy to hold the circles as Nessum was still fighting against his was killing me. Holding myself up with the blade of Trevina as I spoke, I was also feeling the weight of the ley magic as it moved with me. Manus was curled up and lying on the ground with his head filling Abbey's lap. She was caressing him. Every bit of energy I used was being filtered through him in order for me to handle the sheer amount of it.

"Condition?"

"It seems that Nessum has abused her over the years, Karackos. She has no real power left." The crowd mumbled and churned as I spoke. "He drained most of her magic and gave her only the illusion of power in return. She will be of little use to you."

He stomped inside his circle, his leathery wings flipping back and forth. He glared at me. "Did you know of this prior to our arrangement?"

"Not that it matters, Karackos—you asked me nothing of her powers. It wasn't in our agreement." He grumbled, not angry but defeated. "Like I said...not that it matters, but no, I did not." His attention turned back to me. "I have an alternate to your prize," I said and turned and swept my hand to the circle holding Nessum.

"What gibberish are you talking to this Demon?" Nessum growled.

I kept talking to Karackos but looked behind him to Foras. He nodded. "The Dark Angel in exchange for Feldema. I will make him the same offer. He can choose."

"Choose what?" Nessum shouted. I saw Doran's face finally flood with understanding, as well as a few others.

"Agreed!" Karackos said as soon as he caught on. "Agreed!" His excitement betrayed his overzealous greed for power. The same greed in Nessum that had brought all this on me.

"All the same conditions apply? At no time will Nessum be allowed to have enough power to harm me or mine. If you let him out of servitude, those same rules apply. I will be made aware?"

"Yes, yes...make him the deal." He was rubbing his hands together in anticipation.

I did my best to turn without showing pain or weakness. I would not be able to hold the circles much longer.

I dropped Karackos' circle and let him follow me to Nessum. "I make you this offer, Nessum. I make it only once, and you have very little time to consider. I will drop the circle soon and you will die." His anger sprang forth and black, spongy wings spread from his body, pushing physically at the bubble. "If the circle falls you get no choice, Nessum—you will lose your head to Trevina's blade. I give you leave to choose otherwise. You can choose to be bound to the Demon Karackos as familiar from this time forth."

"Bound to a lesser Demon?" He coughed as he spoke. "As a *familiar*? I would rather die!" He held his head high.

"So be it." I spun the blade again and brought it up. It was my magic holding the circle, so my blade would go through it and not break it. Nessum was trapped.

I swung.

Just before the blade reached his neck, he shrieked, "No! Stop! I'll do it!"

I stopped. "Last word here, Nessum. No more chances." I really wanted him dead, but I wanted out of Karackos' indenture as well.

"Fine!"

Karackos struggled forward. "You know the words, bind yourself to me freely."

"I freely bind myself to you, Karackos. I surrender my power and my liberty to your service. I will follow you and you alone." The words came out from behind a fierce grimace.

Karackos jumped in glee. "You may drop the circle now, lady Keena. He will no longer attempt to harm you or yours, will you, Nessum?"

"Not while I am in your bondage. But that will not last forever." He stumbled forward toward Karackos, as though being pulled. Karackos huffed but Nessum kept his gaze on me, eyes burning with a promise of retribution. I wished he hadn't changed his mind. I would have preferred him dead. They moved back to the circle in which I had summoned Karackos. I sent them back in a puff of thick, black smoke.

As soon as Nessum was gone, Feldema collapsed, completely stripped of what little power remained. The bystanders were all silent, watching, the sounds of the battlefield died down to only the hum of the ley line.

"Keena?"

I was looking at Jordan—but it was Tynan's voice I heard from behind me. His voice laced with confusion and tenderness.

The voice of a man who remembered he loved me.

Jordon's gaze went over my head. I felt Tynan moving closer.

Jordan tensed and then looked back to me and nodded. "The spell is broken." The words were a mere whisper on his lips. "This should be interesting."

I turned. My heart exploded. His clothes were splattered with blood. His stride was unsure. He was remembering, trying to piece together the last months. The emotions so plainly crossed his beautiful face. "You set me free?"

The crowd had started milling about. Others were talking and cleaning up the area. Someone helped Feldema from behind us. I was aware of all this but I could only look into those huge, dark-blue eyes.

I wanted to jump for joy and scream in anger. I wanted him back. I wanted him free. Jordan placed his hand on my back for support. The reassuring touch reminded me that this too was out of my control. Tynan was back. And what that meant for the three of us would have to play out in time.

Tynan had stopped a few feet from us. His breathing was slow, his hands frozen at his side. He didn't seem to know what to do. Jordan pushed me from behind. "Go to him, Keena. He needs you now."

I took a step forward. My legs were shaky. I felt a tear make its way down my cheek. I wanted him back. Now that I saw that look in his eyes, I knew I would never give him up again. "Tynan."

He swept me into his arms. The warmth of his embrace gave me strength. "Oh God! I've missed you!" I took his face in my hands and held it still for a moment. I needed to look at him, to hold him. I pressed a single kiss to his forehead. I didn't comprehend how much I had missed him until I felt his body against mine, felt his heart pounding in his chest. I wept openly into his shirt. "I had to, Tynan. It was my only chance to break the bond. I wanted you to be happy."

"Did I not seem happy to you? I knew I had lost something. I couldn't put my finger on it. But I missed something—I missed love. I missed you." He pressed his lips to mine and kissed me as though he would never get the opportunity again. I returned the fervor of that passion.

"You have much to answer for, *mon guerrier*. Much to answer for." He looked over my head to the half-Demon behind me.

"You don't know the half of it," Jordan said.

Tynan pushed a loose stand of hair from my face and gave Jordan a commiserating nod. It felt so good to be in his arms. "She is a handful, isn't she?"

Doran and the other Witches who had been helping me hold the circle were on the ground as if they had been thrown. One of Doran's consorts tried to help her up, but she shooed him away. "Bring her to me, Lord Tynan."

Tynan did as he was told and carried me to her, setting me before her. I was so weak I couldn't stand on my own, my legs folding as I sank tiredly before Doran. Jordan kneeled, positioning himself behind me so I could lean against his strength. Tynan knelt at my side to openly declare his renewed position.

Doran placed one hand on my shoulder and she lovingly smiled at Tynan. With a raised hand, she hushed the crowd.

"Keena, Priestess of the Wild, child of the twenty-first daughter of Agnus the Betrayed, born under the full moon, I claim you and hold you duty-bound to the Kith as High Priestess. In one year and one day you shall succeed me and assume your birthright as leader of the council and conscience of the Kith. The prophecy comes to fulfillment before the eyes of the gathered and seals you to us.

"Be well and be wise, my niece."

The End

Also by Mari Freeman

෨

Beware of the Cowboy

About the Author

୬

Mari Freeman lives on her horse farm in central North Carolina. When not penning romantic erotica, she enjoys horses, hiking, traveling, good food, and friends. An outdoors girl at heart, you can often find her by the pond with laptop fired up, fishing line in the water, and her imagination running wild.

Mari's favorite stories include Alpha females in love with even more Alpha males. She finds the clash of passionate, strong willed personalities fascinating. She writes contemporary, paranormal, and a little science fiction/fantasy.

Mari welcomes comments from readers. You can find her website and email address on her author bio page at www.ellorascave.com.

Tell Us What You Think

We appreciate hearing reader opinions about our books. You can email us at Comments@EllorasCave.com.

Why an electronic book?

We live in the Information Age—an exciting time in the history of human civilization, in which technology rules supreme and continues to progress in leaps and bounds every minute of every day. For a multitude of reasons, more and more avid literary fans are opting to purchase e-books instead of paper books. The question from those not yet initiated into the world of electronic reading is simply: *Why?*

1. *Price.* An electronic title at Ellora's Cave Publishing and Cerridwen Press runs anywhere from 40% to 75% less than the cover price of the exact same title in paperback format. Why? Basic mathematics and cost. It is less expensive to publish an e-book (no paper and printing, no warehousing and shipping) than it is to publish a paperback, so the savings are passed along to the consumer.

2. *Space.* Running out of room in your house for your books? That is one worry you will never have with electronic books. For a low one-time cost, you can purchase a handheld device specifically designed for e-reading. Many e-readers have large, convenient screens for viewing. Better yet, hundreds of titles can be stored within your new library—on a single microchip. There are a variety of e-readers from different manufacturers. You can also read e-books on your PC or laptop computer. (Please note that Ellora's Cave does not endorse any specific brands.

You can check our websites at www.ellorascave.com or www.cerridwenpress.com for information we make available to new consumers.)

3. *Mobility.* Because your new e-library consists of only a microchip within a small, easily transportable e-reader, your entire cache of books can be taken with you wherever you go.

4. *Personal Viewing Preferences.* Are the words you are currently reading too small? Too large? Too... ANNOYING? Paperback books cannot be modified according to personal preferences, but e-books can.

5. *Instant Gratification.* Is it the middle of the night and all the bookstores near you are closed? Are you tired of waiting days, sometimes weeks, for bookstores to ship the novels you bought? Ellora's Cave Publishing sells instantaneous downloads twenty-four hours a day, seven days a week, every day of the year. Our webstore is never closed. Our e-book delivery system is 100% automated, meaning your order is filled as soon as you pay for it.

Those are a few of the top reasons why electronic books are replacing paperbacks for many avid readers.

As always, Ellora's Cave and Cerridwen Press welcome your questions and comments. We invite you to email us at Comments@ellorascave.com or write to us directly at Ellora's Cave Publishing Inc., 1056 Home Avenue, Akron, OH 44310-3502.